WORLDS APART

"To change the subject, do you know whom I met in Cannes yesterday?" Jacques smiled and winked. "Mademoiselle Halstead."

Robert felt relieved not to discuss his mother further and seized the opportunity to speak of something besides *Kristallnacht*. Miss Halstead had left him intrigued, and he admitted that the memory of her had lingered on the edges of his mind long after she had left him at her hotel. She was, without question, an attractive young woman, but it went beyond looks. He sensed in Miss Halstead a vital energy and sense of purpose. He had also found her intelligent, though somewhat argumentative. He smiled at Jacques, "Did you? And how was she? Is she still planning to go to Spain?"

"In two weeks, I understand." He shook his head. "I don't think this news photography is a very feminine occupation."

Robert shrugged. "She seemed feminine enough to me. I think we should have Miss Halstead to dinner." It crossed his mind that getting to know Adria Halstead might prove an adventure in itself.

"So you are going to give Miss Halstead a taste of the good life before she goes to the battlefields?" Robert chuckled. "It's the least I can do."

JANET ROSENSTOCK

NEW ENGLISH LIBRARY
Hodder and Stoughton

Many thanks to Margharita
Collins-Munro for the help
researching costume and
fashion

Copyright © 1987 by Free Lance
Writing Associates Inc., D. Adair and
J. Rosenstock

First published in the United States of
America in 1987 by Pocket Books

First published in Great Britain in 1987
by Judy Piatkus (Publishers) Ltd

New English Library paperback edition
1989

British Library C.I.P.

Rosenstock, Janet
  Worlds Apart
  I. Title
  813'.54[F]

ISBN 0 450 49731 3

Printed and bound in Great Britain
for Hodder and Stoughton
paperbacks, a division of Hodder and
Stoughton Ltd., Mill Road,
Dunton Green, Sevenoaks, Kent
TN13 2YA (Editorial Office:
47 Bedford Square, London
WC1B 3DP) by Cox & Wyman Ltd.,
Reading.

Part
1

Chapter One

1

THE *Queen Victoria* APPEARED pure white from a distance. The ocean liner looked like a virgin vessel gliding across the glassy, azure waters of the Gulf of Lyon, toward the docks at Marseilles. But distance is deceiving. On closer inspection, the stains on the ship's smokestacks appeared as great gray blotches like sprawling amoebas. There were fine scratches on the mahogany rails, and the worn decks bore the evidence of thousands of shuffling feet. The *Queen Victoria* was not a new ship but she had a stately elegance, a worn beauty like an aging but well-dressed dowager, powdered and perfumed, the lines of a privileged life evident in her face.

The sofas that filled the ship's lounges were fat and plush, the dinner service in the first-class dining salon was delicate Rosenthal china, the glasses cut crystal, the tea service heavy, ornate sterling. The staterooms were spacious and comfortable, designed for those accustomed to service and style. It was an eight-day voyage from New York to Marseilles, eight days of shuffleboard, scheduled dining, walks on deck, idle conversation, and cool mornings on the Atlantic spent bundled in deck chairs sipping beef tea. The passengers on the *Queen Victoria* were not unlike the ship: beyond their prime, but well dressed and tasteful.

Initially Adria Halstead had felt a trifle out of place. First, she had neither the *haute couture* wardrobe of the other female passengers nor the glittering jewels; second, she guessed she was younger than the other first-class passengers by at least twenty years.

Among them were Lord and Lady Gupta, an elderly Indian couple. Lord Gupta was a Rajput prince who wore Western garb and spoke in perfectly rounded Oxford English. Lady Gupta had pale skin, white, wavy hair, and dressed in saris woven with silver and gold threads. Unlike those Indians prominent in trade who affected a higher caste by painting a red mark on their foreheads, Lady Gupta had a genuine, full-karat ruby set into her skin. On a Westerner it would have looked garish, but on Lady Gupta it appeared entirely natural, and it served to define her origins as clearly as if her family tree were printed on her iridescent sari.

There was a white-haired professor from Harvard and his wife Lilly. Dr. and Mrs. Nathanial Pierce, their place cards read. They were First Family–Back Bay Bostonians, refined and quiet.

And there was Jacques Cardon, a wealthy wine merchant who traveled regularly between New York and France; an aging actress named Katherine Finley; a Southern senator and his wife: and an elderly British writer who traveled with his Siamese cat, Alfred North Whitehead.

All of them were well traveled and all of them were obviously used to the leisurely rhythm and refinements of first class. She would not have been traveling first class on the *Queen Victoria* had it not been November, when the fare was more reasonable than during high season. Adria had joked before leaving New York, "It will be my chance to see how the other half lives."

But her mother hadn't understood her comment, and certainly her father wouldn't have either. "We have lots of well-off friends," her mother thought, and her father would have muttered, "You've been traveling in heady company all your life." And that was partly true. But knowing people who traveled first class to Europe to winter on the Riviera was one matter; actually doing it was another. And, Adria thought with satisfaction, I enjoyed it. I loved having the steward draw my bath. I adored sitting at the captain's table, and I loved dressing for dinner. That wasn't all, of course. What she had really enjoyed was being on her own.

Her mother was particularly critical of her dress. To compete with her wealthy friends her mother spent hours pouring over fashion magazines and shopping for

4

fabric, then underpaid a seamstress to create duplicates. Despite such thrift, Adria could remember times when the money ran out before the end of the month because her mother had bought expensive accessories for some outfit. So in lieu of high fashion, Adria had adopted the Bohemian dress of her contemporaries in Greenwich Village. And instead of pretending—as her mother so often did—she opted for looking like what she was, a photographer, an artist of sorts. And, she thought happily, not trying to put on airs worked. She felt accepted by her fellow passengers and this gave her a new self-confidence.

As they headed into Vieux Port, the older docks, she could see the white, modern buildings of the city rising against the backdrop of the mountains and glimpse the hilltop sanctuary of Notre Dame in the distance. It looked a quiet, beautiful city, but Adria knew that distance gave Marseilles, like the *Queen Victoria,* an appearance that was deceiving.

Her father would have been outraged had he known she was landing there alone. "Hell holes," was his phrase. "Tangiers, Naples, Marseilles, Panama—they're all the same. Filthy hell holes full of criminals." Then he would add, "San Diego's the only decent port city in the world! That's because it belongs to the U.S. Navy."

No, her father wouldn't approve, but Adria was adamant. She had traveled a great deal, but never on her own. She would land in Marseilles, she would take the train to Villefranche, and she would surprise her father. It wouldn't be a total surprise, of course. He knew she was coming. But he would expect her to phone so he could send a driver. He wouldn't guess that she had decided to take the train and he didn't in fact know what ship she had taken. Adria inhaled, bit her lip and closed her eyes. There was, in fact, rather a lot he didn't know at this point.

Adria stood outside the huddle of gray dock buildings. She had slipped her beige wool shawl off her

5

shoulders and felt entirely comfortable in her stylish, short tan skirt and matching low-cut blouse. Rather than having a saucy hat perched on her head, she wore a paisley headband which allowed her thick auburn hair to fall back and tumble over her shoulders—a Bohemian touch to set her apart from the fashion plates.

The November sun had warmed the temperature to at least sixty-five, a good fifteen degrees warmer than when the ship had docked several hours earlier. November 5, 1938. My independence day, Adria thought to herself. She imagined her own résumé neatly typed on white paper.

Adria Louise Halstead, age twenty-three.

Graduate of Barnard College, New York. Born in Boston, Massachusetts on January 4, 1915. Daughter of Admiral Nelson Halstead. Traveled extensively. Occupation: photographer for *News Views Magazine.*

Adria smiled thoughtfully. The last line pleased her immensely, and though she had ostensibly come to France to visit her father, she had really come to launch her career.

"Allo, mademoiselle!"

Adria looked up to see a bashed-up 1935 Ford that sported a tilted 'Taxi' sign. The toothless, swarthy driver beckoned her with a crooked finger and a leering wink. Adria shook her head, sending him on his way without her in spite of the fact that she needed a cab to take her to the station and that taxis seemed in short supply. The majority of the first-class passengers with whom she had traveled were being met by a long line of chauffeur-driven cars. Adria set her two suitcases down dejectedly. She would simply have to wait for a taxi driven by someone who looked somewhat more trustworthy.

"Ah, Mademoiselle Halstead! Aren't you being met?"

Adria turned toward the cultured male voice, her large, hazel green eyes seeking a familiar face. The question came from Jacques Cardon, the wine merchant from New York with whom she had been seated

6

at the captain's table on the fifth night of the voyage. She took him to be in his mid-forties, a round man with a bald crown and graying, wiry hair that formed a fringe around his head. His large frame rested on short, thin legs; indeed, he was shorter than Adria by nearly two inches. "I'd intended to take the train to Villefranche," she replied, then added, in a slightly dismayed tone, "but I can't seem to get a taxi to take me to the station. It's chaotic."

"Oh, *mon dieu!* It is France! In any case, my dear, the train is an abomination! Rattle, clack, rattle, clack!" He waved his hands in the air expressively. "It takes hours, it stops everywhere. How do you say, a milk train! You must come with me. Monsieur Wertheim's car, which comes to fetch me, passes directly through Villefranche. Oh, do come. I'm certain he would not mind at all."

Adria hesitated for only a moment, inwardly relieved. "If you're certain he wouldn't mind. I don't want to impose."

"Jacques!" Robert Wertheim pushed through the milling crowd. He grinned when he saw his old friend and hugged him as soon as he was within reach. Then with a knowing smile, he acknowledged Adria. "Ah, Jacques is a connoisseur of fine wine, and no mean judge of beautiful women." Releasing Jacques from the bear hug, Robert stood back and waited to be introduced.

"You surprise me! I thought you would send the car! You've driven yourself?"

Robert shrugged and arched one brow. "And why not?"

"I'm embarrassed. I've invited Mademoiselle Halstead to share your car as far as Villefranche. But I am also rude!" Jacques turned quickly to Adria, "Mademoiselle Halstead, allow me to introduce Monsieur Robert Wertheim, a producer of the finest red wines. He is most certainly the first competitor of the Baron de Rothschild!"

Robert bent from the waist and kissed Adria's hand

7

with a flourish. "The pleasure is entirely mine," he said with European formality.

"I really couldn't impose," Adria protested, knowing full well she not only could, but wanted to.

"Impose? It is not an imposition to chauffeur a beautiful woman! Though I may not have room for your trunks."

Adria shook her head. "I only have these two suitcases and my shoulder bag." The latter was heavy, and anchored at her side because it contained her tripod.

"Ah, so you are planning to buy all new clothes in Paris!" he laughed gently, "Women often arrive in France without luggage, but they leave with trunks and boxes galore."

Adria smiled and found herself slightly intrigued. This Robert Wertheim spoke English impeccably, but he also had that "European approach" to women—flowery compliments, penetrating looks. "I don't think so," she replied. "By necessity, I tend to travel light."

"You are not here to vacation on the Côte d'Azur?" Again, his eyebrow rose with the question.

Adria shook her head. "I'm here for a short visit with my father. Then to pursue my assignment."

Robert Wertheim smiled faintly. "I shall hear more of this mysterious assignment in the car." Turning abruptly he snapped his fingers at a bored taxi driver whose vehicle was stopped behind his sleek Rolls Royce. "Here, my good man. Load this luggage in the boot!" The driver climbed out of his cab and followed Robert's directions. Robert paid him and the man tipped his beret respectfully. Adria noted that although he was blocking traffic, no one honked or cursed Robert Wertheim's car. Clearly, this was a man used to giving orders and to having them obeyed without question.

Robert opened the car door for her and bowed slightly. Flowery, curious, and perhaps arrogant, she thought, but far better than a leering taxi driver in a strange city, and there was no denying Robert Wertheim's good looks. He was tall and muscular, well tanned, had thick brown hair, and penetrating, deep blue eyes. He was resplendent in a well-tailored, three-piece beige suit. She took him to be thirty, perhaps a few years older.

Jacques Cardon sprawled across the back seat and Adria sat in the front with Robert. The car, she admitted, was not just "any" car. It was a Rolls Royce Grand Touring car; admiring the mahogany and silver interior, Adria inhaled the smell of rich leather.

When Robert Wertheim closed the car doors, the teeming streets of Marseilles became a silent panorama composed of winding cobbled roads, hanging wash, narrow doorways, and all manner of traffic, from donkey-driven carts guided by old men to overburdened trucks. Robert expertly guided the vehicle through the dockside congestion, and where no road could be seen before, a path opened up as people and vehicles made room for the gliding Rolls as if its occupants were royalty. Soon, they reached the main highway.

So solid was the Rolls that each bump, curve, and minor obstruction was smoothed out as if this vehicle rode on a special magic cushion. "This car is wonderful," Adria felt prompted to say.

"Ah, there's no automobile like it," Wertheim agreed. "But do you know Rolls Royce stories? It is a car with its own folklore."

"No, I don't," Adria confessed.

"Well, I'll tell you one about this very car. Two years ago, just after I bought it, I was driving in Brittany when the axle broke. I phoned Rolls in England, and they instructed me to have it taken to a certain garage. They then put me up in a most elegant inn, and twenty-four hours later, informed me my car was repaired. When I went to the garage, I was informed there was no charge. I said, 'Surely there is some mistake, the axle was broken.' I was told, 'You were

9

mistaken, sir. The axles on Rolls Royces do not break.' They had flown in a replacement overnight with three experts to install it."

Adria laughed softly at the story, and she laughed again when Jacques Cardon told a story about a pedestrian in London hit by a Rolls Royce who apologized to the driver.

After a short time, Adria told them, "You needn't speak English for me. I do speak French."

Robert laughed, "But, Mademoiselle Halstead, my mother tongue is English. I was, in fact, born in England. I have a French-speaking father and an English mother. To make matters more confusing, we are of German-Jewish heritage. Tell me, does your father live in Villefranche?"

Adria nodded her head. "In a manner of speaking. He is headquartered there. He's the commander of the American Naval Force in the Mediterranean."

"Admiral Halstead! How stupid of me not to have recognized the name."

Adria stared at her lap. No doubt her father was well known. He had a distinct talent for making his presence felt.

"But you haven't told us about your assignment," Robert Wertheim pressed. "Does this mean you are what the magazines call one of the new career women? Are you a writer?"

"I'm a photographer. I'm going to Spain to cover the war for a magazine." She smiled because she truly enjoyed telling someone she was actually on assignment, even though she had only sold five photographs and knew that Andy Martin wouldn't have hired her if he hadn't been her mother's childhood friend. But I'll prove myself, she vowed. Besides, her male competitors had all said it was impossible for a woman to get such an assignment. Well, nothing was impossible, and in a sense Adria felt she had already proved that much.

"Spain could be very dangerous, especially for a woman," Robert Wertheim suggested, turning toward her slightly. "It's not a play war, you know."

10

Adria glanced at his elegant profile. Was there no end to it? Men, even men she hardly knew were always trying to protect her. And God only knew what her father would say when she announced her intentions. He had, after all, opposed her going to college. Later, when she chose to study photography, he had opposed that as well. He had given in, of course, and in the end he'd managed to convince himself that she would end up a society-portrait photographer able to utilize and enhance his many contacts. His first and only contribution to her career had been arranging for her to take photos of President Roosevelt when he officiated at the graduation ceremonies at Annapolis last year. Not what her father had expected, the photos hadn't been the usual still poses, all stiff and formal. They were candid, her first attempt at the innovative photographic style made possible by the new German cameras. They had turned out well, so well that Andy Martin had given her the assignment in Spain.

"I see no reason why going to Spain is more dangerous for a woman than for a man," she said tersely.

Wertheim glanced at her. "Let me rephrase my comment. The dangers will be different. In some respects a woman might have certain advantages, but in other respects there will be more difficulty. It is, you might say, a matter of culture."

"I suppose you think all Spanish men are leering skirt chasers," Adria quickly responded, then added, "I can take care of myself."

"I am surprised your father would consider letting you go," Jacques said from the back seat. He hadn't fully heard her response to Robert.

"Where I go is of no more concern to my father than where he goes is of concern to me," Adria replied, folding her arms across her lap defensively. It wasn't true. Her father would try to stop her and she was already preparing for the moment when she would have to stand up to him. And his activities deeply concerned her. Hadn't she heard all the rumors of his infidelities? But then, how often had she been with her father? A

11

total of less than two years she calculated . . . and those years were made up of a week here, a month there, two days and four days. Yet, he expected a say over how she spent her life, worse yet, assumed he knew her and dared to predict her taste, her thoughts, her ideas.

"Is your mother still in the United States?"

Fishing, Adria thought. Robert had probably heard stories. Admiral Nelson Halstead had no doubt garnered himself a reputation in the south of France. He loved parties, he loved being with the rich, and he was very much a ladies man. No assignment could have suited him better. The Riviera was a playground, and Nelson Halstead was an avid player.

"Woman's place is in the home" was clearly his message to his daughter. "Don't run around with that bunch of chippies," he used to warn her when she was in college. But whom did he run around with? When he wanted to philander, he certainly didn't want a homebody. He was obviously grateful for the large number of women who were not virtuous—'chippies,' as he called them.

Adria sat in silence for a time, looking out the window at the beautiful landscape just west of Toulon. Jagged, semiarid mountains, wild flowers, white houses which seemed to be built into the cliffs. She had been told by one of her classmates that the coast around Ste. Maxime and Villefranche was even more breathtaking. She would have looked forward to it more, but Adria could not escape the fact that every mile the purring Rolls Royce traveled brought her closer to her father. She could already feel her antagonism growing side by side with her desire to see him.

"How do you feel about the situation in Europe?" Robert asked, almost as if he sensed her desire to think about something besides her family.

"I think there will be a war," Adria answered.

"You mean a war outside the fighting in Spain?"

"Yes. That's one of the reason's why I want to go to

Spain. I want to see for myself. I want to experiment with candid photography."

Robert Wertheim seemed more interested in her political views. "If there is a war in Europe, do you think America would become involved?"

"Mr. Cardon may disagree with me, but I think America will stay out of it. The pacifist movement is very strong."

"The American Navy doesn't seem pacifist. If they are, why this show of force in the Mediterranean?" Jacques Cardon asked.

"The president and the military might want to go to war, but they can't without congressional approval. And Congress is isolationist."

He smiled. "A very astute observation. Photography and politics, do they go together?"

"Yes."

"And tell me, which side in Spain do you intend to photograph? The victorious Fascista or the decimated Loyalists?"

"Both."

"Then you had better not stay in France too long. The Loyalists are losing."

Adria took a deep breath. "I don't intend to stay long," she replied, once again thinking of her father. Then too, she had heard her former classmate, Christina Barton, was here as well, and Adria certainly didn't want to run into her. Seeing her father would open enough wounds.

2

"GOOD GAME," NELSON HALSTEAD called out. His voice was deep, and even when he shouted in good humor it was evident he was a man used to bellowing orders. He ambled toward the net, aware as always of his posture. Age had thickened his body, but exercise turned much of his weight to muscle, except for a slight paunch covered by skillfully tailored clothes.

Nelson grabbed the orange terry towel that had been casually slung over the end of the net. He wiped his brow, then his light gray brush cut. Too old to jump over the net, he thought a bit ruefully.

Christina Barton strolled toward him. Her bobbed blond hair bounced, he could easily imagine the swing in her neat little rear. She was, as the navy expression went, "built like a masonry brick outhouse."

"You really played well," she gushed. Her hand smoothed her glaring white tennis skirt.

"I used to play a lot at Annapolis." He grinned and reminded himself that he had graduated first in the class of 1913 and that Christina Barton probably hadn't been born when he was bounding around the courts at the Naval Academy.

"Buy me a drink?" Christina asked coyly, batting her heavy lashes.

Nelson could feel the chemistry working, and as surely as he nodded and took her arm, he knew he'd be in bed with her by ten P.M. He pressed her arm to him and squeezed it lightly, pushing his age, his paunch, and his daughter's imminent arrival from his mind. He would phone headquarters in Villefranche and explain that he was detained in Nice by an emergency. That spiffy young lieutenant, William Cutler, could meet her and get her settled in a hotel. Damn! He wished he knew just when she was coming. But he consoled himself with the thought that he hadn't seen Adria for over a year, so if she arrived before he returned, the extra few days of separation wouldn't make any difference.

I am, he rationalized, the youngest admiral in the U.S. Navy. I'm estranged from my wife. And, after a second thought about Christina's age, he added, this is the south of France, where anything goes.

He smiled warmly at Christina Barton as he pulled out her chair at the terrace bar. Young she was, but also sophisticated and wealthy. She introduced him to American expatriate society in Cannes, Nice, and Villefranche, seeing to it that he dined with the likes of the Aga Kahn, the Duke and Duchess of Windsor, and Anthony Eden, all of whom had homes on the Riviera. In short, in addition to being bedworthy, Christina Barton could help further his career. She made him, and thus the American naval presence, known and respected.

And that's what it was all about, Nelson thought. President Roosevelt had sent the fleet on a mission, and that mission was to evacuate refugees from war-torn Spain while impressing the Germans with a show of American naval strength. "Roosevelt wants to exercise a subtle form of gunboat diplomacy," the secretary of the navy had instructed him. "He wants the krauts to look down the barrel of our best 45 millimeters! He wants to let them see our fastest cruisers and battle-ships. He wants us to make our presence known in the Mediterranean. And by God, Nelson, it's a good assignment. Hell, you can only beat the climate on the Riviera at the 11th Naval District in San Diego, but in San Diego you can't touch the social life of Cannes!" How right the secretary had been!

Christina Barton crossed her legs, allowing her skirt to rise a bit and reveal her tanned, dimpled knees. She had long legs, and though he couldn't see her thighs, Nelson Halstead knew they would be sensational. He shifted his weight. The chairs on the terrace of Le Club Anglais were tiny, not built for a man of his bulk. "I love it here," Christina said, leaning back in her chair and studying the list of mixed drinks.

Le Club Anglais overlooked the clear blue sea and the white sand of the Côte d'Azur. The panoramic view from the terrace included sailboats, swimmers, and sun worshipers. Nelson looked around impatiently for the waiter. The food and drinks were served in an all too leisurely style, and Nelson willingly admitted that the European pace often annoyed him. One had to put up with these things, he reminded himself. After all, the club had been built by the British, a splendid replica of other clubs that could be found from Hong Kong to Cairo. It was the favorite haunt of the international set because it possessed the four "E's"—it was exclusive, expensive, elegant, and English. Once upon a time, he supposed, he might have been barred entry, but now both he and Christina Barton were welcomed. He because club privileges were extended to American naval officers, and she because she was the daughter of a former U.S. senator who had parlayed a modest family inheritance into a fortune, and who was well known around Washington as the head of a large industrial lobby working for the likes of ITT.

A warm breeze played with the fringe of the pastel yellow umbrella over the small round table. Christina ran her tongue around her full lips and looked at him. She definitely had bedroom blue eyes, and, just as definitely, she was one of those girls with a taste for older men. "What'll it be?" Her high, firm breasts were obvious through her white cotton knit sweater, and he wondered if they were all hers. God he hated it when he undressed a woman and found out she was wearing a padded bra or falsies.

One of those long-nosed, snooty French waiters stood by, pad and pencil in hand, barely acknowledging their existence. "Something exotic, I think. Yes, that's it, I'll have a Singapore Gin Sling," she said, smiling at the waiter's stone face.

"Bourbon on the rocks for me," Nelson said, ignoring the waiter. Le Club Anglais was about the only place in Nice you could get bourbon, and though he had his own cache of Jack Daniels, he missed it when dining out. They didn't call the south of France "the English Coast" without reason, and the Brits drank Scotch.

Christina took a short breath and reached across the glass table top to take his hand. "Are we having dinner tonight?"

He winked at her. "Why not?" He'd tell her about Adria's visit tomorrow. After all, it would be harder to explain Christina to Adria than Adria to Christina. "Where do you want to eat?"

She shrugged, "I'll leave that up to you." Christina

16

looked into his eyes steadily, "Do you know Monsieur Dubois? He owns the Hôtel de la Mare, that quaint little hotel in Villefranche."

Nelson nodded. He wasn't exactly sure what Christina had in mind, but he hoped to God she wouldn't suggest they go to the Hôtel de la Mare. It was full of naval officers, and though it was well known as a discreet rendezvous for wealthy civilians, too many of his own officers lived there. Villefranche, near the village and fortress of Eze, was not only his headquarters but where the fleet was located. He felt safer cavorting here in Nice twenty miles away, or better still in Cannes. Of course, he lived in Villefranche. Indeed, he had a house there, a very well placed one next door to Anthony Eden's winter refuge. He frowned at her. "I don't know Dubois well—why?"

Christina pressed her lips together and leaned across the table conspiratorially and whispered, "They say he's a German spy. I've heard he keeps carrier pigeons on the roof and that's how he communicates with his German contacts."

Nelson felt a wave of relief, together with a glimmer of interest. He wondered where Christina Barton, a seemingly empty-headed American society Miss, had heard about Monsieur Dubois. Already under surveillance by O.N.I., the Office of Naval Intelligence, the man was most certainly a spy. "I'm sure France is full of German spies," he answered lightly, "and Germany is probably full of French spies." Spies, war, and politics were not what he had on his mind just now. Certainly he didn't want to discuss them with Christina.

"I just thought you ought to know. After all, a lot of your officers live at the hotel."

He laughed, hoping to get her off the subject, but still a little curious. "Where do you hear all these intriguing rumors?"

"I heard this one from Robert Wertheim. You know him? He's terribly wealthy and frightfully good looking. His estate adjoins the Rothschilds' estate."

Nelson grimaced. "He's a Hebe. Hebes see fascists under every bed."

She giggled. "He's so rich—well, they're so rich,—I don't think they think of themselves as Jewish. They're very respected, you know, and very influential."

Nelson nodded. Truth be known, he wasn't interested in Germans. Like the French government of the day, he considered Communists to be the greater threat. But he had no intention of discussing politics with Christina. "You don't have to worry about the navy," he said reassuringly. "We know what's going on, and we know where. Now, where shall we have dinner?"

Christina smiled and leaned over again, "Let's be wicked and drive to Cannes."

He nodded eagerly. If Adria appeared, she could wait. Mentally, he ran through his other responsibilities. He would have to phone and check on the arrival of the *Raleigh*, but apart from that small chore, he was quite free. In his mind he conjured up a small, discreet hotel where he and Christina could go after a long late supper. She was going to be good in bed; he could tell by the way she walked.

3

DESPITE ITS NAME, THERE was nothing worldly about L' Hôtel du Monde; it was utterly and completely French. Indeed secluded, it was located on a small cul-de-sac two blocks off the famous Promenade de Crosette, and regrettably its windows offered no view of the Gulfe de la Napoule, nor the wooded rolling hills behind the ancient city of Cannes. Nelson Halstead smiled broadly at the thought that Phoenicians, Celts, and Romans had all occupied Cannes, and doubtless they'd all shacked up here. That's what invading navies did. Show me a decent port and I'll show you a place that's seen illicit sex through the centuries, he said silently, amused. He rolled over and leaned on one elbow. One thing he certainly liked about the French was their attitude when you checked into a hotel. The clerk had asked for his passport, but not for Christina's. That simply wasn't done in Cannes, where discretion was the better part of keeping your job.

Nelson gazed at Christina and wondered how many more times he would bed her. Her bobbed blond hair was disheveled, her breathing deep and quiet. It pleased him that she slept on her stomach, as he appreciated the view of her lovely, round, white ass tightly wrapped in the sheet.

Last night he had discovered that she was twenty-three, not twenty-five. He shrugged; what did it matter as long as she was over twenty-one and legal? And, he thought proudly, now she had been well and truly laid. Doubtless her previous liaisons, and certainly there had been others, had all been with overanxious college boys, fresh and inexperienced. A woman like Christina needed a man, not a boy. He was pleased to oblige, despite a slight twinge of guilt—she was the same age as Adria.

He reached over to the bedside table and fumbled for his Camels. Certainly the night had been worth it. He felt twenty years younger, relaxed and better able to cope with the impending visit of his rebellious and sometimes bitter daughter. Christ, Adria was twenty-three, she ought to understand by now that some things just don't work out.

Christina stirred and rolled over. Silently he mourned the disappearance of her bottom, though he admitted her front was nearly as enticing. She blinked open her blue eyes and smiled sleepily at him. "You're awake." She sighed and lifted her long, graceful arms, encircling his neck.

"But I have to go." He bent down and teasingly bit her hard little nipple. All women liked that. Christina liked it a lot.

"Once more?" He felt her hands on him, and he could all but feel her long legs wrapping around him. Such a responsive little bitch, he thought, even as he felt the warm rush of his own blood. She moved

19

beneath him, and his resolve to get an early start back to Villefranche totally gave way. He ran his hand over her flat belly and down between her thighs. She moaned and lifted herself up.

He was quick . . . too quick. But he'd been slow the night before, though now, in the morning light, she made him feel like a pup again, anxious and unable to concentrate. Usually, he thought about the baseball scores, or mentally ran through his latest set of orders, but feeling Christina wiggle beneath him he thought about her instead. Consequently he burst forth in seconds, completely unable to control himself once his hands had slipped beneath her rear. "Sorry," he mumbled. But she didn't seem to mind, and he decided not to linger.

As he dressed, Christina Barton lay in bed nude, her pert little chin cupped in her hand, her wide-open eyes staring at him. She had the expression of a pleased cat. "Will it be long before we can get away again?"

"No, just a few days. My daughter's coming. The trip is a graduation present. I've got to show her around, get her started on some sightseeing. I'll send her up to Paris for a few days, then I'll call you." He had neglected to mention his daughter's age. Probably Christina thought she was fourteen or fifteen, and that the graduation was from high school.

"You didn't tell me Adria was coming!" Christina said, suddenly sitting up.

Nelson Halstead froze in the act of pulling his pants up. "Adria? You know her?"

Christina smiled now and ran her fingers through her hair. "Of course I know her. We went to school together. I remember now, she asked me about the Riviera."

Nelson managed to straighten up and scowl at Christina. "Christ, you should have told me."

She arched her eyebrow, "Would it have made a difference?"

He knew his face was flushed. God, he hated surprises, and finding out that Christina Barton was a friend of Adria's qualified as not just a surprise, but as an unpleasant shock. "I don't suppose it would have," he allowed, "I'm just taken aback. You and Adria don't seem to have a lot in common." He pulled on his pants and looked at her nude body from head to toe. Not at all. And he mentally added, not with her mother either, the pristine Julia Halstead.

Christina laughed. "I didn't say we were bosom buddies, darling, I said we knew each other. Trust me, I wouldn't think of letting Adria find out about us. But she knows I'm here, and I expect she'll look me up."

Nelson wondered if he looked as relieved as he felt. She got added points for having a sensible attitude. "I won't worry," he told her. He turned and looked in the mirror. He stuffed his shirt into his trousers, put on his tie and jacket and then his hat. The sleek-fitting uniform entirely hid his paunch. Not only did he feel younger, he looked decidedly younger than he was. "Only a few days," he said turning to her. "Now while I'm out of port, you stay in dry dock."

Christina giggled. "You're silly," she said winking. "But intriguing, very intriguing. My father says that one day soon you'll be a rear admiral, perhaps even the top admiral in the fleet."

Nelson Halstead exulted in her prediction—former Senator Layton Barton was a man of influence, a man in a position to make that kind of prediction a reality.

"Did your ship get back from Spain? I heard you ask about it on the phone."

Nelson nodded. "Yup, and there's a new carrier on its way from Newport News to enforce our presence—one of our new big jobs, very impressive. When it arrives I'll take you aboard for a tour."

"You might start tongues wagging."

He shrugged, "Your father deals with the navy department and you're my daughter's friend. As long as you don't flirt or get playful it'll be all right." To emphasize his point he strode to the bed and slapped her playfully on the bottom. She wiggled seductively, "And none of that," he said, shaking his finger as he turned.

"Call me tomorrow," Christina suggested.

"I will," he replied as he twisted the knob on the door. Pretty kitten, he thought. Definitely good for a long run overhaul. And now that he thought about it, what did it really matter that Adria knew her? In fact, he thought, it might even be an advantage.

Chapter Two

1

ADRIA SAT AT THE glass-top table on the terrace of Villefranche's Hôtel de la Mare. Her auburn hair fell to her shoulders, its ends turned under to caress the collar of her china blue cotton blouse. She wore a slim-line matching skirt, a print headband, and low-heeled leather shoes. Abstractedly, she fingered her antique gold locket. Inside was a picture of her mother and father on their wedding day, her father looking young and proud in his ensign's uniform, her mother angelic in her satin and lace.

Adria looked up, forcing her thoughts away from the picture and all it represented. She gazed up and concentrated on the rolling, brush-covered hills that rose to meet the clear blue sky behind the hotel. Below, a rocky descent led to the white sand and the sea beyond. The hills were dotted with white red-tile-roofed mansions, and below, the two- and three-story buildings of the village. In the harbor, six American ships lay at anchor, their dull gray a striking contrast to the profusion of colors that characterized the Côte d'Azur. Adria inhaled the delicious air, clear and heavy with scent of carnations, and returned her gaze to her father.

She had arrived yesterday and been met by young

Lieutenant William Cutler, who got her a room. Patiently, if with apprehension, she had waited for her father to return. Now they had been together for an hour, and what had they discussed so far? His annoyance that she hadn't told him exactly when she was coming. His tour of duty. His hopes for the future, descriptions of his favorite young officers—always offered with the words, "you'll like so-and-so, I hope you might get together." He'd gone into great detail about one of the cruisers he was sending back to Boston for new fittings, and he had made a few passing comments about Germany's military build-up and how he felt it was all for the best—"let the krauts hold the Ruskies in check." About her he had expressed little curiosity. He asked about her final marks and grunted when she told him she had scored all A's. He asked if she'd gone up to Annapolis for any of the season's social events, and when she answered no, he mumbled that she was missing everything. Pointedly, he hadn't asked about her mother.

"Looking good," Nelson Halstead announced as he raised his glass of whiskey and toasted her. "See you brought your cameras; you ought to be able to get some good pictures up at Eze—it's an ancient fortress, great rock formations."

Adria frowned. "I'm not terribly interested in rock formations." It was the beginning; she was starting to feel irritated. Of course he refused to recognize the fact that a woman could have a career—what women had were hobbies, something to keep them busy till they got married and gave birth to sons.

"Well, then you'll get lots of pictures in Paris. Great museums, something to show your children. You may think it's common, but not every girl gets a trip to Europe as a graduation present."

"I don't have children and I'm not going to Paris."

He raised a bushy brow. "Not going to Paris! Hell, why did you bother coming to France! Let me tell you, you're passing up a chance to study history, to get to

23

know French culture. You'll be bored out of your skull laying around here on the beach for a month! What a waste!"

Adria bit her lip. Their argument was inevitable. Why not sooner than later? she asked herself. "I'm not staying here for a month," she declared.

He grumbled, "And where *are* you going? You know damn well I haven't got time to prance around Europe with you. I've got a job to do here."

"I didn't ask you to go anywhere with me. I can go where I please. Alone." Damn, I sound too angry, Adria thought, silently rebuking herself.

He scowled at her. "Not as long as I'm paying for it. I don't hold with girls your age traveling alone."

Adria avoided her father's eyes and twirled her napkin nervously around her index finger. "You're not paying for it. I have a job and I have an assignment." She was going to count to three and wait for the explosion; she didn't get past one.

"What the hell?" He fairly spit out the words.

"I'm going to Spain. Andy Martin's given me a job. He thinks my work is good."

"You're going to Spain over my dead body!" her father blustered. "I have connections you know. I can fix it so you won't be allowed into Franco-held territory, and that's most of Spain!"

"Then I shall go to Loyalist Spain—I'm sure you don't have any connections with the Communists! I have a job, and I'm damn well going to do it, as you would say!"

"You have a job with that meddling Socialist fairy, Andy Martin! I'll have that son of a bitch's balls for bookends!"

"You can't hurt him, and you know it. I'm going to Spain, Daddy. I'm going one way or another, and I'm going alone."

His face was red and he gulped his whiskey. "I suppose it was your mother who arranged this? Is she seeing that bastard again? God damn it! Adria, Andy

24

Martin—and, I might add, your mother—have no idea what Spain is like."

Adria stiffened. "Mother isn't seeing anyone. And it doesn't matter what mother or Andy know or don't know. I know the dangers . . . why can't you get it through your head that I'm an adult?" She was beginning to shake. How dare he accuse her mother of infidelity! He was probably sleeping with half the women in Cannes!

"I knew this trip was a mistake," he muttered.

"I would have come anyway."

He finished his drink and signaled for a refill. Adria let out her breath, unrolled her napkin, and folded it neatly. His facial color returned to normal, his tirade had subsided; he'd have another drink and then he'd begin on some totally mundane subject. They couldn't discuss anything important without fighting, and he always withdrew from their fights, pulling back, regrouping his arguments. It's because I'm a woman—he wanted a son, he always wanted a son. She couldn't count the times he'd actually said it to her. And he wanted her to marry—he wanted her to marry a young naval officer who could be his son. She watched silently as he drank his second drink slowly and in silence. Then he cleared his throat. "How was the train trip down?"

"I drove with a gentleman I met on the ship, a wine merchant from New York and the man who picked him up, a Monsieur Wertheim."

"Robert Wertheim? He's the second richest man in France."

"He was very nice," she said carefully. "He's worried about the whole European situation. His mother is in Germany visiting; he's trying to persuade her to come back."

"If I were a Hebe I'd be worried, too. But the Germans are harmless. Hell, why do you think we're here? We're here to remind them to behave."

"Harmless? They could cause a war, forcing the Czechs and threatening Poland."

25

"Who gives a damn about Poland and Czechoslovakia? If you get your ideas out of that rag that Andy Martin publishes, you're reading left-wing alarmist crap to take America's thoughts off the real menace—and that's Russia. Look, you needn't think that's just my view. It's the view of the French government too."

Adria finished her wine and put down her glass. "I'm really tired. I think I'll go to my room and clean up, maybe take a nap."

He nodded. "We're going out to the ship for dinner. I'll introduce you to some good looking young officers —you don't have to worry about them, they wouldn't try a thing with the admiral's daughter."

Adria didn't smile. God, did he actually think she was still a virgin?

"All right," she murmured, thinking, if he were the last man on earth, I wouldn't go out with a naval officer. She had made that vow years ago, and much to her father's unhappiness, she had stuck to it.

2

MADAME ABRAHAM WERTHEIM WAS the dowager of the Wertheim family and a genuinely elegant woman. At fifty-one she had tissue-paper skin, perfectly coiffed blue gray hair, and pale blue eyes that solemnly studied everyone and everything.

On her fiftieth birthday she had allowed her portrait to be rendered by a well-known but discreet artist. The end product, a delicate painting in pastels, depicted her sitting demurely in front of her grand piano, long graceful hands folded peacefully in her lap, wearing a pale blue chiffon dress with a finely pleated wide peplum collar that fell over her shoulders. Behind her on the wall of the conservatory in the Wertheim chateau were the portraits of her ancestors. These, though sketchily reproduced in her own portrait, clearly illustrated Madame's strong sense of family and continuity.

In addition to English, which was her mother tongue, Madame Wertheim spoke perfect German and French. She was the daughter of a titled British family whose only famous member had been Benjamin Disraeli, prime minister to Queen Victoria and the first Jewish prime minister in British history. Well, almost Jewish. Isaac d'Israeli, the prime minister's father, had long since lapsed in his faith when little Benjamin was born, and the future politician and writer was baptized in the Christian faith. Not so for the rest of the family, who remained Jewish, though in fact only a few family members ever attended synagogue. If asked, Madame Abraham Wertheim would have described her family as secular and of Jewish heritage.

A cousin of Isaac d'Israeli had married into the Frankle family, the founders of the Kensington Insurance empire. Philip Frankle married a wealthy German Jewish heiress named Eva Obermann. Madame Abraham Wertheim was their daughter, the former Anna Myra Obermann Frankle.

Abraham Wertheim, Madame's late husband, had an even more distinguished family history. The Wertheims were not quite as rich as the Rothschilds, but they commanded similar respect. Abraham Wertheim's grandfather had been born in the Jewish ghetto of Frankfurt am Main in 1760, some fifteen years after the birth of Mayer Amschel Rothschild, the founder of the Rothschild banking empire. As Jews could not own land at the time, the most respected endeavors for a young man to pursue were rabbinical study, medicine, or finance. In turn, young Moshe Wertheim attempted all three, settling on finance by the time he was thirty-one. He had begun as a simple money-lender and advanced to become a financial advisor to the Hapsburgs. Late in life he founded the original House of Wertheim. Moshe's sons, inherited the House of Wertheim and eventually, like the family Rothschild, were made barons in the Austrian Empire. One son emigrated to America, founding Wertheim Investments,

Inc. in the shadow of the Federal Building on Wall Street and across the street from the revered House of Morgan. The other son married a ravishing and talented British actress, Carla Samuelson, and their son, Abraham, married Anna Myra Obermann Frankle, thus uniting the German-American investment house to the British insurance firm. Abraham enhanced the family holdings by expanding into banking, and as a hobby into vinticulture. Abraham's hobby became a passion, and the passion resulted in Wertheim Wines, now known all over the world.

Madame Wertheim, who thought the title baroness was ostentatious—more so since the demise of the Austrian Empire—had given birth to two sons, Robert and Charles. Charles lived in England, where he oversaw the family's British holdings, while Robert remained to manage the family's banking, insurance, and wine production on the continent. The family's American interests were managed by Jakob's heirs, Karl, Michael, and Joshua Wertheim. Each had married into a different German-Jewish-American family. The American "cousins," as they were called, included Strauses, Sachses, Goldmans, Speyers, Seligmans, and Loebs.

Though he traveled often to Paris, Robert Wertheim's base of operations was the huge Wertheim estate near Nice. Madame Wertheim divided her time evenly between the estate, her son Charles's country home in Scotland, and the house of her German relatives, the Obermanns. Once every two years, in the spring, she booked a suite on the *Queen Mary* and traveled to New York for a two-month visit with "the American cousins."

The Wertheims, like the Frankles, the Obermanns, and the 'American cousins,' had possessed wealth for generations. They considered themselves different not only from other Jews but from most other people. They were internationalists in that they thought of several countries as "home," they were multilingual and superbly educated, and they moved among a few people of their own ilk. Anna Myra Wertheim had never seen a dirty dish, an unmade bed, or walked through an unkempt garden. She had been privately tutored, her pastimes were genteel, and she could not envisage any other kind of life.

In October of 1938, she announced her intention of visiting her relatives in Germany. "This might not be the best time," her son Robert had advised.

Madame had only smiled, "But I always go to Germany in October."

"They could come here," Robert had suggested.

Madame would have no part of it. She would go, and stay till the middle of November. In November her German relatives would go to England, and in December they would go to the Caribbean and she would go to England. When she returned from England, her German relatives would come to the estate in France. Madame was not one to break her habits. This she explained to her son in no uncertain terms, and so, against his better judgment, she left for her month-long visit on October 14th.

Hitler, about whom Madame Wertheim knew little and cared less, was no more than an uncouth aberration who fluttered into her vague understanding of the world beyond the four estates she frequented. Not that she had not noticed the rise of militarism on her previous visits, nor was she ignorant of the fact that Hitler had been elected chancellor. But her friends all said it would pass, and Madame, if she had one failing, was politically naive.

Madame Wertheim was not privy to, nor would she have understood, the message sent from Gestapo headquarters at 11:55 P.M. on November 9, 1938.

The message read:

Berlin No. 234404 9.11.2355
To all Gestapo Stations and Gestapo District Stations:

This teleprinter message is to be submitted without delay:

1. At very short notice, *Aktionen* against Jews, especially against their synagogues, will take place throughout the whole of Germany. They [the perpetrators] are not to be hindered. In conjunction with the police, however, it is to be ensured that looting and other particular excesses can be prevented.

2. If important archival material is in synagogues, this is to be taken into safekeeping by an immediate measure. [It is to be retained for display in a special museum which will detail the history of this degenerate people.]

3. Preparations are to be made for the arrest of about 20,000-30,000 Jews in the Reich. Wealthy Jews in particular are to be selected. More detailed instructions will be issued in the course of the night.

4. Should in the forthcoming *Aktionen* Jews be found in possession of weapons, the more severe measures are to be taken. SS Reserves as well as the General SS can be mobilized in the total *Aktionen*. The direction of the *Aktionen* by the Gestapo is in any case to be assured by appropriate measures.

Gestapo II Müller

This teleprinter message is secret.

267 synagogues, 815 shops, homes, and estates, 20,000 arrests. *Kristallnacht*—the night of broken glass, a night of destruction, a night of fear, and a night which Madame Wertheim would always remember, though perhaps for different reasons than most.

At the time, she was sipping a peach brandy aperitif and was listening, eyes closed, to a private performance given by the Gutten String Quartet. Then the serenity was interrupted by a knock on the door. The maid screamed, and suddenly the room was filled with uniformed men. Madame heard someone call them "Gestapo."

The officer in charge had ordered them to get their coats and come along. He actually had a gun, and he waved it at them. But Madame noted he paid them little attention. Instead, he greedily eyed the room, which was filled with priceless art treasures. Madame Wertheim was too stunned to be afraid, and too angry.

They had all been put into a truck like cattle and brought to a building where their pictures had been taken, and the others had been fingerprinted. But when the officer routinely asked for citizenship, Madame had replied—and quite correctly—"British."

"You will be dealt with later," she was advised.

Madame Wertheim, dressed in a full-length blue gray silk evening gown and sheltered from the dampness by a long, rich Russian sable cape, was directed to a long wooden bench and told to wait. At first she was stunned by the sheer grimness of the place, its odor of cigarettes and sweat, and the acrid smell of coffee. All of this was unnerving enough, but the noise level, as well as the sights that were paraded before her, shocked her to the depths of her well-developed sensibilities.

Black-uniformed men pushed, shoved, and manhandled their well-dressed victims. They shouted obscenities, they spoke vile German, and they were rude beyond all of Madame's imaginings.

"We are German citizens! We have done nothing!" an elderly man protested. He was sworn at, and when he refused to move and insisted on calling his solicitor, he was half dragged along one corridor.

Two people were brought in screaming—Madame Wertheim stared at them. They were not well dressed, and the black-uniformed men kicked at the man and shook the woman, whose nose was bleeding.

"They were scissors!" The woman continued to protest in spite of her injuries. "Only scissors! I was defending myself, I am a seamstress! Scissors are not a weapon!"

31

"You are under arrest for carrying a weapon, you Jewish whore!" The Gestapo officer grabbed her by her long dark hair and pulled her away shrieking, her screams echoed off the stone walls as she and her tormentor disappeared down a dimly lit corridor, away from the long bench, out of Madame's line of vision and eventually out of her range of hearing.

Down the long, endless corridors the hapless victims were marched. How many? Madame lost count. Somewhere she could hear the clinking of cell doors closing . . . and where had the Obermanns been taken? Were they in one of the cells? She shook her head, trying to reconstruct the jumbled events of the evening.

Eventually, a man was sent to sit next to her. His hair was long and tangled, and he smelled of garlic. Instinctively, Madame had moved down the bench, hearing only his mutter that he was a scholar. In the hours and days that followed, it was he she would most remember. But now she was brought into a small room and directed to sit in a wooden chair opposite a Gestapo officer whose uniform was highly decorated with medals.

"Why are you in Germany?"

Madame looked at him almost uncomprehendingly and replied slowly, "Because it is November," then thinking, "I always visit my relatives between October 15th and November 15th."

"Who are your relatives?" he demanded.

"The Obermanns . . . Isobel and Myron Obermann. They are here, we came together."

"You were arrested together."

Her cousins were in jail then? What could this mean? Was this why Robert had advised her not to come?

"Their property has been seized. They are enemies of the Third Reich," the man told her.

Madame almost gasped, but she restrained herself, wondering again what it all meant. Did it mean they had nothing?

"All property belonging to disloyal Jews has been

seized. All Jewish property is being reclaimed in the name of the Third Reich!"

Madame stared at him. Who was this vulgar animal? Who were the others? Where did they come from? And how had they come to be in such positions? "Disloyal?" she said, trying with all her will to sound rational in the face of all that was happening. Could one be rational surrounded by irrationality? "Myron Obermann's father was an officer in Kaiser Weilhelm's Army. You have made a mistake. He is a loyal German citizen."

"There is no mistake, Jewess," he snapped at her in a harsh tone. "You gave your citizenship as British. May I have your passport?"

Jewess? No one had ever called her a Jewess. Indeed she had never even been to a synagogue, and never spoken to a rabbi. Madame tilted her head and lifted her chin, "I am a British subject," she said with dignity, as she opened her handbag and handed over her passport.

"You're a Jew. And you will no longer be allowed entry to Germany."

His words stunned her as much as the events of the evening, which were still churning in her mind. In a way, she felt she had seen only a collage of images and heard only a cacophony of sound.

Oh, there had been difficulty during the Great War, of course. The German side of the family had remained loyal to Germany and the French, American, and English sides, loyal to their respective countries. Visits had been curtailed, but everything had returned to absolute normalcy immediately after the armistice. No one save Myron's father had ever served in the military of any country. In fact, the only time in the history of the family that a nation's business had created real hardships had been during the American Civil War, when the "American cousins" had found themselves at odds.

The Gestapo officer thumbed through her passport and then threw it down on the table in front of her. The boor didn't even look in the eyes. He stamped a paper. "You will be escorted to the train. You are being deported from Germany."

"My cousins?"

"Are at our disposal."

Madame Wertheim opened her mouth, and out of habit touched the diamond broach at her throat. Disposal, what did he mean?

3

THE RAMBLING THREE-STORY chateau in which Robert Wertheim and his mother resided was three and a half kilometers off the winding road that stretched between Eze and Nice. The grounds were partially hidden behind a wall of graceful acacia trees and protected by a twelve-foot, wrought-iron fence. Beyond the chateau with its red gingerbread roof stretched vast acres of vineyards that prospered under the warm Mediterranean sun. It was here that the grapes that produced the more common table wines were grown. In Bordeaux were other vineyards that yielded finer wines also sold under the Wertheim label, but it was here, on the Côte d'Azur, that the Wertheims made their home.

The main house was immense. The inlaid tile foyer was as large as most homes and the reception rooms were cavernous, with high ceilings. It could have been an art gallery. All the walls were covered with woven medieval tapestries and paintings by Renoir, Cezanne, and Toulouse-Lautrec. The largest reception room, the massive dining room, the huge living room, and the kitchen—which was big enough to suit a hotel—took up most of the first floor. The second floor held four bedroom suites, a library, and a study. The third floor consisted mainly of guest bedrooms and their adjoining baths. Beneath the mansion lay the famous Wertheim wine cellars, row upon row of wooden racks stocked with dusty bottles of fine vintage wines from all over the world, as well as from the Wertheim vineyards in three French provinces.

Beyond the main house, in a large, thatched-roof dwelling, the many household servants resided, while the groundskeepers were housed in various cottages dotted about the estate. During the harvest, the numbers of workers swelled, but even under normal circumstances the Wertheims were served by twenty-five house staff and seventy-five grounds staff. The servants had much to do when family visited from England, Germany, or America. Then, hoards of small children scurried about creating havoc and getting into mischief. But most of the time the staff simply maintained the estate and served only Robert Wertheim and his mother.

Once Robert had suggested that they could well do with fewer employees, but Madame would hear none of it. "Some of them were born here," she protested, "They're like family to one another." This was true, but nonetheless, Robert sometimes felt as if he were an anachronism, a medieval lord in the twentieth century, and in many ways Robert Wertheim preferred his smaller Paris apartment. Still the climate of the Côte d'Azur, the aroma of fresh blossoms, the miles of vineyards, and the proximity of the estate to the wide, white sandy beaches were compelling. Thus, when in Paris he longed for the estate, and when at the estate, he longed for the anonymity and freedom offered by the city.

In order to make himself more comfortable in the chateau, he spent much of his time in the second-floor study adjoining his bedroom suite. It was here that he always read the newspapers, communicated with Paris, and wrote his correspondence. The study was among the smaller rooms, and the shelves of leather-bound books gave it a pleasant aroma and warmth. He recognized the absurdity of living alone with his mother in such an immense house, but reminded himself that his mother would have had difficulty living any other way.

Robert put down his morning paper and sipped his coffee. Had his mother been home, he'd have been taking tea with her. He closed his eyes and wondered how her recent experience had affected her. From all accounts she had witnessed a brutal experience, unlike anything she had ever seen before. He silently thanked heaven that he knew she was safe, indeed that all his German relatives were safe and planning to leave Germany within the next few weeks.

His mother had called him from Paris the moment her train arrived from Berlin. She had sounded distant and distressed, but clearly still in command of herself. Tears, hysteria, or expressions of fright were not in his mother's make-up; she was too dignified, too steeped in her own traditions, and too convinced of her own superiority. "We'll discuss it all later," she had said, simply informing him that she would have her chauffeur-driven Rolls Royce bring her back to the estate. She was due at two P.M.

Clearly his mother had been outraged as well as subjected to a rare look at the world beyond her own highly protected environment; just as clearly she was worried about the family in Germany. Like his aunts Hester and Willa, and his cousins Deborah and Gabrielle, his mother was utterly sheltered, and completely unable to deal with those who came from outside her sphere. Indeed, her favorite phrase was, "Are those our kind of people?"

The same was not true of the Wertheim men, who traveled widely, associated with all sorts, and sometimes womanized with the most unlikely types. Marriage, however, was a different matter. The Wertheim men tended to marry late, and to choose distant relatives or the daughters of other wealthy Jewish families. Then, sometime between the ages of forty-five and fifty, they sired two children.

Of course it wasn't entirely wealth that created what his mother called "the Wertheim environment." There were wealthy Jews galore in America—men who had made fortunes in real estate and investments, in retail stores, in movies, and even in crime. No, "the Wertheim environment" implied more than mere money. It implied "old" money, education, a genteel way of life, an aristocratic bearing. Most of the Wertheims recognized their Jewishness in a remote and detached way, and no Wertheim had the slightest hint of the bargainer, the tradesman, or the blatantly acquisitive. Nor did the Wertheims exhibit the outrageous taste so often associated with "new" money. Those of the Wertheim ilk, for example, always dressed tastefully, but never to attract attention. It was true that his mother had a sable coat, but she wore it only when being entertained by her relatives or to the opera. Her wedding ring was gold, a single band. She never wore more than one piece of jewelry at a time, and more often than not she dressed in soft, subdued colors.

And if the men of the clan were different from the women, the women were unique among their sex. They were proud, but delicate; they lived in a world of discreet teas, house parties, and artistic and cultural enjoyment. The most ordinary experience they ever had was to give birth, and even that was done in stoic silence. As soon as the crying infant emerged, it was placed in the arms of a wet nurse, to be reared by tutors and nurses, and eventually to be sent away to the finest of private schools if male, or have the finest of private home instruction if female.

Robert Wertheim was thirty-one. In his late teens he had often wondered if his egalitarian leanings, his interest in politics, and his social concerns were not somehow the result of having been nursed by some incipient revolutionary. But as he grew older he knew that his values had been formed by his exposure to a changing world. At Eton he had experienced the subtleties of anti-Semitism, and a thousand questions formed in his mind. His second year at Oxford brought him into contact with the brilliant Jewish scholar Aaron Rosen, and Rosen had set him on the path to understanding. Even though Robert had been born Jewish, he underwent the struggle of the convert, emerging from it with an understanding of his own ignorance of his people, a people who after nearly two thousand years in the Diaspora still held common values, rituals, and beliefs. He visited Jewish communities in the Ukraine, in Salonika, and in Palestine. He saw unity in their diversity and after his travels he was easily attracted to Zionism. His new-found faith and his goals he kept secret from his seemingly content mother and brother. It was he who needed a cause. Now he knew that he would break the Wertheim pattern; indeed he had already secretly begun to sow the seeds and to give full rein to his adventurous spirit. Travel had supplemented his education, business had sharpened his instincts, and anti-Semitism had been part of his consciousness for years. If his mother had been shocked by the brutal, animal violence of *Kristallnacht*, he was not. For many years now he had lived with a sense of impending danger, not only sensing the fanatic evil of Fascism but knowing it would grow to a powerful force.

Robert Wertheim drained his coffee cup and poured another from the steaming pot on the silver tray.

"Am I intruding?" Jacques Cardon paused in the doorway of the study.

"Not at all. I was only reading the papers."

"It's good news that your mother's safe."

Robert nodded thoughtfully. "She's very confused by what's happened. I think it'll be a long while before she settles back into her cocoon."

"I'm certain it's been a dreadful experience."

Robert studied his friend. "Dreadful experience" was something of an understatement.

"Yes," was his only reply.

"To change the subject, do you know whom I met in Cannes yesterday?" Jacques smiled and winked. "Mademoiselle Halstead."

Robert felt relieved not to discuss his mother further and seized the opportunity to speak of something besides *Kristallnacht*. Miss Halstead had left him intrigued, and he admitted that the memory of her had

considered herself a charitable person. There was a word . . . a Yiddish word that Anna had heard from one of the servant girls . . . *schnorrer*, that was it. It was used to describe a person who lived off the charity of others. It was applied to men who took their meals from friends, who slept in beds for which they did not pay, and who begged for a living. These were men without any employment. They had no money, and as she understood it, always claimed they had given up worldly goods in pursuit of learning.

Anna had been thinking that the self-styled scholar was a *schnorrer*, when a fat, rude Gestapo officer had called out in German, "Bring in the next filthy Jew." Anna had instinctively turned toward the man, who, to her way of thinking, was the only person who remotely fitted the description. But it was not the scholar they had brought . . . it was Hannah Baer, who neither practiced her Judaism nor was in any way filthy. It was then that Anna had begun to understand, and the enormity of her realization had shaken her almost as much as the reality of the evening's events. It made no difference to the Gestapo; a Jew was a Jew was a Jew. She, the Obermanns, and the ill-dressed, ill-groomed *schnorrer* were all the same. But of course it *was* different for her. She was a British subject, a foreign national as the Gestapo officer had put it. So her fur was not taken, nor was her plain gold wedding band or diamond necklace. And though she was jostled and escorted to the train station by peasant idiots, she was essentially unharmed. The Gestapo officer had seemed surprised that through it all she carried her head high, looking down on them as God had most certainly intended her to do. Nonetheless, her encounter with the *schnorrer* troubled her.

As Anna Wertheim submerged herself further, she knew that something had happened to her inside. A week ago she and the *schnorrer* had less than nothing in common. Today they were both Jews. What was that word that Sarah the downstairs maid had called non-

Jews by? *Goyim*, that was it. She whispered the word to herself. "The Germans are *goyim*," she said aloud. And in a strange way, saying it made her feel better.

She closed her eyes and soaked for another ten minutes. Then she called for the maid, who helped her out of the tub and assisted her in dressing and arranging her hair. At promptly four o'clock, as had been her custom for twenty years, she joined her son for afternoon tea in the rose garden.

Robert kissed his mother tenderly on the cheek. "You look well," he hedged.

She sighed as the maid poured the tea and proffered cream and sugar, which she never used. Anna Wertheim waved her away, not wanting to speak in front of the servants. "I'm better now that I've bathed. That's how it made me feel, Robert—unclean, violated."

He nodded, knowing full well that all things considered, she had been treated well.

His mother frowned and toyed with the delicate handle of her Spode teacup. "What will become of Hester and the girls? The Obermanns . . . in jail, under arrest, can you imagine? Robert, what will become of them?"

"They've already been released. They're being forced to leave Germany, of course, but they have money in America and in England. They don't have any immigration problems . . ."

His mother bit her lip and shook her head. "It's an outrage! Imagine being sent away from your own country. Myron was an officer in the last war! They're as German as any German . . ." She paused. "They're as German as the *goyim*."

Robert smiled in spite of his grim mood. "Where did you hear that word?"

"I'm not entirely ignorant of Yiddish—or of the world," she replied in a defiant tone.

"At least they have a place to go. They may lose what they had in Germany, but it's small by comparison . . ."

"Comparison to what?" she prodded.

"In comparison to what those who can't leave will lose. Those without money, those whom no country will accept."

"Like the scholar . . ." she said softly.

"Who?"

"A man who was arrested, a truly disgusting man."

Robert ignored his mother's comment. "You need not worry, our relatives and their friends will have no real problems. It's the Jews without someone to sponsor them in America, the ones without money, who will suffer."

"But from what I saw only the wealthy were arrested —and the scholar of course."

Robert shook his head. "This is only the first wave of arrests. But hundreds of synagogues were destroyed, shops and businesses torn apart, and over thirty Jews were murdered. The wealthy were arrested, but other Jews were set upon and beaten. And if they defended themselves, they too were arrested."

Anna frowned, recalling the seamstress with her scissors. Somehow she had thought the woman was someone's servant and had been arrested by mistake. "But they won't keep them in jail forever, and how on earth can they arrest all the Jews in Germany?" Anna asked after a moment.

Robert shrugged. What should he say to her? They'll kill them? He said. "I suppose they'll restrict them to certain places, perhaps put them in camps of some sort."

"That's inhuman."

"It's happened before."

"Oh, you mean the pale. Robert, this is the twentieth century, not the eighteenth. And we are talking about Germany, not the Ukraine. I don't think the German people would allow such a thing, darling." She shook her head. "Germany is simply not being governed by cultured men anymore; I know it can't last. Then all those stupid laws will be repealed and life will return to normal. You'll see; the Germans will rise up and object to what happened. Wanton destruction! It's a waste. I mean, I know so many Germans who aren't like that . . ."

Robert merely nodded as if to agree. He didn't feel that his mother *could* understand the deep-rooted anti-Jewish feeling that was evident all over Europe. Still, he felt that behind her outrage and her optimistic dream of the Germans overthrowing Hitler, something had affected her, something that had to do with her sudden use of a Yiddish word. "Do you want to talk more?" he asked gently.

She shook her head. "Not now," she replied sipping her tea. "I have to put it all in perspective."

"Then, to change the subject, I've invited a guest to dinner tomorrow night."

"Oh, someone I know?"

"No, a girl that Jacques met on the ship. Mademoiselle Halstead."

"Halstead?" His mother rolled the name in her mouth.

"Her father's in command of the American navy here." He paused before taking the leap. "She's a photographer for an American magazine. She's on her way to Spain to take news photos of the war."

His mother looked at him steadily. "A photographer, how nice. Your aunt Hester used to develop her own pictures, you know. It was one of her favorite pastimes."

Robert smiled. "Miss Halstead doesn't take pictures as a hobby. She sells them. That's how she earns her living."

"You mean she supports herself? She has a . . . job?"

His mother looked puzzled, and Robert smiled even more broadly. "More of a profession, I should think. Photography is an art form, you know. But yes, she does support herself."

Madame Wertheim tilted her head slightly and smiled sweetly. "I think it might be very interesting to meet such a young lady. Yes, by all means invite her.

44

You know, Robert, I've been thinking that I lead too sheltered a life."

Robert nodded. His mother was full of surprises.

2

IT HAD RAINED BETWEEN five and six in the late afternoon, a gentle, springlike rain, though in fact it was mid-November. Adria Halstead was called for at the Hôtel de la Mare at seven P.M. by a silent, uniformed chauffeur who drove the same long black Rolls Royce that Robert Wertheim had driven from Marseilles to Villefranche. The automobile purred along the winding six-mile drive to the Wertheim estate.

As an orange sun dropped into the sea, Adria could see the droplets of crystal rainwater clinging to the leaves of the roadside shrubs. Caught in the rays of the setting sun, the drops were like a thousand tiny prisms that turned the landscape into a magical profusion of rainbow-coated branches. She rolled down the window of the car and inhaled the smell of the damp, rich earth. With that sweet, distinct aroma came memories of carefree spring days, days spent with Jeff Borden in Central Park.

Jeff Borden had a ruggedly handsome face, broad shoulders, and a square, muscular body. He always looked disheveled, as if he slept in his clothes, which, in fact, he often did. His eyes were soft brown, his light hair sun streaked, and his hands were immense, bearlike paws. At slightly under six feet, he could have been a woodsman, a construction worker, or a truck driver. But he wasn't any of those—he was an artist with four cameras dangling round his neck. He had an eye that saw his pictures before he developed them. He knew before the camera clicked exactly what the finished product would look like.

He had taken a picture of her in a sunlit garden looking up at a huge weeping willow. In that photo she looked like an innocent virgin, which indeed she had been. But in another taken later the same day, her white slip strap was falling off her bare shoulder, her hair was a tangled mess, and he had somehow caught her with the expression that revealed her inner longing; that of wanton female desire. "This one is my virgin," he laughed holding up the first photo, "and this my whore," holding the second.

Jeff Borden. Around the newsroom everyone called him "Billy the Kid." It was a silly nickname that Adria always assumed had grown out of his ability to steal pictures—to take candid shots or sometimes catch people in a revealing moment when in fact they had expected a formal portrait.

Adria had met Jeff Borden when she was in the last year of her training. He worked at the *Sun Times* then, and she was sent for six weeks to follow him around, take pictures of what he took pictures of, to help in the darkroom, and to play the sorcerer's apprentice. At first he was unfriendly, then he warmed to her, though he criticized her work meanly. Impatiently he told her she should go back to taking pictures of kids on ponies. Still, they were drawn to one another. She could all but feel his hands on her flesh, smell his masculine body, feel the pressure of his muscles. . . . She shivered. Last she had heard, he was in Germany working for *Life*. "Damn," Adria murmured under her breath, did every woman think so much about the man to whom she had lost her virginity? Not that it was a one-night stand; in fact their relationship had gone on for months. It had gone on until Christina Barton happened onto the scene.

The Rolls glided to a stop and Adria forced her thoughts back to the present. The chauffeur opened the car door and ushered her inside the front door, where she was met by the butler, who bowed deeply and directed her to a powder room off the main foyer. "Perhaps mademoiselle would care to freshen up," he suggested.

Adria smiled and nodded, assuming this was more

tradition than an implication that she looked wilted from her quite comfortable journey. She looked around the powder room, which was furnished with plush carpets and antique dressing tables and mirrors, studying her image in a long floor-to-ceiling mirror that hung against one wall of the room.

Adria had chosen a slim-line, off-white wool skirt that fell almost to her trim ankles and a russet silk blouse. Her alligator shoes and matching purse had both been given to her by her father after his last trip to Panama. Her auburn hair reached her shoulders, and her large, hazel green eyes dominated her heart-shaped face. Perhaps her lips were a bit full . . . but then, she decided, no one was happy with their every feature.

Abstractedly, she smoothed her skirt, then thoughtfully touched her camera bag for a moment as she prepared to leave the powder room. It contained one of her most highly prized cameras, a German Leica for candid shots. She had agonized over the propriety of bringing the camera with her. She'd been invited to dinner, and hesitated to take photos without an invitation to do so. Still, Adria was not unaware of the opportunity this invitation presented. This was one of the richest families in Europe, probably in the world. *Life* might even buy the photos, and in her mind she could envisage a two-page layout: "Life Visits the Wertheims," photos by Adria Halstead. I'll never be invited back, she thought. Then she decided it didn't matter. If they agreed to a few dozen pictures in the course of the evening, it would be worth it. Uncouth or not, she made up her mind to ask. Couldn't the Wertheims say no like other people if they didn't wish to be photographed?

Adria emerged from the powder room and followed the butler down the long corridor toward the main reception room. The house was fantastic, she thought, though the lighting left a lot to be desired.

"Mademoiselle Halstead," Robert Wertheim greeted her with a warm smile, lifting her hand to kiss

47

it. Waiting his turn, Jacques Cardon also stood and kissed her hand.

"Mademoiselle Halstead, may I present my mother, Madame Wertheim." Robert directed her to a woman she could only have described as "regal." Adria smiled, and instead of extending her hand as so many American women did, simply bowed slightly at Madame Wertheim to indicate her respect. And respect it was! Madame Wertheim, who could have afforded the crown jewels and the most expensive clothes in Europe, was dressed quite plainly in a powder blue dress adorned only by a single strand of pearls. And, Adria noted, apart from her wedding band and one diamond, Madame's long, slender fingers were ringless.

But it was more than Madame Wertheim's simple but elegant taste that intrigued Adria. Robert Wertheim's mother was, for her age, an extraordinarily beautiful woman who exuded a kind of aura of calm and sophistication. Adria could not look at her without wondering if Madame's extraordinary presence could be captured on film.

"I'm pleased to meet you, my dear," Madame Wertheim said quietly. Then added, "Oh dear, you carry so many bags, you should have left them with Samuel."

Adria set down her camera bag. It was gauche and impolite to presume that she could use a social invitation to insinuate herself on this family and then sell the pictures! She pressed her lips together, Jeff Borden's words echoing in her ears: "You're too damn polite to be a decent photographer, Adria. You can't push and shove, you couldn't bring yourself to go out and take pictures of a grieving widow! You have to learn to take advantage of people, to be nasty and take risks. What's more, you have to learn that you're married to those cameras. They're an appendage and you never go anywhere without them."

"That's my camera bag," Adria replied after a moment. "I like to have it with me all the time."

48

"Oh, but it's perfectly safe," Madame Wertheim looked a bit puzzled.

Adria opened her mouth to answer, but Robert spoke instead. "Perhaps she wants to photograph us, mother."

"Oh, dear, whatever for?" Madame asked in a bewildered tone.

"I would imagine she could sell the pictures," he replied.

"Sell?" Madame spoke the word as if she had never heard it in her life, as if the concept were totally unknown. "Who would want to buy our pictures?" she asked after a moment.

"Selling pictures of the famous is quite lucrative, and it is Miss Halstead's profession," Robert explained matter-of-factly.

Adria protested, "I wouldn't dream of taking pictures without your consent, but I do take my camera everywhere."

Robert laughed gently. "I can't think there's any harm in it. But not tonight. If you come tomorrow I'll take you around, you can photograph the estate and me . . . wine tasting, riding, and tending my vineyards like the simple millionaire I am." The idea amused him, and he decided it had two advantages. The first was the opportunity to spend an entire day with the lovely Miss Halstead, and the second was to annoy his brother, Charles. Always the stuffy Britisher, he would be horrified at the appearance of photos in an American magazine.

His eyes twinkled mischievously, and his tone held just the right expression of irony, Adria thought. "All right." She tried to control herself, not wanting to look as eager as she felt. Besides, photographing Robert Wertheim would be a coup, but she wanted Robert's mother on film too.

"And might I take some pictures of you as well?" Adria asked bluntly.

Madame Wertheim cleared her throat and simultaneously fingered her pearls . . . "I shall have to consider it," she replied. Then added, "I wonder if there is some advantage."

Robert studied his mother silently. She was hardly the consummate bargainer. He couldn't imagine exactly what she meant by "advantage," but he decided not to pursue the subject. He turned back to Adria and offered her his arm. "Dinner is being served."

Adria floated on air. After all, she had photographed the President of the United States, but she had arranged this one, not her father.

Dinner was taken in the main dining room and took the better part of three hours, during which time one cocktail, two wines, and a choice of liqueurs were served in addition to hors d'oeuvres, salad, soup, and a main course of chateaubriand with delicately roasted vegetables.

"How does your father feel about your going to Spain?" Jacques Cardon inquired as they sipped their cognac.

Adria thought for a moment and decided to answer honestly. "He objects and says he can use his connections with the Franco government to stop my entering Franco-held territory. So, I'm afraid I shall be restricted to the Republican side of the war."

"Your father has connections with the Franco government?" Robert Wertheim asked, arching his eyebrow.

Adria half shrugged. "The way I understand it, the American navy has permission to dock in Franco-held ports in order to take out foreign refugees, but the Republicans won't allow that."

Madame Wertheim looked distressed, "But won't that be dangerous? Aren't the Republicans Socialists and Communists?"

"They're anti-Fascist, Mother." It was a gross simplification, Robert thought, even as he said it. But if he had tried to explain that Royalists, Socialists, Commu-

50

nists, Anarchists, and Jewish volunteers were all fighting on the Republican side against Franco—despite their own ideological differences—it would only further confuse his mother.

"That does make it difficult," his mother murmured. "I've never really understood the war in Spain."

"And how do you intend to travel?" Robert asked, turning back to Adria.

Adria shrugged, "I don't know, across the French border I suppose. I have my press card of course, but I might be turned back. I've heard it's rather sticky."

"Why not let me take you by yacht to Barcelona? It's still held by the Republicans."

"Oh, I couldn't. Besides, it's dangerous, you said so yourself."

"I love the sea. I've been planning a voyage, and I fly a French flag. After all, neither side is at war with France."

Madame Wertheim only sipped her brandy, looking first at Robert, then at Adria.

Adria wasn't certain how to respond, finally simply asking, "Are you certain?"

"That's settled then," Robert announced, "May I show you our garden? You can take pictures of it tomorrow, but I must tell you that in the moonlight the statues take on a kind of reality they lack in daylight."

"I should like that very much." Adria allowed him to take her hand. He walked straight and tall and his hand was warm and slightly moist. He was a handsome man, she acknowledged, and he was quite obviously attracted to her. A fleeting thought of Jeff Borden crossed her mind. It was coupled with feelings of vague longing, a touch of regret and a kind of hunger.

3

JACQUES CARDON HAD GONE upstairs when Adria left, but when Robert entered his study on the second floor to have a brandy nightcap, he was surprised to see his mother. "I would have thought you were tired," he said, pouring some brandy into the snifter. "Do you want some?"

Anna Wertheim shook her head.

"How did you like Miss Halstead?" he asked.

Anna Wertheim smiled knowingly. Her son thought her entirely naive, but she had not missed the expression on his face when he returned from the garden. Clearly her son was smitten—as her cousin Hester would say—with Miss Halstead, though Anna wasn't sure how smitten. "She's very pretty," Anna replied truthfully. "I like her because she seems honest and forthright."

"She's intelligent," Robert added. "Something of a rebel I suspect."

"Will she make much money selling her pictures of you?"

"A few hundred I should think."

Anna smiled. "Imagine having a few hundred of one's own money—I mean money earned."

Robert frowned, "I'm not sure what you mean."

"Oh, I mean how wonderful to have a talent for which someone will pay you. I think it must be very satisfying."

"I suppose it is."

"All my life I've just taken it for granted. Until lately. Robert, do you think people really know what's happening in Germany?"

The sudden shift in conversation caught him off guard. He assumed the connection was the fact that the Obermanns' German assets had been seized. "People know what they want to know," he answered. Then with more openness than he usually had in conversations with his mother, "Anti-Semitism is on the rise,

52

Mother. Not just in Germany, but here in France, too. Those of us with influence will have to use it wisely." He didn't go into details. There were things he didn't want his mother to know yet.

"If Miss Halstead took my picture and wrote an accompanying story about my being deported from Germany, do you think it would help people in America to understand what is happening in Germany?"

Robert smiled slowly. So that was what his mother had meant by advantage. "You've always guarded your privacy," he offered.

"I am prepared to give it up if it might help."

Robert nodded. "It would help," he replied without elaboration.

4

SURPRISINGLY, ADRIA HAD AWAKENED rested and refreshed. The night before she had spent long hours thinking of Jeff Borden and Robert Wertheim, as well as of the photographs she was now taking.

Robert Wertheim had something of Jeff's raw masculinity, she had decided, though raw was not an adjective she could apply to any other facet of Robert's persona. He was terribly suave and polished, and she was never quite sure if he was laughing with her or at her. His eyes were compelling and they seemed to lock on to the listener. They were intelligent eyes, eyes that betrayed kindness and humor. And when he talked, Robert Wertheim's hands moved expressively. Instinctively, she knew she had to be careful with a man she suspected of having so many secrets.

But it was more than that. Robert Wertheim came from a world of privilege and stability. A world where marriages lasted forever, where homes were elegant memorials to generations past, a world where there was so much money that no one thought much about it. She, on the other hand, came from a broken home. Her childhood had been lived out of a suitcase, and money had always been a concern. Many high-ranking officers who had gone to Annapolis came from monied families, and their meager navy salaries were supplemented by outside income. But Nelson Halstead came from a midwestern farm family, and her mother came from a poor Boston family—"lace curtain Irish," as they were called. Her maternal grandfather, Bull Malloy, had been a ward boss on Boston's South Side, and he'd managed to garner considerable political influence. When his new son-in-law showed academic talent and expressed a desire to go to Annapolis, he'd used that influence with a newly elected Irish American senator from Massachusetts to obtain an appointment. Nelson Halstead had done well, but, Adria thought ruefully, he still had to live on the three hundred and fifty dollars a month paid to an admiral. She remembered one brag of a Du Pont who had gone to Annapolis: "I earn less in the navy than I pay my manservant." And Adria could not deny that both her parents were social climbers. Her mother constantly lived beyond their means while her father sought out those of influence who could help him climb the ladder of advancement. In a sense the navy, with its own society of rank, suited him. Moreover, high-ranking officers were often guests at the homes of the wealthy, though of course the wealthy did not visit them. One was present as a sort of military attaché, a glittering presence in full-dress uniform. All of this was why Adria had adopted the style of the artist. It was classless.

In all honesty, what troubled her about Robert Wertheim was the difference in their backgrounds, their needs, and no doubt in their desires. Her youth enabled her to taste forbidden fruits, but she knew she had to become independent and she suspected the road to independence could not be walked with a Robert Wertheim. Then Adria laughed. Why so serious about Robert Wertheim? He seemed attracted to her, but certainly nothing had happened beyond meaningful glances.

During their stroll in the rose garden she had expected advances, though initially he had been philosophic, almost poetic. He had guided her among the statues, pointing out his favorites. "There she is," he said, looking at the graceful lines of Venus, "my alabaster snow white beauty, against a black velvet sky." His voice had grown low and seductive, and Adria remembered thinking, "Here it comes. In a moment he'll try to kiss me."

But just as she readied herself for his romantic inclinations, he abruptly changed the subject to politics. He talked about the presence of the American navy, asked her penetrating questions about politics in America, talked to her about her father's views, and asked her in detail what she thought about fascism and developments in Germany. Adria realized in retrospect how much she had told him and how little he had told her. She was loathe to admit how little she knew about anti-Semitism in Germany, indeed how little about Germany in general. "I want to go there," she had said, but she had failed to mention that she wanted to go less to observe fascism than because Jeff was there.

Adria glanced at her watch—it was now nearly three. The day with Robert had passed quickly, and, she admitted, she had hardly thought about Jeff Borden. Robert Wertheim had seen to it that she enjoyed full privileges at the estate. And now, dressed in full riding attire, he sat astride a beautiful black Arabian stallion, looking truly distinguished.

"You look much too formal," Adria joked as she focused her Leica. "Muss up your hair a little and canter by that stream." As he did as she asked, she called out, "Why haven't you ever married?" The question caught him off guard and he leaned forward, a quizzical look on his face, just as she began taking pictures, five candid shots in all, in rapid succession.

"Because no man in my family marries before he's forty-five," Robert answered. "But I see through you —you only asked to catch my expression!"

"I confess," she acknowledged nonchalantly. "I always talk to my subjects so they won't look all stiff and posed. That's one of the advantages of these new

35-millimeters—they're fast. The new speed is really changing photography." She finished off the roll of film, the fifth she had shot, including the one in the rose garden with his mother. He'd been wonderful, changing clothes for different activities, and exhibiting great patience with her suggestions to make it all look more natural. "I think that's it," she called out.

He wiped his brow and dismounted. "Good, let's go have some cold white wine and cheese on the terrace and discuss getting to Barcelona. You know, this modeling business is more tiring than I imagined."

Adria laughed. "You're just not used to it." Then, "Forty-five seems old to marry," she said out of sheer curiosity, as he took her arm.

"Well, it's not a rule. It's more a matter of taste."

"And then you shall marry a twenty-year-old?"

He laughed. "No, I shall marry my fourth cousin who is no more than ten years younger than I."

"An arranged marriage?" She felt a twinge of regret.

"No. And then again, I might not marry her at all. I might run off with a show girl, perhaps even a photographer."

Adria blushed and felt confused. He pulled out the little white wicker chair for her. "Help yourself to the brie," he offered, pouring her a glass of chilled white wine.

"You're trying to embarrass me." She leaned over and tried to return to the conversation. "Is marrying a cousin a matter of taste, too?" she prodded.

"Who else is there?"

"I would think you'd have no trouble finding any number of women."

"Women yes. Wives are a different matter."

Adria didn't allow her expression to change. At least he was being honest. "So marriage is a matter of tradition and for your pleasure you choose from a cast of thousands?"

He laughed, "Not exactly thousands. Taste enters into pleasure, too."

Adria blushed again because his eyes were penetrating, and his words seem to convey the promise of a seduction to come.

"I can be ready to sail on Monday," he said, changing the subject. Then disarmingly, "Pay no attention to me, I'm a terrible tease."

Adria returned the smile. "Monday suits me just fine." Sipping her wine, she realized she would be overjoyed to get away from her father's overbearing presence. "You don't have to worry; by necessity I'll be traveling light."

"It's not a long voyage."

"I really do appreciate it."

"Oh, you're not getting off so easily. I have a package for you to deliver in Barcelona."

She tilted her head slightly. "As long as it's legal."

"I assure you it is. I'd go ashore myself but my Spanish papers aren't in order."

"I understand."

Robert smiled and bit into a cracker spread with the ripe brie. She was beautiful and intelligent, but she didn't understand at all. And that, he knew full well, was for the best.

Chapter Four

1

THE PACIFIC OCEAN ALWAYS seemed to be frothy, turbulent, and blue green; the Atlantic was often an angry steel gray; but, Adria thought, the Mediterranean had a hue and personality all its own. Gentle waves caressed the miles of white sand beaches and the sea itself was at times almost turquoise, turning to azure where it was deeper, and to a shimmering, glistening reflection of the dying sun at eventide.

"You like the sea," Robert Wertheim observed, as he stood by her side on his luxurious hundred-and-fifty-foot yacht the *White Jewel*.

Adria allowed the light breeze to blow through her

hair, making no attempt to brush the loose strands off her forehead. She felt calm and relaxed, lulled by the motion of the vessel. It didn't seem possible that she was traveling into a war zone; this luxurious transport would surely be in violent contrast to what she would encounter in Barcelona.

"I've always lived by the sea," she finally answered. It seemed a more romantic way to respond, though she might well have said, "I always lived on naval bases": Norfolk, where her father had trained raw recruits; San Diego, the 11th Naval District, where he had taken young officers from Annapolis and put them through their paces on a wooden battleship that sat absurdly on a grassy knoll overlooking the harbor; Oakland, where they had lived on Treasure Island and her father had presided over the majestic *Lexington,* commissioned in 1927, the first of three new giants that were the pride of the fleet. Then there had been Providence, Rhode Island, Quincy, Massachusetts, the Brooklyn Navy Yard, and Pensacola, Florida—an assignment that guaranteed you a place in heaven since it was said to be hell on earth.

"You must have had an interesting childhood," Robert Wertheim commented.

Adria nodded, "I was alone a lot, and I traveled a great deal."

"You have no brothers or sisters?"

She shook her head. Her parents had separated when she was fifteen, but in the years that preceded their decision to part she was certain they had not made love.

"I only have one brother," Robert revealed, "but he's lived in England for many years."

"Does your mother always remain with you?" Adria fished. Madame Wertheim fascinated her.

"No, she divides her time between London, Germany, Paris, and the estate, with periodic journeys to the United States. But I think she considers the estate her real home, and now, of course, she can't go back to Germany."

"You're fortunate to have such a good relationship with her."

"You don't have a good relationship with your mother?"

It wasn't an easy question. Her relationship with her mother was strong, but not always good. "I do now," she replied with honesty. And thought, because I'm four thousand miles away. She stared into the sea allowing silence to fall between them.

In fact, her relationship with both her parents was rocky. Her mind drifted back to her father. He clearly hadn't thought she was serious when she'd told him she was going to Spain. When he discovered that she had already made arrangements, he had gone into a rage and ranted on for nearly an hour. Part of his anger centered on her manner of travel, beginning with the immorality of an unmarried young woman sailing alone with an unmarried man—and a Jew. And surely his anger was fired with his frustration. He couldn't pull strings. He had no influence with a man like Robert Wertheim. Realizing this, he had gone on to shout about the dangers, the uncertainties, finally ending with mutterings that amounted to little less than a blatant assertion that war was for men only.

Nor had Adria herself been kind. She had shouted back that he had no right to suggest she was immoral when he was infamous for sleeping around, that she was old enough to make her own decisions, and finally, that he could take his rank and his navy ideas and go to hell. Then she had fled before the hot tears of anger ran down her face. "I'm a grown woman," she remembered screaming. "It's not my fault I became one when you weren't around!" It was a vicious comment, one intended to wound, and Adria knew she had hit the mark. Her father had stomped away, and though she knew he was still furious, she also knew she had made him feel guilty and that for days he would be depressed. It was the back side of love, she thought. When you knew someone well, and you loved them dearly, you had a greater ability to wound.

"The sun's setting," Robert commented. He took her arm and they walked to the other side of the yacht so they could enjoy the panoramic view of sea and shore.

Sitting amid a profusion of flowered bushes, white houses with red tile roofs climbed the hillsides, perilously clinging to rocky plateaus or huddled in tiny clearings, while across the placid water the sun was sinking into a gold-striped sea that touched the Algerian shore. Adria shivered as the cool evening breeze came up.

"Should I have the steward bring your shawl?"

She laughed lightly, "I only have a jacket." She thought for a minute how shocked he had been at her lack of luggage. She had only one skirt, a blouse, a sweater, and a jacket for formal wear. Her other clothes amounted to only two blouses and two pairs of culottes, together with minimal undergarments. Both pairs of her shoes were flat and practical. She had stuffed all of her belongings unceremoniously into a hiker's pack. Her heavy camera bag with her three precious Leicas, film, collapsible tripod, and filters was far more necessary than a wardrobe. Jeff, of course, would have carried even less. He used to joke that when his clothes reached the point of no return, he simply discarded them and bought new ones.

Robert signaled the white-clad steward and requested Adria's jacket. Then, quite casually, he slipped his arm around her shoulders. Adria didn't object. Indeed she had felt certain he would make advances to her on their journey, and waiting for him to make his move had filled her with apprehension. Her father's prejudiced objections had so angered her that she knew she might go to bed with Robert Wertheim simply to spite her father. Her father wouldn't know, of course, and going to bed with a man to get even with your father was unfair to the man in question. Then again, Robert Wertheim knew that when she left him in Barcelona they would probably never meet again; how much fairness did he want? Could she allow a man to make love to her, knowing it would be the first and last time? Would closing her eyes and allowing her sensations to rule her be a violation of her memories of Jeff? Adria didn't try to think through the answer. It would be like everything else in her life: she would decide when the moment came.

"Here we are." Robert took her jacket from the steward and slipped it around her shoulders. "We'll eat in an hour," he told her. His arm was no longer around her, and she was puzzled that he actually seemed to move away from her.

"As soon as the sun sets, I'll go to my cabin and freshen up."

He nodded. "You'll sleep like a baby tonight. There's nothing like a night at sea."

She inhaled, "And the fresh air does make me sleepy." Perhaps she was mistaken. Perhaps he wouldn't make a pass at her.

"I'm going below for a while." He took her hand and squeezed it. "I'll see you in an hour in the salon."

Adria nodded and watched him disappear down the narrow stairway toward the sleeping cabins. She felt vaguely disappointed.

2

ROBERT WERTHEIM LAY ON his bed, staring at the blue-shaded light on the bulkhead as it swayed gently with the movement of the yacht. He and Adria had enjoyed a delicious meal of fresh prawns and delicately prepared saffron rice. They had drunk a bottle of vintage red wine, a Grands Echézeaux, and after dinner he'd had two brandies, but still sleep wouldn't come.

Adria Halstead was a temptation; a young, animated woman with a clear lust for life and adventure. She wasn't like any woman he'd known before; she was intelligent, original, and obviously creative. She was quick to discuss politics, quick to offer informed opinions, and just as eager to learn and add to her own store of knowledge. The women he usually encountered were more like hothouse plants; watered, pruned, and harvested in a stifling environment. And the others, those women with whom he sometimes took casual pleasure, were consumed with their appearance and sought only their own vision in his eyes.

She had the round, pleasing curves of a model, but she was concerned with far more than her image, pleasing though it might be. In fact, he found her something of an enigma. She appeared happy and optimistic, but there were moments when she seemed seized by a contemplative melancholy. Of one thing he was certain: she was reaching out, trying to grasp onto life. He could see she wanted to transcend the ordinary, and to excel. But as she herself said, her art and profession depended on being able to capture on film the kind of pictures that would replace a thousand words; pictures of common people and events that were, by circumstance, made extraordinary. She talked about another woman photographer, a Margaret Bourke-White, who worked for *Life* magazine and who had pioneered what Adria called "the photo essay." "That's what I have to do in Spain," Adria had explained, and in her eyes he saw an intensity, a toughness, and passion for her work. Yet beneath the surface, he sensed, she was emotionally vulnerable, and his suspicions were confirmed by their conversation at dinner.

"You moved a lot as a child," he had commented when she told him about her travels and the many schools she had attended.

"I never formed long-term relationships," she confessed. "I had to make new friends wherever I went."

"I can't quite imagine that. I went to boarding school with the same friends for years, and then a lot of us ended up at the same university. Then, too, I had cousins I was with in the summer and all the children who grew up on the estate."

"And your brother," she had said almost enviously.

62

Robert remembered laughing. "We're not much alike, but that's another conversation." Then he had looked into her eyes seriously. "You must have been lonely growing up."

Adria nodded as if contemplating his conclusion. Then after a short silence she said, "I guess I was. I always had the feeling that I shouldn't get too attached to people, because if I did, I'd miss them when I left."

Her expression had spoken volumes, and not wanting to open wounds, he'd changed the subject abruptly to tell her about his brother, Charles.

Abstractedly, he reached up and flipped off the light switch. Sleep, he must try to sleep. Adria would deliver the new books on which the codes were based, and that was important. But for him, the real danger would begin only after Barcelona. He reprimanded himself for letting his lovely passenger distract him. All day he had thought of trying to make love to her, but he had rejected the idea despite her clear attraction to him. Making love to her would be pleasant for both of them, pleasant and possibly hurtful. She wasn't, he decided, the kind who could "kiss and run," as the Americans were always saying. His own instincts told him that if he made love to her, once would not be enough though twice would be impossible. She would join other writers and photographers to record the final days of the war in Spain, while he was, in reality, on his way to Algiers via Las Palmas, where he would pick up twenty illegal passengers. He closed his eyes and willed himself to sleep. Miss Halstead had certain charms, but an affair, however brief, might present him with unneeded responsibility. And no woman, he thought, should become involved with a man in his position. It wasn't fair to initiate love, when death hovered over him.

BOLDLY FLYING A FRENCH flag, the yacht nonetheless traveled mostly at night during the last twenty-four hours of the voyage. Robert ordered the lights extinguished, and except for one navigation beam, the vessel slid through the water in darkness, clinging close to shore and maintaining radio silence.

On the 15th of November Robert Wertheim's yacht sailed into Puerta de la Paz—Port of Peace, in Barcelona. Under the circumstances it was an incongruous name, Adria thought as she trudged toward the Columbus Monument on the Reales Atarazanas, a block away from the docks.

She thanked heaven that her hiker's pack was light. Robert had put her aboard a government boat far out in the harbor, and in a makeshift customs shack she had stood for over an hour and half while her credentials were checked. Still, the officials seemed friendly enough.

Catalonia, the province of which Barcelona was the capital, had declared itself autonomous at the outbreak of the war three years ago. Now it remained the last major stronghold of the Republicans in Spain, and no doubt Robert Wertheim was quite correct when he told her its days were numbered. She surmised that the officials were hospitable largely because, although Spain was crawling with writers, most members of the working press were now in Fascist-held territory. The Republicans could boast the presence of the literati— mostly novelists and poets—but whatever they produced would reach the public long after the war had been decided, and if they wrote for magazines, they were magazines with a small circulation. But pictures appearing in large daily newspapers and periodicals with vast distribution did more to influence popular opinion in America. And popular opinion was important since the Republicans were still trying to raise men and arms, and to seek justice through the intervention of other countries.

In its dying days, with its streets teeming with refugees, and its bombed ruins, the remnants of Republican Spain could use all the help it could get, Adria concluded. Though the outcome seemed sadly inevitable, what *was* left undecided were the details of the lives of ordinary people. Where would the refugees go when Barcelona fell? When would the houses be rebuilt and the ravages of modern warfare be repaired? Who would treat the wounded, and, in the end, what kind of government would the Fascists eventually mold? Barcelona, indeed all of Catalonia, would surely suffer for its recalcitrance, for being the last holdout, and for proving in blood that it was the most loyal of the regions.

Adria paused beneath the monument in the square and carefully unfolded the little map of the city Robert had given her. "Try to get a room at Casa Linda," he had advised. "It's a small hotel and caters to the press. You'll be safer there, and in case of attack the cellar is deep and well stocked with wine. The press corps likes to drink, don't they?"

She had smiled and agreed.

It was just before the government coast patrol veered alongside the yacht that he had given her the package. "This package is extremely important," he had told her seriously, "though if you are searched and if it is opened, neither you nor the security officials will realize its importance. I beg you, no matter what you think, see to it that it is delivered according to the instructions I'm going to give you."

She had laughed. "Are you a spy?" But he hadn't laughed, only pressed her arm and said earnestly, "I can't answer any of your questions, I can only assure you that the package will not get you into trouble. But I must extract your promise that no matter how strange it seems to you, it will be delivered."

"Where shall I deliver it? You haven't marked an address."

"The person to whom it goes is a transient. You will take it to the Restaurante el Cid on the Avenida de Flores. Simply ask for Raúl Saltrez. He will either be there, or they will know where to find him. Please deliver it only to him." Robert had then marked her map with the location of the restaurant and returned it to her.

"Anyone can give any name," Adria had protested. "What does this Raúl Saltrez look like?"

"Like a bird of prey," Robert had answered, then more thoughtfully, "Tall, thin, dark with sharp features. His nose is his most distinctive feature though his eyes are quite compelling. You will, however, find him to be a man of few words."

"It seems simple enough, hardly worth all the trouble you've taken to get me here."

He had smiled warmly and reached down to touch her hair gently. "The pleasure was all mine."

Adria had smiled back, still feeling puzzled and regretful. She was certain his eyes caressed her, but he had gone no further, and now that the coast patrol boat was bearing down on them it was too late to begin that which for all real purposes had ended.

Still he had surprised her in the final moment. He put his large hands on her shoulders and bent to kiss her, brushing her cheek with his lips and then kissing her mouth almost as if they had been lovers. "If we meet again," he had said, looking at her with his large, intent eyes, "we'll be different. Time will have passed and with it any carefree moments we might have had."

"I don't understand you," she had murmured.

He smiled, though it was not a happy smile. " 'Dover Beach,' " he had answered. "Do you know the poem?"

"No."

"It's by Matthew Arnold. Read it—and remember me."

"I will."

"Buena suerte, Adria—good luck, in Spanish."

But now the mystery of Robert Wertheim and his package seemed all the more puzzling. The officials had searched her luggage. The package, casually wrapped, contained nothing more than three issues of *McCalls*, an American women's journal, not even the most recent issues. The officials had shrugged with disinterest. Women might well be expected to carry such magazines, but Adria found herself totally intrigued by the contents of her parcel. Still, she remembered Robert's words, "Deliver it, no matter how strange it may seem," and she vowed to follow her instructions.

But first I must get settled, she told herself. She hurried on down the street hoping that the Casa Linda had a room and was not much farther.

She paused momentarily as she passed a square that must have taken a direct hit only recently. Small piles of rubbish still smoldered, and a huddle of ill-dressed, elderly workers lethargically dug away at the ruins of what must have been a stone building. She wondered what it was like being in an air raid, of knowing that death could at any minute fall out of the blue Spanish sky. The very thought caused a rush of adrenalin in her system, mixing uneasily with her suppressed apprehension. This was Republican Spain! This was late 1938, the war that had brought America's leading intellectuals to worship at the altar of a distant political cross was winding down. I wasn't here for the beginning, Adria thought, but I shall be here for the end.

4

THE CASA LINDA WAS located on a small side street just off the Ramblas, a well-known promenade that once boasted sidewalk cafés and graceful shade trees, but which now was shattered, many of its landmarks in ruins. The hotel stood a mere three stories, but it was built around a charming patio that was completely hidden from the street. The hotel had vacancies, but not till Adria had made it plain to the concierge that she was willing to pay in American cash did he admit it.

The room she was given was on the second floor and overlooked the patio's old fountain, crumbling tile floor, and gay profusion of tropical plants. Adria could almost imagine being serenaded by a guitar-playing lothario beneath her window, but she knew full well that here in Barcelona, for the moment, romance and music had faded into the background.

Robert Wertheim had been right; the hotel was filled with American press. It was, she decided, a good environment for her, even though the other members of the press corps were male, and could be described as condescending at best. Still, she wasn't a correspondent, she was a photographer, and that meant that for the most part she was not in competition with the gentlemen.

One trip to the hotel bar had given her ample introduction to her temporary companions. She had met Wilson Henry from the *Trib*, a short, round, bald man in a rumpled gray suit, and Marty Harris from *Time*. A thin and nervous man, Marty Harris talked exactly the way stories in *Time* were written, his words spewing out as if from a machine gun. As she had suspected, Harris and Henry were the only two from major publications. A shy young man who said he was covering the war for a Harvard literary review, Leonard Fineberg kept referring to his "friend," Stephen Spender. Then she had met Irv Cohen, a short, intense Jew who admitted instantly that he was a Communist, and who was writing articles for the *Daily Worker*. Two and two, Adria couldn't help thinking. Henry and Harris were either anti-Loyalist, or they didn't give a damn who won; Feinberg and Cohen were pro-Loyalist and cared passionately. All four of them had ogled her and practically giggled when she'd told them she was a photographer. Certainly there were other American writers in the hotel as well, but Adria suspected they would fall into the same camps. After twenty minutes in the bar she returned to her room and consulted her map. It was time she kept her promise to Robert Wertheim.

Following the directions to the Restaurante el Cid, Adria made her way across the square, frowning as she came to an entire block which had been bombed. Here children played in the rubble, collecting whatever they could find that might be useful. One small boy carried a tattered straw basket into which he piled bits of charcoal for a fire while others searched out bits of metal or crockery which had escaped the destruction with only cracks and chips.

It was a good picture, and she moved out of their direct view to take a few candid shots. It was always better if you could get the pictures before you were noticed—especially with children. Best to catch them in that one second as they looked up from their activities, surprised, perhaps even startled. A little girl with long scraggly hair, wearing a smock dress that was several sizes too large, obliged. Adria smiled to herself; she had caught the child absolutely wide-eyed with an expression of panic on her face. It was going to be the kind of photo that made American mothers weep—the kind of photo that sells magazines.

Adria smiled and the little girl's expression changed too. Adria replaced the lens cap and hurried on. It was twilight, and since she was walking she wanted to get to the restaurant before dark.

Two more blocks and she entered what appeared to be an industrial area. Its bombed-out warehouses looked eerie in the dying light, and glassless windows stared at her like hollow eyes. One side of the street was completely untouched, the other flattened and barren. Then, to her relief, she saw the sign and hurried inside.

The Restaurante el Cid was airless, hot, and steamy. There were few individual tables, most were simply long wooden ranch tables where food was obviously served "family style." Adria looked about. There were no women in the restaurant, only men in clothing that clearly defined them either as industrial or dock workers. Uneasily, she sat down at one of the few small round tables, avoiding eye contact with the other customers though she was only too aware of the stares directed at her. The waiter eyed her somewhat suspi-

69

ciously as he hovered over her, and he apologized, explaining that they had only coffee, rolls, and rice. "*La guerra*,—the war, señorita, there are terrible shortages."

"Café," Adria replied, then tapping his arm and beckoning him to lean over, "Is there a Señor Raúl Saltrez here?"

The waiter's facial expression didn't change. "Not now."

Adria took a breath. She wanted to be rid of the package. Somehow she didn't feel free to explore Barcelona and get on with her business until it was delivered, even though its contents seemed so totally unimportant. "Will he be back soon?" she asked, glancing at her tiny gold wristwatch.

"Maybe, for what do you want him?"

"I have a package for him."

"I can take it," the waiter suggested.

Adria shook her head. "No I must deliver it personally."

The waiter, looking a trifle disappointed, shrugged. "Maybe he comes soon," he suggested. "You can wait."

Her coffee came and Adria sipped it slowly. It was only lukewarm and was thick with sugar. An hour passed slowly and again Adria checked her watch, wondering if there were still cabs in Barcelona, or if she would have to walk back to the hotel alone in the dark, in this city under seige. Silly, silly, she chastised herself. How can you photograph a war if you're afraid to be out after dark? Still, her parents' childhood warnings rang in her ears: women who got "into trouble," as they always put it, brought it on themselves. They shouldn't have been out alone at night, shouldn't have been in "that" neighborhood, or near "that" bar, or alone in "that" dancehall. Still, there was no denying that the other customers were a rough lot and that the streets of Barcelona were new to her.

"Señorita?"

Adria snapped up and looked into the eyes of a tall,

emaciated man whose age could have been anywhere between twenty-five and forty. He wore stained blue trousers and a crumpled blue shirt that was open at the neck. He was sharp featured, and her immediate reaction was that he did indeed look like a bird of prey. He would have made a good subject for a picture with his dark and intense eyes, his lips narrow and pressed tight, and his nose long and sharp, making him intensely ugly, but equally as interesting.

"I am Raúl Saltrez."

"Adria Halstead." This man did not look as if he could possibly be a friend of Robert Wertheim's. They looked to have come not just from different worlds, but from different planets. He pulled out the chair across from her and straddled it.

"I have a package for you, from Robert Wertheim." He nodded. "May I have it?"

Adria reached down into her bag and withdrew it.

"Was it inspected at customs?"

Adria nodded.

"It makes no difference."

He took it from her and didn't bother to say thank you. "I have to be going," Adria said, looking past his shoulder out into the dark, ominous street. "It's getting late." She waited, hoping he might offer to see her back to her hotel. Though he himself looked none too trustworthy, she convinced herself he must be all right if he were a friend of Robert's. But he didn't offer. Pulling herself together, Adria stood up. "Is there some place I can get a cab?"

He shook his head. "How did you get here?"

"I walked."

"You'll have to walk back," he said without concern. The waiter appeared again and set down a plate of steaming rice in front of Raúl Saltrez. It looked like a glutenous mass, but the steam that arose from it reminded Adria she hadn't eaten since breakfast. She extended her hand and he shook it tightly. "Goodbye," she said, walking toward the door and wondering why she was being so polite.

Adria stepped out and took a breath. Damn! there wasn't a light anywhere! The street lights had obviously long since stopped functioning, and all the buildings must have been using dark curtains to prevent their lights from being easy targets. Adria walked briskly. At least there was a full moon and she could make out the street signs and see where she was stepping.

One block—Adria stepped off the curb and startled at a skittering sound. Instinctively she gasped as a huge, dark rat crossed her path, skuttling toward a puddle of putrid water. Adria shivered and hurried on across the street. After four blocks she heard the footsteps behind her. Unconsciously, Adria began to walk faster, and the footsteps hastened too. She forced herself to slow down, but the steps behind her remained rapid.

Adria was vaguely aware of perspiring and of being cold at the same time. When she broke into a run, the footsteps ran too, and she felt a sense of rising terror. Could it be a robber? They must be common in a city under siege. A rapist? Any one of the men in the restaurant had looked capable of it.

She turned down a street that was not on her direct path to the hotel. Perhaps the footsteps that seemed to be following her, indeed trying to overtake her, would go the other way. She slowed to a walk, intensely aware of her low heels clicking on the cement and of the softer, but easily heard sound of whoever followed. Adria's heart beat wildly and again she turned a corner, mindful to head back the way she knew before she became lost in the tangle of shadowy streets.

Why in the name of God was there no one around? Didn't Barcelona have police? The steps seemed louder now, closer. Adria began to run again and the steps ran too. Her legs felt like rubber. I used to be able to run faster, she thought.

Then there was a long, animal wail . . . no, not an animal, a machine of some sort. It echoed through the darkened streets and Adria ran faster. An air raid siren, that's what it must be. Still, she couldn't stop and listen for the droning of planes; the footsteps were nearly directly behind her and fear and panic willed her on. Strange she couldn't turn, stop short, and confront whoever it was, but she couldn't, and in those fleeting seconds she felt angry that she was so frightened and so vulnerable.

A strong arm grabbed at the sleeve of her jacket, then encircled her from behind, bringing her to an abrupt, breathless halt. Adria closed her eyes as she felt herself being pulled into an alley. Her scream brought only a quick slap across the face. Though the face of her attacker was invisible in the pitch black that eveloped them she could hear him breathing hard and feel his damp flesh as his strong arms grasped her. He was dragging and pulling her, forcing her into a building, then down a darkened staircase into the pitch blackness of a dank, musty room. Adria screamed again, but he forced her to her knees, and for the first time in her life she felt lightheaded and dizzy. "Oh God, don't hurt me!" she heard herself plead. "Please don't hurt me."

Chapter Five

1

CHRISTINA BARTON'S PATERNAL GRANDFATHER had emigrated from Bavaria in the late 1800s. The family name had been Brockhaupt, but an emigration official, weary of foreign spellings, christened a confused Karl Brockhaupt with the name Barton. "Much more American," he was reputed to have said, as he appropriated the name of his neighbors and bestowed it upon the newly arrived German.

Karl Brockhaupt, reborn Carl Barton, settled in Philadelphia's Germantown and eventually married Greta Schultz, whose family also sprang from Bavaria. Their son, Christina's father, had gone on to become the head of his own multi-million-dollar construction firm, then a U.S. senator, and was now a wealthy and influential Washington lobbyist. On the stage of American political opinion, ex-Senator Barton was labeled "right wing" and an isolationist. But those who knew him well knew he was openly pro-German, had business dealings with large German industrialists, and had traveled to Germany with his daughter three times since Hitler's seizure of full power in 1933.

But ex-Senator Barton was not a foolhardy man. As the Fascists became less popular at home and abroad, he dropped his public affiliation with the German-American Bund. But he kept it in secret; when Christina had been sent to the Bund training camp at the Deutschhorst Country Club in Sellersville, Pennsylvania, in the summer of 1936, she had used an assumed name.

Christina Barton smiled at herself in the mirror and ran her fingers through her almost white blond hair. She was surely a fine example of Aryan purity—she was just the sort of woman that the Führer praised and that now the German people worshiped almost as goddesses.

Vaguely she wonc ed how much her father knew of her involvement. But surely he would approve; why else would he have sent her to Deutschhorst? Still, her father did not know she had been recruited for German intelligence that summer, nor know that she was told to resign from the Bund in order to "keep her record clean." Nor, she thought, did her father know about the man who had recruited her and who was now both her lover and her control. Christina had obtained her first assignment in her senior year at Barnard. That assignment was to get to know Adria Halstead, and through her, to meet Admiral Nelson Halstead. Initially Christina had both succeeded and failed. She had befriended Adria only to learn that Adria was somewhat estranged from her father. Then, because she was a woman who had to prove herself constantly, Christina had seduced Adria's boyfriend, Jeff Borden. Adria did not speak to her as a result. But when Nelson Halstead was assigned to the Riviera, Christina had a second chance and immediately followed him to France. Much to her control's delight, she had not the slightest difficulty seducing Nelson Halstead. "Now," Erich Schmidt told her, "the trick is to turn your affair into a permanent relationship."

Christina, who had loved Erich since their summer together at Deutschhorst, initially objected, but Erich convinced her it made no difference to him. "You may even have to marry him," Erich told her, "but if war comes, the marriage will place you in a most valuable position."

"But you and I?" Christina asked.

"Will make a short-term sacrifice to be of service. We're young, we have the rest of our lives."

Christina had argued that Nelson would tell her nothing of importance, but Erich countered that for centuries "pillow talk" had provided the best intelligence information. "And this liaison is for future use," he told her, "there to be activated when needed." Christina had stored Erich's words. She did not believe America would become involved in a war with Germany, but still, Erich was right. Plans had to be in place, and she accepted her own role, pushing all other thoughts from her mind.

She shook her head as if to dispel further thought, then returned to combing her hair. The ladies lounge of Le Club Anglais was decorated in hues of flattering pink, and the lamps, that shone up from crevices in the walls like ancient torches gave off such a subdued light that even the most wrinkled skin looked young again.

Finishing her hair, Christina Barton, with practiced skill, applied ruby lipstick to her kewpie-doll mouth and blotted with a tissue from her purse. She checked the gold Benrus watch on her wrist. It was ten to eight; Nelson would be waiting outside. The man was always early by at least ten minutes.

Even though the nights were cool, the café society of

the Côte d'Azur flocked to Le Club Anglais to dance on the terrace and sip cocktails under the cloudless sky. Dinner was served inside in the spacious dining room, where conversations were muted by the tinkle of crystal and fine silver.

"Time to fume," Christina told her image in the mirror, and surely Nelson Halstead would be angry. He would be furious that Adria had actually left for Spain with Robert Wertheim, and when he heard that she herself had been with Robert Wertheim the night before their departure, he would be even angrier.

Christina smiled at herself. It wasn't as if she had planned it, merely that the opportunity presented itself and she had sense enough to take advantage of it. She had been on her way into Le Club Anglais when she had all but collided with Wertheim in the parking lot. As they strode toward the terrace bar together, Christina hastily reminded him of their introduction many weeks ago at the Aga Khan's garden party. Clearly—though it miffed her to admit it—he didn't remember her. Still, he was the perfect gentleman. He feigned a flawless memory, then, embarrassed by the truth, asked her to join him for a drink.

Christina readily accepted, and made certain that Mrs. Carrington-Steele saw them. A gossip of the first order, Mrs. Carrington-Steele could positively be counted on. Later in the evening, when Robert Wertheim was long gone, Christina followed Mrs. Carrington-Steele into the ladies lounge and there confided in her.

"Christina, darling!" A pearl-bedangled Mrs. Carrington-Steele gushed. "How do you do it? I mean, you're the talk of Nice! First Admiral Halstead, now that devastating Mr. Wertheim!" Mrs. Carrington-Steele rolled her eyes heavenward, and her second chin wiggled to punctuate her enthusiasm even as her giant bosom heaved beneath her apricot satin dinner dress.

Christina had blushed appropriately and pressed a finger to her lips. "If Nelson found out about Robert, he'd simply have a fit," she confessed. "Now you will be a dear and not say a word, won't you?"

Mrs. Carrington-Steele nodded. "Mum's the word," she pronounced. That had been several days ago, and Christina felt certain that Nelson Halstead would have heard the story by now.

Christina peered out the crack in the door of the ladies lounge and spotted her admiral being seated at one of the many tables around the edge of the terrazzo patio. His expression was grim and he looked anything but relaxed.

Christina turned once more toward the mirror to smooth out her form-fitting gold lamé skirt and fluff up her low cut, gold-trimmed chiffon overblouse. She wore long, amber beads around her neck and matching earrings that hung below her short hair. She casually slung her red fox stole over her arm so that its two little heads caressed her hips when she walked and its tiny clawed paws swung along in midair, and forced a smile of devastating innocence as she opened the door and glided toward her prey. She approached Nelson Halstead from behind and gently squeezed his shoulder. He jumped, startled by her approach.

"Darling, you look like a face on Mount Rushmore. Whatever is the matter?" Nelson grunted, and, not waiting to be helped, Christina slid into the chair opposite him.

"That's not much of a greeting," she chastised. "After all, I have missed you."

"Not too much, I gather."

Christina pouted. "I don't know what you mean."

"I think you do. It's not bad enough that Adria's run off with that Wertheim, but I hear you were out with him just before they left."

Christina pressed her lips together and looked at Nelson seriously. "It was nothing," she said truthfully. "I met him accidentally and he asked if I'd have a drink with him."

"You expect me to believe that? I heard you were here with him till nearly midnight."

Christina suppressed a smile. The story begun by Mrs. Carrington-Steele had certainly been exaggerated as it passed from mouth to mouth. In truth she and Robert Wertheim had parted within half an hour of their meeting. "It was hardly that late," Christina protested. "In any case, I was simply asking after Adria. You know, she never did try to look me up."

"Good thing." Nelson picked up the menu and then laid it down with irritation. "Where the hell is that waiter!"

Christina reached across the table and gently rubbed the inside of his wrist with her index finger. "Don't be cross and don't be jealous. There's nothing between Robert Wertheim and me—that's the truth. You're the only man I care about."

He looked up and across at her, his expression changing as his eyes dropped to watch the slow motion of her finger rubbing the inside of his wrist. The very touch of her finger was incredibly suggestive. He started to say something, but her lips parted and she wet her lower lip with her tongue and whispered throatily, "I want to be with you tonight." His mouth went dry and he could feel his desire for her rising.

He half smiled at her and nodded. Then, once again in command, barked at the passing waiter. "A double bourbon and a gin sling for the lady."

Christina smiled, "That's better."

"Sorry—Adria's going off has upset me."

Christina nodded and tried to look understanding. "I had hoped to see her," she lied. But if I were standing next to her, she wouldn't speak to me. Christina's mind wandered back to a hot, steamy night in New York. She'd been in bed with Jeff Borden. He'd called her an alley cat, but he wasn't beyond playing the Tom even though he and Adria were living together and it was Adria who had introduced them. I hadn't counted on her coming in and finding us, Christina thought. But it *was* delicious. Taking a man out of another woman's arms always made her feel powerful, and her brief liaison with Jeff Borden was a real exercise in power—because he was clearly in love with Adria. Adria, of course, left Jeff and neither ever spoke to her again. Christina had wanted the pleasure of discarding Jeff, and she was livid that he had turned away to pine over Adria.

One always gets a second chance, Christina thought. Just thinking about Jeff and Adria made this whole affair with Nelson Halstead almost enjoyable. Adria would be furious. Unconsciously, Christina smiled.

"You have that kittenish look again," Nelson Halstead commented as the waiter put down their drinks.

Christina pressed his wrist. "Anticipation," she whispered.

2

ADRIA STRUGGLED AGAINST THE bare, sweaty arms that forced her to the floor. Again she whimpered, "Don't hurt me," but she could barely hear her own voice.

"Señorita!" he shouted almost into her ear, but before she could reply or even muster the strength to struggle again, the sound of a long whistle filled her ears, like the glorious exploding rockets at a Fourth of July celebration. But this whistle ended not with a sunburst of bright red against a black sky but with a deafening explosion that rocked the ground under both their feet and brought down timbers from the ceiling, filling the shallow basement with dense dust. Adria screamed as she fell to the floor, no longer struggling. In her fear she was hardly aware of whether the weight that lay across her was human or one of the beams from the ceiling. She gasped and coughed in the dust, choking on her own salty tears as well as on the foul air.

The weight stirred, rolling off her just as another whooshing whistle filled the air. Like the first it delivered its payload nearby, and the vibration rocked beneath her as she clawed her hand into what she discovered was a dirt floor.

"Aquí," the male voice said urgently. He tugged on her, pulling her roughly across the floor, away from where she thought the ceiling beam must have crashed. Then in rapid succession, one bomb crashed after another, each exploding missile obliterating the sound of the ominous whistle the first two had issued as warning.

She was aware of him pushing her under some sort of wooden table to shield her from the falling debris. She closed her eyes in spite of the fact that it was pitch black, and with each burst and explosion clung to her attacker's muscular arms. Adria shivered, her tears mixing with the dust and filth of the warehouse basement.

Another resounding explosion, and a gust of fresh air. Adria opened her eyes, looked up, and saw the gaping hole in the ceiling, and beyond it the unmistakable tongue of flame.

"Venga usted!" In the dancing shadows Adria saw him. He was of medium height and rugged looking, a streak of dark ash cut across one cheek like a scar, and his leather vest gaped open, revealing a dark, hairy chest.

He pulled her roughly from under the ancient wooden table and pushed her toward the mud stairs he had dragged her down only moments before. The door had swung closed on its heavy rusty hinges. Adria coughed violently as the smoke from above began to fill the underground room, screaming when a flaming timber dropped a few feet away. Her companion struggled with the door for only a second, then with a heavy boot, he sent it flying. He pulled her hand, dragging her from the smoke-filled inferno out into the night, which had become illuminated by the explosions.

Mobs of screaming people filled what had been an empty street. Four, perhaps five buildings were blazing tinder boxes, and in the distance she could see that other parts of Barcelona were also aflame.

Instinctively she felt with her free hand for the

camera round her neck. Miraculously the lens cap was still in place.

"Alto!" Adria shouted, for the first time resisting being pulled along. "Stop!" she said again, afraid she had used the wrong Spanish word.

He did stop, and Adria wrenched herself loose from his grasp and pulled the lens cap off. There was no time for a light meter reading, but she knew that there was enough light emanating from the fires to capture the flickering shadows of destruction. All her training in the dark paid off as her fingers moved swiftly to set the lens opening and exposure time.

"Cristo!" she heard him curse. With her camera to her eye she panned around and locked on him full frame. She saw a wide smile had broken across his face. His white, gleaming teeth were in marked contrast to his swarthy, soot-coated skin, which was marked by streaks of perspiration. A deep gash on his forehead oozed blood, and a wisp of thick, straight, dark hair fell across his brow. Adria changed her lens opening and pushed the button. This man, whoever he was, had just saved her life. Moreover, she was no longer alone with him.

"No matter what the situation—even if you're scared out of your mind, you have to get the camera in place and shoot!" Jeff Borden's words filled her mind.

"Un momento," she pleaded. The eye of her camera had caught a lone child pulling a scraggly, wolflike dog on a rope. It was a little girl, in a torn dress with a pack on her back. Adria took three shots and then could not resist turning her camera on a clattering wagon that was overburdened with household goods and children who clung to its sides like limpets to a sea rock.

"Venga!" her male companion urged, grasping her elbow and pulling her along. But Adria shook him off. She followed reluctantly on her own, pausing now and then to take another picture.

Gradually the scene began to change. In the distance a siren sounded that Adria took to be the all-clear, and ancient fire trucks headed down the streets to fight the fires.

The light that enabled her to take pictures gave way to an eerie, pink, smoke-screened sky. And still she followed the man, though he now simply walked silently by her side.

As it was now too dark to continue taking pictures, she paused to replace the lens cap on the camera. Then looking into his face asked, "Who are you?"

Again the broad smile, and unexpectedly a bow from the waist. "Carlos Barrera Solana, Señorita."

"Why did you follow me?"

"I was sent from the restaurant. The air raid alert was heard on the radio a few moments after you left. Saltrez sent me to see you to shelter."

"You speak English quite well. Why didn't you call out to me or say something? You scared me half to death."

"Señorita, when I am angry or in a hurry, I forget my English."

Adria again looked into his eyes and fell in pace with him. She inhaled the odd, chemical smell that permeated the air. She had noticed it before, but now it seemed stronger, apart from the smoke. Adria sniffed, "What's that smell?" Then she sniffed again, hoping he would understand.

"Cordite," he replied. "From the bombs."

Adria nodded. "I'll be all right now," she told him.

"I'll see you to your hotel," he stated.

"You probably saved my life."

He half laughed. "Probably," he allowed.

Adria again cast a sideways glance. He wore ill-fitting wool trousers, heavy leather boots, no shirt, but only an open leather vest. His face was angular and his eyes softer than his mouth except when he smiled. His hair was thick, dark and black. In all, he was an exceptionally handsome man. She wondered if, like so many Spaniards, he was part Gypsy. Perhaps it was only the way he was dressed.

They rounded several more corners until the hotel came into view. "Come in," Adria invited. "You've cut your forehead, let me put some antiseptic on it and a bandage."

"It's nothing."

"It needs to be washed."

He laughed, "I need to be washed."

Adria found herself smiling back. "It's possible for you to bathe if the water is still running."

He stuffed his large hands in his pockets and followed her through the deserted lobby and up the stairs.

"This part of town is almost untouched," he commented as he followed her in. "I suppose the Fascista know where the foreign journalists stay."

Adria went into the bathroom and turned on the water. "It works," she announced, standing in the doorway. "Go ahead, have a bath."

He nodded and disappeared inside, closing the door behind him. Adria went to her bag and withdrew a bottle of Scotch. She rarely drank straight alcohol, but she needed it now to steady her nerves. Though she had momentarily recovered long enough to take photos, the bombing raid was returning to her now with full impact. She shivered, and without hesitation poured herself a jigger and drank it straight down. Then, gratefully, she sank into a chair and put her feet up on the bed. Her clothes were utterly filthy from the warehouse floor. Her hair was tangled, and surely her face was as smudged as Carlos's.

She leaned back and closed her eyes and smiled. In her camera was a roll of priceless film, and for the first time she knew every one of her shots was good. What's more, she knew she had crossed over a threshold: in spite of fear she had gone for her camera. It had been as automatic as breathing, and taking the pictures had temporarily jolted her out of her fright.

The door to the tiny bathroom opened and Carlos appeared wrapped in a bathtowel and carrying his clothes in a bundle. Adria looked up at him not knowing what to say. The sudden intimacy of their situation seemed a surprise.

"I'll wash these later." He grinned and let his eyes examine her more closely. "You have not told me your name."

She found herself blushing under his gaze. "Adria," she stumbled. "Adria Halstead."

"Adria . . ." He rolled her name off his tongue, giving it a Spanish accent. Then he ushered her toward the bathroom. "It is yours."

Adria pulled herself up and gathered clean clothes from her pack. "There's Scotch," she said, indicating the bottle and disappearing into the bathroom.

"More scarce than gold," she heard him say as she closed the wooden door and turned on the water in the shower.

Adria washed her hair and covered herself in lather. Letting the lukewarm water run over her, she wondered what she would do with her unexpected guest. She emerged fully dressed, her damp hair falling in ringlets to her shoulders. Carlos was stretched out on the bed, the towel still covering him, a glass of Scotch in his hand and a relaxed expression on his face.

"I'll call down to the desk and order some food," Adria offered.

Carlos nodded his agreement. Then he tossed his bundle of clothes toward her. "Tell the maid to have them washed and dried."

Adria opened her mouth to protest—then, embarrassed, mumbled, "I don't have anything for you to wear."

His laughter filled the room. "Then I shall remain here."

"But . . ."

"We'll talk all night if you insist. Ah, American women are so strange. Do you think I need a woman so badly that I would molest you? I don't force myself on women." He grinned. "I don't have to."

Adria felt the warmth in her face and reprimanded

herself for the vestiges of childishness she knew she still manifested. But it was more than that. There was something about Carlos that reminded her of Jeff, something strong enough to make her recognize her own vulnerability. She turned away and picked up the house phone. She clicked it four times before anyone on the desk answered.

"Food for those who can pay in dollars," Carlos said when she had ordered. "There are a million refugees in Barcelona," he added ruefully. "How fortunate I am. I am one of the very few who will spend the night with a bottle of Scotch, a full belly, and a beautiful American photographer."

"You're cynical," she said.

"I'm a poet, one of a dying breed. We're being murdered for our songs. It was all we had to fight with."

"The war's not over yet. There's still talk of an independent Catalonia."

"And talk is all it is." He picked up her empty glass and poured her a drink. "No man should drink alone."

Adria mixed the warm Scotch with water from the decanter on the bedside table. It still burned her throat and filled her chest. She hadn't eaten since morning. Morning—was it only twelve hours ago that she had stood with Robert Wertheim on the deck of his yacht? It seemed like weeks ago.

She responded slowly to the knock on the door. The maid came in and set down the tray. Adria handed her Carlos's clothes and Carlos gave her instructions in Spanish. A dark look on her face, she disappeared, closing the door behind her.

"She relishes in serving Americanos. When Barcelona falls she will run into the streets and proclaim the Fascista."

"I thought everyone in Barcelona was Loyalist."

Carlos laughed, "It's a city of rats, and when their compatriots march in they will swarm up out of their holes and rejoice."

Adria uncovered the tray and handed Carlos a plate of steaming paella. She took the other and surprised herself by eating as rapidly as if she had been starved.

He opened the red wine and poured them both full glasses. It mixed in Adria's stomach with the Scotch and made her lightheaded, almost giddy.

"Tell me about your poetry," she requested. Her sobriety was slipping away.

He finished eating and put his plate on the table. "Poetry is to be heard, not described."

"Can you recite some then?"

"Do you understand Spanish?"

"Much better than I can speak it."

Carlos began his recitation slowly in a mixture of Spanish and English.

> *Viva la revolución!*
> I touched your soft flesh,
> caressed your flaming lips, and
>   buried my sword in your moist depths.
> I gave myself to you.
> *Viva la revolución!*
> Children weep for their dead
>   mothers, half men, men without
>   legs, fill the streets.
> They gave themselves to you.
> *Viva la revolución!*
> The rivers run red with blood to
>   the sea. The once fertile valleys
>   are black, scorched by fire.
> My country was consumed by you.
> *Viva la revolución,* you are a seductive whore.

Adria was transfixed. Like the poet Pablo Neruda, who had recently left Spain, Carlos's use of language was raw and sexual. Adria blushed not at the words of his poem, but at the way he had spoken them and of where his gaze had concentrated.

Carlos laughed and stood up, the towel that covered him dropping to the floor. Her eyes fell on his hard, tight, muscular buttocks and she could not turn away. When he had retrieved his cigarettes from the dresser, he picked up the towel and wrapped it around himself before turning around.

He laughed at her, "I've shocked you. I keep forgetting—I live with so many others that nudity is taken for granted. War has a way of eliminating modesty."

Adria concentrated on his dark eyes. I want to know more about this man, she thought. I want to know why he's here and what he's fighting for. She waited till he had lit his cigarette and settled back onto the bed. "Tell me when you first got involved in the fighting," she prodded.

He grinned at her, "I see you *do* want to talk all night."

Adria moved restlessly, seeking comfort; then her eyes opened suddenly. The first light of dawn shone through the open window and with it had come an early morning chill. Carlos loomed over her, his towel wrapped and knotted round his waist. She shivered, not knowing whether it was the early morning cold or Carlos's nearness that had awakened her.

He took her hands and pulled her to her feet. "I don't displease you, do I?" he asked.

Adria felt the blood rush to her face as his arms encircled her, pressing her to his near-naked body as he kissed her neck. "You fell asleep in the chair," he whispered.

The feel of his lips sent another shiver through her. Carlos exuded a raw sensuality, and she felt herself responding as his hands worked on her back in movements between soothing massage and knowing caresses. Then he unbuttoned her blouse and pushed her lacy undergarments aside. Lips on her breasts and silent urgent embraces. She went limp in his arms.

I should tell him I've only ever been with one other man, she thought. He ought to know that I knew that man for months before we made love . . . What will he think of me? For an instant she hesitated and almost pulled away from him. But her strength was gone, and wave after wave of warmth swept over her until she was only aware of a building desire that drew her to this man.

He led her to the bed and, discarding the towel, fell on her hungrily, covering her with intimate kisses.

Adria put her arms around him and held him tightly. She was wildly aroused as he stroked her body and whispered words in Spanish. Rough and direct, his muscular body moved against her, and she lifted herself willingly, plunging into sensations and memories as he took her. In the full light of day she would notice her nail marks on his back, and she would remember kissing him so passionately that she bit him. He would call her a tigress and he would confess that he had thought such passion came only from Latin women.

3

IN ALGIERS ROBERT HAD been told to load supplies and continue on to Cairo. He had docked several hours ago and only slightly rested he now made his way through the winding streets.

The air was heavy with the smell of dung, the smoke from evening cooking fires, and the aroma of exotic spices: roasted caraway seeds, cumin, and essence of almond. In the distance *muezzin* called the faithful to worship from the minarets of a hundred mosques, the calls mixing incongruously with the music of popular instruments, the mournful call of wailers, and the singsong beckoning of local shopkeepers. Midway up the dusty street, the low, squat, white building labeled *Al-Ward* in Arabic stood out among the maze of mud houses. Its peeling whitewash invisible in the darkness, at night it possessed a certain grandeur. On either side of its guarded entrance, huge roses were painted on the white walls because the name *Al-Ward* meant "The Rose." The doorway itself and the edge of the tile roof were strung with gaudy colored lights of the sort used on American Christmas trees. Robert pushed past two men in the doorway.

Inside, the *oud* player moved his fingers gracefully and tilted his head to his own tunes. But his eyes were strangely dull as he stared out at his noisy audience, as if he faced an empty room with his Egyptian lute. Next to him the *kanun* player sat with his instrument—a lap zither—between crossed legs. He did not look up at all. Only the drummer who played the ancient, goblet-shaped *darabukaah* seemed involved. His dark eyes flashed as he lecherously followed the movements of the scantily clad belly dancer who clicked her finger cymbals as she turned and whirled, simultaneously rolling layers of subtle flesh and swinging her hips. Her dark skin glistened as perfumed oils mixed with perspiration and she thrust herself suggestively forward and backward.

As for the patrons, the movements of their eyes were hidden by dark glasses, or shadowed by the combination of heavy eyebrows and low-slung burnooses. What light there was came from low-watt bulbs on a high ceiling and was filtered through layers of sweet, acrid smoke. Pungent Turkish cigarettes mixed with the unmistakable odor of hashish.

Unlike a nightclub in Europe or North America, this Egyptian version was totally populated by men. The only females were the belly dancer and a few whores who were restricted to the back room adjacent to the bar. If aroused by the gyrations of the dancer, patrons could, for a small price, avail themselves of these time-worn ladies on one of several plush chaises-longes.

Robert Wertheim glanced at his watch and again eyed the entrance. As usual Ben El Lazar was late. He stared into his black coffee and wished he had ordered a drink. Moslems or not, many patrons were drinking. Of course Cairo had long been corrupted by the British and the French, and its population was mixed in spite of the many minarets raised like lone guardians toward the sky. And, he mused, for a true believer hashish was as off limits as alcohol.

"*Shalom,*" a low voice muttered in his ear as strong fingers grasped Robert's shoulder. Robert turned his head slightly and looked into the solemn face of a burnoose-clad Ben El Lazar.

"I was watching. You didn't come through the front entrance."

Ben Lazar shrugged and sat down. Like thousands of other Arabs on the streets of Cairo he wore desert garb and dark glasses.

"You look more Arab than the Arabs," Robert commented.

"I could say the same of you, though on close examination your blue eyes would give you away."

Robert did not answer.

"And what cargo do you bring me tonight?" Ben Lazar asked, arching his eyebrow slightly above the frame of his glasses.

"Twenty souls," Robert answered. "Eight children and twelve adults. Six men."

Ben Lazar shook his head. "Six men to look after eight children and six women. You make my life difficult."

"The women are strong and two of the children are fourteen, both boys and both capable."

"Capable of what? Tilling the soil? They aren't capable unless they can shoot a gun and throw a grenade without a second thought. But that comes later in a training camp. First they must get to Palestine."

Ben El Lazar was a commander in the Haganah, and before changing his name to that of an ancient ancestor he had been a sergeant in the British army. He was a tough man. His face had been turned to leather by the desert sun, and Robert thought his heart might well have atrophied, too. Lazar's work was to smuggle Robert's cargo of fleeing Jews past British lines into Palestine despite the reign of terror conducted by the Mufti. Aliyah Beth, the organization for which Robert worked, supplied the funds to settle the refugees as well as the funds to bribe the Mufti's men. Robert would have preferred not to work in secret, but it was imperative that his involvement be kept under wraps. Aliyah Beth was well known but its backers were not, first because they would have become targets for assassination, second because had the British and French governments discovered the involvement of their citizens, funds would have been frozen. The British were strict about immigration to Palestine. They wanted the Arabs as allies against the Germans should there be a war, and to ensure that, they made promises to limit Jewish settlement in Palestine.

"The price has gone up," Ben Lazar said without expression. "A thousand a head now, my friend. And still some will be betrayed and murdered. This is a bloody business and I've heard the price on both our heads is higher. Ah, how they would love to find and eliminate the source of our funds."

Robert stared into his coffee again. The faces of the children stood out in his mind. The baby, Hannah, was less than a year and still suckling from her young mother's breast. Two-year-old Adam was a heart-stealer whose small hand had found its way into Robert's day after day while they had been at sea. "Will they be safe?" he queried.

Lazar shrugged and smiled slyly. "Only if I can slit the throat of Al-Hussein first."

Robert felt suddenly nauseated. "The middle man?"

"Who appears to have been playing both sides of the fence."

"And the last group I brought?" Robert asked anxiously.

"Half made it to Palestine."

Robert's fist automatically doubled in anger. He could see the faces of each one of them, but he resisted the temptation to ask which had been killed. He knew that his expression revealed his emotions, his eyes misting over.

"You are too soft," Lazar said. "Do not mourn the

dead, celebrate the survivors. It is with them we will build a new nation."

"To me they are all important," Robert replied. Perhaps he was soft, but Ben Lazar was too hard. Robert sipped his coffee. Active Jews were divided. Some Zionists felt that the creation of the State of Israel was the highest priority; they regarded the British as their enemies and had no compunction about spilling English blood. Peter Bergson, a Palestinian who was a leader in the Irgun Tzevai Leumi, the armed, anti-British organization founded by Menachem Begin, was such a man. Others, like Robert himself, felt the most pressing task was saving Jewish lives. He believed the British could be pressured or negotiated with, and he did not favor using terrorism against them. The problem for both groups was money and political backing. No nation had yet condemned Hitler's policies, and influential American Jews were reluctant to donate to either the moderate or militant Zionists. Like his own brother Charles, they saw little difference between the Haganah and the Irgun. Those involved in smuggling Jewish refugees into Palestine against British policy were painted with the same brush as those who offered armed resistance.

"Have you sufficient money to pay the new price?"

Robert nodded. It was an absurd question. In this case he would most certainly use his own money, as he had often done. But then, Ben Lazar had not the faintest idea who he was, knowing only that he had a boat, or access to one, and that he worked for the Aliyah Beth. He knew him only as "the fisherman" and he thought him to be French.

"You will meet me here tomorrow and I will bring the necessary amount."

Ben Lazar nodded. "Tomorrow," he agreed. Then added, "In cash." Their arrangements complete, Ben Lazar took his leave.

Robert sat for a time sipping his coffee and abstractedly listening to the music. His involvement with Aliyah Beth had originally been limited to cash donations; then he had begun traveling to the ghettos of Poland, Greece, and the Ukraine. He came to know his own people and to understand the threat they faced. His long discussions with Aaron Rosen replayed in his mind and he gradually realized that the struggle for a Jewish homeland was *his* struggle.

Chapter Six

1

THE STREETS OF BARCELONA were filled with bands of marauding children, pale skin stretched over bony frames, dark eyes made huge by gaunt faces. There were a million refugees in Barcelona, six hundred thousand of them children with outstretched arms and thin, unsmiling faces. Forty thousand a day were fed by the Quakers; the rest survived on a few ounces of lentils and rice, on rodents—if they could be caught—and on rain water.

The Casa Linda was like a fortress. Foreign currency bought comfort, and there Adria and her fellow journalists sought refuge from the horrific reality of a city under siege.

During those days Adria became one with her cameras, beginning to experience a strange sensation when she shot the grieving, the dying, and the dead. It was as if a curtain dropped around her mind, as if everything were blotted out save her consideration of focus, light, and technique. With the camera to her eye, a dying baby and weeping mother might have been a bowl of fruit or a bottle of wine. Composition dominated everything—till she stopped shooting. Then she often wept or became physically sick. There were times when she could not even look at her own developed pictures.

Carlos remained with her at the hotel for a time, then came and went, returning sometimes only after several days. Each time he seemed more weary than before. She questioned him, but he put her off and only replied, "I am fighting for my country. That's all you need to know."

Adria stood at the hotel's entrance and shivered. An hour ago an old woman had brought a note from Carlos—"Be ready with your cameras, and pack your things. I'll meet you in front of the hotel at 11 P.M."

"Where are you," she whispered under her breath as she drew her recently purchased shawl tighter. It was a little after eleven. An hour earlier, a light rain had begun falling and the smoke that rose from smoldering fires all over the city—the legacy of last night's bombing raid—mixed with the mist, blanketing Barcelona with an eerie fog.

Adria took a few steps from the hotel's entrance and turned to search the street. She jumped when Carlos's hand touched her neck from behind.

"Where did you come from?" she asked peering into his face.

"I came through the building next door—did I startle you?"

"Yes."

He took her arm, "Is that everything? Did you check out of the hotel?"

"I didn't check out. Why should I?"

"Because you're not coming back."

"I should pay my bill . . ." It flashed across her mind that she had just accepted what he said without question. Not only had she grown to trust him completely, she was in a way dependent on him, her guide through this terrible hell. His fingers grasped her arm tightly, preventing her from turning back.

"Forget your bill. You'll have better use for your foreign currency and letters of credit."

"But I should—"

"Do you want to go to the front or not?" he asked somewhat impatiently.

"You arranged it? Of course I want to go."

"Then stop worrying about your hotel bill. When we get back—if we get back—we'll have to go elsewhere. The Fascists are going to walk right into this city and to

survive we'll have to fade into the population or make a
run for the French border."

She started to protest that she would be quite safe,
but she realized he was talking about himself and that
he assumed she wanted to be with him. And I do, she
told herself quickly.

"You'll find out what it's really like," he said.

She could still hear the bitterness and anger in his
voice. "Have I done something wrong?"

"Wrong? You? No, my Lady Bountiful, you've done
nothing wrong. You've been most generous with your
foreign liquor. Now I will return your generosity. You
can come and share our sour wine, putrid rice, and stale
bread! In that hotel you are a tourist. It is like watching
a war from inside a bulletproof bus. All around you
there is suffering, but you aren't part of it. So I am
going to take you to the front and then bring you back
here to stay with my friends."

He stopped suddenly and moved in front of her. She
could just make out the hard expression on his face.
"That is what you want—isn't it?"

Adria nodded, a wave of guilt passing through her.
People were starving all around her, but her foreign
currency had been able to buy food on the black
market. Those who ran the blockade at night in yachts
and rowboats to deliver small amounts of food, alcohol,
and cigarettes would accept only American dollars,
British pounds, or gold coins.

He stared into her eyes for a long moment, then
stepped aside and again took her arm. "There's a truck
waiting for us on the far side of the park."

They walked across the crowded park where the
homeless lived in tents and ramshackle huts made from
cardboard and cloth. Adria could not help wondering
what the park had looked like before its transforma-
tion. Had there been flowers and grass? Then sadly she
wondered if there would ever be vegetation here again.
The hungry were even digging up roots to boil for
nourishment.

The truck was parked by the curb, and Carlos called

out in Spanish to the driver who waved back and started the sputtering engine. From the rear hands reached out to help Adria up. Carlos threw her pack ahead of her, and he followed her inside.

In the darkness bodies moved to make room for them and Adria and Carlos sat down, their backs to the side of the open vehicle. In seconds they were moving and within half an hour they had left Barcelona behind and were headed down a bumpy dirt road.

Away from the city the fog disappeared, and in the weak moonlight Adria could make out the faces of her traveling companions for the first time. Dressed in uniforms and wearing helmets, they looked like frightened children going off to a play war. They were young, so young she felt ill.

"Do they get weapons at the front?" she asked.

Carlos actually laughed. "Weapons? They have their hands."

"You mean there are no guns?"

"Only those taken from dead men. My dear American, at the beginning of this glorious campaign there were only thirty-seven thousand rifles for all of Catalonia and not enough ammunition to make full use of those."

Adria again searched the youthful faces of the soldiers. One grinned back at her and the rest looked away.

Carlos's hand reached behind her neck and rubbed it gently. Then he pulled her closer, so her head was resting on his shoulder. "It's a long ride; try to get some sleep."

Adria wanted to look into his eyes, but couldn't. The question she so often asked was again on her lips. "Carlos, what do you do? Do you go to the front to fight?"

"Ah, do you think I am a coward who sends others?"

"No."

"But you are curious?"

"I want to know."

"I go behind enemy lines. I am a saboteur."

96

Adria emitted a slight groan from deep inside her throat. Last week a train had been blown up near Lerida in Fascist-held territory. Everyone had been killed, soldiers and civilians alike. Carlos had been gone when it happened. She fell silent and in a moment Carlos touched her forehead with a kiss.

"You see, there are things you don't want to know," he told her.

2

DRESSED IN BATTLE FATIGUES with her face smeared with dirt, Adria stood in line amidst some fifty-odd men and waited for the daily ration of watery soup and hard bread. They were a mile from the Ebro river, the line between the Republicans and the Fascists.

All day she had been at the front, or as close as the Republican commander, Enrique Lister, would allow her to go. She had photographed the wounded in underequipped field hospitals and she had taken a series of photos of the burial detail as they set about their grim task. She felt bone weary as she waited in silence with the others. It took no insight to know this was a beaten and dispirited army. Vaguely she wondered what kept them going day after day, week after week.

"Adria!"

She turned sharply to see Carlos coming toward her, her pack and his slung over his shoulder. "We have to go," he told her.

Adria frowned. She felt like a sleep walker. "I was just waiting for some soup."

"You can have something to eat later." He grasped her arm and pulled her out of line. "I mean now."

Too tired to argue, she followed as he led her away from the encampment and up a steep, rock-strewn path. She forced one leg in front of the other and grasped low bushes as the climb grew steeper. "Where are we going?" she finally asked.

"Back to Barcelona," he replied.

So tired she now felt giddy, Adria laughed, "Are we walking the whole way?"

He turned to her angrily. "Stop making jokes and just try to keep up, will you?"

They reached the top of the hill and Adria stopped, panting. "Wait," she begged. "Just let me get my breath."

"Tardón, Tardón—slow poke," Carlos muttered.

"What *is* the hurry?"

Carlos moved her around and pointed to the valley on the far side of the hill they had just climbed. At the end of what looked like a long dirt driveway was a small plane. "It's dangerous to have it exposed," he said. "An enemy plane might see it."

"We're flying?"

"It is the means of transportation used to drop me behind lines, but now it will take us to Barcelona."

"Why now?"

Carlos glanced at his watch. "Because very soon the Fascists will attack. I don't expect the line to hold any longer."

He had been behind the lines, so she didn't question his information. They might be losing, but the Republicans still had halfway decent intelligence information on enemy troop movements. "It's December twenty-third," she said. "What about the truce?"

Carlos shrugged. "There will be no Christmas cease-fire. The pope's negotiations failed. We heard it on the radio."

"I was hoping he'd succeed."

"It would only have been a short reprieve. Now come *on!*" Carlos led the way down and she followed, half walking, half sliding toward the little plane that waited in the clearing.

3

IT WAS MADAME WERTHEIM'S custom to visit with her eldest son Charles in England during December and then rendezvous with her younger son Robert in Paris for the New Year holiday.

Robert had returned from his long voyage on the 15th of December and gone first to the Riviera, remaining until December 28th. On the morning of the 28th he had left for Paris, choosing to drive his silver Peugeot sports car rather than take the train.

Robert and his mother had spent a simple holiday. They had gone to a special New Year's Eve performance of Mozart's *Marriage of Figaro*, and after the opera had shared a midnight supper in a private salon at Maxim's. On New Year's Day they visited with the Rothschilds. The day following the holiday, January 2, 1939, was a Monday, and so Madame Wertheim went to the salon of her couturier, Gabrielle Chanel, to be fitted for her spring and summer wardrobe. That evening she and Robert ate dinner at his apartment, and then he drove her to the railway station so she could return to the estate, planning to follow in a few days.

Robert stepped out of the gare de Lyon and, brusquely tossing his silk scarf over his shoulder, headed for his car. The weather was surprisingly damp, and as he looked heavenward, wet snow began to fall. The great white flakes melted instantly as they hit the ground, as if touched by a magician's wand. Robert dashed across the street, and once on the other side, withdrew his black pigskin driving gloves from his pocket. Head down, he turned the corner onto the dark side street where he had parked the Peugeot.

The snow and the dim light obscured his vision, but as he came closer he noticed that the car was leaning to one side and that it was dented and scratched. He bent down to check the tires and saw that they had been slashed. Robert moved to the curb side of the car and

froze. Etched on door were the words, *"maudit juif"*—
"cursed Jew."

"Bastards," he said under his breath as he ran his
fingers along the scratched-out words. But how did they
know? The question formed in his mind simultaneously
with the realization that he had been followed, singled
out . . .

"Dirty Jew Communist." Robert straightened suddenly as two hulking figures emerged from the shadowed doorway. They were hooded, and he could see
them clutching heavy batons.

Robert turned quickly and began to run, almost
slipping as he sprinted across the street toward the
Seine. He yelled for help at some passersby near the
station, but they looked at him blankly, then turned
their backs. No time to think. Should he try to run into
the station and yell for the gendarmes? No, the batons
might well be police batons and his pursuers might well
be off-duty police officers who belonged to the Cougalards or some other Fascist street gang.

Robert turned his head slightly—they were large and
he was faster. He turned again and suddenly was half
blinded by the glare of headlights coming right for him.
He dove round the corner at quai de la Rapée, putting
a lightpost and a small kiosk between himself and the
oncoming car. He rolled and slid down the sidewalk,
scrambling to his feet as the car careened around the
corner, skidding into the lightpost and exploding into
flame.

He didn't pause. His foot pursuers were still coming,
shouting obscenities into the night. Robert rounded
another corner and darted into the shadows to catch his
breath. His heart was beating wildly, sheer terror
causing waves of adrenalin to surge through him.

He turned into an alley and turned again into the
darkness of a deserted street, his eyes darting left and
right as he searched for an escape route or a place to
take refuge. He turned again and ran, then stopped,
paralyzed as, he realized he had run into a cul-de-sac.
He could hear the feet on the wet street, and seeing a

light in a third-floor window, he stopped and began pounding on the door.

Robert heard their footsteps, then their heavy panting. He felt a loose cobblestone with the toe of his shoe and he quickly picked it up. As he did so, the swoosh of a baton went by, just missing his head. Robert swung his fist straight up in front of him, catching one of his assailants in the face. Stone met flesh and bone, and with a groan and a grunt one hulk slipped to the ground. Before Robert could swing again, he felt himself kicked in the ribs and he crumpled over, trying to roll away and protect himself. A giant fist hit him in the face and blood mixed with cold perspiration. A sharp pain rippled through his head and the profile of an earless man flashed before his blurred vision. Then he passed out.

"Your eyes are the color of the sea," Robert said, looking down at Adria. They were stunning eyes—green with a gold ring around the pupils. Hypnotic eyes, the kind of eyes that could make a man forget himself—tempting eyes. They were dancing to Cole Porter and he was holding her close, wanting to be closer, wanting to kiss her deeply and carry her back to his cabin.

She smiled up at him with full, tempting lips and her magic eyes danced with humor. "You're a flatterer," she had replied. But she hadn't withdrawn from him, and he knew she wanted him, too, and that made it harder. But she was on her way to Spain and he was on his way to transport refugees to Palestine. He had important work to do and she had an assignment. Tomorrow she would be gone and tonight was too late to start an affair he wanted to last forever.

"Dear heaven," Robert heard a female voice through a fog of pain.

"Adria?" He wasn't certain if he said her name or just thought he had. Terror seized him. He couldn't

101

move or speak nor open his eyes and confront his circumstances. The world was dark and he was totally immobilized.

4

"AND NOW WE WAIT," Carlos told Adria.

He took her to a basement room in what had been an apartment block in Barcelona. Destroyed by the relentless air raids, it was now nothing more than a pile of rubble, but to one side there was an entrance that led down a flight of stairs, and off the darkened corridor there were rooms. Miraculously, the ceiling had not caved in, and because it offered shelter in a city where hundreds were forced to sleep in the streets, every room was occupied by as many people as could cover the floors at night. Their room was shared with two of Carlos's friends, Diego and Anita. Its sole amenity was a potbellied stove with a chimney pipe that was thrust through the roof.

Day after day, Adria gave Carlos precious dollars and he roamed the black market, returning with rice and sometimes a bottle of cheap wine. At night they huddled together beneath a coarse woolen blanket and made love in the darkness.

Carlos could be as soft and gentle as he could be passionate or cruel. He was, Adria decided, the most complicated man she had ever known. Sometimes by the light of a flickering candle, while she sipped wine and drew the blanket about her, he read his poems, his voice deep and hypnotic, his images of war deeply sexual. One night he read her a poem by his friend Pablo Neruda, *"España en el Corazón,"* which had been published and distributed to the Republican soldiers.

Adria leaned against the wall and stared into the fire. It was January 24th and she felt restless and frustrated. She had sent her last pictures to Andy Martin over a week ago, and now she could send no more because the fighting had grown so close and the air raids so frequent that the airport was closed.

"What are you thinking about?" Carlos asked.

"My pictures," she answered. "I can't send any more."

"My country is being murdered and you worry about your pictures?"

Adria frowned. Lately he had often taken that tone with her.

"How fortunate I am to have found an American!" he said looking at Diego and Anita. "She has dollars to buy us food and she keeps me warm at night—as warm as any Spanish whore could." He turned and leered at her. "Perhaps warmer." Then he added, "And such a talented American—so free to pursue her dreams!"

Adria wondered if the pain she felt showed in her eyes. She glanced at Diego and Anita, who looked away in embarrassment.

"I will write no more poems," he said evenly, his eyes fastened on hers. "You may go on taking pictures, but there will be no more poems. Lorca, the greatest of our poets, is dead, and Hernández is being tortured in a Fascist prison. His blood gives meaning to his art."

"You can still write. We don't have to stay here and wait. We could make it to the French border." As soon as she said it, she knew it was the wrong thing.

Anita and Diego had gotten up, and Diego mumbled something about getting some air. Carlos didn't even turn away when they left. He stood and stared at her, his eyes clouded with anger.

"Yes, we should run away," he stormed even before the door closed behind his friends. "Then you could totally support me, you could even give me a new nationality! No, my dear American angel, I have a country and I will not leave it."

He hates me for giving to him, she thought as she watched his dark eyes narrow.

"'En el principio es la palabra'—in the beginning is the word. The Fascists are coming and they will burn

103

our poems because words are revolutionary. Hear Mussolini's slogan, 'To believe, to obey, to combat.' Those words are the antithesis of 'Liberty, equality, fraternity.' Fascism has no ideology, no positive force. It is entirely negative. That is why I will write no more. But I will not run away either, I will not let you turn me into a coward."

Adria closed her eyes so she could not see his face.

In one stride he was at her side, his large hands touching her throat, brushing the blanket to her shoulders. "My beautiful, untouched, American angel. You sleep with me because you feel sorry for me, because you know I am a man on the short end of a Fascist rope who will not live to see his thirtieth birthday!"

"No—" Adria tried to protest, but his mouth covered hers and his hands sought her beneath the blanket, both warming and chilling her.

"You give and I take," he whispered. His voice was bitter and his hands were not gentle as he clawed at her clothing, exposing her breasts.

"So lovely in the light—enough of making love to you in the darkness." He rubbed one nipple roughly between thumb and forefinger and kissed the other.

Adria groaned and tears filled her eyes as her arms encircled his neck. "I want you to take," she murmured and even as she said it, she knew it would anger him further. He would have preferred rape, just as he would have rather stolen her money. But Carlos was neither a thief nor a rapist. He was filled with pride, a pride circumstances would not allow him to exercise.

He moved his hand from her breast to between her legs and she moaned as he entered her. All thoughts were gone as she was swept away by the pure sensations of their lovemaking. Carlos shuddered and collapsed on top of her, panting as if he had temporarily expelled the devil that taunted him. In a moment he moved off her, pulled the blanket over them, and drew her close. He lifted his hand and stroked her cheek, then her forehead, brushing the damp strands of hair away. His hands were as gentle now as they had been hard and probing moments before, when even so she had responded.

"I'm sorry," he whispered as he withdrew his arm and propped his head up so he could look down into her face.

"You needn't be."

"I am. I'm sorry we didn't meet when I was a whole man, sorry each time I hurt you for being kind, sorry for both loving and hating you."

"Do you hate me?"

"Sometimes. I hate you for losing yourself in your work when mine is fruitless. I hate you for coming from a country still vital and filled with the spirit of revolution when mine is dying, and I hate you for loving me because there is so little left of me to love."

Adria nodded silently and touched his lips with her fingers. He had explained his conflicting emotions more concisely than she could explain hers. In the last two months, she thought ruefully, I've exposed myself to a hurtful relationship, a relationship that can only end tragically. She looked down so he could not see her eyes. They'll betray me, she thought. He'll look into my eyes and he will know I don't truly love him. She inhaled deeply and felt overwhelmed. Carlos was bitter because he felt he had used her, but in reality she had used him. Oh, the physical attraction was real enough, but what was even more real was her own guilt. She wanted Carlos to hurt her, she wanted to suffer because everyone around her was suffering. She was an outsider, and when it was over she had a country to go home to, but they did not.

5

JEFF BORDEN AMBLED ALONG the puddle-filled streets of Nice. Beneath his wrinkled trench coat he wore tan slacks, a plaid, open-necked shirt, and a V-neck tan pullover. He had neither rubbers nor a hat, but he didn't much care if his head were wet. He carried only a small shoulder bag, but round his neck he wore three cameras.

Nothing worse than a resort when it rains, Jeff thought as he surveyed the dismal, deserted streets. In January the so-called "garden of Europe" was being watered, and the hundreds of flower stalls that normally lined the streets had been boarded and shuttered, leaving only a collection of unattractive little huts. He came to a bedraggled horse wearing a dripping straw bonnet. The animal shifted its loose bones and pawed the cobblestones, waiting for its master to return.

Jeff paused long enough to photograph the horse, then pulled his trench coat around him and continued on his way. He felt frustrated and angry. Nice, after all, was a detour, and he chastised himself for taking it. He should have gone directly to Spain, but he had wanted to see Adria. Then he discovered she had left her Villefranche hotel many weeks ago, and when he sought out Nelson Halstead, he was told he was on leave and could not be contacted. Finally, he began searching for Christina Barton. But she, too, was absent, and the maid at her villa did little but shrug, as if Christina's comings and goings were far too complicated to understand.

"Shit," Jeff mumbled as he turned away from the horse and stuffed his hands in his pockets. He cast a suspicious look at the sky and decided it was about to rain again. He didn't even have a hotel room yet, nor, he remembered, had he eaten since early morning. Putting off the hotel momentarily—after all, this was hardly the height of the tourist season—he entered a small, elegant-looking restaurant. What the hell? he thought. He was on an expense account, and if the portions proved too delicate, he would simply order more. That, he had discovered, was the real trouble with expensive French restaurants. He himself preferred peasant fare: a loaf of garlic bread, a bottle of wine, some cheese, and a pound of rare roast beef.

The waiter eyed Jeff with distaste in a way only the French can muster, and Jeff considered leaving. But he heard thunder followed by heavy rain on the stone streets. *"Combien de personnes?"* the waiter asked, looking over his shoulder.

"One," Jeff answered flatly. *"Une."*

The long nose sniffed and the waiter guided him among the tables, seating him in the rear. Jeff folded his large frame into the absurdly small chair and immediately searched for his cigarettes. It was then that he heard the crystal laughter, laughter so familiar that he turned his head, searching the dimly lit room.

They were sitting by the window, Christina Barton dressed to the nines in a tight violet dress and Nelson Halstead out of uniform. They were holding hands across the table and she was playing to him while he responded like a schoolboy. Jeff did not bother to be discreet. He simply stared at them and wondered what he had seen in Christina that even warranted a one-night-stand. It had been a meaningless liaison, but it had sent Adria away.

Nelson Halstead stood up and pecked Christina on the cheek. He didn't need to kiss her passionately, Jeff thought. He'd probably had it all before dinner and was now taking his leave to go back to Villefranche. He watched as Halstead left the restaurant, donning his raincoat at the door. Jeff waited until he was gone, then without a moment's hesitation strode across the room. "Join me for wine?"

Christina looked up and paled slightly. Glancing toward the door to make sure Halstead was gone, she smiled weakly. "Whatever are you doing here?"

"Passing through. Come on Christie, let's have a drink."

She stood up and almost reluctantly followed him to his table. "Just one, I have to go soon."

"Mummy waiting up for you?" he asked sarcastically.

"You know perfectly well I'm alone this season."

"Sure, daddy's home playing fund-raiser for the Bund and mummy's book-banning club is in full session."

"You're quite loathsome," Christina replied.

He smiled engagingly. "What'cha got going here, Christie baby?"

"What I do is hardly any concern of yours."

"First me, now Adria's old man. You know, you have hidden talents, lady. Tell me, what have you got against Adria?"

"Nothing. Whatever makes you ask such a question? Nelson means something to me. As far as Adria is concerned, well, it's coincidental."

He lifted his eyebrow and lifted the glass of wine the waiter had poured. "Where is Adria?"

"She's gone to Spain, ran off with a very handsome, wealthy Jew named Robert Wertheim. Her father was furious." Christina smiled. Jeff would be jealous and she liked that.

Jeff shook his head. "I can't say I know Robert Wertheim personally, Christina, but I certainly know who he is. As it happens, he was attacked in Paris by Cougalards, the French version of the Ku Klux Klan, and is in the hospital in a coma. The Paris papers are full of the story, so I know damn well he's not in Spain with Adria."

"Well, he took her to Spain on his yacht."

Jeff ignored her barbs. It wasn't all that easy to get to Spain, even though since Barcelona had fallen the frontier had been opened and some two hundred thousand Royalist troops, the last remnants of the defenders of Barcelona, had poured across it. "When did she go?" he prodded.

"The end of November, as I recall," Christina replied.

"Christ, she must still be in Barcelona." He felt a twinge of apprehension, but then told himself that nothing would happen to an American journalist.

"Are you here just to see Adria?" Christina asked, lifting one brow.

"No, I'm on my way to Spain."

"Isn't that a bit dangerous?"

"I got Spanish papers in Germany from the Fascists. I'm going to photograph a new Spain, a Spain under Franco."

"Well, I suppose Adria is still there," Christina said without concern.

The waiter appeared and Jeff ordered dinner. Christina made no move to leave. Normally he would have been delighted to have female companionship—any beautiful woman would do—but not Christina. She was beautiful all right, but hard as nails. There was something evil behind her blue eyes, something he sensed but couldn't define.

6

ON JANUARY 26TH, BARCELONA did not fall gloriously, with fighting in the streets and resistance at every intersection. Instead, it fell whimpering, a city starved into submission. Fleeing Royalist troups bypassed Barcelona and headed directly into the mountains for the French border. Royalist supporters in the city waited, while others who had hidden their preferences flooded the streets to greet the Fascist tanks.

"Please, Carlos, we could get to France," Adria remembered pleading. But it was no use. Carlos muttered about fate and destiny, said he could not run away anymore.

Two days after the Fascists came into the city, they were all arrested. Miserable and frightened, Adria found herself in a Spanish prison.

"Did you know that Carlos Solana once tried to assassinate General Franco?

"Perhaps you helped him.

"You know of course that Carlos Solana wrote tracts against the government? Did you know he was part Gypsy? Did you know he was a murderer?

"And you yourself are a spy, are you not?

"Admit it, it will go easier for you."

Over and over and over the same questions. Over and over the same answer: "No. I am an American citizen. I am not a spy. Please contact the American embassy."

Beba! Drink! The old woman held the rusty ladle to Adria's lips and again pressed her to sip. Adria allowed her tongue to lap a mouthful of the warm, sour water, forced herself to swallow. Then she shook her head and the old woman muttered and returned the ladle to the bucket.

Adria sank back against the cool, damp cement wall of the cell, closing her eyes against the sun streaming through the small window. Lethargically she scratched her head. She itched night and day, and though she could not see the lice, she could feel them. Adria shivered. Days and nights had melted into one another and she was rapidly losing track of how long she had been here.

At first she had thought it was all a nightmare from which she would awaken. Then she realized it was all too real. Now, after twelve—or was it thirteen—days and nights, fear mixed with hopelessness and hunger turned her numb, too weak to protest or cry. Still, the events of the last two weeks ran through her head, playing like a fragmented horror film on the shaky screen of her mind.

She, Carlos, and the others had been dragged from their room, loaded into trucks like cattle and brought to the old prison. They were immediately separated and Adria found herself tossed into a cell with twenty other women, women with dark, expressionless faces who eyed her suspiciously and made no attempt to converse. For two days and two nights she crouched in the corner, afraid of her cellmates, too terrified to sleep and acutely aware of the vermin skittling in the darkness. They had taken her belongings—her precious cameras, her passport, her clothes. She had only what she was wearing.

110

On the third day she had been taken by two burly men into the office of a uniformed officer who asked her questions for hours, but who seemingly did not listen to the answers.

"I'm an American citizen," she had protested. "I'm a photographer. You must notify my embassy! I'm an American citizen." Tears of anger, of fear and frustration had run down her face. But she was returned to her cell, again and again, so often she knew the questions by rote.

On the sixth day she had been taken to a small balcony that overlooked the courtyard; there in its center was a scaffold and by it a line of blindfolded men.

"Carlos!" her scream filled the courtyard and echoed off the ancient walls. He turned toward her voice, but he could not see her.

Then the sallow-faced officer who had questioned her appeared. He pressed her camera into her hand. "You will photograph the hangings," he ordered. Adria shook her head, knowing her dry lips were parted and that her face betrayed her horror and revulsion. Her hands began to shake and again tears began to tumble down her cheeks.

"You will do as you are told." Adria felt the sharp point of the guard's bayonet press into her back.

Carlos was marched to the base of the scaffolding.

"Take his picture now!" the officer demanded.

Adria lifted the camera. She could move it slightly to the left and take the fortress wall. She could jerk it suddenly blurring the picture. She could fail to focus properly. Through her long-distance lens his face was so close that for a second she felt she could reach out and touch it. He had been badly beaten and she could clearly see his puffy eyes. His hands were not simply tied, but swathed in bandages through which blood oozed. There was a slash across his chin and another beneath his left ear.

Then something happened. Adria's hand steadied and she began to focus, to frame the picture. Carlos's face was centered—*click*. The noose was placed round his neck and his face filled with terror—*click*. The trap was sprung and his head tilted sideways, his mouth opened in a squelched scream, agony gripped him and his body dangled, legs kicking in midair. *Click, click, click* in rapid succession.

"What a pity you have no movie camera," the officer said bitterly. "Another picture, señorita. The last."

Adria took the picture, then let out a moan as she dropped the camera to dangle round her neck. Now she was human again, and she doubled over and retched violently. She swayed, but did not faint. Male hands roughly supported her. Her camera was taken, and she was half dragged back to her cell.

Again on the ninth day she was interrogated. Again she protested and was told, "You were in Barcelona and in the company of a wanted man and his companions. You are a spy." She was returned to her cell, and since then no one had come even to ask her questions.

Adria ran her tongue around her lips and again the old woman pressed water on her; the same old woman made her eat the sloppy rice gruel that was given to them twice a day. At night she cradled Adria's head in her lap and muttered over and over, *hija, mia hija—* daughter, my daughter."

Adria shook her head and again counted the times she had been interrogated. Again, she tried to remember how long it had been; it must now be February 12th, she reasoned with effort.

Adria dug her fingers into the dirt floor of the filthy cell. "I don't want to die!" she screamed out. She began rocking back and forth, clutching her knees. "But I'm going to," she whispered. She was going to die in this horrible place and nobody even knew where she was. Beads of perspiration dotted her forehead, and the old woman bent over her with concern.

"*Fiebre*," she mumbled, touching Adria's forehead.

The word meant fever and Adria nodded. Perhaps she had gotten typhoid from the water; certainly she had dysentery. She was always going to the slop bucket in the corner of the room, her stomach knotted in cramps. She felt lightheaded and almost drunk. Her hair was a mass of tangles, her face was filthy, with white streaks where her tears had fallen. Her dress seemed to rot on her skin and she was bitten in a hundred places. A catalogue of illnesses ran through her mind—cholera, hepatitis, smallpox. No, she couldn't get smallpox, she had been vaccinated against it. Absurd thoughts ran through her mind as she pictured her mother's face. Her mother had once thrown out twenty-five pounds of flour because she had seen a weevil, and now her daughter was glad of weevil-ridden rice gruel because it temporarily quieted her cramps and filled her empty stomach.

"Lie down," the old woman commanded in Spanish. She pulled Adria down and nestled her head in her lap. She wrung out a rag in the bucket of drinking water and put it on her forehead, then she crooned some song as if Adria were her long-lost child.

An hour, perhaps two, passed. Adria was not certain. Sleep came and went and dreams burst forth with such realism that she had difficulty separating her sleeping from her waking. One moment she was with Robert Wertheim and another she was recording Carlos's death.

The cell door was opened and two officers pulled her away from the old woman. "Come!" they said as they pulled her to her feet. Adria was propelled down the long, shadowed corridor even as the old woman screamed in the distance. She was dizzy and her eyes rebelled when she was taken into the sunlit courtyard. Before her loomed the scaffolding, and she resisted as the guards dragged her along.

"No!" she screamed over and over. As sick as she was, she knew she was not dreaming, yet as she struggled she grew even more lightheaded. She blinked her eyes, then accepted the neutral blackness as she passed out.

Chapter Seven

1

ADRIA SAT ON THE edge of the immaculate, white-sheeted bed, her bare feet touching the cold tiled floor. Her body cried out to lie down again, to slip into blessed sleep, but her sense of reason warred with the weariness. Something had happened. The stone-faced nun who urged her to sit up seemed anxious to be rid of her. Hope surged through Adria. Were they preparing her to leave this awful place?

The nun emptied the backpack that Adria had brought with her the day of her arrest. Its contents were dumped onto the bed and the nun picked up each item, reciting its name in Spanish and returning it to the pack. Finished, she pointed to the cameras and tripod, then to Adria's purse and finally to her passport. Satisfied with her inventory, she folded her arms across her chest and asked, *"Esto es todo?*—this is everything?"

Adria nodded, uncertain as to whether the woman had made a statement or asked a question. In her mind she was still trying to piece together the events of the last two days. She only vaguely remembered being taken across the courtyard before losing consciousness. She recalled being stripped by two huge women and having her hair cut short. Too weak to protest and still feverish, she had passed in and out of dreams and nightmares. She remembered the coal tar being applied to her head and she recalled being fumigated with a vile-smelling concoction before being bathed and dressed in a nightgown. She was then brought to this room where she was allowed to sleep in between visits from a doctor who gave her several shots. She was fed properly and given clean water. And this morning the grim, unsmiling nun had brought all of her belongings and ordered her to dress. Adria glanced uneasily at one of her cameras and wondered if the film of Carlos's hanging was still there, waiting to be developed. She shivered involuntarily.

"Stand up and get dressed!" the nun ordered in Spanish. Adria pulled herself up, her feet flat on the black-and-white tiles, and steadied herself by holding on to the edge of the bed. She sorted through her clothes and began to dress under the nun's watchful eye. Hooking her skirt, she felt the slack of at least two inches and only then realized how much weight she had lost. Dressed, she pulled a comb through her short wavy hair. No doubt cutting it had made it easier to get rid of the lice, but she could not imagine how she looked; it had been weeks since she had seen herself in a mirror.

Adria stuffed her belongings into her backpack and tied it securely. She hung her cameras around her neck and indicated she was ready to leave.

"Follow me," the woman muttered.

At first Adria walked slowly, as if she were blind and feeling her way, but gradually her knees began to steady and her sense of balance returned. She followed the nun down four corridors and through a ward with beds on each side of the narrow aisle. When they emerged on the other side of the ward, they stopped in front of an office. "In there," the nun told her.

Adria opened the door and stepped into the airy, sunlit room. Her eyes moved quickly from the officer behind the desk to the familiar square, muscular, tanned man leaning against the wall by the window. His hair was sun-streaked and his clothes slightly rumpled. A cigarette hung from his mouth, and he eyed her almost mischievously. The officer behind the desk stood up, and standing next to Jeff Borden, he looked like a dwarf.

"Miss Halstead?" the officer asked. Short and swarthy, he sported a tiny mustache. He bowed from the waist and smiled with slightly yellowed teeth.

"Yes." Adria couldn't take her eyes off Jeff. She had once thought she never wanted to see him again, but at this moment she wanted nothing more than to fling herself into his arms. But what was he doing here? And how had he found her?

The officer picked up a paper from his desk. He read from it in halting English. "I'm afraid an error in identification was made. My government would like to apologize for any inconvenience you have been put to. You are free to go."

Inconvenience? Thirteen days in a Spanish prison, Carlos hanged before her eyes while she was made to take photos of his execution—and the others, what of the countless others moldering and starving in their cells? Adria's mouth was dry and her eyes wide. Her lips parted, but Jeff had taken her arm and his fingers dug into her flesh as if he understood what she was thinking. The message was clear enough—keep quiet or we won't get out of here.

"Miss Halstead is most grateful," he said before she could speak. "We'll be leaving Barcelona immediately. Thank you again for your help."

"Un momento," the officer shuffled through his papers. "Miss Halstead must sign for the return of her belongings."

"Of course," Jeff responded.

Jeff held her steady and by force of his unspoken will, she said nothing. Her hand was shaking as she scrawled her name across the line reserved for her signature.

The officer inspected it and waved his hand. "You are free to go."

Jeff guided her down another corridor, out through double doors, and down the stone steps into the sunlight. He propelled her steadily along toward the hotel, searching the streets for a cab.

"Jeff!"

He turned to her and pressed his lips together. "Not now," he cautioned. Then added, "It took a lot of bluff to get you out of there. I don't want you to talk till we're across the French border, and I mean it. We are being followed, Adria."

She glanced behind her, but the sun seemed blinding

and the streets were full of pedestrians. Still, for once she followed his lead in silence, allowing herself to concentrate on the smell of fresh air, the sight of the sky, and the warmth of the sun—such little things—but at this moment they seemed to mean so much. She felt like crying, like running, almost like singing. The word "freedom," once abstract, had now taken on new meaning and new reality.

At the hotel Jeff picked up his bag and paid his bill. Then he took her directly to the bus station. During the long ride she slept, her head on Jeff's broad shoulder, her mind reliving the nightmare of her incarceration.

They crossed the French border at noon the next day and immediately took another bus to the village of Norbonne on the Mediterranean coast. Adria did not question Jeff. For the moment she was content to let him make the decisions and guide her.

"It's off the beaten path," Jeff announced as they approached the small country inn, "not that it's tourist season anyway." He helped her out of the cab and continued to talk, as he had throughout her waking moments. His conversation was cheerful, and, she felt, designed to distract her from her thoughts.

Perched on a cliff that overlooked the sea and the white sand beach, the inn was a scant two stories high. It was built around a courtyard filled with flowers and each room had two balconies, one overlooking the sea and the other the courtyard. It was run by an elderly couple who exhibited no curiosity about them in spite of the fact that they were the only guests.

Their suite contained a large bedroom with two beds, a living room, and a private bath. The furniture was overstuffed and comfortable, the beds had handmade quilts, and the walls were painted a cheerful white and yellow.

"We'll stay here for a couple of days," Jeff told her, "maybe a week. Give you some time to unwind."

Adria nodded and sank into one of the chairs.

"I'll go down and get a bottle of wine and some

cheese," he told her. Then turning, "Do you mind staying alone for a few minutes?"

"No," she smiled weakly. "I'll be fine."

The door closed and Adria caught herself in the full-length mirror; she stared as if at a stranger. Her auburn hair, no more than three inches long, waved and curled around her face. Her clothes hung on a frame at least fifteen pounds lighter. Her skin looked sallow and her eyes were still ringed with fatigue. No wonder Jeff wanted her to come here to rest and recover; he must have been shocked. She half smiled. He hadn't shown it. He got points for being such a good actor.

Jeff opened the door and smiled, "You do look awful, but a few days down on the beach and you'll be fine." He waved the bottle of red wine and pulled the cork with his teeth. Then he began unwrapping a treasure of cheese, hard-boiled eggs, cold meats, and bread. "Wine's good for you, lots of iron. Got to get you eating and get some of the meat back on your bones."

Adria sank onto the sofa. Though she had not eaten for hours she wasn't really hungry. She guessed she was fed so little in prison that she'd grown used to less. "How did you find me?" she asked.

"When I checked into the Casa Linda Marty Harris from *Time* was still there; he told me you'd been there but moved out with some strange-looking Spanish guy."

"Carlos Solana."

"Yeh, I know. He's pretty well known. Anyway, I made inquiries and finally some woman came and told me she heard I was looking for you." Jeff was eating now, and he went on between mouthfuls of bread and cheese. "She said you'd been arrested. Well, you know me: I like to start at the top. I had to go to Madrid anyway to interview Franco, so I told him his people in Barcelona had mistakenly arrested the daughter of an American admiral and that there was going to be hell to pay if I didn't get you out before they found out about it. A little bluff, but I made it sound good. When I got back to Barcelona they said they'd "found" you. I didn't want you blabbing and getting all self-righteous because the fact is you were with a nest of well-known and wanted saboteurs. Hell, Adria, your poet Carlos once tried to assassinate Franco. One slip and you'd have been back in prison like that." He snapped his fingers for emphasis.

Adria leaned against the pile of cushions on the sofa, abstractedly feeling the material with her fingers. Her eyes were closed and she could hear the surf pounding a few hundred yards from the balcony of their room. "It was horrible," she whispered.

Jeff was sitting in a nearby chair, filled wine glasses in hand. He pressed one into her hand, "Want to talk?"

"I don't know if I can." Her eyes filled with tears and her throat tightened. She turned her head away from Jeff toward the balcony as she struggled to gain control. Then slowly and softly she began, "They.. . . they hanged Carlos. They made me watch. They made me take pictures."

"No shit!" Jeff put down his glass. "Christ, Adria, is the film still in your camera?"

Jeff was already on his feet and examining her cameras. "I've got my development kit," he said, barely able to hide his own eagerness.

Adria looked at him wide-eyed, tears running down her face. He'd been so sensitive up until now, but suddenly it was as if he had forgotten her ordeal. "Leave it alone," she said, trembling. "Jeff, you don't understand!" She began to shake.

Jeff gave her a hard look, one she knew from the days of her apprenticeship. "Your boss will want these photos, Adria. We're talking about a well-known writer here. I'm going to take them in the bathroom and run them through the solutions and see what you've got. Probably you messed it up anyway."

Adria covered her face with her hands. "I didn't," she murmured. "I wanted to, but I couldn't."

Jeff disappeared into the bathroom. Within half an

hour she heard him shout, "Christ Adria! These are the best pictures you've ever taken! Shit! They're dynamite!"

He was standing in the doorway holding a wet print with his tongs. "Look at what you've done! Damn—as soon as they dry I'll take them to the post office for you." He held the print up to have one more look. "Talk about realism!"

"It *was* real!" she screamed at him across the room. She was shaking all over and she gripped the edge of the sofa for support. "I don't want to see them, ever. I wish you hadn't developed them!"

Jeff returned the prints to the darkened bathroom to dry. Then he came to her side and touched her shoulder gently. "You'll get over it," he said firmly. "I'm still mailing them to Andy Martin."

Adria looked up into his face, now serious. He looked distressed and she knew he was trying to understand.

Jeff squeezed her shoulder. "Lady, you've come a long way. You couldn't have taken those six months ago." His eyes locked on hers. "That's what happened to you, isn't it? You couldn't stop yourself from taking a good picture."

"Yes," she admitted looking away from him. Then slowly turning to face his steady eyes, she shook her head. "I don't like it," she admitted.

"It has to be," he answered. "In that moment when your real talent is born you lose part of your humanity." He fingered his own camera lovingly. "You can't save the world, Adria. You can only record the truth."

Adria leaned back again, surprised. He did understand.

STILL LEANING ON A cane, Robert Wertheim climbed painfully out of the cab and hobbled toward the front entrance of his brother's London town house. This was the visit planned before the attack, and one he vowed would not now be unduly delayed.

The people on whose door he had pounded that night in Paris had summoned the authorities, and the sound of the approaching police vans had frightened off his would-be killers. He had been taken to the hospital and there remained unconscious for three days. Awake, he found to his dismay that the Paris papers had all carried the story and his picture.

In his pocket the police had found the address of a singer, and they had notified her to come to the hospital to identify him. Celeste Deschamps had come immediately and, of course, once his identity was known, the attack became headline news, and his name was linked with Celeste's romantically. One story was unfortunately captioned, "Chanteuse hurries to injured millionaire lover's side."

But far more frustrating was the insistance of the police that he had merely been robbed and vandalized. In spite of his importance there was no investigation into the activities of the Cougalards, whose hooded figures roamed the streets beating Jews and Communists and whose attack on Robert had obviously been carefully planned. As he had suspected, the authorities turned their backs in such cases. He wondered if the symbol of French justice—her scales balanced—wept at the reality of what was now happening in France.

On the bright side, there were no long-lasting physical effects from the beating. He sustained a concussion, three broken ribs, a black eye, a broken leg and a badly twisted ankle. But he would heal, and now he felt more committed than ever to the cause that had brought him to see his brother.

Eaton Square was one of London's distinctive addresses. Close to High Park, St. James Park, and Buckingham Palace, its stately town houses were built in the Parisian style. It was a fair trip from the marble steps of Charles Wertheim's Eaton Square home to the hustle of Lombard Street where the offices of Kensington Insurance were located, but it was much closer to the City of Westminister where Charles, the soon-to-be-Lord Wertheim, now spent far more time. A gifted businessman, highly educated, and multilingual, Charles Wertheim now lent his considerable talents to the Secret Intelligence Service (MI6), the most elite of His Majesty's intelligence services.

The door was opened by Stanley, his brother's archetypical British butler, who ushered Robert in silently, but with a friendly nod.

The blue parlor was a magnificent room. Its high ceiling was a muted painting of the sky, the floor-to-ceiling windows were draped in blue-and-white silk, and a crystal chandelier was suspended from the ceiling by a long gold chain. The furniture was Louis XV, satin covered, regal and elegant. Every table held a bouquet of fresh flowers, every heavy gold candelabra held fresh blue candles.

Charles Wertheim was shorter than his brother by several inches, slightly paunchy, and balding at thirty-five. His eyes were brown, not blue like Robert's and Madame Wertheim's. He wore gold wire glasses, and was dressed conservatively in a dark, three-piece suit, expertly tailored to mask his slightly overweight physique.

Charles walked with the slight swagger of a confident man, sure of himself in all matters, solid in his opinions, staid in his morals, and quick of mind though restrained in action. Emotion played no role in his decisions; he was calculating and controlled.

Robert, on the other hand, was emotional, quick to act, always the rebel. He too was talented in business, but he was far more of a gambler and tended to make judgments on the basis of his own good instincts.

Charles stood framed in the doorway of the parlor for a minute. At ten in the morning he wore a red velvet smoking jacket and dark trousers. He shook his head at the sight of Robert. "My, you are a bit of a mess," he said carefully.

Robert simply shrugged. "I'll be well soon enough."

Charles moved across the room and sat down on the chair opposite his brother. A bottle of brandy and two snifters sat on the leather-top table between them. Not bothering to ask, Charles simply poured two drinks.

Robert took a sip of the amber liquid and wondered how to begin. Certainly Charles was going to bring up the matter of Celeste, their half-sister, the love-child of their father, Abraham, and a French actress. Both Celeste and her mother had been looked after by Abraham before he died. Their own mother knew nothing of course, but in the tradition of the Wertheim men, Robert and Charles had been told.

Charles had been angered and outraged at his father's indiscretion, but Robert regarded the affair as a symptom of their father's humanity.

"Sheer weakness," Charles had told his brother. "But a chapter closed."

It had not remained a closed chapter for Robert. He had sought Celeste out and remained friends with her, seeing to it that she lived well and had anything she desired. He encouraged her career and he treated her as his sister, though he was equally careful to shield his mother from knowledge of her husband's infidelity. That was why he had her address and phone number, why she had come to the hospital.

True to form Charles brought up the subject immediately. "I trust you are happy that you have gotten your picture in all the Paris papers and are now linked romantically with a woman who is your illegitimate sister," he said sarcastically.

"I didn't ask to be attacked," Robert countered, somewhat angrily. "Should I have told the press she was my sister?"

"Good Lord, no," Charles snapped.

"Mother doesn't suspect anything and that's all that matters. Such stories die fast."

Charles sniffed. "Let us hope so."

Robert saw no need to preface the reason for his visit. "I haven't come to discuss Celeste or the attack or even anti-Semitism in France. Charles, the issue is Palestine."

Charles leaned back and withdrew his pipe from his pocket. He tapped it on the silver ash tray, filled it with tobacco from the silver humidor, and then lit it with a flourish, puffing smoke into the room. "I wondered when you would come," he said slowly. "Surely you didn't think that British intelligence is unaware of your activities."

"I supposed they knew. They probably have a rather thick file by now." Robert was well aware of Charles's intelligence connections.

"Rather," Charles said drily.

"You have political clout and you're about to be knighted. Charles, you've got to use your influence to have the immigration quotas to Palestine increased." Leaning over, Robert knew he sounded as intense as he felt.

Charles inhaled. "It will not please you to know that the quotas will be tightened. I've heard that only seventy-five thousand Jews will be allowed into Palestine over the next five years."

"Seventy-five thousand over five years!" Robert stormed. "There are two hundred thousand German Jews who need a homeland now! And what about Polish Jews, Hungarian and Russian Jews? Do you understand what this restriction will mean?"

Charles sucked on his pipe, then expelled more smoke into the air. "I can hardly support the work you do," he said, letting the emphasis rest on "you." "The Haganah and The Irgun are constantly harassing the British army. They're little more than terrorists. You can't expect Downing Street to want to import more trouble into Palestine—they have quite enough already. Besides, the Arabs complain constantly; you know how vital their cooperation might become. If there's need for increased immigration, I know we'll do the right thing."

"Is that the royal 'we' Charles? In the name of heaven, anti-Semitism is rampant in the British military. The British have always favored the Moslems—they favor them in India and they favor them in Palestine."

"Because they will be needed as allies if your predicted war comes to pass."

"Hindus and Jews can't fight, is that it?"

"I would suppose that element of reasoning exists in the planning rooms of Whitehall," Charles allowed.

"Personally, I think you just don't want to rock the boat. It's clear that being 'Sir Charles' means more to you than fighting this planned restriction on immigration to Palestine. As for the need, I can tell you it already exists. Where are the Jews of Europe going to go, Charles? America won't take them without sponsorship. Canada turns them away and Argentina and Venezuela will only take the technically skilled. Perhaps you intend reviving the idea of settling Jews in Uganda? As for the Arabs, I can tell you that they're now accepting a thousand dollars a head to settle Jews—Arab landowners are only too willing to sell to Jews who have money. The situation is growing critical. I think you have a moral obligation at least to try. What do you propose to do?"

"I don't propose to do anything. So far there has been no official declaration of a limitation on immigration. There's a good chance it will be scrapped."

"I doubt it," Robert replied, white-knuckled, turning his back on his brother. He'd struggled out of a hospital bed to come here to enlist his brother's help. Now he felt angry and more defeated than when he'd been beaten to the ground a few days ago. "You're a disgrace, Charles. You could use your influence to lobby successfully for your own people. The very least you could do is complain about the Mufti. He may wear a burnoose, but he's as Fascist as any SS officer and a crook to boot."

"And you want the British army to protect illegal settlers from the Mufti and his followers?" Charles thought about the militant Amin al Husayni, Mufti of Jerusalem, for a moment. He had fled to Lebanon now, but the Palestinians still revered him as their leader. The Mufti violently objected to further Jewish immigration to Palestine and any move on the part of the British to help the Jews would bring violent reaction from the Arabs. Charles shook his head, "No, Robert. You're being short-sighted. If we did what you want, the British army would have both Arabs and Jews throwing bombs at them."

"I think the British should look twice at their allies. If the need arose, the Mufti would sell them out."

"Really. I admire you, Robert. You have such a gift for seeing into the future." Charles pressed his lips together in a sarcastic smile and raised one eyebrow.

"You're a condescending bastard. You act as if you had no idea what's going on in Germany. I never thought I'd live to see the day when mother knew more than you about world affairs."

"Mother had an unpleasant experience from which I'm certain she is quite recovered."

"You're becoming too British, Charles."

"If by that you mean I think before I act and try to examine all issues logically, I take that as a compliment. Your problem is—and always has been, I might say—a tendency to think of yourself as some sort of Robin Hood. You rush around saving the world in little pieces from your protected castle in Sherwood Forest. And you have the blundering audacity to think you and your friends are the only ones to be even slightly concerned with the fate of the Jewish people. I should think you would understand that getting rid of Hitler and Fascism is the obvious way to make Europe and the Jews secure. Personally, I think British policy is designed to do just that."

"It's a policy of appeasement."

126

"Nobody wants war," Charles retorted in annoyance.

"I think the Germans do," Robert replied quickly. He turned and picked up his briefcase from the leather-covered table. "I should have known I couldn't talk you into anything that involved taking action."

"Where are you going now?"

"Off to tilt another windmill," Robert answered sharply.

"Simply because I disagree doesn't mean you can't stay the night."

Robert shook his head. "I'd rather go to a hotel."

Charles shrugged. It wasn't the first time the two of them had parted in anger, and he took for granted that it wouldn't be the last. "Do as you wish," he muttered.

Robert turned and left, listening to his own footsteps click in the long hallway as he showed himself out.

3

ERICH SCHMIDT WAS FIVE feet eleven inches, but slight, with blond curly hair and blue eyes. Though not as muscular as he would have liked, he was wiry and athletic, a record-breaking sprinter built for speed. And in the back of his mind he harbored the idea that his more brawny compatriots were not only slower on their feet, but also slower of wit.

His father, an early devotee of Adolf Hitler, had immigrated to the United States in 1930 when Erich was twenty. As he had attended Columbia University, his slangy English was easy and natural. No one would have guessed his German origins; he had no discernible accent and he knew America and Americans well. In the five years he had lived in The United States, he had traveled the country thoroughly and assessed both its strengths and its weaknesses. When he returned to Germany in 1935, he presented himself to the elite SS and was immediately assigned to the counterintelligence services, the Sicherheitsdienst. Known simply as the SD, it was headed by Heinrich Himmler.

After a year of indoctrination and training Erich was sent back to the United States to teach at a summer camp run by the German-American Bund. It was there that he had met, recruited, and trained Christina Barton.

His central job was to act as liaison with French Fascist groups and to observe and report all movements of the American navy in the Mediterranean through several agents he controlled. Ostensibly the latter would have been a job for the Abwehr—the military intelligence service headed by Admiral Canaris—but the SD had its own mandate to check on the Abwehr and to compare all information it garnered with that gathered independently by the SD. That Germans found themselves spying on one another didn't bother Erich Schmidt at all. It was too well known that the exceptionally competent Admiral Canaris was no great lover of Hitler, nor was Canaris a true adherent of Fascism.

In Berlin the February rains had carried ice pellets, and winds had lashed the populace as they sought shelter from the damp cold. But here on the Riviera the rolling hills had once again been renewed by gentle rains. They were already a sea of green punctuated with the buds of fast blooming flowers. It would be an early spring—late March and April here in Cannes, May in Paris, when the chestnut trees that lined the Champs Elysées would burst into flower. *Freulich wie Gott im Frankreich*—happy as God in France. It was an old German saying with which Erich could not agree more.

Erich smiled to himself, ran his fingers through his short hair, and knocked on the hotel room door. He was not surprised that Christina Barton called out for him to let himself in. She was fond of greeting him from the bed where she lounged in seductive, lacy lingerie.

Truth be known, he did not find her as attractive as she found him. He much preferred the beautiful blondes who inhabited the several Nazi breeding centers, existing solely to be impregnated by SS and SD like himself. Their offspring would form the new master race. Thus he could satisfy his carnal desires and serve his country at the same time. The added advantage was that there were no emotional ties to the breeders, and Erich Schmidt regarded himself as a man who ought to avoid such ties.

But he did have a certain fondness for Christina. Perhaps more important, he understood her. Christina Barton's profound insecurity was at the root of what appeared to be nymphomania; she seduced men because she had a constant need to prove herself. At the camp in Pennsylvania she had had to seduce him because he was the instructor. A fellow student would not have been good enough. Almost immediately he realized how to control her and how to satisfy her sexual appetites. He had also seen how useful such appetites could be if channeled properly.

He opened the door and found her as he expected. She was lying on the bed in a black satin slip. One strap hung down over her left shoulder, exposing the curve of her breast, and the slip rose up high on her bare thigh.

"It's been weeks," she chided. "Surely you could have come back sooner."

He walked to the bed and sat down. On the night stand he saw the full bottle of Scotch and the glasses. He poured himself a drink, then turned to face her. "Your admiral does not keep you busy?"

Her round, full lips formed a pout. "You know I can't stand him," she murmured. Her hand reached out and clasped his arm. "I wait only for you. I only make love to him because of you."

"Sex does not replace information," he said, reaching out to touch her breast. She enjoyed being toyed with, having the tables turned.

"I have all the information you asked for."

He smiled and spread himself out beside her. His hand grasped her white thigh and he pinched her. "In your head, or have you written it down."

"It's in the drawer. You know I can't remember all those things."

Lethargically he rolled over and opened the drawer and withdrew a small spiral notebook. He sat up and took out his own notebook. Without haste he put her information into code, then ripped out pages and took them into the bathroom to burn them in the sink.

When he returned she had removed the slip and lay naked beneath the covers. He quickly stripped under her watchful eyes, then climbed in beside her.

"You always make me wait," she complained.

His hands touched her intimately, "That," he said coolly, "is what you usually like best."

Chapter Eight
1

THE STREETS OF VILLEFRANCHE seemed comfortably familiar to Adria despite her short first stay, and returning to them felt wonderfully like coming home.

Madame Lejeune, who ran the tiny boutique near the sea wall, greeted Adria like a long-lost friend, and along with the two blouses she purchased, Madame Lejeune insisted on giving her two tiny ivory containers of dried perfume. One had a hand-painted carnation on its lid and the other a rose. Adria opened the one bearing the carnation and found inside a heavily scented salve. "It's like a garden full of carnations," she said with delight.

"A little something for my returning customer," Madame Lejeune replied.

Adria tucked away the gift in her purse and picked up the bag containing her blouses. She bid Madame Lejeune good-bye and continued along the winding street toward the village post office. Jeff had made her promise to meet him for lunch.

In the postal box she had rented before leaving for Spain, Adria found three pieces of mail. One was a letter from *Life* accepting her photographic layout on the Wertheims and offering her five hundred dollars for the exclusive right to the photos. The second was a letter of praise from Andy Martin, it asked her to return briefly to the United States and hinted at a permanent contract and a substantial raise. The third was a mysterious parcel of newspaper clippings from the Paris papers. They all concerned Robert Wertheim, the attack on him, and the singer who came to see him and with whom he had left hospital. Inside there was a short note which read, "Darling, knowing how interested you are in the elusive Mr. Wertheim, I just knew you would want these clippings." It was signed simply, "C.B." and a postscript read, "Sorry we didn't get together, but I know we'll be seeing a lot of one another soon."

"Christina," Adria said, as she threw the note aside and glanced quickly at the clippings, which she then folded and put in her bag.

The café next to the post office was cozy and warm. True to Jeff's taste, it served simple, but filling fare. Jeff had ordered a rare roast beef sandwich soaked in gravy and as usual, ate as if it were his first meal in weeks.

"Are you interested in Wertheim?" Jeff asked as he watched the disturbed look on her face.

"He's an interesting man," Adria hedged. Truth be known she *was* surprised to learn that Robert was apparently involved with a nightclub singer, though if the picture of Celeste Deschamps looked anything like her, she was certainly most attractive. Robert's involvement with another woman certainly explained his behavior; in fact, his loyalty made Robert Wertheim all the more admirable. What bothered her more was Christina's statement about seeing a lot of her soon.

"What do you suppose she meant by that postscript?"

Jeff soaked the last of the gravy on his plate with his bread and took a huge bite. He shrugged and tried to look mystified. Christina was Nelson Halstead's surprise. He changed the subject, "Are you going back to New York?"

Adria nodded. "After I see my father."

"Then what?"

"I'm hoping Andy won't assign me to one place. I'd like to go to Italy . . . maybe to Berlin."

Jeff put down his fork and smiled warmly. He reached across the table and covered her hand with his. "I wish you would come to Berlin. I get lonely, you know."

Their eyes locked momentarily. Then Adria turned slightly. "I have to see my father this afternoon."

"If you go to see him, you're going to fight. Adria, why don't you just drop your old man a line and save yourself the aggravation?"

Jeff's advice rang in her ears as Adria sat across from her father on the terrace of the Hôtel de la Mare in Villefranche. She didn't admit she had been in prison in Spain, though she did tell him proudly that she had sold the layout on the Wertheims to *Life* and that her editor at *News Views* was happy with the photographs she had taken in Barcelona.

Her father accepted her information without comment. He seemed distracted, Adria thought, as she watched him sip his drink. He moved uneasily, then said, "I have something I want to discuss with you." He seemed to be looking beyond her and out toward the ocean.

Adria frowned. "Discuss" was not usually a word her father used. "Oh?" she replied, trying to mask her apprehension.

"I've decided to divorce your mother."

He continued to stare into his drink. Adria gripped her own glass. Divorce? It had never occurred to her that her parents would actually divorce. "Has Mother agreed?" she asked.

"Not yet, but she will." Nelson Halstead leaned forward, for once looking Adria in the eyes. "We've been separated for eight years. I know you've always wanted us to get back together, but it won't work, Adria. It couldn't."

Adria set her glass down, feeling slightly numb. Did

her father understand how much her mother needed him? Did he have the slightest inkling what a divorce would do to her? Her mother was an Irish Catholic. To be separated was, if not desirable, at least acceptable, but divorce did not exist in her mother's world. Oh, her father could obtain a civil divorce, but the church would never recognize it.

Adria shivered slightly—What was the old saying?—"the straw that broke the camel's back." She felt that way now. She had been through too much, seen too much, felt too much in the last month. Her father's assertion was like pouring salt on an open wound. "What do you want," she asked coldly, "my blessings? You said you wanted to discuss this with me, but you're just telling me what you've already decided!" She felt her face flush with growing anger.

"I had hoped you would understand."

"I understand that you've been unfaithful! I understand that you're not giving a second thought about what this will do to Mother." Adria pushed her chair away from the table. She was angrier than she should have been, and even as she heard her own voice rising she wondered at herself.

"Your mother is stronger than you think. She'll adjust."

"And *you're* weaker than I thought."

Strangely, her father did not reply. His features were set and she knew that he, too, was angry. For a few moments they sat in silence, then he asked, "Will you be going home now?"

Adria nodded. "For a few weeks. Then I'm hoping to go to Berlin."

"Isn't that where that Borden fellow is going?"

"Have you been keeping tabs on me?"

"Well, you did come back from Spain with him."

"Yes, he's going back to Berlin." Adria fumbled in her purse for a cigarette. She didn't often smoke; now she withdrew one and hastily lit it.

"Are you, ah, seeing him?"

Adria looked across at her father. The question was

133

prompted by more than curiosity. He didn't like Jeff Borden, never had.

"Yes," Adria answered evenly. "Perhaps we'll live together in Berlin."

Her father's face grew red and Adria pushed the chair farther away and stood up. "Don't play the moralist with me, Father. You go your way, and I'll go mine." She turned curtly and walked away, confident that this time she had won an argument. It was true that she saw Jeff every day, but it was not true that they intended living together or even that they had resumed their love affair. Jeff had surprised her. He seemed to understand that she needed time.

It was four hours later that Adria found herself sitting opposite Madame Wertheim in the living room of the rambling chateau. Madame had heard she was in Villefranche and asked her to tea.

"I'm so sorry Robert is still in London. He'll regret having missed you," Madame said as she poured the tea from the heavy silver service.

"I'm sorry to have missed him as well," Adria lied. Truthfully, now that she knew about his relationship with Celeste Deschamps, she didn't want to reawaken the strong attraction she had felt for him. In any case, they would once again have been going in different directions.

Wearing a light ivory dress, Madame Wertheim wore a single strand of rich amber beads and now and again fingered them as if rolling them between her fingers helped her think. "I had your American magazine sent to me. I saw your pictures taken in Barcelona—they were very good. The faces of the children made me cry, you know. I want you to know I'm very impressed with your art. I consider it art even if you insist on calling it work."

Adria blushed. "Thank you. Your respect means a lot to me," she said sincerely.

"I know you could not have taken such pictures without going through a great deal, my dear. I wish I had a way of expressing myself. Is your work cathartic?"

Adria nodded. "Very much so, though sometimes it frightens me."

Madame Wertheim frowned. "I'm not sure I understand."

"I mean I become totally involved taking the photos —with technique. It's as if I'm separated from the reality of the horror by my camera. Sometimes I can't even look at the pictures afterward."

Madame nodded. "Ah," she said slowly. "I think I understand. I see suffering and I try to give money to help, but I feel as if I am separated from the whole world by my money, by the way I live. It's an incomplete life," Madame confessed, a faraway look in her clear blue eyes. "Lately I have begun to wonder if a person can appreciate happiness if there is an absence of unhappiness. Once I was unhappy and when it was over, I felt more in love with life than ever."

Since Adria's first meeting with Madame Wertheim, the woman had fascinated her. Now she found herself wanting to confide in her. "I was in a Spanish prison," Adria said hesitantly.

Madame frowned slightly and gently touched Adria's knee with her hand. "Tell me everything," she requested. "I want to know the story behind all your photos."

Adria began hesitantly, but as she talked she felt herself relax, and surprisingly she also discussed her father and mother. Jeff knows I've fought with my parents and that I've been resentful, but I've never confided this much to him, she admitted silently. The reason was suddenly obvious. Jeff was often insensitive and brash, passing judgment too quickly. On the other hand, Madame Wertheim listened carefully to her every word and seemed to understand what was behind her statements. Rather than drawing conclusions, she drew Adria out and caused her to reflect on her feelings.

"My father told me today that he is divorcing my

135

mother. I got very angry and we fought. But I knew it was coming—it was no real surprise. I was angrier than I should have been," Adria confessed.

Madame half smiled and touched her hand. "If you promise you will never tell anyone—not even Robert— I will tell you my secret."

"I promise."

"Many years ago I discovered my husband was having an affair with a Paris showgirl. I was angry, even bitter. But I didn't confront him; I buried my anger and became even angrier because I was mad at myself. I learned her name, where she lived, how she lived. I thought one day I would embarrass them; I imagined over and over how upset Abraham would be. Then she had Abraham's child and I was devastated because it was a girl, and I had always wanted a daughter."

"Did you confront them?"

Madame shook her head. "Never."

"It must have hurt you terribly if you loved him."

Madame smiled, "Oh, I did not love him the way you think of love these days. Ours was an arranged marriage and over the years it is safe to say that we grew to like one another very much."

"In spite of his affair?"

"After," Madame admitted. "You see it was not really the affair that made me angry, but the fact that he was free to do such a thing and I was not. It's not the same these days—women can have a life and a career apart from men." Madame smiled. "Perhaps what makes you angry is your father's freedom—perhaps you fear you will become like your mother."

Adria nodded. Yes, she did fear becoming dependent, then being rejected.

"But you are not your mother, my dear. You won't have the kind of marriage she had, and I think you love your father very much. I think you have to consider what really makes you angry."

"What happened to me in Spain made me angry, too."

"Of course! And to make matters worse, you were rescued by a man, and that reminded you how vulnerable women can be. But I think your friend would have gotten you out of jail if you had been a male colleague."

Adria thought for a moment. Yes, Jeff probably would have done it for a male friend, too. "I just don't want to be treated like a child because I'm a woman."

"Nor do I," Madame Wertheim responded. "Robert wants me to leave Europe and go to Martinique where I'll be safe. But Robert doesn't understand. I'm sure you were incensed by what you saw and experienced in Spain, just as I was incensed by what happened to me in Germany. I felt defiled; worse, I felt helpless."

"Yes, I did, too."

"Because you couldn't stop the Fascist bombs, and because you had to leave others behind?"

"Yes."

"Again it is anger at yourself. It will pass when you realize that your photographs are a way of waging war on the Fascists. My dear, you are in the front lines and you are doing something to fight this plague of ignorance. I can only donate money; I don't have your talent."

Madame's blue eyes were intense, and Adria blushed.

"Don't be so modest. I envy you. You are a new generation of woman. I feel even sorrier now that I had no daughter. I would have liked one like you."

Adria pressed Madame's hand in hers, feeling as if she had been paid the highest of compliments. "May I write to you now and then?"

Madame Wertheim smiled. "I wish you would."

2

A SPRING BREEZE BLEW gently through the trees of Central Park. The carefully tended bed of tulips were in full bloom. On Manhattan's crowded streets, usually harried New Yorkers had shed their heavy winter clothing and they smiled at one another to celebrate the first really warm day.

Adria was in no great hurry as she strolled along Broadway and then turned onto 47th Street. It was three in the afternoon, and already the flashing marquees proclaimed films starring movie favorites—Shirley Temple, Myrna Loy, and Tyrone Power.

She had boarded a Pan American clipper in England yesterday, having sailed across the channel the previous night. Unlike the long relaxing ocean voyage, the plane trip was both nerve-wracking and hectic. There was no hot food, the turbulence was frightening, and the plane landed and took off many times, stopping in Shannon, Iceland, and Gander, Newfoundland, before arriving in New York. Furthermore, the sudden time change left her disoriented. It seemed that one minute she had been in England thinking about Europe's concerns, and the next she found herself on 47th Street where the newspapers sported pictures of film stars rather than headlines of impending gloom and pictures of Hitler and Mussolini.

Europe was consumed with talk of politics and war, but New Yorkers seemed optimistic that the terrible pressures of the Depression were lifting, that the bat of Babe Ruth and the pitching of Lefty Gomez would take the Yankees to the World Series, and that Clark Gable and Carole Lombard would live happily ever after. America, free and protected by the oceans, danced to new tunes while Europe seemed to be preparing for the last waltz.

Adria stopped in front of the *News Views* building. She peered into the glass window, taking quick stock. She was wearing a cream-colored suit, a silk scarf, and flat leather shoes. Her ever-present cameras hung around her neck and her short hair blew loose in the afternoon breeze. Pleased with her professional appearance, she inhaled and pushed through the revolving doors into the terrazzo-floored lobby.

Time had begun publication in 1923, and one of its founders, Henry Luce, had established *Life* in 1936. A year later, *News Views* had come on stream. Both magazines owed their birth to the growth of pictorial advertising and to the German Leica. The new miniature cameras, with their wide-aperture lens and high-speed shutter, made it possible to take top-grade photos under any conditions. "Pictorial Journalism" was the new phrase, but like all such phrases it failed to explain what had passed before.

Andy Martin, the editor of *News Views* had grown up on the south side of Boston and gone to school with Adria's mother. He wasn't Irish, nor had he come from an immigrant family. Nonetheless, he grew up in a neighborhood where the population was ninety-nine percent immigrant, and it was there that he began thinking about "picture magazines."

"Literacy in English ought not to be necessary to understand what's going on," he used to say. But in reality, Andy Martin had only a passing interest in helping the illiterate understand world events. What he possessed was a good capitalistic outlook and instinct. If millions of Americans were either marginally literate or non-English-speaking, they represented an untapped market.

In elementary school he began working as a newsboy for the *Boston Globe*, and by the time he graduated from high school, he was running down photos for the city desk. "In those days," he used to say, "newspapers didn't have photographers. If there was a murder or a death, you had to go and beg for a photo from the grieving widow."

In his twenties Andy Martin had graduated to cub reporter and from there to city editor at thirty-five. He was a tough newspaperman, but eternally frustrated by the staid *Globe,* so he left to take over a New York tabloid. Its size, use of pictorials, and advertising push inspired him. He stayed for ten years and learned everything there was to know, from advertising sales to layout. Next he worked for *Mid-Week Pictorial,* a forerunner of *Life;* then he rallied his friends, borrowed thousands, and launched *News Views.* The idea was to tell stories in pictures as *Life* did, but the new magazine would also feature slightly longer captions, some news stories, and a slightly moralistic and generally liberal editorial involving some aspect of social justice.

Andy Martin had bought Adria's pictures of the Roosevelts then, at her mother's urging, had promised to purchase her coverage of the war in Spain. In the end, Adria thought happily, he had done more. He had bought all her photos and complained when she sold the Wertheim photographs to *Life.* Now he wanted an exclusive contract with her and seemed willing to let her pick her own assignments.

Short, balding, and overweight, Andy Martin wore thick glasses and spoke hurriedly. His office was a tribute to confusion: he believed in vertical filing, in working late, and in pinning anything and everything on a virtually invisible bulletin board. Adria could not recall when she had seen Andy Martin with his suit jacket on. Usually he was behind his desk, feet up, phone at his ear, with his jacket slung casually across the top of an overflowing waste basket.

Adria tapped lightly and Andy Martin motioned her into his glass-enclosed cubicle. He was on the phone—his office looked and smelled exactly as she remembered it. "Okay, Sam, see if you can get some shots of people on top of their houses—or better yet, a cute dog being rescued." He rang off and looked up at Adria. "Floods," he said by way of explanation, motioning to a chair. "A spring ritual and a never-ending source of great photos." He grinned and laughed. "One year we got a photo of a whole house floating down the Mississippi and on the roof was some old lady sitting on her rocking chair. Damned if she didn't float right under the Eads Bridge in Saint Louis looking completely unperturbed."

"What happened to her?" Adria asked.

"Oh, she was rescued a few minutes later, but it was a great picture."

Adria half smiled.

"You have a good trip?"

"It was a quick trip, too quick maybe. I'm not sure how I feel about flying."

"Better get used to it. There's no time to take ships these days. How ya been, Adria? How's your mother?"

"I'm okay," she answered, then added, "I haven't seen Mother yet."

"I didn't mean you had to come directly here when I asked you to come back posthaste."

"I thought I should. In any case what we discuss is important to what I tell her."

He raised his brow. "Regrettably that's true," he said thoughtfully. He turned to the sideboard with one swift movement of his swivel chair, opened the cabinet, and withdrew a bottle of Scotch and two paper cups. "How about a refresher?"

"Thanks. Andy, is there something wrong?" Usually he wanted to get right to the point.

He took a long swig of his drink and refilled the cup. "You're mother was here yesterday. I was surprised as hell to see her."

"Here?"

"In this very office. Said she had come down to New York to meet you. I'm supposed to tell you she's in the Wellington. Actually, I'm supposed to fire you and send you right over there." His face was utterly emotionless.

"Fire me? You said you were happy with my work."

"Happy is an understatement. Your work is terrific. Your photos sell *News Views*."

"I don't understand."

"Your mother's worried about you. She wants you to stay with her and forget going back to Europe."

Adria's mouth went dry.

Guessing her reaction, Andy added quickly, "I told her you were doing a great job and that no matter how much I like her, I'm not firing you."

Adria let herself exhale. She took the proffered paper cup and sipped at the Scotch. How could her mother do such a thing! It made her look like a little girl in front of her boss—a man who had no time for "little girls." "I'm sorry. I can't imagine why she would do something like that."

Andy shrugged. "She says you're living an immoral life in Europe. She told me you were seeing Jeff Borden again."

"We're friends. My father must have written her. Damn!" Adria pressed her lips together. Then, without looking at Andy Martin. "He's divorcing her. That's the real problem. She wants me at home because she can't stand the thought of being alone."

"I want to sign contracts with you, and first I want you to work for a week down in layout with Mike Simpson and Crane Laird, who does captions, so you'll have a personal relationship with the people on this end. Then I want you to hightail it back to Europe." Martin took a deep breath. "Your mother and I are old friends. I gave you a chance because she asked, but Adria, I run a tight ship here and I haven't got the time or inclination to make allowances for the personal life of my staff. So, right off the top I need to know if you're willing to take this on."

Adria nodded. "I'll be down in layout within the hour and on the clipper back to Europe whenever you say. I want to go back, Andy. My career means everything to me."

Andy Martin furrowed his brow. "Go easy on her. I don't think your mother realizes what a career is, or even that you have one. Until yesterday she still thought I was employing you because I was doing her a favor. Fact is, I knew you had talent the first time I saw your portfolio."

"Thank you."

He poured himself another drink and smiled. "And don't let the boys downstairs get to you. They love teasing women and they don't get much opportunity."

Adria stood up and smoothed out her skirt. Her mother was waiting, and though she didn't want to see her while she was still angry, she knew she had to face her.

Andy Martin gulped down his second shot. "Be here at eight tomorrow morning," he suggested. "Spend the evening with your mother; try to make her understand."

"I will," Adria promised, but she knew that no matter what she said, her mother's conclusion would be the same—"I need you, and you're deserting me."

3

ADRIA WALKED WEST ON 34th Street to Eighth Avenue. She had been to the New York Public Library and the Empire State Building. She had passed an hour in Macy's and now she walked slowly, or as slowly as one could without being trampled. It was nearly five P.M. and office buildings were emptying, their human contents spilling out into the streets like bees released from the hive. Car horns and screeching brakes were New York fare, as were cursing taxi drivers. In the distance you could always hear the wail of a siren, and the aroma of fresh-baked bagels, the smoke from a million furnaces, and the perfumes of elegantly dressed women combined with the noise to make the crowded streets an assault on all the senses. On Eighth Avenue Adria caught a bus heading toward Central Park. It was packed, and she stood all the way to Columbus Circle.

She was putting off seeing her mother. Strong and stubborn, her father was someone she could fight with. Never angry, her mother was always hurt.

"But I am justified in being mad at her," Adria whispered under her breath. Perhaps Madame Wertheim was right. Perhaps her anger was less at her parents than at her own feeling of powerlessness. She had been powerless in prison, but she was also powerless to do anything about her parents' divorce. "Foolish," she muttered to herself. Her parents would have to work out their own lives. Still, she was tired of forever being the rebel. They were so overprotective—so unaware that she was a grown woman. "She had no right to ask Andy to fire me," Adria thought. But even as she thought it, she knew when she brought it up her mother would manage to make herself the victim.

Her father wanted Adria to marry. Her mother wanted her to stay home, to stifle her sense of adventure. And neither wanted her to see Jeff Borden. Somehow their objections seemed to make him more desirable, and that, too, frightened her. Was she some sort of a ball always rebounding off the wall of other people's expectations and emotions?

Adria took a long, lingering look at the park. The trees all had new leaves, and the lawn was green from the March rains. Then she turned and slowly walked down Seventh Avenue, past Carnegie Hall and toward the Wellington.

Julia Halstead had long auburn hair streaked with gray and she wore it rolled in a huge bun. Her face was angular rather than heart-shaped like her daughter's, but Adria had her eyes, green, with gold rings round the pupils. Still an attractive woman, Julia Halstead had a good figure and a fine Irish complexion, but her expression made her seem older than her years. Her mouth was her most revealing feature. In her youth her mouth had turned upward, but in age it revealed a woman who had too long pressed her lips together, too long considered herself a martyr. Julia sat on the edge of her bed in the hotel room, her hands folded in her lap, her eyes downcast.

Adria looked out the nine-story window. Toy cars vied with toy trucks at the intersection on a street that seemed less than real. "Have you ever looked at my work, Mother?" she asked.

"Of course—but you don't understand."

144

"I do. I understand that you went to Andy Martin as if he were my high school teacher instead of my employer. I understand that you tried to get me fired."

"Adria, you could get a job in Boston."

"I have to go back."

"It's dangerous. I worry about you."

Adria inhaled. "Life is dangerous. I'm sorry you worry, but it's my career."

"What if there *is* a war?"

"I've been in a war. Didn't you see my pictures of Carlos?" Adria turned, her face stormy.

"Carlos? Oh, that poet who was executed."

Her mother would have fallen off the bed if Adria had replied, "my lover," and she resisted the temptation. "I had to watch him being killed. That's how I got those pictures."

"They're horrible. I couldn't look at them."

"You can't hide from all the horrible things in life, Mother."

"I couldn't take pictures of something like that. You're like your father—you're hard."

Adria shook her head. "No," she whispered, though her mother didn't seem to hear.

Her mother straightened up. "So you're going to leave me just like your father. Adria, you know you're all I have left."

"I have to go, Mother. It has nothing to do with the way I feel about you. I have to get away from both you and Father. I have to stand on my own two feet."

"You're going to go to Germany and be with that Jeff Borden. He's not good for you, Adria. Besides, running away from home and into the arms of some man is not standing on your own two feet."

"I'm going to Germany for my *job*." Talking to this possessive woman, a woman alone and afraid, was like talking to a wall.

"Don't lower yourself," her mother said. "Remember who you are." By that her mother meant "don't become sexually involved unless safely married." And Adria wondered, Who am I? One answer came clearly:

I am a photographer. Adria fingered her camera, then lifted it to focus her long-distance lens on the street below. Light and shadow—movement and pattern. The cars were in a configuration that looked like a puzzle from above.

"There's a portrait studio in Boston that needs a photographer. I heard of the opening from Admiral Leighton's wife, Bitsy Leighton, you remember her? She was always so fond of you. I'm sure she would speak with the proprietors if you would reconsider."

Adria snapped the picture and advanced the film. That was her answer.

4

"I MADE MY REQUEST August fifteenth," Adria said with irritation. "Today is the twenty-ninth and I still don't have my press accreditation card for the three-month period beginning September first." The male voice on the other end of the phone line responded only by asking her to wait a minute. Adria sighed. The Germans fancied themselves efficient, but their red tape accounted for endless hours.

"Why didn't you apply for twelve-month accreditation when you arrived May third?" the voice asked.

"Because I didn't think I would be here longer than six months," she replied wearily. The press officer answered only with a grunt and a plea for yet another minute. Adria held the phone loosely, and with her other hand continued to arrange the photographs in front of her. It seemed at least five minutes before the press officer returned to the phone.

"Your application is being processed. If you have not received it by the first of September, come into the office and we will issue you temporary identification papers."

Adria murmured insincere thanks and hung up. "Temporary identification papers," she said aloud with disgust. That would most certainly take all morning.

She stood up and stretched, then walked to the

window and looked out. It was a gray day and a hint of fall was in the air.

There were days when Adria thought Berlin was the most depressing place she had ever been. Even in the grim days before its fall, Barcelona had not been so depressing. There had been defiance, and Adria often recalled Carlos's words just before they were caught. "They have defeated us and they may now try to kill all of us, but they cannot kill our ideas. Even if they conquered every free nation on earth, the idea of freedom would live." But Berlin made her wonder if indeed Carlos had been only a hopeless romantic. Here the idea of freedom seemed quite dead.

The Nazis might be slow and inefficient with paperwork but they were deadly efficient when it came to routing out those deemed enemies of the state. Jewish men, women, and children lived under extreme restrictions and many had been arrested. Poverty-stricken Gypsies, homosexuals, and the mentally ill had been interned and, in one documented case, brutally murdered when they were herded into a building and the building was set afire. Lawyers, judges, and Catholic and Protestant clergymen who spoke out against injustice had been arrested. Neither she nor any other journalist in Berlin knew how many were interned, but every journalist had some contacts who were dissenters, and gradually those contacts disappeared, victims of nighttime arrests. The government did not issue lists of those detained, nor was either the victim or the press given reason for detention.

The People's Court did, however, receive considerable publicity. In 1934, Hitler had become incensed when three of four defendants accused of setting the Reichstag fire had been acquitted by the German Supreme Court. Within a month of the acquittal he took the power to try treason cases away from the Supreme Court and vested it exclusively in the Volksgerichtshof—the so-called "People's Court." It soon became the most dreaded tribunal in the country. Made up of two judges and five others chosen from the

SS, party officials, and armed forces, there was no appeal from its verdicts. Moreover, its sessions were usually held in camera. In the time since Adria had been in Berlin, two prominent society matrons were among those convicted and publically beheaded for alleged crimes against the state.

If it were possible to believe that all those arrested had actually been plotting against the state, Adria might have believed there was resistance to the Nazis, but such a conclusion was not possible. Indeed, it was the absence of organized resistance that so depressed her. Oh, there was rumor of an organization called the White Rose that Jeff insisted existed, but if it did, Adria considered it a case of too little, too late.

Her own view was that Nazism flourished, and that on the whole the German people accepted it and indeed relished its discipline, militarism, and ritual trappings. Throughout the long, warm summer she had witnessed parades, mass meetings, rallies, and militaristic athletic competitions. The flowers in Berlin's many parks vied with the red-and-black swastika-covered banners of the Nazi Party. The fashionable women who shopped at Ka De Va wore silver and gold swastikas round their necks, and small children traded in their hoops and balls for wooden guns and marched side-by-side with their older brothers. Line upon line of goose-stepping, jack-booted military units were everywhere, and they played to street audiences who seemed mesmerized by the scent of power. In Berlin there were two kinds of Germans—the majority who seemed to accept the hysterical and sometimes numbing rhetoric of Hitler and his henchmen, and the silent who feared for their lives. "The vise," as Jeff put it, "was being twisted tighter."

Adria glanced at her watch. It was nearly five o'clock, though the dark clouds made it appear later. Berliners in the street below hurried to do their shopping on the way home from work. What had happened to this city that a few short years ago had rivaled Paris for its unrestrained gaiety?

Adria turned from the window. There were decisions that had to be made and she knew she was putting them off as surely as she was putting off selecting which of the photographs on the table to send Andy Martin. She stirred her lukewarm coffee and took a sip.

The apartment she shared with Jeff was small—a living room that served as dining room with an alcove kitchen, a bedroom, and a bathroom which doubled as a darkroom. The used furniture was utilitarian and comfortable, but Adria found its dark color disheartening. Last night's dinner dishes were still piled in the sink of the closetlike kitchen, and there were four dirty coffee cups on the table. Prints, suspended from lines with clothes pins, dangled across one corner of the room, and the American newspapers for the last week had accumulated untidily by the chair. "I ought to clean up," she said aloud, but she felt gripped by the lethargy of indecision.

Her eyes fastened on one of her photos. It was of Jeff, standing by a tree in the park and talking with a small child. He was good with children and he seemed to like them. Adria bit her lip and fought back tears. "But do you want a child?" she asked the photo.

She had been in Berlin for only a month when they had resumed their relationship. Beginnings are so easy, she thought. It came back to her in a flood of warmth.

"I've waited for you to recover from Spain," Jeff had whispered. Then he had kissed her tenderly. "I love you and I want you back." They moved in together, but they kept their relationship a secret from the rest of the Berlin press corps.

Still, there was something wrong—something that had been wrong from the first night they spent together. It was true enough that sometimes they sought one another hungrily, and it was just as true that she could not claim to be unhappy. But she knew she didn't feel real passion, and it troubled her. Perhaps, she rationalized, passion always slips away in time. Perhaps she didn't love him. She shivered at the question she always feared, its answer doubly important now. And what

149

about his feelings? She couldn't quite imagine how Jeff was going to react.

Not that she had been stupid. Before they had resumed their relationship she had gone to a doctor and been fitted with a silk worm, the latest contraceptive device. It was, as the doctor explained, intrauterine and, "as safe as anything we've tested."

But this morning he confirmed her own conclusion. "You are pregnant and I can only assume the silk worm was involuntarily expelled. It happens in about ten percent of my patients as I warned you initially."

Adria hadn't been surprised. This morning she had forced herself to smile at the doctor, but now she admitted aloud, "I don't know how I feel." On one level the thought of having a child pleased her, on another it was disturbing. The timing was wrong—all wrong. And how would Jeff feel? They had never seriously discussed marriage. Was that what she wanted?

Adria clenched her fist and closed her eyes for a second. The doctor had offered an abortion, easy and safe in Germany. "We have to talk," she said to Jeff's picture, and vowed that they would, right after dinner. It was at least a decision to make a decision, and Adria returned to sorting her latest photos.

After her doctor's appointment she had taken pictures at yet another "managed" event. The Germans had announced the unveiling of a new factory and held a news conference. The journalists were taken on a tour of the factory and given the opportunity to take photos of Goebbels with the equipment and the happy workers. Gone were the days of searching for the opportunity to take a candid photo of some important German. Spontaneous news gathering was replaced by carefully released memos. No one would talk, and sometimes she knew she was followed and watched. She felt stifled and angry and realized this, too, was part of her dilemma. Jeff might not agree to leave Berlin, but she would not have a child here.

Adria stood up and once again examined Jeff's latest

prints. How did he do it? Among the journalists and photographers in Berlin, Jeff alone seemed to have a sixth sense for where and when something was going to happen. He alone had good candid shots.

Adria reexamined her own pictures. She had, after many weeks of prodding and planning, obtained a meeting with Hannah Reitsch, a well-known test pilot, confidante of Hitler, and operator of a glider school where young pilots were trained. Her pictures were not bad, but they lacked spontaneity, since Reitsch would only pose stiffly with her planes and her students. I didn't catch her as a woman, Adria lamented. She knew she had failed to reveal something hidden, something distinctively feminine. Still, the photos did reveal a certain truth—Hannah appeared as much a machine as her planes, and her angular face displayed nothing if not the ruthless determination to sublimate all else to her work. Vaguely Adria wondered if Hannah Reitsch ever made love.

Adria turned away from her pictures when she heard Jeff's key in the lock. She smoothed her peach-colored linen skirt, and shook out her now shoulder-length hair.

Jeff lumbered in, his trench coat dripping, his sandy hair soaked. Rain drops still clung to his nose. He smiled broadly and discarded his coat with a slight curse for the inclement weather. Brandishing a bottle of red wine, he advanced on her cheerfully. "We're going to celebrate," he announced, giving her a bear hug.

Adria looked up into the face that always cheered her. In spite of his photographic coups, she felt no real jealousy, though the competition between them sometimes surfaced in the form of good-natured ribbing. She smiled weakly. "And what are we celebrating?"

Jeff grinned. "Something big, but I can't tell you."

She wiggled out of his arms. "You know something I don't? Jeff, what is it?"

He shook his head, "No way. But I'll tell you this: the resulting photo layout will appear in every newspaper in North America, maybe even the world."

151

Adria fought to look nonplussed. He was certainly onto something, but if she prodded he would be even less talkative. "Hitler's going to pose nude for you?" she guessed coyly.

He laughed and shook his head. "Better than that." He wet his lips and opened the wine. "How about a couple of glasses?"

Adria went to the utility kitchen and returned with two glasses. He eyed her lecherously and pulled her down onto the sofa next to him, kissing her hard. "You're turning into a real hedonist," she joked as she leaned against him. "This isn't proper before dinner." But his sudden good humor distracted her and she gave in as if running from her own mood. Why dampen his spirits? There were so few joyful moments.

His large hand rested on the top button of her blouse. "There won't be any time after dinner," he replied with a wink. "I'm leaving town for a week, maybe two."

Adria's mouth opened in surprise, but he closed it with a passionate kiss and pushed her back on the soft cushions of the sofa. She closed her eyes and put her arms around him. His hand moved beneath her skirt and she pressed herself to him. At times a little rough, he always aroused her quickly. If she felt something was lacking in their relationship she knew it wasn't pleasure in their love-making. They *were* hedonistic, and she felt their hedonism was due in part to Berlin. One felt driven to satisfy all appetites—to go against the grain, to thwart the driving, maddening, puritanism of this coldly military city with its regimented population of automatons whose hands so eagerly lifted in salutes to the Führer. Would she and Jeff be like this somewhere else? It was yesterday's question, but today the answer took on new meaning. I can't talk to him now, she thought. There won't be time and he's leaving. As soon as he comes back, she promised herself, I'll tell him. And it will be better, she rationalized. His leaving will give me some time to sort out my own feelings.

Jeff kissed her closed eyelids as he removed her last bit of outer clothing, leaving her in a white slip that offered no resistance to his explorations. "You won't even miss me," he predicted. "First we'll make love, then I'll take you out to dinner, and then I'll leave."

Adria shook her head. "I will miss you."

He kissed her breast and began moving against her, the heat of his body exciting her. "Probably I'll be home in a week," he offered. "And boy, will you be surprised."

Chapter Nine

1

THE COMMUNICATIONS ROOM OF the Berlin Press Center was muggy, airless, and filled with smoke. Hastily hung wall maps indicated the whereabouts of the German troops, and red marker pins were steadily advanced by the fat German press officer with each new bulletin from the front. Then the bevy of reporters rushed to their phones or lined up to use the teletype machines, updating their stories.

The Italian reporters kept to the northeast corner of the room, the small crew from the Russian papers huddled together in the opposite corner. The British and French were absent, having fled for the border at the first announcement of hostilities with Poland. Officially England and France were now at war, and their reporters and photographers were declared *personae non gratae* and given twenty-four hours to cross the frontier or risk imprisonment. But the Americans were sacrosanct—save the reporter for *Time* who had been previously expelled—and they lolled about the round tables on the far side of the room and sipped black coffee or drank warm German beer.

"It was obvious it was coming," Keith Jackson said with bravado. He gulped from his cup and put his feet up on the chair opposite.

"If it was so obvious, my boy, why weren't you in Poland to get the story firsthand?" Bill Hanson challenged.

Adria stared into her coffee. There wasn't much else to do. The foreign press had gathered in the press center and here they sat, waiting to be fed whatever news the Germans decided to release. Those who were filing for dailies would be constantly changing their stories, but she worked for a monthly and thus felt no sense of urgency. When she wrote the story that would accompany whatever photos she might eventually take, it would at least have some perspective.

Keith Jackson was from the *Chicago Journal* and Bill Hanson a photographer from the *Philadelphia Post*. Although Adria had wanted to be alone, she had taken a chair at their table because the other tables were all full.

"Where's Jeff?" Hanson asked, poking Adria's arm.

Adria looked up. Of course she couldn't be sure, but gut instinct told her that Jeff was in Poland. Somehow he had gotten wind of the invasion and had been allowed to travel with the German press. As surely as she sat here she knew that once again he had scooped everyone. The rest of them would have to wait to be invited by the Germans to view the devastation. Still, she didn't quite know how to answer the question. Finally she shrugged and simply replied, "Out of town for a few days."

"Son-of-a-bitch!" Hanson said, slapping the table. "He's done it again. He's in Poland isn't he?"

Adria met his eyes. "Maybe," she answered honestly.

"I'll bet he found out about the invasion from Fräulein Greta von Merk. General von Merk's daughter. Jeff's been hustling her for months now, bedding her down now and again. She's gotta be his source. Hell, he's always where its happening before it happens," Jackson said bitterly.

"It's got to be Greta," Hanson agreed, shaking his head and pressing his lips together. "She must have tipped him and she must have used her influence to get him up front with the German press corps. Christ! He sure has a way with German girls."

"It's his blond hair," Jackson responded meanly. "Borden's the perfect Aryan."

Adria didn't dare look up, she felt immobilized, too stunned to speak. Greta? Yes, she had seen the general's tall, blond, and blue-eyed daughter on several occasions. She was Christina Barton's type, in a way.

"Are you all right?" Jackson leaned toward her, the light reflecting off his thick glasses.

Adria shook her head. "It's hot in here." Was this all just gossip—or professional jealousy? "Jeff wouldn't sleep with someone just to get a scoop," she said defensively. But her own voice was uneven, and she knew that deep inside she suspected it was true. There was no denying that Jeff had been scooping everyone else for months. She might deny it to herself, but Jeff *was* an opportunist.

"Sure he would," Hanson said glumly. "He'd do anything to get a story—especially an exclusive. Anyway Greta's not hard to take. I wouldn't say he's making a big sacrifice."

They all laughed. Adria pushed back her chair and stood up. She felt as if she were in a trance.

"Leaving?" Hanson asked. He looked her up and down. "You were the only bright spot in here," he lamented.

Adria ignored him. "I'm going out. It's pointless waiting around here."

"Sure, go out and take pictures of concerned Berliners on the first day of war."

Adria edged past them. "It would be an improvement over waiting to be told what we're supposed to write and photograph."

"Gee, honey, you might miss your free trip to the front. I'm sure that eventually the Germans will want more coverage than Jeff alone can provide."

"I'm tired of 'free trips,'" she muttered. Her mind was flooded with thoughts of Jeff. She could not forget his cocky claim that his pictures would be in every paper—he knew he had the jump on everyone and now, with a sickening feeling, she accepted how he gained his information.

Adria pushed her way out into the warm September sunshine. She hurried toward the park, determined to take pictures, to feel her camera in her hands, to photograph Berliners on the first day of war. Hanson's wasn't a bad idea. She settled down on a bench opposite a large pond and cleaned her lenses. Ready, she began to walk around the still water. In the distance, a small German boy caught her attention. He skimmed a balsam model plane across the water, made rat-a-tat-tat sounds with his mouth, then scooping his plane up, he directed it to bomb a water lily.

Hidden by the shrubbery, Adria snapped her pictures using her long-distance lens. The child's face was intent, and her camera caught the small swastika pin he wore on his lapel. "Rat-a-tat-tat!" drifted through the silence once again.

The sensation of her camera distracted her from thoughts of Jeff until she snapped the final shot and turned away. "Playing war just like I've been playing house," she thought. At that moment she knew she would give Jeff the opportunity to defend himself, but she felt just as certain that he wouldn't bother. She touched her swelling stomach gently. "We're on our own," she whispered to her unborn child.

2

ADRIA SAT IN THE semi-darkness of their apartment and waited. Jeff had phoned and said he was at the station, that he'd be home within the hour.

She leaned back and closed her eyes, wondering if it would have been better if he'd surprised her. No, she decided, it didn't matter. For a week she had rehearsed what she would say and imagined Jeff's responses. She was tired of thinking about it, tired and confused.

And what of the child? Abortion had presented itself

a hundred times in her thoughts and a hundred times she had rejected it. She'd been brought up Catholic and she supposed that had something to do with her reluctance. The night before last the child had moved in her womb and she had known for certain that she would not have an abortion. It was a living being and she could feel it and love it. Other women have raised children alone, she told herself. I can do it too.

She looked up at the sound of the key in the lock and a crack of light from the hall illuminated the floor in front of the door. "Adria!" Jeff's voice called out.

"I'm right here."

He flicked the switch, flooding the room with light. "Why the hell are you sitting in the dark?"

He was framed in the doorway, a bouquet of flowers in one hand and a bottle of champagne in the other. He grinned boyishly. "I was thinking," she replied. The words she had planned fled, a week's rehearsals for this meeting melted away, leaving her mind blank.

"What—no festivities planned? Hey, I expected a celebration! Or at least an enthusiastic welcome!"

He closed the door behind him and took several long strides across the room. He held out the bouquet and smiled. When she didn't respond, the smile was replaced by a look of concern. "What's the matter? You look like you've seen a ghost. Are you all right?"

Adria lifted her eyes to meet his. "I think you should save the flowers for Greta . . . or did you go there first?" Jeff's face flushed and she waited for his denial.

"I didn't go there first because I wanted to be here with you."

She let out her breath. To his credit he hadn't lied, and probably wouldn't. "You're an opportunist," she said. Parts of what she had planned to say came back in a rush.

Jeff put the flowers and wine on the table. He took off his coat and slung it across a chair. Touching his upper lip with his tongue, he looked at her as if trying to decide how to respond. "I just do my job," he said evenly. "And I do it damn well."

It was the opener. "Are you telling me you have to sleep around to do your job?" Adria could hear the hurt and anger in her own voice.

"I'm telling you that I do what is necessary to get a story."

"And what story were you after when you slept with Christina?"

"We've been through that! Hell—everybody sleeps with Christina. As a matter of fact, she's your old man's latest fling. Ah, maybe that's it. Maybe I'm too much like your father."

Adria stared at him in disbelief. Christina and her father? The memory of Christina's hypocritical smile came into focus.

I shouldn't have said that, Jeff thought looking at her stricken expression. It only confused the issue. "I'm sorry to be the one to have broken that news to you—no I'm not! Damn it, Adria. Grow up! Men do these things! I could hardly turn down the daughter of a German general. Hell, Adria, she didn't mean a thing to me. I love you."

Adria struggled to her feet. Her father's deception, the thought of Jeff with Christina and Greta, and her own physical condition combined to push her near hysteria. She felt like screaming, but at the same time felt too weak. "You don't know the meaning of the word 'love,'" she murmured.

"You're being childish."

"I want more from a relationship than you can give." She moved toward the bedroom. Jeff didn't know it, but her bags were packed.

"You'd have done the same thing if you'd had the opportunity."

"No," she answered.

"Come on, Adria. I remember your photos of Carlos. You had a thing going with him, and you may have been forced to take those pictures of his execution but once you got the camera in your hand, your real passion took over. Good pictures, those."

"I was forced to take them. It was a matter of

survival. My camera saved me from breaking down. The only thing I *could* control was the camera! Jeff, those pictures of Carlos are very painful for me. It's not the same as what you've done, and no amount of rationalization will make it the same." She turned away, her eyes filling with tears. "I'm leaving," she shouted as the bedroom door closed behind her.

Adria leaned against the door in the darkened room and let her tears run freely down her face. Should she tell him she was pregnant? No. He had forfeited any right to be a part of her life. He wouldn't want a child anyway; a child would inhibit him.

"I'll leave you alone till you calm down," she heard him say through the door. Then in a few minutes she heard the front door open and close.

She opened the door and saw that he had indeed left. She walked to the phone and dialed for a cab. There was a train leaving for Milan at midnight and she planned to be on it.

3

THE TRAIN EDGED ITS way along another hairpin curve bringing it another mile closer to Milan. From the window, Adria could clearly see the snow-capped Alps rising like an impenetrable wall of jagged stone. Through the open doors that separated her compartment from the corridor she could see out the windows opposite. It was straight up on that side, while on her side of the train deep valleys and fog-filled gorges fell steeply to indeterminable depths.

Adria leaned back against the white doily pinned on the blue-cushioned seat. Her last conversation with Jeff replayed in her mind again and again, keeping her from sleep. Adria checked the time. It was two in the afternoon, but it looked like early evening. A light drizzle had begun to fall and the raindrops seemed to be clinging to the window, quivering with the motion of the train.

She was alone in the compartment and for that she

was thankful. Every now and then she cried a little and she was certain that she looked as bad as she felt. Her head ached dully and her eyes were surely red and puffy. "Think about something else," she whispered to herself.

I'll make England my base of operations, she thought. I'll rent a house in a London suburb and hire a nanny to care for the baby. She tried to conjure up a mental picture of the house, the nanny, and the child. She would come home from an assignment and a child would rush into her arms and devour her with kisses and hugs. "Don't think I don't want you," she whispered. "I do—I do. And we'll be happy together."

Next Adria forced herself to think about Italy. She wanted to do a photo series on Mussolini, then travel to England via France. It would be a complicated journey. England and France were now at war with Germany and Italy and she would have to go through Switzerland.

Adria thought about Mussolini. She hoped to get pictures of him with his family and she had special hopes concerning his daughter, who was said to object to the path her father followed.

Yes, Milan was the logical place to start. It was there that the Italian Fascists had built their party headquarters. She reviewed her notes, then closed her eyes again. She would work till it was time for the baby to be born . . . but then, like an invading army, Jeff's face again forced its way into her thoughts.

Adria opened her eyes to dispel his image. The path the train inched along was now even steeper and more winding. She could see the front of the train as it curved around. Fascinated, she twisted around in her seat to watch the train—now a creeping snake climbing slowly, almost painfully.

Then to her horror, she saw an explosion between the third car and the engine. Instinctively she grabbed onto a brass rail by the window and screamed. As if in slow motion, one car pulled another as one by one the train's carriages were jerked from the track and flipped on their sides. A few separated under the terrible force of gravity and broke loose, rolling down the barren mountainside like beads from a broken necklace. Others hung in a tenuous chain, clinging to the side of the mountain. Adria hung on tightly and closed her eyes as her carriage began to rock with the force of the car in front. Once, perhaps twice, she felt the sickening motion. Then the car flipped.

Adria grasped the rail with all her might to keep from being tossed on her head. The screams and shrieks of other passengers filled her ears and her luggage fell from above as she tried to shield her head with her free arm.

"*Dio!*" a voice yelled.

"God help us!" someone else shouted.

The far end of the car struck a huge rock, and Adria felt the jarring blow as the car bent around and then came to a crashing halt caught between two giant stones on the mountain side. A single, horrible, stabbing pain traveled from her neck to her toes as her head was jolted by the impact. She blinked, struggling to hold onto consciousness, but it was no use. She let go of the brass rail and tumbled down the side of the upside-down carriage to crumple on the curved ceiling.

4

NELSON HALSTEAD WAS TEMPORARILY installed in what the British called "a residential hotel." Just off Grosvenor Square, a short drive from the British admiralty. It hardly deserved the designation hotel—with or without the word residential in front. In reality, it was a great sprawling mansion that had been converted into twenty-two bed-sitting rooms, elegantly furnished with antiques. There was no restaurant and no pub, and Halstead was obliged to walk several blocks to drink and to take his meals.

Shortly after the German invasion of Poland, Halstead had been ordered to England to await further orders. These had assigned him to the post of American liaison to the British admiralty, and his initial reaction was less than joyous. "I wasn't meant for a desk job!" Nelson Halstead blustered, as he drained his glass of bourbon. "And I hate England! The climate's putrid and the British have two speeds: slow and stop!"

Christina smiled indulgently from the dressing table. She was watching him pace in the mirror. "Darling, you haven't examined the more positive aspects yet."

"Positive? Christina, Stalin has signed a pact with Hitler. That means the Fascists and the Commies are going to be working together—*are* working together," he corrected himself. "Russia has already invaded Poland." Personally he found the Russian-German alliance hard to accept, but now he put it out of his mind. "I know that at the moment the French and the English are playing at war—buying time, really. But eventually it will warm up and I doubt the U.S. will stay out. The good promotions are at sea, Christina, where the action is."

Christina turned slowly to face him. Her little white slip had ridden up and her thighs were fully exposed as she crossed her long legs. "But we'll be together, and as soon as your divorce is final we can get married. Darling, I talked to Daddy and he thinks this liaison position is just the thing for you. He thinks it will give you all the right contacts, and when the time comes for a supreme Allied naval commander . . . well, you would be the logical choice."

Nelson frowned. Had Christina's father something to do with his orders? The thought mollified him somewhat. "I suppose there could be advantages," he allowed.

She slithered off the stool and walked over to him. Her hands pressed his face and she lifted her full lips to his for a kiss. "I just had a terrible time getting out of France, darling. Just everyone who is anyone was leaving. We've been apart for weeks—"

Nelson kissed her and she tugged at his tie playfully. "Look at this lovely room." She waved her arm at the

Victorian charm of the high ceilings, the inlaid mahogany tables, the giant four-poster bed. "Pity to waste the bed," she laughed lightly and led him to it, then sank to her knees on the floor in front of him, her head obligingly between his legs. Her big blue eyes looked up. "I want to know everything about you and your job. I want to be the admiral's lady. Darling, I want to know everything and do everything for you." She caressed him hotly in a way that made him instantly erect. He grappled for her, but gave in easily enough when he realized she intended to pleasure him. It was something special that she did, something he could not resist, something that made him feel young again. He grinned, fondled her hair, and leaned back, allowing her to work her magic.

He groaned with pleasure when she had finished and embraced her as she crawled up and into his arms, covering him with her warm little body. "When is your first meeting with the admiralty?" she purred softly.

"Next Wednesday," he replied groggily.

"Let's be together after," she suggested. "You can tell me all about it."

He laughed and pushed his hand inside her loose-fitting slip. "Now why would you be interested?"

Christina closed her eyes. Erich had taught her how to turn her feelings off, how to think only of him when she was having sex with someone else. He had spent months teaching her how to give a man supreme enjoyment. "Because I care about you," she lied, "and I want to know all about your work. If we're to be married, we should share everything."

"Julia never took any interest in my work," he muttered.

Christina smiled. "I'm not Julia."

5

EACH TIME ADRIA INHALED, she was vaguely aware of the odor of vinegar and chlorine, but before she could force her eyes open, she drifted off into yet another vivid dream. Her mother was cleaning, she was in the hospital having her tonsils removed, it was laundry day and her mother was soaking her playclothes in bleach and muttering about how little girls shouldn't climb trees and get their clothes so dirty. In another sequence she was sitting by a long turquoise blue swimming pool with Robert Wertheim. He leaned across the distance between them and was about to kiss her when her dream faded.

Her eyelids seemed too heavy to open, but she wiggled her toes trying to reassure herself that she could still move. Carlos's face appeared and he walked toward her, his arms extended. Adria tried to run toward him, but she couldn't move because arms held her down. Then his face became contorted and he was dangling on the end of a rope. She screamed and again hands and arms restrained her. But whose arms and hands? She was alone.

Adria tossed again. Jeff was calling her, pleading with her to come back, and she was running down a long corridor away from him. As clearly as in real life she could hear his footsteps on the stone floor.

Open my eyes and end it—open my eyes and shut out the dreams . . . but perhaps she could not open them. Filled with fear she forced them open, and stared into the sculptured face of a white-clad nun whose wimple bore a large red cross.

The nun smiled and jostled her arm slightly, then turned and called out over her shoulder in a language that sounded familiar but which Adria could not seem to fathom.

This was no dream. She was in a hospital. Where was Jeff and where was she? Her thoughts were muddled and her eyes, still heavy with sleep, began to close again. But the nun shook her again and Adria forced her eyes open. Did they want her to stay awake?

In a minute a man dressed in white appeared. "Ah," he exclaimed, then added a phrase in the same language spoken by the nun.

Adria shook her head, and was aware of a sharp sudden pain.

"You do not speak Italian, signora? If the answer is no, just blink your eyes," he requested in broken English.

Adria blinked.

He smiled comfortingly. "You've been in a train accident. Do you remember?

Again Adria blinked.

"Ah, well, you will. Now we want you to try to stay awake for a while. You will be all right in a few days, signora, and gradually your memory will return, together with the power of speech. You've had a concussion, and there are some bruises. You may have a very stiff neck for several days as well." He smiled, "The neck will be painful I'm afraid, but it is not serious, just some pinched nerves, which will stop hurting when the swelling goes down. It is the medication that makes it difficult for you to speak.

Adria searched his face. A train accident? She tried to remember, but all she could remember was the rain in Berlin and Jeff angrily shouting at her, "I won't sacrifice my career for you. I will do what I have to do to get a story."

Adria fought against sleep. The doctor moved away, but the nun stayed on duty, shaking her gently when her eyelids began to close.

Adria moved her hand across her stomach, then with a sudden return of memory, thought of her pregnancy. She gurgled and pushed, forcing her lips to form the question. "Baby?" she managed, almost surprised by the hoarse sound of her own voice.

The doctor returned immediately, his expression serious. "I'm sorry," he said, touching her shoulder. "But you have had a miscarriage."

Adria groaned, but could say no more. She felt tears form in her eyes.

"The child could not be saved. But you are young and there is no damage to your internal organs. You can have other children."

The tears continued to flow and Adria closed her eyes in spite of the nun's shaking. She forced the words, "Leave me alone," from her mouth, then turned on her side, as once again memories began to return painfully.

"She will be all right now," she heard the doctor say. Without turning to look, Adria knew they had left.

6

IT WAS THE TENTH of November, and in London the cold, bitter rain seemed to fall unceasingly, and when it wasn't raining, it was foggy. Buildings smelled of mildew, sheets were damp, and even in potbellied stoves the coals sizzled and smoked because of the moisture. The temperature seldom dropped below forty degrees, but the lack of sun made it bone chilling.

Bundled up in a lined Burberry, high boots, and a broad-brimmed rain hat, Christina Barton walked purposefully beneath a pink umbrella through Regent's Park and toward the elephant's enclosure at the Zoological Gardens. Under her breath she cursed at every puddle. What a stupid place to meet! Erich could not be reached.

Christina pushed through the doors of the huge enclosure and silently cursed again. It smelled worse than any barnyard.

"Peanuts?"

Christina turned toward the vendor who huddled in a blanket just behind the door.

"Not so many people in this weather," he commented, offering a toothless grin. "They'll be glad to see you, they will. Did you know when there ain't no crowd they get all depressed?"

Christina looked at the wizened old man disparagingly. When they met publicly she and Erich always tried to choose a crowded place, or if that could not be arranged, a place where they could be absolutely alone. On any other day this would be overflowing with school children, but today it was raining too hard. This was the worst of all meeting places, and here was a witness who would surely remember a woman with a pink umbrella. No, I'm being paranoid, Christina thought. Who would ask? She opened her handbag and took out some change. "I'll take a bag of peanuts," she agreed.

The exchange made, Christina walked farther into the enclosure. The odor of straw, shit, and decaying vegetable matter was overpowering.

"And fancy meeting you here." Erich stepped out into the main aisle.

Christina frowned. He must have come in the other entrance and been waiting down toward the cage with the baby elephant. "It's disgusting in here," she said without hesitation.

"But private," he muttered.

"Not quite." Christina tilted her head toward the vendor, but Erich only shrugged.

"I would rather go elsewhere," she said, "somewhere we can at least have hot tea."

He took her arm obligingly. "Why not? There's a tea room just across Park Road."

Together they went out the far exit, Erich guiding her along. He seemed unusually cheerful, Christina thought, and certainly unusually relaxed.

"I have a gift for you," Erich told her as they approached Park Road. Instinctively, he restrained her, pulling her back so she would not be splashed by a passing car.

The traffic light changed and they hurried across the street into the warmth of the tea room. Erich helped her off with her coat and requested they be seated in the rear, which offered a small alcove.

"And when do you intend giving me this gift?" she asked.

"When our tea comes."

Christina leaned forward in her chair. "You're being mysterious."

The waitress plunked down their tea and a plate of doughy-looking cookies, then she disappeared.

"Ideal," Erich said, lighting a cigarette. "The service is so bad in British restaurants you can be utterly uninterrupted for hours."

Christina half laughed. Erich, like Nelson Halstead, suffered from Anglophobia.

"She brought the tea quickly enough."

"But she won't be back for hours." He reached inside his coat pocket and withdrew a tiny package. "Don't open it now," he instructed.

"What is it?"

"The latest in miniature cameras."

Again Christina frowned. "What for?"

"What information you glean from conversations is interesting, but not entirely vital. I have it on good authority that your friend returns from meetings carrying a briefcase. What we need are photos of the documents it contains."

Christina's lips parted in protest.

Erich covered her hand with his. "You always knew this would grow more complicated, my dear."

"But when can I do it?" she questioned sharply.

"When he sleeps. And if he is not a sound sleeper, there are some powder packets enclosed with the camera that will ensure his rest. All you need do is take the briefcase in the bathroom and quickly photograph the contents. You will then place the film in one of the canisters I am going to provide you with and make the drop."

"Drop? Does that mean we will not be meeting?" She knew her voice held a slight tone of panic. She longed for him and even today she hoped they might go somewhere and be alone for a few hours.

Erich smiled. "We will meet now and again. But our game grows more critical, my dear, and we must limit ourselves for safety's sake."

Christina nodded. She hadn't really counted on war—but of course she was American and America wasn't at war. Still, she had somehow thought her job would consist mainly of repeating her conversations with Nelson. Somehow, photographing documents—secret American and British documents—seemed more involved. Nelson did indeed bring them home, in a locked leather briefcase handcuffed to his hand. He usually left the case on his desk and when she left, or sometimes before she arrived, he opened the case and reviewed what was inside. "He keeps the case locked," she told Erich. "Obtaining the keys could be very difficult."

"And so this," Erich said, handing her a small block of what looked like candle wax. "You only have to obtain them once. Make an impression in the wax and take it to this address. Within an hour you will have a duplicate key."

"Are these documents so important?"

"Yes." He looked into her eyes and she looked back. "Are you having second thoughts?" he asked without blinking.

Christina shook her head.

Erich smiled. "Good. You see, you couldn't just give it up now, my dear. We have far too much information about your father and his activities."

Christina stared at him. Never, ever had he threatened her in any way or questioned her loyalty. But then again, she had never hesitated. Christina smiled confidently, "You have no cause for concern," she assured him. Left unspoken was her vow to herself. I come first, she swore.

7

November 15, 1939

Dear Adria,

First I really must reprimand you. When you leave one country for another—indeed when you

169

travel at all—please keep me informed and please inform the U.S. embassy of your intentions. Need I remind you that there is a war going on? Imagine my surprise when I finally succeeded in getting a long distance call through to Berlin and discovered you had left. On a more practical level, how can I forward your expense money if I don't know where you are?

Naturally I was glad to get your wire and learn that you were all right, having suffered only minor injuries. Although there has been no confirmation, you probably know that the Italian authorities suspect the train was blown up by anti-Fascists. Perhaps when you leave Italy for Switzerland it would be better to hire a car, or perhaps you can go by boat across Lake Constance.

Your last Berlin pictures were interesting, to say the least, and I liked the idea of photographing ordinary Germans on the first day of war. Leave it to the dailies to run battle pictures. I do have to admit, however, that Borden's photos of the Polish cavalry divisions meeting the German panzers told a story all their own and struck a chord of real sympathy here. Medieval warfare meets modern technology and all that.

I like the idea for your Italian photo stories. Just keep the material coming.

My final news concerns your Spanish photos. We've been approached by several groups raising funds for Spanish refugees to allow the photographs to be shown and prints sold at an exhibition. Do I have your permission to pursue this?

That's all for now and keep up the good work.

Andy

Adria folded the letter and put it in the pocket of her suitcase. It was the first long communication she had received since being released from the hospital in Milan two weeks ago. She had wired Andy from the hospital twice, once to tell him she was there and recovering, then to tell him she was going on to Rome. He had responded with concern—or as much as could be expressed in a ten-line telegram.

Adria closed her suitcase and looked around the Rome hotel room which had been her home for two weeks now. It had absurdly high ceilings and was decorated with heavy red brocade drapes and large pieces of ornately carved furniture. This is what I needed, she thought to herself, time to be alone. Every day she had risen early and gone out to take pictures, and every night she had returned to her hotel tired enough to sleep without dreams. Now and again as she watched small children playing in the park she felt a wave of sadness sweep over her, but in the end she convinced herself that things had worked out for the best. No matter how much she had rationalized, she knew that a child needed a father and she knew, too, that she and Jeff could not have made it together. If we hadn't separated in Berlin we would have ended it later, she told herself.

Next to her suitcase was a packet of photos for Andy—a photographic essay entitled, "The Return of Caesar." It also contained a letter telling him she was going to the south of Italy for Christmas and then on to Paris.

Better to spend the holiday in a warm place where she would not be reminded of turkey dinners, Christmas trees, and family reunions. In a sense her choice was perfect. Italians celebrated Twelfth Night rather than Christmas, and by then she would be on her way to Paris. No, on a warm Mediterranean beach with palm trees and white sand she would not even feel as if it were Christmas. And certainly, she thought with conviction, she was not going to go to England and spend the holidays with her father and Christina Barton. In any case, if she did get to England, she might not be able to return to Paris, and she wanted to remain on the continent to photograph the effects of war as long as possible.

171

Adria reached for the phone on the bedside table and dialed the desk. Best to be at the railroad station on time, now that Mussolini had ordered the trains to run on schedule.

Chapter Ten

1

"YOU WOULD HARDLY KNOW there *is* a war," Adria had written to Andy Martin last week. The same thought occurred to her now as she sat down for a cup of coffee at one of the many sidewalk cafés that lined the Champs Élysées. It was March and Adria had been in Paris since January waiting for the promised mobilization and move against the Germans. All of France was caught up in what was termed the *drôle de guerre,*—the phony war. France and England moved in slow motion toward the inevitable battlefield encounter.

In fact, Adria found the situation in France very perplexing. The French had declared war on Germany but instead of pursuing Germans, they pursued Communists and indulged in an unprecedented—for France —anti-Semitic campaign. Those newspapers sympathetic to the government rationalized that Germany and Russia were allies and thus rounding up Communists and Communist Jews was an obvious step toward self-protection.

"As we are invincible to attack," the papers insisted. "We must be certain to curtail the activities of our enemies from within." Endless references were made to the Maginot Line and the protection it offered. Even the American press ran articles on the vast superiority of the French army.

Adria ordered her coffee and opened her bag, smiling to herself as she began taking notes on the assignment she had just completed. There were dissenters in France and she felt satisfied that she had found a rather interesting example.

Last week she had been talking to a reporter from *Le Monde* and he had suggested she might talk to a young general named Charles de Gaulle. "You may not like him," Marcel Trudel warned. "He's rather pompous and formal, but I think you'll find him an interesting photographic subject and a man with unique views." Marcel had given her the number where she might contact this general. "You won't find it difficult to get an appointment. He seeks publicity."

Marcel had been right on all counts, Adria thought as she mentally thanked him for the lead and reviewed her interview.

General de Gaulle claimed that the French army was unprepared to fight because there was no unified command. Moreover, he argued for aggressive tank tactics, tactics which would match the ability of the Germans. "Past glories," the general lamented. "We rest on our laurels and pray that our former hero, General Pétain, will return to unify a hopelessly divided country." As good as his copy was the general's irresistible nose, especially in half-profile.

"But surely the Maginot Line cannot be penetrated," Adria suggested, sensing the comment would bring a quick and interesting change of expression to his face. Beneath the long nose, the general's thin lips curled into a smile, the eyes flashed, and the chin lifted slightly. *Click.*

"My dear young woman, the Maginot Line might possibly have stopped an invasion of France in the fifteenth century—though even that is doubtful—but it will not stop planes that will fly over it nor panzer divisions that may drive around it. Let us continue to cheer and feel relaxed because we have finally managed to build fortifications suitable to protect a medieval lord—I daresay the Maginot Line is slightly superior to a moat—but let us try to remember that we have entered an era of modern warfare. Please note the success of the fine Polish cavalry in turning back the German panzers."

Adria snapped away. She didn't mind that he answered her with nearly venomous sarcasm, nor that he considered her questions idiotic. With a subject such as this it did not hurt to play naive. In the course of his short retort, she caught his ironic smile, his droll humor, and his aristocratic bearing. Instinct told her that although this general was not currently in favor, one day he would be extremely important.

Adria added a little more sugar to her steaming coffee and finished the notes she would file with the photos. Experience had taught her that it was always best to make notes while events were fresh in your mind. Satisfied she had written down everything, she carefully placed the notes in her handbag.

A warm breeze ruffled the fringe on the green umbrella above her table. It was only the end of March, but already tulips and irises had begun to bloom in the park across the street, and she looked at the expanse of green lawn dreamily.

"Adria?"

She jumped at the sound of her own name and turned to face a smiling Robert Wertheim. His eyes studied her and she thought he looked more boyish than the young sophisticate she had first met in Marseilles and sailed with to Spain. Vaguely his relationship with the singer came back to her. Facing him now, she smiled, slightly embarrassed by her previous girlish expectations. "This is a coincidence. I didn't expect to see you again," she said hesitatingly.

"Mother told me you visited her, but that was over a year ago. Why have you come back to Paris?" Without invitation he sat down opposite her.

"I've been in Germany and Italy for the past year," she replied. "I'm afraid war will soon come to Paris. It's the city Americans are most familiar with, so it's important I be here." She shook her head at her own words. "I sound like a vulture," she admitted.

He laughed, his blue eyes alive. "Not many would agree that the danger is real, but I do. Wanting to be in the right place to practice your art is not predatory. I've

174

seen your photos of Spain and I saw an issue which had photos of Berlin. You're very good, you know."

He was wearing dark trousers, an open-necked shirt with a print ascot and a black beret. His eyes were openly admiring, and though he was commenting on her work, he was looking at her in that way men reserve for women they find attractive. She realized that for the first time in many months she was conscious of her looks. She too was dressed casually, in a green cashmere skirt and sweater. Her three-quarter-length brown and green plaid jacket was slung over the back of her chair. "Thank you," she said softly, responding to his compliment.

"Where do you live?" he questioned. "Is it far?"

Adria shook her head. "A few blocks away, on the Rue Jacob."

"I will only be here for a few days. Spend the afternoon with me, will you? I'm sure you think you know Paris, but let me show you *my* Paris." His eyes were intent and he leaned toward her.

She wondered if she should ask about the singer— no, that would be too prying. Adria frowned slightly. "I have to make some phone calls," she hedged. Actually she wanted to change her clothes and put on some make-up. "Could we meet back here in an hour?"

"Why don't I just come with you?" he said, standing up and offering her his hand. Reluctantly, Adria nodded.

Her so-called apartment was no more than three tiny rooms located in a once elegant house that had now been converted into smaller units. The sitting room was furnished sparsely with a cushioned wicker sofa and chair. Her bedroom held only a bed and nightstand, and her kitchen was converted into a darkroom. A line was strung across the living room and from it photos held by clips were left to dry like clothes on a line. In one corner a pile of newspapers threatened to tumble down, and a half-open magazine was draped over the arm of the chair.

"I'm afraid it's rather cluttered," Adria said as she opened the door. "I'm not at home very much."

He smiled indulgently and seemed to sense her embarrassment as he followed her in. "I could fix you some coffee," she offered.

He shook his head. "I've had enough for one day. Have anything stronger?"

Adria blushed slightly. "I'm afraid not."

"Then I shall just wait patiently and without benefit of liquid refreshment," he said with a wink.

Adria indicated the sofa. "Make yourself at home," she invited as she retreated to the bedroom.

Robert sat down and looked around. The apartment was furnished with only the bare essentials and certainly it lacked any signs of domesticity. He wondered if Adria had always lived this way, or if she had changed since being in Spain. He leaned back against the faded flowered cushions of the furniture. He had hardly recognized her in the café. Her auburn hair was as beautiful as ever, but she had worn no make-up. Not that she needed it, he thought. Her eyes were still beautiful, but the innocence of youth had left them, and she seemed as preoccupied as he had been at their first meeting. Had it only been a year? She seemed more than a year older, she seemed mature and somehow more solid. Certainly she was a girl no more. Now, he thought, she was a woman.

When Adria emerged, her hair had been brushed back and she wore a linen suit with a stylish straight skirt with box pleats. Her jacket sleeves were wrist length and she wore suede, low-heeled shoes. She no longer dressed like a Gypsy, he noted wryly.

"I'm sorry my place is so small and I have nothing to offer you," Adria apologized.

He shrugged good-naturedly. "It's utilitarian; I would expect nothing more or less. I think you have more important matters on your mind."

"True, I'm seldom here except to sleep."

He took her arm as they emerged together into a

176

sunny Paris afternoon. "You have much to tell me," he suggested as they walked down the street. "I think your life has changed since we last met."

"It's changed," Adria allowed. Her thoughts strayed to Berlin. Jeff had not tried to contact her and certainly she had not written to him. It had ended when she walked out on him in Berlin, and since she had lost the baby there was nothing to make her reconsider her decision. She would not, however, discuss Jeff or the baby with Robert. "Once I think I believed I could somehow remain behind the camera and always be the observer," she said. "I can do that when I'm in the act of taking pictures, but when I've put the camera down, I get involved. In that way I've changed."

"I'm glad. You can't stay impartial," he replied, putting his hands into his pockets as they walked.

"I did deliver your package in Barcelona." Adria wondered how much he knew about her experience in Spain. Of course she had told Madame Wertheim a great deal, but that did not mean Madame had confided in her son.

"I know," Robert replied. Then, suddenly changing the mood, "How about lunch at my favorite bistro?" He laughed, "Were we in London I would say pub— but in any language this place has good food and a nice atmosphere."

"I'm starved," Adria confessed as she fell into step with him. He seemed different, but she could not explain why.

2

"LOUIS XV RECEIVES THE credit, but it is Francis I to whom the French owe a debt of gratitude," Robert said as he and Adria descended the steps of the Louvre. "He built the Louvre, remodeled Versailles, and created the national library. He was the Renaissance collector and the builder of chateaux."

"And Louis XV?" Adria asked.

"He gave his name to spindly legged furniture—valuable, artistic, but really terribly uncomfortable to sit on."

"You're joking. You really like it. I saw Louis XV furniture at your home," Adria countered.

"Bought by my grandfather. You never saw my room or my study. Let me assure you I have soft, plump leather chairs and sofas that beg to be sprawled on. The rest of the house is like a museum, but you cannot *live* in a museum."

Adria smiled and recalled that on the way to Spain he had spoken ruefully about the life he led. "Like a medieval lord," he had joked. She hadn't commented then, but she did now. "You can afford to reject luxury," Adria suggested, "because you have everything."

He looked at her quizzically. "Do you think I have everything?"

"You're one of the wealthiest men in the world. You can have whatever you want."

He laughed gently. "You know little of what I want if you think that. Then he turned to face her, a mischievous smile creeping up. "Can I have you?"

Adria blushed deeply. "I didn't mean that sort of thing," she stammered, "I meant possessions."

His eyes suddenly seemed to change hue, as if he could see through her. "Can't a woman be possessed by a man?" he asked in a tone that sent a shiver up her spine.

Adria looked away, afraid he would see her desire. "You're teasing me," she said with a smile.

He adjusted his beret and linked arms with her. He was joking, she told herself. Best to brush it off. Adria stopped and turned back toward the Louvre. On the steps an old woman with a black kerchief and an intriguing face was selling flowers. Adria lifted her camera to frame her portrait. Robert waited patiently until Adria again fell in step beside him. She had crawled back into her shell, drawing her career around

178

her like a protective curtain even as she walked with Robert Wertheim.

"I'll be leaving France soon," he told her, "though I expect to be back."

"You've joined the army?" she ventured.

He half smiled. "Not exactly. I've joined the British forces." I cannot tell her it is the intelligence service, he thought to himself.

"Why the British?"

"Well I *am* British, and they made me an offer I couldn't refuse." He smiled wryly and took her arm, guiding her toward a cab. "So you see, I will be gone soon, and my last desire is to spend the next week with a beautiful woman. You're beautiful—will you oblige this last civilian wish?"

Adria again felt desire mix with reluctance. It was the oldest line in the world. Tomorrow I'm going to war, so sleep with me tonight. "I doubt I could fulfill all your expectations," she said honestly.

"I'm not sure what my expectations are. Dinner tonight, perhaps a covered boat ride down the Seine. Tomorrow I should like to go to all the tourist spots we haven't visited today. You see, when you live in a city you don't get to see it as tourists do. I want to be able to remember Paris."

"You speak as if you think it will be destroyed."

"I know it will never be the same. Come with me, Adria. I need to be with someone."

Adria nodded, unable to refuse the pleading in his voice.

"Maxim's for dinner?" he asked.

"I'm afraid I don't have the wardrobe."

"Then come to my apartment. Some of Mother's clothes and jewels are there. I think you are about the same size."

"I couldn't wear your mother's things," Adria protested.

"Of course you could—she wouldn't mind at all. As a matter of fact, my mother is intrigued with you."

"It's mutual."

Robert laughed lightly. "Most people feel that way."

3

THE MAGNIFICENT DRESS ADRIA had chosen now hung limply from the hanger, its shimmering threads glistening in the winter sunlight that peeked through her bedroom curtain. According to Robert, its fabric had been hand-woven in Morocco, and the dress itself cut and designed by Madame Wertheim's personal couturier, Gabrielle Chanel. "She makes her the latest fashions every year, but half of them mother never wears," Robert confided. "Mother thought this one was too young for her, but on you it looks stunning," he said with admiring eyes.

How it actually looked on her, Adria could not say. But she knew it made her feel elegant as well as beautiful. The design was feminine and seductive, but its white lace collar cast an aura of innocence. The only jewelry she had worn was an old-fashioned topaz pendant framed in gold and hanging from a gold chain.

They had dined in a private room at Maxim's, with waiters hovering over them like bees over honey. Cold vichyssoise was followed by a salad delicately dressed with spicy oil and Roquefort cheese, then by the main course of thinly sliced veal in a magnificent sauce with slivers of paper-thin mushroom bits. They ate slowly, talked, and drank Chateau Lafite-Rothschild. Robert had raised his crystal glass in a toast. "To my competition," he had said as he swished the wine in the glass and inhaled its delicate bouquet.

"I should have liked a Wertheim wine," Adria said.

Robert raised his eyebrow and smiled. "Regretably we make only reds, and veal calls for white."

Adria nodded, remembering now that he had told her the Wertheim vineyards did not produce white wine. She sipped slowly and watched Robert Wertheim, so at ease in this rich atmosphere. She herself felt slightly uncomfortable even in the presence of the long-nosed waiters who seemed to watch slyly which fork was used for each course and just how the spoon was held. "Here," Adria offered, "you would never guess France is a nation at war."

"To my knowledge, Maxim's does not engage in wars. I suspect that one evening in the near future Nazi officers will be dining here, and I assure you, the waiters will judge them, too, by their table manners and the vintage wine they request."

"You can't think that France will fall so easily?"

"I do. It's a land divided, a country without the will to fight. Even as we sit here talking, the government leaders are trying to bring back General Pétain from Spain to take over the reins of power. The man is old and senile; he can't unite France and he won't fight."

Adria frowned. "The American papers all say France has the best army in Europe."

"No doubt the French army is superior to the Polish cavalry, but it's vastly overrated. What France has, with rare exception, is strutting generals and bragging, overconfident politicians."

"You sound like a general I photographed yesterday. De Gaulle was his name."

Robert moved his expressive hands. "I have heard of him. A tyrant perhaps, but essentially right about our military strategy. Maybe something will come of him. He certainly has the right name for leadership."

"I've always thought names play a role in success," Adria suggested.

"Like horoscopes. Tell a person that he's fated to be a natural leader and it certainly helps make him one."

"Then General de Gaulle should succeed on two counts," Adria laughed. "When I photographed him I asked the month of his birth. He told me he was born on November 22nd and is a Sagittarius. He proudly explained that it's a sun sign and Sagittarians are known for leadership and independence."

"Ah, how can he fail? I'm sure Hitler's astrologists will warn him against a general so well named and strategically born."

"I'd heard that Hitler has astrologers."

"Indeed. Astrologers who have convinced him that he is fated to lead because he was born on the cusp between Aries the ram and Taurus the bull. And certainly Hitler believes in the power of names. 'Hitler' has a strength 'Schicklgruber' certainly lacks. But it is really his generals who will make it happen."

Adria smiled and repeated "Schicklgruber," dropping the inflection on the middle syllable. "I don't think he'd have gone as far with that name," she agreed.

"It was his mother's name; he's illegitimate. Going back to astrology for a moment, do you know about Karl Ernst Krafft?"

Adria shook her head.

"He's a German astrologer. He predicted an attempt on Hitler's life a few years ago and warned the SS. When the attempt was in fact made, the German papers made a lot of it. It was then that Goebbels hired astrologers for the Ministry of Propaganda."

"I have a hard time believing that people with power set store in subjects like astrology."

Robert winked. "Do you want to know a secret?"

She nodded and leaned closer.

"Churchill has astrologers too. He uses them to second-guess Hitler's soothsayers. And I fear that the Canadian prime minister, William Lyon Mackenzie King, is a total devotee of the occult. Rumor has it that he not only consults the stars, but that he has conversations with his dead mother."

"I'd say the fate of the world is in the hands of some strange people."

Robert laughed. "An understatement, but it's always been true. When we've finished our meal, I'll show you the most magnificent view of Paris you will ever see," he offered as he changed the subject. "At night the Seine is like a black velvet ribbon of darkness traversing a sea of sparkling diamonds."

He had taken her to the Palais de Chaillot, which had been built for the 1937 International Exhibition above a two-hundred-thirty-foot hill originally prepared for the construction of a never-built palace for the king of Rome, son of Napoleon. From the statue-guarded terrace they enjoyed a splendid view of Paris, a view most often used in daytime as the backdrop for Diana Vreeland's *Vogue* models or the chic, bored-looking ladies of *Paris Match*.

Then they had a nightcap at a small, secluded café and Robert had returned her by cab to her rooms. He had kissed her gently on the lips when they had parted, and promised to call the next day.

Adria climbed from her bed. It was nearly eleven and she headed for the kitchen and some much-needed coffee. Robert Wertheim had been the perfect gentleman as always, treatment which mystified her on one hand and pleased her on the other. He teased, he hinted at lovemaking, but he did not attempt it. Perhaps, she reasoned, she was a stand-in for someone else. Or perhaps he too recognized the gulf between them. "It's better," she told herself as she poured the black coffee. She felt prepared to play Cinderella, but unprepared to play the prince's lover. There were too many memories of Jeff and Carlos playing on the edges of her mind. Then, too, there was the whole situation of war and the threat of an invading German army. Her experience with Carlos had taught her the danger of living for the moment, yet she still felt that terrible twinge of apprehension—a small voice still whispered, "a moment is all you might have."

A quick, irritated knock at the door snapped Adria out of her thoughts. She tied her robe around her and went to the door. There her neighbor, a short, fat, bald Frenchman gesticulated wildly with his hands at more than twelve baskets of roses that filled the hall.

"Take them inside, mademoiselle!" he said with a sweeping motion. "Roses in winter! Such an extravagance! And in wartime!" Adria supressed a smile. Robert Wertheim had all the makings of an ardent suitor, after all.

4

IN THE HEARTH THE fire flickered, winking at her. Adria sat on the thick russet carpet, her legs covered by a cashmere blanket, and she leaned back against a pile of huge, multicolored cushions. Robert, who had been sitting nearby, was stirring the fire now, trying to rouse it once again into dancing flames.

The lights in his study were out, and only a candle burned on the table. The blackout curtains were drawn, and the room was still. Adria inhaled a mixture of aromas: the fine leather of the books that lined the walls, the smell of Robert's pipe, the charcoal from the fireplace. She sipped her cognac and closed her eyes. Tomorrow he was leaving for England.

"When you first said you would be working for the British I pictured you in Whitehall behind a desk. You won't be behind a desk will you?"

He turned toward her, surprised. "No," he answered, "no, I won't be behind a desk."

"Tell me," she pressed.

"I really don't know what my assignment will be. Possibly I'll return to France to coordinate some form of resistance."

Adria stared into her glass. "That will be terribly dangerous."

Robert sat down beside her and drew the blanket around his own legs. His arm went around her and Adria leaned her head down, resting it on his broad shoulder. She felt warm and comfortable, her misgivings slipping away. Perhaps he was all he seemed to be, perhaps he could be trusted. Then she thought of the headlines in the Paris papers—of the beautiful face of the singer with whom his name had been romantically linked. His lips caressed her hair and she closed her eyes. That he wanted her was obvious—but for what? A short interlude? An affair? It was too late for an affair because tomorrow he would be gone. They only had one night, and one night was not enough.

"Your hair is soft," he murmured. "It smells sweet, like flowers in spring." His fingers moved on her shoulder, the sensation promising more. Adria turned toward him and the tips of their noses touched, then their lips.

The first kiss was quick and tentative. Then he drew her closer and she could feel the pressure of his mouth on hers, the full passion of his embrace. She shivered in his arms, acutely aware of a rush of conflicting sensations—desire, fear, tenderness, sadness, joy. She pressed against him, letting herself go for an instant, then she broke the kiss and turned away. "Please," Adria protested softly. "You're leaving tomorrow. I didn't mean to lead you on . . ."

"If I weren't leaving, would it make a difference?"

She moved her head slightly. Their noses were almost touching, their lips were a breath apart, and his eyes questioned her, held her transfixed. "I don't know," she breathed.

"Would it make a difference?" he repeated.

"Perhaps," she allowed.

"What are you afraid of?" His lips brushed her throat, then her ear. Again he was looking at her, his deep blue eyes steady, penetrating.

"I'm afraid of the war," she whispered. "Afraid of not being able to sort out how I feel because I'm afraid for you. It's the urgency—it causes mistakes. It's no different for you." Her hand brushed his cheek gently and he seized it, pressing her fingers to his lips.

"I understand," he said moving away slightly. "You're right, of course." He avoided her eyes and chastised himself for slipping. She was not the kind of woman you bedded for a night and then left. But God, he admitted to himself, he did want her. But as much as I want her, he thought, I want her for more than one night. "All's fair in love and war" was a rotten cliché. There was nothing fair about their having to separate, yet he had commitments and he knew he would honor them.

Adria silently let her head drop again to his shoulder.

The brandy, the fire, the warmth of another human being. It was all there could be for now. "I'm sorry," she said quietly.

Robert did not answer, though he continued to hold her. He wondered if she wanted him as much as he wanted her. Sometimes it seemed that way, sometimes not. How often had he seen pure desire in her green eyes? How often in the last week had he felt her growing nearer to him? But he had witnessed other sentiments, too, seen pain as some memory flashed through her mind. He wanted to hold her, to mend her, to pledge undying love. But he knew that if he did, he might cause her the greatest pain of all.

Part
2

Chapter Eleven

1

ADRIA PUSHED OPEN THE dormered window and breathed in the warm July air. It was only seven o'clock, but the streets of Paris already hummed with activity. She watched as women crowded the small fruit market across the street and shopkeepers rolled up their awnings, signaling the beginning of a new day. She looked about her room and sighed. A half-open wardrobe trunk bulged with her clothes, and partially-filled boxes seemed to chastise her reluctant preparations. Still, the time had come to go. The war was happening elsewhere, and her presence in occupied Paris was growing more difficult by the day.

As an American citizen she had been able to remain without too much hindrance after France had capitulated thirteen months earlier. The first German occupiers had placed no restrictions on her work. She had photographed the German entry into Paris and their grand parade through the Arc de Triomphe, capturing the anguished looks of anti-Fascist Parisians and the proud pompousness of pro-Fascists, who were almost immediately catapulted into positions of authority by the occupying forces, in pictures that had filled the pages of *News Views*. But now the Germans prevented her from photographing anything that showed the dark side of the occupation. She was again forced to record only what the Germans wanted recorded.

Adria went into the tiny kitchen and turned on the gas burner. While waiting for the coffee to perk, she slipped into her clothes and ran the brush through her hair.

How quickly it had all happened! Never a day passed when she didn't remember that Robert had been right. The French had no will to fight, and their magnificent

Maginot Line proved to be less intimidating than a child's play fort. The Germans had simply gone around it, then swarmed over it like ants over a stunned prey. Resistance had melted, Paris had been declared an open city in mid-June, 1940, and France had sued for "Peace with Honor" within days. Following that, the new government of Marshal Pétain declared it would remain in France to look after "domestic affairs," and it was agreed that the south of France would not be occupied. Then, to no one's surprise, the British sank the French navy to keep it from falling into German hands, and Marshal Pétain broke off relations with England, declaring that "France has never had, and never will have, a more relentless enemy than Great Britain." "Collaborators," the loyal French whispered when they spoke of the Vichy Government; then "traitor" became the slogan scrawled on the sides of buildings.

Adria finished her hair and applied a small amount of make-up. She glanced at her closet and saw Madame Wertheim's beautiful gold dress. This morning she would have to wrap it and send it to Madame in the south of France. She chastised herself for not returning it sooner, though Robert had urged her to keep it. And she wondered this morning, as she did almost every morning, where Robert Wertheim was and what he was doing. Had he been at Dunkirk? Was he in London? Her mind wandered back to the week they had spent together during the tense, but strangely untouched days of the phony war. He had wined her and dined her, confided in her and flirted with her. They had gone to the theater, strolled through the gardens of Versailles, taken trips into the countryside, discussed every subject imaginable. And they had kissed passionately, come close to being lovers, then held themselves back in the face of separation. "I wish we hadn't," Adria whispered to herself. Now that he was gone she wanted real memories, not the taunting frustration of imagining how it might have been.

The knock on her door startled her out of her

reverie. She answered, "One minute," and crossing the room, opened it a crack.

"Mademoiselle Halstead?" The petite young woman who stood on the threshold had expressive, almond-shaped eyes, dark curly hair, and a deep, throaty voice. She was well dressed in a spotless white silk dress, a cocky little black cloche, black shoes and bag. A warm smile softened her angular face. She was truly a beautiful woman.

"Yes," Adria replied somewhat mystified. The woman spoke with a French accent, but Adria had few visitors and none were French. Cautious, they stayed away from Americans in occupied Paris. But there was something familiar about this woman's face, and Adria opened the door.

"May I come in?" the woman asked in English.

Adria nodded and opened the door wider, despite a flash of caution. She had heard of some French coming to Americans for help, then turning on them and accusing them of spying. Sometimes she wondered if there were as many members of the underground as there seemed to be collaborators. She had been warned again and again by the press attaché at the embassy, "Don't place yourself in a compromising situation."

The young woman stepped into her apartment and Adria closed the door, automatically looking down the hall to make certain her visitor was alone. "How may I help you?" Adria asked.

"You could start by giving me a cup of coffee," the young woman replied with a smile. Her eyes surveyed the apartment carefully before she sat down. "I shall only take a few minutes of your time. Please, let me introduce myself. I am Celeste Deschamps."

"Celeste Deschamps," Adria repeated her name, searching her memory. That was it! She was the singer with whom Robert had been involved. Adria had seen her photo. But no wonder she hadn't recognized her; the photo had not done her justice. Adria forced a smile and went to the kitchen to pour two cups of the fresh coffee. "Have we met before?" Adria asked, although she knew they had not. "Or do we have mutual friends?" She was fishing, and none too artfully.

Celeste nodded and took the cup. "We have a mutual friend, Robert Wertheim."

Adria wondered how much her expression changed. Did this mean Robert was still involved with this woman? Adria felt flustered. "Sorry everything is such a mess. As you can see, I'm preparing to leave Paris."

Again Celeste nodded. "Have you had problems with the Germans?"

Adria shook her head. "Not really, but I'm restricted in my work. I'm a photographer for an American news magazine."

"I know."

"You have me at a disadvantage. You seem to know about me, but I know nothing about you."

"Would you say it is safe to talk here?" Celeste asked.

"Safer than most places, I imagine. I doubt I'm watched, if that's what you mean."

Celeste sipped her coffee. "Approaching foreigners can be dangerous," she allowed. "I'm a singer at the Club Morocco. I am also involved with the Resistance."

Adria frowned. "And how do you know you can trust me?"

"I think you have no interest in German success. More, it is a question of making you trust me."

Adria searched her eyes. If she was lying, she did it well. "Did Robert send you?"

"Yes, though I confess he is more than a friend."

Adria tried not to look surprised at the woman's directness. She had assumed Robert's affair with Celeste was over, but clearly she had been wrong. Just as clearly they worked together in the underground. I'm stupid, she thought. I assumed too much from our week in Paris. She suddenly felt quite bewildered and disappointed. But I can't feel betrayed; he never promised anything. Nor did he ever tell me he loved me. She

192

looked steadily at Celeste Deschamps, aware of envy. "Is Robert in Paris?" she asked, not sure she wanted to know.

Celeste wiped her lips with the napkin on the table. "Sometimes. He comes and goes frequently. I've come to you about a simple matter. You're leaving soon and we need to transmit some information. We need a courier."

"I'm hardly trained for that sort of thing."

"It takes no training, and I'm certain it won't be dangerous for you. Please, we have to utilize every opportunity until our radios are delivered. Right now communication with the British is very difficult." She smiled slightly. "We've approached many Americans, and they have all been most cooperative."

Adria nodded silently. "How can I be sure Robert sent you? Why didn't he come himself?"

"You are wise to be suspicious. He told me to remind you of the package you took to Spain for him."

"Yes," Adria answered hesitantly. Celeste could not have known about the package unless Robert had told her. But what did he want her to do now? And what if they met again? Knowing about Celeste, did she want to see him again? Adria bit her lower lip. Helping the Resistance in some way was more important than her feelings toward one man. "What do you want?"

"You must come to this address at six o'clock. Take the metro and change trains several times. I'm sure you won't be followed, but we must be careful."

"If I come at six, I can't get home before the curfew."

"If necessary, you can spend the night and return in the morning. It will give us time to make plans."

Adria agreed and watched as the young woman rose to leave. Perhaps she would not see Robert again, but in spite of Celeste she found herself hoping she would.

First Adria went to the Louvre to lose herself in the crowds, then to a café for a late lunch. When she left the café, she went into Bon Marché, tried on dresses, and then slipped away out another entrance of the store. She rode the metro in several directions, moving through crowds and always watching. On one level she felt absurd and ridiculous playing spy, on another exhilarated, as if she were doing something to fight the Germans no matter how minor her role.

At a few minutes after six she stood before a large town house on the perimeter of Paris. Apart from the single light that burned from a front window, it looked deserted and empty. Glancing once again down the empty street, she walked up the steps and knocked lightly on the door.

"Mademoiselle." The door opened and Celeste beckoned her to enter. Silently she led her to the kitchen and from there down a narrow staircase into a well-lit basement meeting room. The odor of French cigarettes greeted them, and Adria squinted as her eyes adjusted to the sudden bright lights.

"Friends, meet Adria."

Her eyes went to the familiar voice, and her mouth half opened. His remarkable disguise aged him by twenty years, but he was nonetheless recognizable. "Robert!" she said in surprise.

He smiled, held out his hands, and walked to her side. He gave her a hug and a perfunctory kiss on the cheek. Then turning toward the others, "You've met my half-sister, Celeste."

Adria's mouth opened slightly in surprise. "Half-sister," she stumbled. She knew her face was flushed and she felt awkward. But then Robert had no way of knowing what she had thought all these months.

Robert nodded. "I'd have come for you myself, but I've just returned from a trip to the north of France."

"And I did not want to promise he'd be here when I wasn't certain he would get back in time," Celeste added.

There was laughter from the four strange men, and one commented, "Robert knows every beautiful woman in France."

"There will be plenty of time for your reunion later,"

194

Celeste pointed out, "but Ramon has to go, so we had better get on with it."

"Of course," Robert agreed. "Adria, this is Ramon, Michel, Claude, and Henry. We do not use last names."

Adria nodded at them. Claude and Michel had the distinct look of academics, while Ramon might have been a truck driver. Henry defied even a good guess, small and frail-looking, but with remarkable hands. His fingers were long and almost graceful, like those of a master surgeon or perhaps a jeweler. Adria took the chair Robert offered and sat down.

"She's been a courier for me before," he said smiling. "She can be trusted."

"They were only magazines," Adria said.

"Ah, but our code was keyed to one of the articles. It's the most efficient form of code, though the Germans are smarter than the Spanish and often suspect such things."

"Is that how I am to carry your information?"

Robert nodded. "We may have to be slightly more sophisticated. The Germans may well confiscate printed matter as you leave."

Adria could not take her eyes off Robert. She wondered if he saw the admiration and love in them.

"I imagine you'll be able to take your photos as long as they're not of sensitive subjects."

"And how does that help us, Robert? We cannot photograph the key to the code."

"Perhaps we can," Robert said, scratching his chin thoughtfully.

"You have an idea?" Celeste asked.

"Adria could take a picture of Celeste in front of a newsstand. If the right lens is used the publications would be visible and could be enlarged and read. We would then use those publications as the basis for the code."

Ramon half smiled. "A brilliant idea."

"But how will the British know the code?" Adria queried.

Robert laughed. "They already know it; they only need the specific publications. You probably don't understand and I don't blame you. It's complicated, and of course there are different ways to do it." He walked to a table and picked up a copy of the paper. "Now suppose you and I both had a copy of this paper," he explained. "I would broadcast a series of words and you would find the words in your copy. Under a prearranged deciphering system the position of the words might indicate a numerical value. A series of numbers may then indicate certain letters for actual deciphering. That is one system; another involves the selection of phrases. I cannot tell you what system we use, only that it is essential that we have one copy and the British the other. It does not matter what publications are used as long as both parties have copies. In this case we will both have whatever is on the newsstand when the photo is taken."

"I understand now," Adria said. "Well, Celeste, dress fashionably. If I'm asked, I shall say they are for a fashion layout."

"To illustrate the normalcy of the German occupation," Ramon said sarcastically.

Adria lifted her brow, "Isn't that what the Germans want? For the world to think that Paris is as it was?"

"That's the current propaganda line," Ramon agreed. He withdrew a Gitane, struck a match on the corner of the table, and inhaled. "The fact is, this first army of occupation is soft. They're beguiled by Paris, charmed by it. Later, when the SS comes, I assure you that Paris will be under the jack boot."

"That's why we must get started now," Celeste said. "At the moment what resistance there is is disorganized and splintered. But we know, we sense, that our freedom of movement is running out. Soon we will have to be much more careful."

"Wouldn't it be better if all the Resistance groups worked together?" Adria asked.

"No," Michel replied. "We are in communication, but this way it is much more difficult for the Germans."

He smiled and shrugged. "Besides, there are different philosophies—a normal thing for we French. All we agree on is that Germany must be defeated."

"Michel, my fiancé, is a doctor," Celeste added. Then looking at the Michel sitting at the table she smiled. "Not this Michel. In any case, my Michel prefers to work with the Jewish Resistance. But Robert and I have chosen to work directly with the British."

"And De Gaulle has his own intelligence people," Robert told her.

"I heard that," Adria said thoughtfully. Her General de Gaulle was becoming quite famous.

Henry tapped his long fingers on the table. "Ah, Americans are one for all and all for one. But before you condemn our disunity in the face of the enemy, Mademoiselle, consider this: if resistance exists in one body, its head is easily severed and the whole body dies. Better the Germans should have to hunt down a hundred bodies."

Ramon slapped his open hand on the table. "The philosophy of resistance is something I can do without. I see no problem with this plan," he announced, returning to the matter of transmitting the codes. "And that being the case, I've work to do."

"I hadn't thought we would finish so early," Celeste said, glancing at her watch.

Robert stood up. "I'll see Adria home before the witching hour." He grinned at her, "You won't have to spend the night after all."

The old red Citroen rattled along over the uneven pavement. Adria leaned back against the canvas seat and watched the Paris streets emptying as Robert weaved in and out, avoiding known check points. How absurd she had been! Now that she knew the truth about Celeste, she felt free and, in spite of the danger, happy.

"This car is a drop in status for me," Robert joked. "It's the car farmers drive in through the fields."

Adria thought about the plush Rolls Royce he had

driven to Villefranche and the long Daimler he had used in Paris only a few months ago. Her mind wandered back to the magical dinner at Maxim's and to the days in the country when they had walked hand in hand. The Citroen clattered to a stop in front of her building and Robert parked it around the corner and walked with her up the narrow flight of stairs.

Outside the door he gathered her in his arms and kissed her cheek. Adria leaned against him, then moved her face so their lips met. She kissed him, moving her mouth till he responded with passion and held her still closer. "Come in," she whispered, not wanting him to leave.

His steady, serious blue eyes looked down into hers, even as his hands moved slowly and tantalizingly from the nape of her neck to the small of her back. "If I come in, Adria, I'll stay the night."

She nodded. He took the keys and opened the door, then suddenly he lifted her into his arms and carried her inside, closing the door behind them. He carried her to the small bedroom, which was lit only by the moonlight from the clear summer night, and laid her gently on the bed.

"I've waited for you for so long," he murmured, kissing her ear, then, biting it gently, he breathed into it.

His breath on her neck and in her ear sent a shiver of anticipation through her. "I—"

"Sh!" His lips moved across her neck, to her lips, then back to her throat. His fingers moved adroitly as he unbuttoned her blouse and slipped his warm hand inside, cupping her breast and kissing her lips hard. "I want you to belong to me," he told her. "I don't want this to be for one night, Adria. I want it to be forever, for as long as we live." In the moonlight she could see his face; his expression was serious, and she knew then how very much she loved him.

"There will come a time," she cautioned, "when the world returns to normal. I'm not certain I fit the mold of the Wertheim women."

198

He smiled wryly. "When this is over the world I was born into won't exist, Adria. Your world will have changed too." He kissed her neck again and eased her blouse off, then the lace slip that covered her firm breasts. He kissed her taut nipples and moved his hands over her, gently, almost worshipfully, as he finished undressing her. He quickly discarded his own clothes and stretched out beside her, pressing her to him so she could feel the full length of his body against her.

He touched her intimately, moving his hand between her legs, slowly drawing circles on her flesh with his finger, massaging her carefully, then withdrawing and kissing her nipples.

Adria felt hot as he caressed her into a fierce desire. She moaned and tossed in his arms, pressing herself against him, moving with him. Slow and beautiful, he seemed to know her body and how to arouse her to a feverish response. When she touched him, she felt him strong and hard, and lifted herself to him.

"Not too much, or our lovemaking will be shortened," he cautioned. He moved slightly and returned again to her breasts. He kissed one nipple and teased the other between his thumb and forefinger. Then he began moving his hand down, finally touching her most sensitive spot—back and forth—never quite enough. Adria writhed in his arms, breathing heavily, given over entirely to the sensations that surged through her, each one stronger than the last. She wanted him so much she almost cried out. He entered her slowly, teasing her by withdrawing and returning till she wrapped her legs around him and held him to her. He moved within her and against her till they shuddered together, becoming one.

In the still darkness they lay together until the dull dawn separated them and they each returned to their changing worlds.

2

ADMIRAL HALSTEAD SAT BEHIND his massive rosewood desk, framed by the blue curtains behind him. To his left was a huge American flag on top of which an ugly brass eagle sat perched, its wings stretched, metal mouth agape. The size of the room and the red, white, and blue oversized furniture were a testament to the Admiral's pomp and status.

But if power seemed to go with the trappings of the room, he didn't feel powerful now. Indeed, he felt nervous and definitely not in command as he twisted his swivel chair, causing it to squeak. His large hands were folded in front of him and he twiddled his thumbs and kept his eyes down. He had planned to take Adria out to dinner, to ply her with cocktails, and to fortify himself with bourbon before telling her of his forthcoming marriage, but Adria had flatly refused his invitation. Even more annoying, she had been in England for some weeks and had spent most of the time at Tangmere, the Royal Air Force base just north of Portsmouth, or traveling about photographing the devastation wrought by German bombing raids. Reluctantly he admitted that her photographs were good, and though he had not expressed his admiration, he did in fact feel a bit proud of her. He rebuked himself silently for never expressing his admiration—but how could he when she constantly avoided him? It wasn't his fault they weren't close. Well, not entirely his fault.

And, he told himself, her proclaimed independence ought to make this all easier. She had stated flatly that she wanted to live her own life. Well, let her. And as part of the bargain, he rationalized, he should be able to live his.

Now Adria stood in front of the desk, taking in his new office, and he guessed she was avoiding meeting his eyes as much as he was avoiding hers. He'd been surprised when she first walked in. Looking less Bohemian and more fashionable, she seemed altogether more mature than when he had last seen her. "Sit down, Adria. You don't have to stand."

She glanced around and perched on the edge of a tapestried chair. "You're looking well," she offered. Then, referring to the officer who had showed her in, "A new assistant?"

"Not by choice," he replied, jumping at the noncontroversial topic. "He was assigned. A Mustang—you know, worked his way up through the ranks. Not an Annapolis boy."

"Does it make a difference?"

"He's a know-it-all. Makes me feel as if I'm being watched." What he didn't say was that his new assistant had a vast store of practical knowledge, and that the man drove him crazy because he was right one hundred percent of the time.

"I'm sure not," Adria replied. "Why would anyone want to watch you?"

"Oh, I didn't mean he actually spies, I just mean he makes me feel that way." Nelson leaned over, looking her in the eye for the first time. "Are you sure you wouldn't like to go out to lunch?"

"I'm sure. I have an appointment at the war office in an hour."

"Trying to get press credentials to travel with the troops?" he guessed. Then he half smiled. "I doubt you'll get them. It's inconvenient for the military to have to provide for women."

"I already have them," Adria replied icily. It pleased her no end that she had gotten her credentials without so much as uttering her father's name. "It's more a question of finding out where I'm going."

Nelson Halstead only grunted. "Heard from your mother?" he ventured.

Adria shook her head. "She's angry with me because I won't come home."

"She's worried about you."

"I can take care of myself."

For once her father didn't disagree. "Well, I asked you to come here because I have something to tell you."

Adria leaned back in the chair and prepared herself for the news that the divorce was final.

"I'm getting married," he said abruptly. "Now that the divorce is final."

Adria sat up straight again and stared at him. "Married?" Unable to hide her feelings, she blurted, "Couldn't you have waited for the ink to dry on the divorce decree?"

"I've been seeing her for some time. Actually, she's a friend of yours."

Adria knew he was talking about Christina, though in all honesty, she hadn't thought Christina would go that far.

"Christina Barton, ex-Senator Barton's daughter. She said you were friends."

"We are acquainted," Adria said coldly. Then she added, "To marry Christina is ridiculous."

"She's a beautiful, mature, and loving woman," he said defensively.

Adria felt tired as well as angry. "She's my age! And as you would say, 'she's a chippie!'" Her father's face grew red and Adria stood up. "How could you?" she asked.

"I'm certain she is a woman who has had some experience," her father retorted. "But she is not a chippie and I resent your tone!"

His voice had taken on that admiral-to-sailor tone Adria knew so well. She bit her lip hard so she wouldn't cry. Then in as low and determined a voice as she could muster she told him, "I don't care what you do. I never want to see you again!"

Her father stood up and started to come around the corner of his desk. "Adria! Snap out of it! It's over between your mother and me and I am going to marry Christina!"

Adria stepped away, feeling as furious as he looked. The hand with which she clutched her purse was almost cramped and her other hand was doubled as she dug her own nails into her palm. Of all the women in the world! "I mean what I say," Adria murmured as she turned and headed for the door.

"Christina is a lot more mature than you are!" he shouted after her.

Adria didn't respond, but she let the door slam shut. She turned to the young officer who had shown her in and swore under her breath. He, to her surprise, didn't bother to suppress a smile. As Adria hurried out into the gray November day images of Christina Barton and her father flooded her thoughts. She forced them away.

She had vowed not to see her father again, and her mother was in faraway America. We weren't much of a family to start with, she thought unhappily. From now on she would stop lamenting the past and concentrate on the future. When the war was over she and Robert would marry and have their own family, a real family, a loving family. Robert's face came into focus and then the tears began to stream down her cheeks. Where was he? Why hadn't she heard from him? They had parted in July and now it was late August.

3

ADRIA READ ANDY MARTIN's telegram, dated August 30th. "Your photos are rocking the American public, Adria! Keep up the good work! P.S. I'm giving you a raise even though you won't find anything to spend it on in North Africa."

Adria looked around her room. She was on the move again, but this time she would be traveling light. In North Africa it would be army issue only.

"Hope you get there before we have to evacuate," the British officer had told her this morning as he handed over an official-looking buff envelope. "Inside you'll find your identification tags. Wear them at all times."

"Tags?" Adria questioned. "Don't the soldiers have only one?"

He smiled. "You get two, one with your name and identification number and the other to identify you as press. There's also a voucher for military transport, another one for accommodation, and a third entitling you to eat on base. You already have your press credentials."

She had nodded and taken the envelope.

"You'll be flying in at night. I should warn you that it's not a comfortable flight and that roughly a third of the night planes are shot down. Dress warmly. There's no heat, no light, and no oxygen on board. We fly low and we pray a lot."

Adria had tried to smile, but she knew he was serious. Tobruk was under siege. The British Eighth Army had its back to the sea and the only way in or out was by cargo plane. The planes flew many missions each night. One or two landed, most simply made drops of needed medical supplies, food, and ammunition. Unconsciously Adria touched her cameras. Danger was part of her work. Fear and exhilaration mixed easily.

Adria jumped as the damnable sirens began to wail. "I ought to be used to them by now," she said aloud. The Germans bombed every night, night after night. Yet life went on in London and, surprisingly, Big Ben, the Houses of Parliament, Buckingham Palace, and most of the city's other famous landmarks were still standing.

She looked around and grabbed her bag and cameras. The bag contained a change of clothes and two changes of underwear as well as a towel, washcloth, soap, comb, and make-up. It was always packed, always ready to go. Wearily, she lifted her tripod. Her load was heavier now because she didn't dare leave any of her cameras in her room, in case the building took a direct hit. Her three Leicas with their interchangeable telephoto, normal, wide-angle lenses, and synchroflash, and her Hassalblad were vital, and because they were German, were now irreplaceable.

Burdened with bag, cameras, tripod, and purse,

Adria extinguished the light and locked the door behind her. "Jerry" was usually spotted over the coast of England and a radio signal alerted London so that the citizenry had fifteen to twenty minutes to reach the shelters before the first bombs began to fall. Adria got to the end of the darkened hall and nearly ran into a young boy at the head of the stairs. He squinted at her in the darkness.

"You wouldn't be Miss Halstead would you?"

"I am, yes."

"Got a message here for you," he said in a clipped cockney accent. He held out a white envelope.

Adria took it and fumbled for some money. "I can't find my change now," she said flustered. "Are you headed for the underground?"

He nodded.

"Here, give me a hand with some of these things and when we're in the shelter, I'll pay you."

"Glad to help, miss."

Adria handed him her tripod and Hassalblad. "Don't drop it," she warned. "It's a camera."

He took it carefully and followed her down the stairs as they both headed for the nearby underground station with streams of others.

Going to the shelters was a nightly ritual, but now that the RAF had begun bombing Berlin the British seemed to feel better. Not that morale had ever been low, Adria thought. From the beginning those who took shelter in the underground sang, told jokes, and mocked the sound of the exploding incendiaries. An experience I'll never forget, she thought.

Along the walls of the deep subway platforms the British had built rows and rows of cots for those who might have to spend the night. Families camped out on blankets, and street vendors sold hot roasted potatoes on sticks just as they had during the day in Oxford Circus.

Adria found a spot near the wall, dropped her bag, and turned to the lad who followed her. "This will be fine," she said, sitting down on her bag. He put down her camera case and tripod and waited while she fished in her purse for ten shillings. "Here," she said, holding it out.

"Thank you, ma'am," he said with a slight bow.

"You can stay here," she offered the space next to her, but he shook his head.

"I've got some friends who always come here," he imparted, "I'll find them."

With that he disappeared into the crowd, and Adria opened the message he had brought.

Lord Charles Wertheim requests the pleasure of your company at 3 P.M. on Thursday, September 1st, at his home.

There followed his exclusive address. Adria's heart skipped a beat. Did he have a message from Robert? What else could the elusive Lord Wertheim want? She smiled to herself. Robert had warned her about Charles. "Not a bit like me," he had said. "Very stiff, very British."

4

USHERED INTO THE BLUE parlor, Adria perched on a satin-covered chair near an intricately carved antique coffee table. Before her host's appearance, a silent butler brought in an ornate silver tea set, Spode cups and saucers, and a plate filled with scones.

Then, as if on cue, Lord Wertheim appeared in a somber dark suit and tie. If I were to guess this man's profession, I would say he was a banker, Adria said to herself. He had that ultra-conservative demeanor bankers seemed to cultivate. In contrast to the slightly ruddy complexion of most Londoners, Charles Wertheim's skin was pallid, a testament to the inordinate time he spent indoors. He wore gold-rimmed glasses that slipped to mid-nose, and his thinning hair was artfully combed to conceal his growing bald spot. On the whole he looked older than Adria knew him to be. She smiled at him and thought that Robert was quite right. She would never have guessed they were brothers.

"Miss Halstead," Lord Charles extended his hand, took hers and kissed it perfunctorily. He eyed her silently, apparently taking her measure.

Adria wore her heather gray silk suit and beneath it a paisley blouse in hues of subdued green. Her tam was the same green, as were her shoes, purse, and gloves. Her hair fell to her shoulders in a smooth page boy. "Lord Wertheim," she acknowledged.

He cleared his throat and took a seat opposite her on the sofa. He poured two cups of the steaming tea. "You don't look quite as I expected," he allowed.

"And what did you expect?"

"Of a lady photographer? A news person? I'm not sure, really. Someone garish I suspect, perhaps bohemian. Or mannish. After all, you do compete in a man's world and I shouldn't think your profession the most feminine of occupations."

"It's not, but one dresses for the occasion." She met his brown eyes honestly. He certainly seemed the snob that Robert had good-naturedly described and even, in one lighthearted moment, had imitated. Nonetheless, Adria didn't want to alienate him. He was a link with Robert, and though she feigned calm she prayed that was why he had invited her.

Charles leaned back and sipped his tea slowly. "I know very little about you, Miss Halstead. I know you were allowed to photograph my brother and mother—a little over a year and a half ago, was it?"

"November 1939," Adria confirmed.

"And you sold the photos?"

He placed a rather nasty intonation on the word "sold." Adria nodded. "With their permission."

"Personally, I would consider such a thing an invasion of privacy."

Although she sensed Lord Wertheim had little sense

of humor, if any, she couldn't help smiling. "You're privacy is safe. I have no hidden cameras."

He grunted. "I also know you delivered some valuable information to British intelligence when you arrived from France in July, some special photos taken in Paris. I know that because I work for British intelligence."

That Charles Wertheim worked for British intelligence came as a surprise, but she did not reveal it. Had she known she would have contacted him immediately. Adria leaned forward and set her cup down. "Have you heard from Robert?" she asked, knowing she sounded anxious.

Charles nodded. "I've been told to tell you he's fine. He asked me to get in touch with you personally and to tell you that for the next few months communications will be impossible. I'm afraid I can't elaborate on that."

Adria leaned back, relief flowing through her veins. "I worry about him so. I worry he will be caught—and he is Jewish."

"I can put your mind at ease on that score. He has the identity of a non-Jew, a member of the Resistance who was killed some months ago."

Adria nodded and again picked up her teacup. "Thank you for telling me."

"I was afraid you and my brother might have more than a friendly relationship. Of course as soon as I saw you, I knew I was right."

Adria ignored his comment. Doubtless he would have preferred to choose his own sister-in-law. Not that it had come to that yet, but she knew it would if Robert survived. "And your mother? Is Madame Wertheim safe?"

Charles audibly sighed. "My mother is a very stubborn woman. But she is quite safe as long as she stays in the south of France. Naturally I would prefer to have her here."

"I'm sure that would be better."

"You do seem to have some curiosity about my

family, young woman. Tell me—what is your relationship with my brother?"

Adria frowned at him. He was a snob and he was also much too curious. "It's personal," she answered coolly, "and it will stay that way."

"I see. Well, I should warn you that Robert is a bit of a womanizer."

Adria drained her teacup. She didn't want to listen to any stories about Robert now that she knew he was all right. "I must be going, and thank you again." She paused and opened her bag, withdrawing a scrap of paper and a pencil. On it she scribbled an address. "In a few days I'll be moving out with the Commonwealth troops," she told him. "Please, if you have other messages—anything—from Robert, please let me know."

Charles Wertheim accepted the paper and nodded his agreement. "Shall I have a cab come round or can Simpson drive you somewhere?"

"I'll walk."

"It's a long way across the park."

Adria laughed. "I come from Boston. It's a city meant for walking, so I'm quite used to it."

"An old New England family?"

Adria shook her head and her auburn hair swirled. "Lace curtain Irish, I'm afraid."

Charles Wertheim didn't respond.

5

PARIS WAS KNOWN FOR its gaity, Marseille for its earthiness, and Lyon, France's third city, was famous for its sober and solid qualities, Robert mused. Located in the east central part of the country at the confluence of the Rhone and Saône rivers, its appearance and reputation for conservatism would hardly seem to make it the ideal place for the headquarters of an underground war.

Not ideal, but logical. A large city with an abundance of meeting and hiding places, it was industrialized and coming to play a large role in the manufacture of German war weapons. It was just south of the demarcation line, which meant it was not occupied. And most important, Lyon was the hub of all principal rail lines and national highways. Information could easily be both gathered and disseminated.

On the other hand, the SS was active and the city teemed with German informers. The French citizenry of Lyon fell into three categories: those who actively opposed the Germans, those who would neither hinder nor support the underground, and those who were pro-German Fascists. 1940 had been the year of organization with Robert working to establish links to various resistance groups. Now the time for real action was at hand. The Resistance would have to see to it that much of the equipment the Germans were ordering from Lyon factories never reached the front.

All Resistance groups shared three objectives. The first was to publish in order to warn the French against collaboration, to make clear the lies of the Germans and the Vichy Government, and to inform the populace of the progress of the war. The second objective was to aid Britain and the Free French by helping downed pilots escape and by gathering intelligence information. The third objective was sabotage and the actual training of assault troops. As the resistance groups increased their activities, the British-directed networks specializing in espionage also grew.

Publishing came easily to the French, and all groups were now successfully printing and delivering information. Later, people would probably say this was not heroic, Robert thought, but those people would not understand living under the Germans. Children were shot for posting illegal papers, presses were destroyed and their owners tortured and killed. In truth, the penalty for publishing was the same as that for sabotage. Death.

As an Agent for the British SOE (Special Operations Executive) in Lyon, Robert's initial task was to liaison with any group wishing help. Now his role had been expanded. Over the past few months he had arranged for parachute drops containing a variety of new weapons including the new plastic explosive, incendiary pencils, time fuses, detonators, and small bombs. In addition, he made himself available to the most promising of his resistance groups to help plan and actually carry out missions.

Robert stared into his glass of red wine, then looked across the café to the small table in the corner. He smiled to himself. The man was twenty-three or twenty-four, with thick brown hair, round eyes, and an engaging smile. His name was Jean-Pierre Frenay and he was a telephone line-checker. The girl was known to him only as Claudia, and she was with one of the Resistance groups. She was not Jean-Pierre's lover yet, but she was in the process of recruiting him and seemed to find the task enjoyable. Perfect—Jean-Pierre was absolutely perfect. A line-checker could monitor the German telephone lines and obtain information regarding men and arms movements, which could be quickly relayed to sabotage units. For weeks now Robert had been concentrating on the recruitment of dozens of engineers and technicians, men who worked in the highly developed industries of Lyon who could, by virtue of their expertise and positions, help form elite sabotage teams. Up till now his recruits had kept themselves to simple tasks like putting a handful of sand in the gearbox of a German truck, but soon more SOE personnel would be arriving from England and larger and more dangerous plots would be hatched.

Jean-Pierre stood up, leaned over, and kissed Claudia on the cheek. She remained at the table and watched him as he left.

Robert unfolded his newspaper and pretended to read it. Claudia was magnificent, one of the most dedicated members of the Resistance. He thought for a moment about how the French women were distinguishing themselves. In fact, the largest of the Resistance groups, The Alliance, was run by a woman, Marie-Madeleine Fourcade, the beautiful and highly intelligent executive editor of a publishing house. And of course there was Celeste, his own half-sister. She worked tirelessly and handed over a good deal of information in spite of the personal danger.

Without haste he finished his wine and saw Claudia light a cigarette. He smiled at the signal that she wanted to talk with him and he got up and headed the few blocks to the cheese shop. One group met in a shop called La Lingerie Pratique, but since he was in love, he preferred the cheese shop where the decor was considerably less suggestive.

He opened the door and was greeted by the pungent smell of Roquefort as well as by the round-faced proprietor. "Ah, my best customer! I have a fine ripe cheese for you in the back!"

Robert laughed. "I think I can smell it from here." He sat down at a wooden table in the back of the shop. In a few minutes he was joined by Claudia.

"I expected to find you sampling the merchandise and sampling something from André's private cellar."

"I'm quite full from my lunch," Robert replied. "How's your young man?"

"Anxious to help us." She smiled. "He hates the Germans and he is quite aware of the advantages his work offers. Should I bring him to a meeting?"

Robert shook his head. "It's too soon, no matter how sure you are of him."

"He says he has important information now, Robert."

Robert considered her words for a moment, "Then I will meet with him alone," he decided. "You arrange it."

Claudia nodded.

Chapter Twelve

1

FROM HIS VANTAGE POINT on the hill Robert could just make out the four figures as they climbed the railway embankment, Paul the shortest and Raymond the tallest. Of average height, Luc and Henri were engineers, while the other two were mechanics. This was the second and most ambitious mission together for his four most skilled recruits. Like Robert, they all wore black and their faces were covered with soot. In a few moments, when Robert was certain no one followed, he would join them on the embankment to help string the long cord leading to the detonator.

Not the most perfect night, he acknowledged silently. Robert had sent Luc out during the day to check on the location—a bend in the railway track with woods on one side and tall grass and a hill on the other. It checked out with Jean-Pierre's description, as did the train schedule. It was announced that the regular train would be delayed by several hours, implicitly confirming that the way was being cleared for a special train.

Robert shook his hand to relieve his tension, again, scanning the tracks. Sometimes he fantasized about the ideal night for sabotage—it would be windy so the sound of steps could not be heard, it would be near winter when the fall leaves no longer rustled when stepped on, and it would be overcast, with no moon and no stars. Real luck would bring a low-lying fog. He cursed silently the bright moon, two-thirds full. And here, some seventy miles from Lyon, the stars were not obscured by city lights nor a single cloud. On the ground the newly fallen September leaves were brittle. Robert smiled to himself as he thought of the works of James Fenimore Cooper, boyhood reading, in which the snapping twig was the sign of an unwanted presence. But tonight's activity was not a boy's adventure.

This mission could be a real coup for us, Robert thought. The target was a twelve-car arms and munitions train headed for Brest, where rumor had it that the Germans were stockpiling equipment for an invasion of England.

Robert strained his eyes and saw that the team was in place. Directly opposite him Luc and Henri were setting the four explosives, two for each rail, just into the curve so the train would not have time to stop. Paul and Raymond were fifty yards on either side of Robert, acting as sentries and placing two additional charges on the rails. The explosives would be detonated by hand from the woods where Robert now stood. The third set of explosives was set as back-up in case of a poor connection. Robert ruled out a time set device because he could not count on the train being on schedule; more important, they had to make certain it was the right train.

"There will be no passenger cars," Jean-Pierre had told him. "And the Germans will place guard units along the track every three miles. You have only to pick a spot between them." That very afternoon Jean-Pierre had contacted him again with the location of three of the guard units, making it possible for Robert to select just the right spot.

Robert took one more look around. There was no sign of life in any direction and no sounds behind him in the woods. Stealthily he emerged from the woods and ran to reach the steep embankment. Again he stopped. There was nothing. He climbed the embankment. On the other side there were no woods, only fields of tall grass. He frowned and wished the grass were not so tall. Why didn't he hear the crickets?

Luc and Henri already had their packet unwrapped. Robert crouched down. "You know what to do," he said.

They nodded, and Robert ran in a crouched position down the track toward Raymond. Raymond was a novice with this type of explosive. He reached Raymond and crouched beside him. Novice or not, the young man worked expertly. The device was attached and he was placing the detonator cap in the explosive. Robert handed him the wires to put in place and took a large role of wire from his knapsack. "Let's go," Robert hissed, running back toward Luc and Henry where the final connection would be made. Robert whistled a signal to Paul.

A shadow and a sudden answer to a half-asked question: it was too quiet! There were no crickets because there were people! "Run for it!" Robert shouted even though he knew it was too late.

Paul groaned and suddenly the whole area was illuminated by a blinding searchlight hidden in the tall grass.

Robert fell flat and rolled as machine gun fire followed his spotlit body into the darkness. He loosened his Tommy gun from its sling and fired toward the light, which had now found his fleeing companions. Spurts of machine gun fire filled the night air, and Robert fired again toward the damnable light until it exploded in a burst of sparks like a firecracker. His companions were now returning fire as well.

Robert forced himself to wait despite the footsteps approaching him, praying the four would make it through the woods and to the road beyond. His job was to cover them, to make certain they had that chance.

In the moonlight Robert saw movement in the grass to one side of where the light had been. "Shit!" escaped his lips. German soldiers, weapons in hand, swarmed out to the grass like locusts. And there was noise behind him! Turning his head he saw more soldiers coming out of the woods, but they emerged farther to the left of where his companions had run.

The soldiers shouted at him in German to drop his gun, but he fired instead at the outlines of those he could see in the light of the moon. All three figures dropped, but they continued firing. He half ran, half slid down the embankment towards the woods where his team had fled across a bit of a gulley between the railway tracks and the trees. As he ran forward, something latched onto his legs. Robert had that trapped feeling as he whipped around and swung his gun butt at his assailant, then flipped the weapon around and fired a final burst as he ran out of ammunition. He dragged himself forward.

"Over here!" A soldier yelled in German.

"Take him alive!" someone ordered.

Robert's fist doubled as he swung wildly—to no avail. Four soldiers had thrown themselves on him and his gun had fallen from his hands. There was a swift, hard kick in the ribs and wild punches to his body. Instinctively he covered his face and head, pulling his knees up into his stomach to protect himself. His mind raced ahead to the consequences of his capture. He should have turned the gun on himself. His last thought before losing consciousness was incoherent and silly—there had been no snapping of twigs.

2

ADRIA STARED INTO HER coffee and blew gently to cool it. She had learned the hard way not to pick up steaming coffee in a tin mug. Not that the contents of the mug could truly be called coffee. The British didn't make good coffee under the best of conditions and under the worst it became little more than acrid brown water with the requisite amount of caffeine. It was a poor substitute for the strong black American brew offered by the U.S. Navy. Not that the coffee in the canteen was uniformly as disgusting as it was today. On some schedule no one had succeeded in figuring out, the mess cooks were rotated. When Paul Tremblay, the French Canadian, was on duty the coffee was not only palatable, but delicious. He made it strong and added chicory for flavor.

The canteen was crowded with men of all ages, and Adria listened intently to the varied accents and languages of the Empire and the Commonwealth, marveling at the distinct sound of even the English speakers. Near the bar five Australians drank warm beer and talked loudly of their displeasure. They wanted to be home to protect their country from the growing Japanese threat. They resented fighting the Germans in this Godforsaken desert and their views were shared by the New Zealanders, who grimly predicted that soon the Empire and the Commonwealth would be fighting on two fronts. The Canadians had no such fears. Like the Americans, who still refused to enter this "foreign war," they felt protected by the oceans that separated them from Europe on one side and Japan on the other. Still, like the Aussies and the New Zealanders they had answered the call of Great Britain. There were Welshmen and Scots as well, and their accents mixed with those of London, Liverpool, and the Midlands. In addition to those who spoke English, there were Sikhs, Gurkhas, and Goans. No matter what their origins, all the men showed both humor and depression as the days passed slowly by.

Small wonder, Adria thought. Tobruk seemed like the last jumping-off place, a corner of the African continent with its natural colors stripped and stored away. Everything, she lamented, was the color of the coffee: the desert uniforms, the buildings, the desert itself, the tanks, guns, and planes—even the clothing of the local people. Sometimes she wondered if they had stored their long, colorful kaftans away, exchanging them for flowing robes of brown stripes and solid blacks. The occasional trader appeared from out of the desert, his evasion of the enemy lines a mystery, wearing the spotless white of the Moslem men of Mali. Beneath his turban a jet black smiling face offered hard-to-get items. Few such visitors stayed, but if they did their costumes turned brown within a few days. More often the desert people simply disappeared, magically making their way back from whence they had come. For five thousand years or more, in war and in peace, the traders had followed the old caravan trails. Governments came and went, but in the desert, she learned, the traders were eternal.

Unconsciously, she reached down and touched her

own coffee-colored fatigues. Men's clothes, they were the only practical garb. Her long hair was tied back to keep it off her neck in the heat of the day, and her skin, she lamented, was dry from the desert winds. She had used her only jar of *Ponds* the first week in Tobruk, and now at night she used simple vaseline. "And when that's gone, dearie, you can use crankcase oil—good camouflage, too," the Aussie quartermaster had told her cheerfully.

Adria felt a funny wave of apprehension, a second of *déjà vu,* and then from behind a large, friendly hand grasped her slender shoulder.

"Adria, baby! Am I glad to see you! I heard you were here."

She looked up into the square-jawed face of Jeff Borden. He too was dressed in brown, his cameras dangling from his neck and his grin as wide as ever. He leaned over her, his shirt open, beads of perspiration on his brow and upper lip, seeming bigger than she remembered him. "I'm not glad to see you," she replied icily. "And don't call me 'baby,'" she added with irritation. Of course, that was the way all male reporters talked. Women were all 'baby,' 'chickie,' or 'tomato.' She'd take that from others, but she wouldn't put up with it from Jeff.

Unperturbed, he slipped into the chair next to her. "Being the only woman here I thought for sure you'd be mobbed." He grinned again, slapped the table, and ordered a beer from the stony-faced Libyan waiter. "There are other women," she informed him. "Nurses, women army officers, and women in the city."

Jeff laughed. "The ones in the city are either an invitation to syphilis or to the possibility of an Arab knife in your back. The Arabs don't like their women messed with."

"I didn't know you were so well informed on the mores of Arab life," she said sarcastically.

He ignored her. "I get around."

"I can't disagree with that." Adria pushed her chair back, but Jeff put his hand on hers. "Don't go," he asked. "Come on, Adria. This is a small place, you can't avoid me."

"I can try."

"Let's talk about it. Look, Adria, you never understood me."

Adria looked into his clear eyes, resisting their little-boy appeal. "I understood that we had something —or at least I thought we did. I understood that you began an affair with that German girl just to ace out assignments. Jeff, you're a conniving opportunist, you always will be," she said bitterly. There was so much more she couldn't say. This was hardly the time or the place, and in any case, she wondered if even she wanted to open old wounds. Why tell him about the baby when she herself had almost forgotten the pain?

Jeff didn't blink or flush. His fist doubled and he hit the table, though not with the force of temper. "Damn right, Adria. But you're wrong, if you think my sex with her was like my sex with you. And you and I did have something, as you put it. But make no mistake, if the opportunity was there and it was the only way I could get the pictures, I'd do it again."

"Well, I don't want a relationship on those terms."

"Like your mother aren't you? A nineteenth-century romantic. You want declarations of love and undying loyalty."

"I've been through too much to be a romantic, Jeff. My career is all-important to me right now and I'm not being sidetracked anymore," she answered firmly.

"Precisely, Adria. That's the way I feel about my career."

Adria didn't look at Jeff, but she felt relieved that she didn't love him anymore. If she had an obsession besides her work, it was her love for Robert Wertheim. But those memories and hopes were sacred, and there was no need for Jeff to know about him. In any case he would have called it a "one-night stand" and told her she was crazy.

"You look far away," Jeff said.

"I suppose I am," she admitted.

"Adria, we're here together and we're going to be covering the same ground. I'm not asking you to screw around, but I am asking you to be my friend. It would make life easier."

She half smiled. "You have such a genteel way with words," she replied.

"These aren't genteel circumstances. How about it, you going to be my drinking partner once in a while? My confidante? Listen, there's a real shortage of development space and chemicals. I'm willing to share."

Adria nodded slowly. "All right," she agreed, then warned, "But don't start, Jeff. Friends. That's it."

He grinned and quaffed down his beer. "Okay, friends."

3

SECTION IV GESTAPO AND Intelligence Headquarters in Lyon was located in a recently refurbished building that had once held the city jail. A stone building surrounded by high stone walls, it was virtually soundproof.

Robert was rudely brought to consciousness by ice-cold water and repeated slaps to his face. He blinked open swollen eyes to find himself naked and tied to a straight backed chair in front of a Gestapo officer. The man was standing, his thick arms behind him, his fingers grasping a traditional riding crop. Robert did not turn his head, but he sensed there were guards behind him, probably by the door.

"Poulet. Poulet is the name on your identity papers. But that is not your name is it?" The officer leaned over, his cold, dark eyes and loose jowls close.

"It is what my papers say. It is my name." Robert answered.

The riding crop came down on the desk and with a loud slap hit a pile of neatly stacked papers. The fat fist that was doubled around it revealed a heavy gold signet ring.

I must remember everything, Robert thought. I must

220

remember the room, where they take me, what they look like. He forced the fear of pain out of his mind and concentrated on committing the officer's face to memory.

The officer pressed his lips together and moved out from behind his desk. He wore jackboots and he was as heavy from the waist down as from the waist up. Suddenly the riding crop was raised and brought down with incredible force on Robert's naked thighs. He jumped with the stinging pain.

"A mere taste of what will come if you don't cooperate. We'll take you that close to death," he held up his thumb and forefinger to indicate a millimeter or two. "Then we'll let you heal and then we will start again. You'll scream to be killed, to be put out of your misery. You'll beg us to shoot you."

Robert avoided the man's eyes and wondered if he looked frightened. He didn't for a moment doubt that the threats would be carried out, but he also knew that fear could make reality worse and that the Germans used fear well. They worked on the mind as well as on the body. "I am Poulet," he repeated.

Again the riding crop was brought down and this time it struck the welt from the first strike. A thin line of blood appeared. I feel more vulnerable because I am naked, Robert thought.

"You're English!" the German officer suddenly proclaimed. "You're an English spy."

Robert wanted to ask the officer what had brought him to that conclusion. With a shiver he wondered about the others. Had they gotten away? He shook his head as if to clear it. They had fallen into a trap—that much he knew. One of his sabotage team, Claudia or Jean-Pierre, was a traitor to the French cause. Of the six people who knew of the mission, only five knew he was English and worked for SOE. Jean-Pierre did not know. He could thank heaven that no one knew he was Jewish, or he would have been immediately transferred to Germany for interrogation. Vaguely he wondered if being English would offer any protection. When the trap was sprung they seemed to have singled him out; of course the traitor would have told them he was the leader.

The German officer took a step closer to him and leaned over. With his fat fist he grabbed Robert's penis and squeezed it hard. Robert winced. "You're circumcised!" The German shouted. "You're English! All the English are circumcised!"

Under other circumstances Robert might have smiled. The German had looked into his blue eyes and noted his sandy hair. He didn't fit the well-publicized German stereotype of a Jew, who would also have been circumcised.

"So I'm English," Robert admitted as he changed easily to his mother tongue.

"And there are more of you in Lyon!" The German officer's voice rose to a crescendo.

Robert didn't answer.

"Take him to the courtyard!"

The two guards appeared in his peripheral vision, untied his hands, and pulled him roughly to his feet. Both over six feet and heavy-set, they marched him out of the room and down a long corridor. The German officer followed, his heels clicking on the floor.

They pushed him into the dusty courtyard and Robert shivered. It was late September and cold enough that he could see his own breath. Goose pimples broke out on his naked body. The German officer blew his whistle and shouted in German for the prisoners. Through a doorway on the other side of the courtyard, five people were pushed and prodded into the open and made to stand against a far wall.

Robert stared at them, his mouth dry. Jean-Pierre could hardly stand. His body was criss-crossed with whip lashes, his hair was tangled with blood clots, and his face was swollen and battered. Claudia, once lovely, had in twenty-four hours been completely transformed, her hair cropped, and face swollen almost beyond

222

recognition. She was nude, and sought vainly to cover herself with trembling hands. God knew what she had been subjected to. Raymond, Henri, and Paul were also beaten and limping. Paul was the worst, he had to be helped by the other two who staggered themselves. Robert felt suddenly like crying. Luc was not there, his absence confirmed Robert's suspicions about the traitor. Oh, they would say he escaped, but Robert knew the trap had been too well planned, too perfectly sprung.

From the other side of the courtyard a detail of German soldiers appeared and took up firing positions opposite the wall.

"You might save their lives," the German officer suggested as he prodded Robert in the ribs.

The lie that would haunt him fell from his lips, but it was a lie they too would have told, in fact had vowed to tell. "I don't know these people," Robert said.

The German officer smiled for the first time. His teeth were yellow from chewing tobacco. "The girl is young—perhaps used, but still young. Surely you would like to save her life?"

Used. There was no doubt in his mind. The pain in her face, the way she had moved, indicated that she'd been sexually attacked. "I don't know these people," Robert repeated.

The German officer gave the signal and the sound of the guns reverberated off the four walls of the courtyard. Robert winced as the twisted bodies of his comrades crumpled like rag dolls to the ground.

The German officer narrowed his eyes. "We'll find out what we want to know," he said evenly. "And you will wish you had been against that wall with your friends."

4

IN NEW ENGLAND THE rolling hills of the Berkshires would be alive with the fall colors of red, gold, and russet. Children would be preparing for Halloween and the mornings would be frosty and clear, the days bright, the evening crisp and cold. But here in Tobruk the temperature varied little, the scenery even less.

Adria walked along the path that wound around the barracks and led eventually to the headquarters of the British Eighth Army. "What is it?" she asked herself. What had been plaguing her for the past month? She felt nervous and apprehensive, as well as lonely. Every morning she woke up with her stomach churning and her body stiff from lying in one position too long. She silently admitted to herself that she had a feeling of doom, a feeling that something had happened she did not know about. Absurd, she chastised herself. It was simply not knowing, the lack of letters.

She reached the quite ordinary building that served as headquarters and pushed through the screen door and into the outer office. In all four corners of the room clerks typed busily, and overhead a ceiling fan turned slowly.

"Can I help you, Ma'am?" A young officer snapped to attention and looked at her expectantly.

"I'm Adria Halstead, I was told to come in."

"Ah, yes. Just a moment."

He disappeared into another office off the main room, then re-emerged and beckoned to her. "Second Lt. Marshall will see you now."

What bit of army red tape was it now, she asked herself. Probably they'd tell her that the chemicals she requisitioned for the dark room wouldn't arrive for another month. She shrugged and followed the young man.

Lieutenant Marshall stood up and bowed slightly. "Lt. Marshall, Army Intelligence, Miss Halstead."

Army Intelligence? The introduction almost made her smile. Her father always said that Army Intelligence was a contradiction in terms. "Have I done something wrong?" she asked.

"Not at all, not at all. I have a message for you, but I'm afraid it has to be read here and destroyed. Security, you know."

Adria reached out toward the manila envelope. She opened it eagerly and quickly perused the neatly typed letter.

My Dear Miss Halstead:

It is my unhappy duty to notify you that my brother Robert was taken prisoner by the Germans sometime in mid-September. Our sources are now trying to confirm his condition and whereabouts. Rest assured that every effort will be made to free him.

Sincerely,
Charles Wertheim

P.S. This message is to remain entirely confidential, so it is being sent via Army Intelligence with orders to destroy it after reading. Thank you for your cooperation.

Adria reread the short letter twice and her hand trembled. Robert was a prisoner? The Germans would torture him, kill him!

"Are you all right Miss Halstead?"

The young lieutenant had walked to her side and taken her arm. "You look quite pale," he observed.

Why was Charles letter so formal and so uncaring? She felt like screaming. Robert! My God what will they do to him? Black thoughts crossed her mind, horrible thoughts, and she began shaking.

"You'd better sit down. I'm sorry, I'll have to take this now."

For a second Adria grasped the letter as if it were from Robert himself, then let it slip through her fingers as tears filled her eyes.

"Let me call a nurse," the lieutenant offered.

Adria suddenly turned on him, "Aren't there enough dead and dying for them to care for?" Her tears were flowing freely now and she began to back toward the door.

"Miss Halstead." There was pleading in his voice, but he had no gift for command.

"I'm all right," she said twice. "Leave me alone, I'll be all right."

5

FOR THREE WEEKS, NIGHT and day blended into one for Robert Wertheim. The terror of anticipation was replaced by the reality of pain and alternately he had prayed for the relief of death and the hope of life. Then they had put him in a small, dark cell and left him to remember the agony.

The knotted leather whip had always swished before he felt the searing pain across his flesh. For days he felt the dampness of the blood as it gushed from the half-healed wound on his left cheek. Throughout he had always tried to keep his eyes closed and his body loose, tried to force himself into unconsciousness, and always prayed for relief from pain, from the reality of the continuing torture.

"Enough for today," he remembered hearing the commandant shout. "He's no good to us that way. Perhaps some time in solitary confinement will loosen his tongue."

Strong arms had lifted him roughly and he had been dragged unresisting along the corridor. Rather than back to the cell with the others, he was cast into darkness on a stone floor. He recalled the door slamming and the bolt being shot. Then and only then had he opened his eyes and pulled himself up to tend the gushing wound on his face and explore his dark surroundings with cautious, tactile probings.

He had ripped a portion of his already tattered shirt and pressed it to his swollen face, vowing to hold it in place as long as possible. Then he had moved about slowly, mentally measuring his new environment. Eight feet long, four feet wide, and four feet high, he had calculated—a cement coffin of generous proportions. He had found a bucket of water by the door, a drain in the center of the floor, and a single threadbare blanket to shield him against the dampness and the cold.

That had been twelve days ago, and it was as utterly dark and soundless now as on the first day. He leaned back against the wall and touched his cheek, which now bore a rough scab. He wondered why they hadn't killed him. It could only be because he had confessed to being British and they had believed him, keeping him alive in hopes of finding out more about the activities of British intelligence. Or perhaps they had given up and retained him only for exchange purposes.

Had he held on long enough? He had told the Germans nothing. Only he knew that a party of highly trained top secret British agents was landing to assist the underground in their sabotage missions. Only he knew where and when; what day was it? How long had he been held and tortured? How long had he been unconscious after those first few days of beatings? He smiled; by all reckoning the team had landed and had by this time dispersed. Even if they tortured him again, nothing he might tell them would make any difference, except of course his identity. They must not discover who I am, he thought. They would have heard of Charles, and might try to make use of him in some way.

He closed his eyes even though the cell was dark. He had welcomed the solitary confinement because when he was with others he had lived in fear that someone who knew him would be taken and, under torture, identify him. His fellow saboteurs—even the traitor Luc—knew him only by his French identity. But there were others who knew his real identity, those who might even recognize him accidently because they had done business before the war. He could also be grateful that he was held by the SS. They were the bully boys, the men who carried out inhuman tasks but were not as well trained or as thorough as the Abwehr, the German intelligence unit headed by Admiral Canaris. Canaris was rumored to be anti-Nazi, but his men were highly respected and incredibly efficient at gathering foreign intelligence.

Robert spread the thin blanket out on the cement floor and lay on it, then pulled the other half over himself. With his free arm under his head for a pillow, he sought sleep and dreams of Adria. In the dark dampness of this world only his memories and his hopes for the future would keep him sane.

Like a recording, he again heard Adria's soft voice reciting his favorite verse.

Ah, love, let us be true
To one another! for the world, which seems
To lie before us like a land of dreams,
So various, so beautiful, so new,
Hath really neither joy, nor love, nor light,
Nor certitude, nor peace, nor help for pain;
And we are here as on a darkling plain
Swept with confused alarms of struggle and flight,
Where ignorant armies clash by night.

Adria's voice had been low and sad as she recited the last lines of "Dover Beach," and Robert remembered the mist in her beautiful sea green eyes. "You looked it up," he had said, taking her into his arms. It was the poem he had asked her if she knew when they had been traveling to Barcelona.

228

"Yes, I looked it up," she had answered softly as she leaned against him.

Closing his eyes now, he could almost feel the softness of her hair with his fingertips, and if he concentrated, he could feel her sleeping beside him, the quiet rhythm of her breathing in his ear. He inhaled the dampness of his cell and smelled the sea, he touched the coarse blanket and remembered the softness of her breasts . . . "I will live," he vowed.

His vow brought back the face and words of Ben El Lazar, the hardened Zionist who had helped him smuggle Jews into Palestine. "You are an adventurer," Lazar had once told him, "but you have not yet faced yourself because you've not really come face to face with death."

Robert rolled on his side. "I have now," he thought.

6

ADRIA SCRIBBLED THE DATE on her roll of film and realized she had been in Tobruk for three months. "December 1, 1941." she said, shaking her head. "I hope we're not here for Christmas."

"You should go back to England," Jeff warned.

"Is it safer in London with raids every night?"

He continued to preach. "Sure you look cute as hell in your army fatigues, but Adria, you don't belong here. Soon we're going to be eating dust morning, noon, and night. This isn't the Ritz," he said with an expansive wave around their hotel bar, "but when we break out we're going to be bunking in hovels. Somehow I don't think you're equipped to sleep in a trench and eat hardtack."

"You forget—I've survived a Spanish prison, and you're not goading me into returning to England," she retorted.

He shrugged and muttered, "Don't say I didn't warn you."

"You've warned me endlessly."

"Well, if you insist on staying, you ought to learn how to use your camera under fire."

"What do you mean by that? I've been at the front every day."

"I mean you're too slow and you're liable to get your head blown off like Mike Simpson. Poor son-of-a-bitch never learned to shoot on his back or roll with his camera."

Adria looked into his eyes. This was how he had been while training her in New York. Always disparaging, but always trying to get her to improve. "Would you care to give me a demonstration?"

"Sure, we'll go outside, down by that old line of trenches."

She followed him out of the hotel and down the dusty streets to the outskirts of town. The real fighting front was now two miles away, and this area had been prepared for a last stand if necessary.

"Now don't go and waste real film while you're practicing," Jeff said as she started examining her cameras.

"How will I know if I'm doing it right if I don't use real film?"

"You can use it in a few days. In the meantime I'll watch you. I'll know if your hand is shaking. Now look, first I'm going to demonstrate the roll. You have to shoot, drop, and roll fast. It's important for you to roll correctly so you don't hurt yourself or damage the camera. Now, look. Wrap your camera strap around your wrist and hold your camera in your left hand tightly. Take your shot, drop down on your right knee and turn your right shoulder forward. Next, extend your right arm. Think of a ball, Adria. Your arm must be round. Now turn your head toward the left shoulder. Your left hand with the camera drops down in front. You protect it with your forearm if necessary. Your left leg folds under so you can come up in a crouched position. You must commit yourself to the roll. Now watch carefully."

Adria watched Jeff as he took her picture and quickly

dropped down and rolled over like a ball and came up
into a crouched position. Then, to show off, he did it
backward. Adria laughed. "I'm impressed, now help
me try."

"Okay, use this rock in place of your camera, just in
case. Now get down on your right knee. Remember to
extend those arms and make them unbendable."

"Like this?" Adria asked as she let Jeff position her
body.

"Yes, that's it, now lean forward and push with the
left foot. Go!"

Adria felt the hard ground ripple across her back and
saw the sky pass over head as she came to the position
she started in. "Damn it," she cursed. "I'm leaning on
the rock!"

"Better that than your camera. Your balance needs a
little work; otherwise it was a good roll. Try again. I
think you've got the feel of it."

Determined, Adria turned and rolled again, this time
without leaning on the rock. "It doesn't hurt as much as
I thought it might. Just a lot of little bumps going across
my back."

"You'll get used to it."

"Here, let me try it with my camera."

"Not on your life. You practice for a while longer and
you come back and practice tomorrow and the next
day. When that roll is second nature, then you try with
your camera."

She started to argue, but realized Jeff was right. He
had been her teacher, and she welcomed him back in
that role.

7

MADAME WERTHEIM WAS DRESSED smartly in a russet
wool suit. She had discarded the idea of wearing her
sable coat to protect her from the sharp December
winds, and instead chose a wool camel's hair coat and
low-heeled walking shoes. A broad-brimmed hat that
matched her suit tilted fashionably as she walked along,

exploring with interest, slowing now and again to catch her own image in shop windows.

Never, she thought, had she actually walked the streets of Paris, free of chauffeurs, maids, or chaperones. So despite the strutting German officers on every corner, her freedom to stop in front of boutiques and dawdle at will was new and enjoyable.

She halted in front of the old building on the Rue Madelaine and consulted the scrap of paper on which she had written the address. She sighed, pushed open the door, and prepared herself for the climb to the third floor.

Outside the door numbered seven she paused to catch her breath and reaffirm her reasons for this visit. First there was Robert. She hadn't heard from him in months and she was frankly worried. Second, the time to heal old wounds was at hand. She inhaled and knocked firmly, even though her heart fluttered slightly. What would this girl be like? Would she be friendly? Perhaps bitter?

The exquisite creature who opened the door both surprised and delighted her. Small and petite, she had an angular face with dark brows and almond-shaped dark eyes. Her hair was short and curly, and Madame noted that her legs were slender and well shaped, the hallmark of a dancer.

Of course she *was* garishly dressed, in a black sequined top and a shortish black and silver striped skirt that hugged her hips. Her shoes were spike heeled, and her stockings sheer and black. Doubtless, Madame thought, this was her costume since she performed in a cabaret.

The magnificent almond eyes—Abraham's eyes—peered suspiciously at her from beneath the dark brows. "May I help you, Madame?" she asked in a throaty voice.

"Celeste?" Madame questioned, though in her mind there was no doubt.

The girl nodded.

"I'm Anna Wertheim. May I come in?"

Celeste's full lips parted. "Madame . . ." she sounded surprised, perhaps stunned. She opened the door wide and beckoned her in, hastily clearing a chair in the cluttered room. "It's a mess. Oh, I'm so sorry. Here, sit down, please. I will make us some coffee, or would you prefer tea?"

Madame Wertheim sat down and smiled. "Please don't bother, it is quite all right. I should have called I suppose, but I only had the address and the phones are so unreliable these days." She emphasized the words "these days." It was how everyone referred to the Nazi occupation.

Celeste paused and looked at her in silent appraisal. Then, like a worried bird, she again began to flit about.

"Please stop tidying up," Madame requested. "Come, sit down, Celeste. I must talk with you."

Celeste sat down near her, her brow furrowed. "I did not know you even knew of my existence," she confessed in a near-whisper.

Madame smiled kindly. "There was a time when I didn't want to know, my child, but now I think we need each other. Then too, I vowed I would come one day—you *are* Abraham's child."

Celeste automatically reached for Madame Wertheim's gloved hand. "Madame . . . I don't know what to say to you."

Madame Wertheim made no attempt to remove her hand, but with her other touched Celeste's hair. "You have your father's eyes," she said indulgently. There were so many questions, Anna thought, so much she wanted to know. And why had she not come sooner? It was not as if her arranged marriage to Abraham had been a great love affair, and when he took pleasure elsewhere she accepted it without jealousy. So many years . . . How old was Celeste? Younger than Charles, older than Robert—twenty-nine, she decided. Madame smiled, "Did they love each other, your mother and Abraham?"

"I always thought so," Celeste replied honestly, relieved that Madame did not appear hurt.

"I'm glad," Madame replied, lowering her eyes.

Celeste let go of Madame's hand and Madame removed her gloves. "I understand you work as a singer in the Club Morocco. I see also that you are dressed for work. Am I keeping you?"

Celeste shook her head. "I have an hour or so."

"I wanted to see you. I should have come years ago I suppose, when your mother died. But I knew Robert came, though of course I never told him. I'm ashamed that for years I let him do what I should have been doing."

"Madame, you owe me nothing. Nor does Robert."

Madame Wertheim inhaled. "My dear, you *are* Abraham's child, of his blood just as my sons are. And things are different now. The world has changed, so much really. So I wanted to ask you to come home with me. I don't know how long it will be safe, but it's safer than Paris."

Celeste nodded. "Madame, you should not have come to Paris. You know the Germans have already begun arresting Jews."

"So I have heard. But I wanted to meet you and I wanted to know if you know where Robert is. I haven't heard from him in months. It's as if he had dropped off the face of the earth."

Celeste pressed her lips together, and out of habit moved closer to Madame Wertheim and spoke softly. "Robert is with the underground. I don't know for certain, but I believe he was sent to Lyon. We think he is a prisoner . . . or perhaps . . ."

"He is not dead," Madame interrupted. "I would know if he were, in my heart."

Celeste met her calm gaze. "I wish I had your faith."

"Come back with me to the Riviera," Madame urged.

Celeste shook her head. "I cannot, Madame. Robert had his work and I have mine. But you must return to your estate immediately; in unoccupied France you have the protection of the Vichy Government."

"Those strutting turkeys!" Madame said with irony. "They are all traitors!"

Celeste smiled at Madame's sudden show of emotion. "You sound like Robert—or is it that Robert sounds like you?"

"I don't need Robert to know what a traitor is. I have come to my own conclusions, though I should have started learning about the world years ago. Time is precious, my dear. I regret that I have discovered another Anna Wertheim in my body only after so many years of being a hothouse plant, as Robert would say."

"Robert loves you and worries about you."

"And I about him. You know, I have found just the girl for him, too. I hope when the war is over I can get them together."

"I think Robert has already found a girl," Celeste ventured. "An American, a photographer."

Madame's face brightened. "Perhaps he does not need me as much as I think. Is her name Adria by any chance?"

Celeste nodded and smiled. Then more seriously, "He needs you, Madame. You must go back to the Riviera."

Stubbornly Anna Wertheim shook her head. "No, I shall remain in Paris for awhile, to live as I always have for as long as I can. And you will visit me. We will become friends as we should have done years ago."

"I would like to be your friend," Celeste replied. "But Paris is not the only danger, my friendship may be dangerous as well."

Madame did not require an explanation. "I assume that you and Robert are engaged in similar activities. Also that money is always needed for such ventures. I will come back tomorrow with some jewels that can easily be converted into whatever currency is most useful."

"Madame, there is no need. Robert has given generously to our cause."

"Robert is Robert. I want to do something myself. In

any case, if I am arrested my jewels will be confiscated by the Germans. It is far better that what trinkets I have here in Paris be used for a good cause."

Madame Wertheim stood up and smoothed out her skirt. Then she put her arms around Celeste and kissed her on the cheek. "Tomorrow at ten," she promised.

Chapter Thirteen

1

ADRIA EXAMINED HER LATEST photos. They were, she thought unhappily, the last she would see developed. How quickly one got used to the primitive circumstances of war. There was no electricity in the hotel, and weeks ago the water had ceased to run from the taps in the bathrooms. The photographers in the building collected water in buckets and brought it to Adria's room, where all the film for the day was developed. Water had to be used as sparingly as possible, and now they had all been told that even this must stop. From tomorrow on, undeveloped film would be sent out on the dangerous night flights. It was December fifth and Tobruk had been under siege for two hundred and thirty-seven days. She herself had been there for eighty-eight of those days. The front was still so close that the newsmen and photographers covering the fighting drove to it every morning and returned to the city when it was dark.

She slept in her clothes, ready at any moment to evacuate her room for the shelter beneath the hotel lobby. Jeff joked about washing in beer with the British newsmen, and they had all grown used to eating out of tins.

Adria selected the best of her photos, put them in an envelope, and lay down on the narrow bed. She turned off the light and tossed restlessly, feeling the perspiration on her brow and between her breasts. She daydreamed about soaking in a cool bath and washing her hair in a thick lather.

She was on the edge of sleep when the night was suddenly filled with the wail of the sirens. Her eyes snapped open and she pulled herself up in the darkness. Force of habit caused her to shake out her boots in case any scorpions had settled into them for the night. Not wasting time lacing them she simply pulled them on, slung her cameras round her neck, and quickly unpinned her latest negatives, holding them so they would not stick together. Finally, with the practice of many air raids, she grabbed her packed emergency bag in her free hand and headed for the stairs. Others clamored in front and behind her. There were officers quartered in the hotel as well as press.

The shells began to fall before they were all crowded into the shelter. Tonight, as always, bottles were opened and drinks passed around.

Adria sank to the floor among the wine racks and began lacing her boots. Jeff came and sat beside her. He waved a bottle of scotch, unceremoniously took a long swig, and passed her the bottle. She shook her head.

Jeff's hair was uncombed and his wrinkled shirt was open to the waist, revealing his hairy chest. His cameras, like hers, were around his neck. She smiled at him in the dim light and thought that he was, in fact, a handsome man. And if he lacked the ability to act responsibly in a relationship, he had certain other commendable traits, like good humor and dedication. He was intelligent and often fun to be with. In retrospect, she wondered what the weeks in Tobruk would have been like without him.

"You know, I don't feel like spending another night in this dump," Jeff said. He stood up and stretched. "I'm going outside and take some pictures of the bombs bursting in air."

"You're drunk," Adria said, reaching up and pulling on his shirt.

"I'm not drunk, I'm bored."

"Jeff, it's too dangerous. For God's sake sit down."

"What's a little danger? I think you just don't want old Jeff to leave you."

Adria frowned at his loud voice. Rick Shattner, an Australian journalist huddled in the corner, snickered, and the rest of the men simply grinned. "It isn't that," she insisted.

"Good," Jeff said, weaving away from her grasp. He turned and headed for the door.

Adria watched him, then stood up. "Wait, I'm coming with you!" she shouted. The door of the shelter slammed shut behind her and she ran her hand along the damp wall to guide herself up the narrow steps that led into the alley behind the hotel. Jeff lumbered on ahead of her, then turned to offer his hand in the darkness.

"Come on slowpoke," he urged. "There's death and destruction out there, a whole world of pictures."

"Don't joke about it," she replied, allowing him to guide her through the darkness.

A sudden shell lit up the night and Adria inadvertently screamed because it had fallen so close. Jeff pulled her into his arms and sheltered her against a building as flaming debris fell around them. The fire burned brightly and Adria pulled away to look up into Jeff's face. He smiled down at her and ran his fingers through her hair. "I don't know who he is," Jeff said slowly. "But I do know that I'm here and he isn't."

Adria looked away. "He's being held by the Germans."

"He's lucky you love him, Adria. You're a hell of a woman."

"I don't want to talk about it," she murmured.

Jeff leaned over and kissed her on the mouth. It was a long deep kiss and she could feel his hands moving on her back as he pressed her to him. His kiss aroused her—or was it merely that she was lonely and missed Robert so very much. Still, her arms went around Jeff's neck. Then he broke the kiss and kissed her neck, nuzzling her the way he used to.

Adria felt tears welling in her eyes. Inexplicable tears, of confusion, of fright, of fear at Robert's unknown fate. She trembled violently at the emotions loosened by Jeff's kisses and pulled away, shaking her head.

Jeff's eyes locked onto hers, first uncomprehending, then hurt. Adria lifted her hand as if to fill the distance between them. "I can't," she murmured, then turned and ran back down the alley.

2

ROBERT SET HIS BOWL aside and eased himself into a sitting position. He turned his spoon handle up and scratched another mark on the wall. Robert knew he had been arrested on September 17th and placed in solitary confinement five or six days thereafter. As nearly as he could figure he'd lived in silence and in darkness for some seventy-three days. A bowl of food delivered twice a day was his only hint of time, and to date he had received one hundred forty-six bowls. Thus it must be the first of December.

Seventy-three days without so much as the sound of a human voice. Still he felt sane, felt that if freed he could struggle out of his cell and resume his life. Yet never before had he realized how much sanity depended on self-discipline and on the daily exercise of both the brain and the body.

To combat the dark silence Robert had worked out a series of long and laborious exercises in the cramped space available. He did them daily for what he thought was an hour in the morning and in the evening. He thought of Adria, and mentally constructed a home, decorated it, named their children, and planned their education. He invented games, played chess with an imaginary opponent, and sometimes counted the grains of rice in his evening meal. In spite of the utter blackness, he knew every inch of his tiny cell. He memorized the pores in the walls, located the stones under which the draft flowed, and there he dug with his nails, hoping against hope to find a ray of light or hear a distant sound.

Robert again ran his finger over the wall, feeling each of his marks. Deprived of sight and sound he was amazed at how his fingers had grown sensitive to texture and his nose to the slightest of odors.

Robert stretched his body and strained his ears, thinking he heard the heavy boots of the guard. Though he had already been fed, the slot in the door opened. He could see no light, however; the slot was already sealed on the other side when it sprung open on his. "Put the bag over your head!" a harsh voice ordered in German.

Robert steeled himself even as he marveled at the sound of another human voice. Were his days of dark internment to end before a firing squad he could not see?

"Am I to be shot?" he answered, shattered by the sound of his voice.

"It will go easier on you if you cooperate."

Robert took the hood and placed it over his head. "I am ready," he called out.

The cell door creaked and two pairs of muscled arms pulled him from his tomblike cell. No sooner had they pulled him to his feet than his hands were handcuffed and the beating began.

As he was half dragged down the long corridor, he was kicked and punched. He felt almost grateful for the beating—it was human contact. And in spite of the pain inflicted on him, he relished the sound of voices.

When he was half-unconscious his hands were freed and he was shoved into a box, its lid slammed shut. "Here you are, a new home! A real coffin!"

A cold chill filled him and for the first time he felt a surge of true terror. Had he survived seventy-three days of hell only to die, buried alive in an unmarked grave?

He heard them nail the coffin closed, felt it carried on strong arms. Next he knew the sensation of traveling by truck. He rolled in the coffin on each curve and was jolted with each rut in the road. Then again he felt the coffin lifted, he heard them talking about the woods. Cold sweat broke out on his brow and he began screaming and kicking the sides of his prison. Like a small child in a temper tantrum he beat on the sides of the coffin and he was silenced only by a single shot. Panting, he calmed down, his senses suddenly alert.

The nails were being pried open agonizingly slowly. He prepared to thrust himself upward, to kick away the loosened lid, to discard the bag over his head and at least have one last moment of light before he met whatever fate awaited.

But before he could use his own feet, the lid was flung upward. Feeling the air on his face, Robert yanked away his hood and for the first time in seventy-three days he was bathed in sunlight. His hands flew to his eyes, "I can't see!" he shrieked, and held his palms over his eyes even as tears flooded them. "I'm blind! I can't see!"

Roughly, he felt himself slapped across the back. "Shut up." a deep voice hissed. "We've gone through hell to get you out of prison, my friend, so keep your mouth shut until we get you out of France."

Robert shuddered. "I'm blind," he repeated. Fear kept his hands over his eyes.

"I'll tie my kerchief over you like a blindfold," one of the men offered. "You'll be all right, it takes time."

Robert nodded. One was French, one had a limey accent, and the third had an out of place Texas drawl.

How? Why? Questions flooded his mind, though he allowed himself to be led away in silence.

"Good thing you're used to the dark," the Frenchman said. "You'll be traveling mostly at night."

They walked through thick brush for nearly half a mile. Then Robert was thrust into a car, which drove along rough roads for another hour. After that, they entered a house where Robert smelled the mouth-watering aroma of fresh bread.

Seated at a table, he heard the men instruct someone to turn down the lights. They removed the kerchief, but Robert held his eyes closed, afraid to open them even in this dim light.

"Oh, God." He shuddered, his sensitive fingers exploring the wood grain of the rough wooden table at which he was seated. Still he held his eyes shut till courage and curiosity combined to force them open. He blinked, his eyes watered, and he blinked again. The room and its occupants were blurred, but he could see! There were the three men who had brought him and an old woman. She extended a hot cup of coffee to him and he grasped it gratefully.

"I've been in solitary confinement for seventy-four days," he told them haltingly.

"Seventy-six," the limey corrected. "This is December sixth."

"The war?" Robert questioned.

"Isn't over," the Frenchman answered curtly.

"My mother, has anyone heard anything from her?" They both shook their heads. "Our orders are to smuggle you out to England. This operation was planned by the SOE. Sorry we had to batter you so. Had to maké it look good for the Krauts."

Robert nodded. "Bring me up to date. Tell me what you know." He sipped the coffee and felt a sense of wonder as his sight improved, listening to the sound of their voices as if they were the world's greatest orators. Human sound—sight—how much he had missed them!

The Texan was ostensibly a businessman, but in reality he worked for American intelligence and with the French underground. His orders were to return to England. "We'll have to drive most of the night," he told Robert, "but when we reach the airfield, I'll be flying us out."

The Texan was taller than Robert, and heavier. Robert took him to be forty-five or so. He grinned and slapped Robert across the back. "Easy son, I've been flying since I was fourteen. We'll be low, and of course we *are* expected."

Robert knew he must have looked aghast. "What on earth kind of plane is it?"

"Little Waco, son," the Texan said proudly. "Nice and airy, but no need to worry. I have clearance from Jerry. I do a lot of business with the Krauts, and naturally they think a Texas redneck is their kind of people." He laughed and grinned.

"A biplane! In December? Over the channel?"

"We'll bundle you up all nice and warm."

"He's a genius," the Frenchman said with a smile.

"A mad genius," the limey added with a wink.

Robert drained his coffee cup and attacked the bread with a smile at the pilot. "Mind if I have a good last meal?"

"As long as you don't get sick in the air," the Texan cautioned.

3

ON MONDAY MORNING, DECEMBER 8th, 1941, a thousand men were turned away by the naval recruiting office in New York City. It was the same across America. Recruiters could not cope with the million men who volunteered to serve in the armed forces. Irving Berlin's popular song, "I Didn't Raise My Son to Be a Soldier" faded into memory, to be quickly replaced by Kate Smith singing "God Bless America."

In England there was subdued joy in the knowledge that America had entered the war, but apprehension tempered that joy when Britain declared war on Japan. Japanese forces landed in Malaya and Thailand. Singapore and Hong Kong were bombed, and the international settlement in Shanghai was quickly occupied. At Tobruk, the British Eighth Army held on tenuously to this one small corner of North Africa, which, by the day after the attack on Pearl Harbor, had been under siege for 239 long days.

* * *

In London, December 8th was misty and cold. The dampness seemed to permeate everything, and fuel shortages meant that few could heat their homes. The sun was a dim red ball hidden behind low banks of gray fog, and fires from the raids the night before smoldered, blanketing the city in sooty smoke. Still, the pubs were filled with patrons drinking warm beer, Big Ben still chimed forth the hours, and in spite of taking a direct hit earlier, Buckingham Palace still stood, its occupants unharmed.

Robert Wertheim sat in his brother's comfortable den and slowly sipped his Raynal Napoleon 1897 brandy. The smoke from his pipe curled in the cool room and he watched it as it dissipated. It hardly seemed possible that less than forty-eight hours earlier he had still been imprisoned in Lyon. Apart from weariness, he felt almost as if his months in prison had not happened. Robert bent slightly and pulled up the heavy wool tartan lap blanket that covered his legs. A small fire burned in the gigantic fireplace and Charles paced in front of it, his red velvet smoking jacket tied together loosely.

"She's completely mad." Charles paused briefly in his forward march before the hearth. "Mother's in Paris, in danger! Good Lord, she could be living in luxury in Martinique, she could be here with me, or she could be in Scotland on the estate! It boggles the mind," he sputtered.

Robert could not suppress his own worry, but at the same time he knew his mother was far from insane. She must have gone to Paris for a reason. "Is there any way she can be gotten out?"

"She won't leave," Charles said, turning on Robert as if he were to blame for their mother's recalcitrance. "Not only will she not leave, but I've only recently learned that she sold all the jewels she had here and gave the money to the underground."

Robert shook his head. "I'm just as worried as you are, but you know she falls into that category of Jews who have been labeled 'privileged' by the Germans. Perhaps she'll be all right."

Charles grimaced. "Privileged" Jews were being sent to special ghettos, and while the Germans were not actively exterminating them, the ghettos were known to be filled with disease and hardship. How could their mother survive such an ordeal? "A mad mother and a demented brother," Charles grumbled. Then he looked directly at Robert. "You're going back, aren't you?"

Robert laid down his pipe in the ash tray and lightly rubbed the crystal brandy snifter, looking into it, seeming to seek his own reflection. How tempting it was. He didn't want to go back. He wanted to find Adria, make love to her, run away with her, to resume a normal life. But there was no normalcy now. Oh, there were places to run, but how far could a man run from his own conscience? "I'm the best liaison we could have with the underground. I have to go back," he finally replied with conviction.

"You've done more than your share already."

"Perhaps, but I'm going back, anyway."

"I'll have to have you back here when the plans for an invasion are solidified. You'll have to play out the role of the Resistance."

"Of course."

Charles smiled slightly, then almost begrudgingly added, "You'll make my job easier. I have to admit your work is vital. And please try to get Mother to go back to the south of France."

"I certainly will."

Charles grumbled into his brandy but Robert didn't comment. He was used to Charles and he knew that, begrudgingly or not, his brother admired him. "Do you know where Adria Halstead is?" he asked, trying to sound less interested than he was.

"In North Africa with the Eighth Army."

Robert half smiled. She had done as she said she would, she had stayed on the front lines. "She's quite a woman," Robert said with undisguised admiration.

"She knows you were being held by the Germans," Charles said flatly. "She left me her address, asked me to keep in touch."

"Can I send a wire?"

Charles nodded. "She's very attractive," he said, half under his breath.

Robert could not resist. "Why Charles," he goaded, "I didn't think you noticed such things."

4

ADRIA PUSHED THE FLAP of the press tent aside and blinked into the dim interior. The desert sun was blinding and it took a moment for her eyes to adjust to the sudden change. She walked inside and let the flap drop into place behind her. It was hot and airless, but still cooler out of the relentless sun.

On a camp table there was a typewriter and several others sat in their cases on the floor. There were three narrow army cots, a couple of folding chairs, a water cooler, and some paper cups. In the corner was a metal trunk labeled PRESS—VITAL SUPPLIES, and she smiled, knowing it to be filled with bottles of liquor carefully packed between layers of blankets. Hot as it was in the daytime, it was cold at night, and she suspected that both the liquor and the blankets would be needed in a few hours.

Adria sat down on one of the cots and checked her watch. It was four in the afternoon, which meant she'd been up for twelve hours. By seven the whole crew of newsmen and photographers would be back and then the usual nightly discussions would start. People did drift back and forth all day, of course, but she was lucky. For the moment she was alone and she decided to seize the rare opportunity and catch a little sleep. She stretched out and put her arm under her head. Not even the constant sound of shells and mortars was going to keep her awake.

They had begun to move out of Tobruk on December tenth, and by the eleventh they had met up with units of the British Eighth Army at Acroma. The siege was over after two hundred forty-two days. It had cost the British Navy twenty-five ships and a countless number of planes to keep Tobruk supplied with men and material, but it was over, she thought joyfully. At last the British were on the offensive, their morale boosted by America's entry into the war.

Adria thought briefly about Pearl Harbor. She had been stunned when the news had come through. How could the fleet have been trapped? She thought of friends whose fathers were on the *California*, the *Oklahoma*, and the *Tennessee*. Sadly she thought of Admiral Isaac C. Kidd, a personal friend as well as her father's colleague, who had been killed manning a machine gun aboard his flagship, the *Arizona*. Thank heaven the carriers hadn't been there, she thought, though of course carriers would be sitting ducks without cruiser and battleship support. There was no question that it would take time to replace the losses and that until then the war in the Pacific would go badly.

Adria turned over on her back and opened her eyes to stare at the top of the tent. Damn. Now that she was lying down, her mind was replaying the news like a broken phonograph record. Still, events had occurred quickly, and she hadn't had time to digest them or to consider their ramifications.

"Anybody in there?" a male voice shouted.

"Yes," Adria called out.

There was a moment of silence then, "Permission to come in ma'am."

"Yes, come on in." She pulled herself up and ran her hand through her hair. It must have been one of the newly arrived troops. Everyone else barged into the press tent all the time, with or without permission.

The young man stepped inside hesitantly, as if expecting to find her half-dressed. Oh, God, he couldn't be more than seventeen. And as if to confirm her suspicions, half an American comic book dangled out the corner of his shoulder pack.

"I'm supposed to find a Miss Adria Halstead," he stammered nervously.

Adria smiled, "Mission accomplished."

He handed her a brittle envelope. "This just came in over the wireless for you. Sorry for the delay; it had to be decoded."

Adria reached for it anxiously. It had to be from Charles. Nobody else except her father had the clout to send a coded message by radio.

"Will that be all, ma'am?"

Adria nodded, then beckoned him back.

"Yes, ma'am."

She smiled broadly and pointed to the comic book. "I'd tuck that in before an officer sees it," she advised.

He blushed deeply and stuffed it further into his pack. "Thank you, ma'am."

Adria almost giggled when he actually saluted as he left. The flap closed and she ripped open the message.

Safe and sound with Charles. Will go back soon. Don't worry my love. Robert.

Tears of relief ran down her cheeks, and she held the radiogram to her lips and kissed it. "Thank God," she murmured. "Oh, I wish I were with you, Robert. I wish I were in your arms."

Holding the crumpled paper to her breast she lay down again, and this time closed tear-filled eyes with relief and weariness. "We'll survive," she whispered. "We'll be together again."

5

MADAME WERTHEIM HAD TAKEN up residence in her Paris apartment five months earlier, in December, 1941. In spite of the occupation of Paris and the persecution of Jews, she was determined to carry on as normally as possible, to live in dignity, and, if arrested, to meet her fate with dignity. It was not that she wanted to be arrested and deported east, it was simply that she was determined not to hide. Why, she asked herself, should she be different from other Jews? If the Germans chose to treat her differently, that was not her doing. But if she chose to use her connections to leave Paris or flee France, it would be she who was making herself an exception.

As Jews were not allowed to hire household help—though many workers were obligated to work for the Germans—Madame had closed off most of the apartment and utilized only the parlor, the kitchen, one bath, and her own bedroom. To her way of thinking, it was a simple existence. She shopped for fresh bread in the market, occasionally purchased chicken or fish and fruit, and augmented these purchases with tinned oysters from the store in the pantry and champagne from the wine closet. It had taken her some time to learn how to turn on the stove and even longer to master the art of broiling the chicken to tenderness, until she discovered the former cook's recipe file. With the joy of an explorer on an unknown continent she began to delight in cooking, and had she turned dust into gold like an alchemist's dream, she could not have been happier than the day she succeeded in making an entirely delicious *coq au vin.*

Shortages sometimes made certain food difficult to obtain, but Madame had money and letters of credit. The vast Wertheim fortune had been removed from France by Robert shortly after her return from Germany in 1939 and now resided in numbered Swiss accounts and in America. The money in America could not be sent to France, but from one of the Swiss accounts Madame requisitioned a small monthly allowance.

Madame was not unaware of the fact that she was watched, nor had she deluded herself that she would be allowed to remain at large forever. Nonetheless, she had gone about her business ignoring those who followed her. Even now she smiled when she thought about the unexpected and uninvited visitors she had entertained on the night of March thirtieth. It had been an evening of small triumph, despite the consequences.

She had answered the door to an entourage of five elderly men, one of whom was old Marshal Pétain himself, the president of the so-called Vichy Government. They accepted her invitation to tea with surprise and shuffled into the parlor, seating themselves uncomfortably on the edges of chairs. At another time, Madame thought, these officers would come to visit the Wertheims only if summoned, or perhaps through intermediaries, approach the Wertheims for a government loan. She took small satisfaction that at least they appeared suitably uncomfortable in her presence.

"It is few who are honored by a visit from Marshal Pétain, himself," one of the Marshal's aides boasted.

Madame turned sweetly and smiled, "It is even fewer whom I allow to take my time," she countered.

Marshal Pétain snorted, grumbling under his breath. To Madame's thinking he was a senile old goat.

"Madame," he snorted, "you are of grave concern to us."

"France is of grave concern to me," she answered. "There are Germans in Paris, Marshal, have you noticed?"

Marshal Pétain flushed at her words and clearly smarted from her tone, but he did not respond. "I respect your family," the Marshal replied, though he did not look into her eyes. "It is why I am here. Madame, you must leave Paris at once and return to your estate. From there, it can be arranged to transport you to England. For months now we have been protecting you and we can protect you no longer."

"You don't respect my family," Madame Wertheim snapped. "I'm simply an embarrassment to you. What do you do with a woman whose husband virtually paid for your uniforms before the war? Protect me? My dear Marshal, I've seen how you protected France, and I would rather not accept your protection, for I know it will result in betrayal."

"You could be shot for speaking to me like that!" the

Marshal blustered, a dribble of saliva running onto his white mustache.

"Then history will record that I was shot by a drooling old fool," Madame said, standing up. "Gentlemen, leave me to the Germans as you have left France to them. Confiscate my estates, as you will no doubt do, anyway. Marshal, we are both past our prime. I shall die peacefully, but you shall die knowing the history books will call you a traitor."

"I defeated the Germans at Verdun!" he muttered, his old face now red with anger and the blue vein above his right eye pulsating.

"You forestalled them and then gave them all of France," Madame said.

Marshal Pétain had struggled to his feet, aided by one of his officers. "I came here to offer you sanctuary and freedom. You have been most rude."

"The least of my sins," Madame replied.

"You have been warned. You have been offered a chance . . ."

"A chance to be different from the other Jews in Paris? No thank you. I have come to think about these matters a great deal lately, and though I have much to learn, I have decided to begin living."

"I suppose a woman cannot really understand politics. I tell you, you will be arrested."

Madame laughed and took pleasure in the sound. "Then I suspect we shall meet the same fate," she replied. "The Germans will lose this war and you and your kind will suffer even more than they. Traitors do not fare well, Marshal."

The old man turned his back on her and marched out of her apartment. Anna Wertheim closed the door behind him with great pleasure.

The next morning, April 1st, 1942, Madame Wertheim was arrested by a Gestapo officer.

She was allowed to dress and pack a bag, and though she was not told where she was going, she knew it was eastward when the long train with its miserable human cargo pulled out of the station.

Madame sat on her fur coat in the cold boxcar filled with frightened women and children. She cradled a young girl in her arms and recalled years past. How many springs and falls had she traveled this route in a plush private carriage? She recalled the countryside vividly, and she recited its charms to the young girl, helping her to see beyond the wooden barriers.

"A pity there are no windows," she said softly. "The hills are rolling here and at sunset the sky glows pink over the fields."

Because she counted the hours, Madame knew the train had passed through Germany. On the fourth day she was taken off the train with her belongings while the others continued on their uncertain voyage. Much to her surprise, she found herself taken to the old Czech fortress town of Theresienstadt.

6

THERESIENSTADT WAS AN OLD Bohemian fortress town on the banks of the Ohre River. Not a camp like Auschwitz, it was rather a ghetto, an area of special settlement. The last of its original Czech population had been deported early in 1941 to make room for the newcomers. Theresienstadt, Anna Wertheim soon learned, was especially designed by Reinhardt Heydrich to serve as a ghetto for certain categories of Jews: Jews whose mistreatment might result in embarrassment for the Germans at home and internationally. To "qualify" for Theresienstadt, one had to be a leading functionary of a Jewish community, an internationally known writer, scientist, musician, artist, or university professor, a German-Jewish veteran of the Great War, a German Jew over sixty-five, the Jewish partner of a mixed marriage, or an extremely wealthy Jew with family and funds outside Europe. A propaganda film was made for distribution abroad, showing Theresienstadt to be a lovely little town—"A Settlement for Our Jews," the Germans proclaimed. The town was also shown off to dignitaries from the International Red Cross.

Dr. Paul Eppstein, who had been in charge of Jewish immigration for the Reichsvereingung—a Nazi-appointed Jewish Central Organization—had been made Judenaltester, or elder of Theresienstadt.

In spite of the fact that everyone called it a ghetto, it was not a ghetto like those of the Middle Ages. Essentially, it consisted of two fortresses: a large garrison and a small military prison, one on each side of the river. When Theresienstadt, or Terezin, as the Czechs called it, had become part of the Czechoslovakian Republic, the small fortress had remained a prison but the larger fortress fell into disuse.

Around the two fortresses a small town had grown up. It had an attractive town square, but in general the town was drab and dull. Gray stone buildings dominated, and there were no flowers, no lawns, and barren trees. When it rained, rivers of mud covered the ground, and when the rain stopped, the thick mud dried into rutted paths marked by boots and bare feet. Of the two hundred twenty-one buildings in the town— the two fortresses, the barracks, and some two hundred houses—only a few had electricity and fewer still running water.

By the time Anna Wertheim arrived, in April, 1942, the camp had been open six months. Built to house ten thousand, it held six times that. Homes originally built for four persons now sheltered as many as sixty. The Hotel Victoria, the town's best building, was used to house the SS. It was separated from the surrounding buildings on the square by barbed wire.

Although she should have felt depressed, Anna felt pride in what she heard and saw in Theresienstadt. The Jews had taken over the administration of the ghetto, organized a laundry, a bakery and a food depot, built a sewer system, and closed contaminated wells. All this in spite of the fact that the vast majority of Terezin's inmates were elderly and came from families that were active in business, religion, or administration. Few of them came to Terezin with useful skills, but they were challenged to survive and Anna could feel the acceptance of that challenge in the air itself.

Regardless of age or the station held in their former lives, everyone worked. Women who had lived all their lives being waited on by maids now cleaned and scrubbed clothes in the laundry, or worked long hours baking in the communal kitchen. Men who had never held a hoe, shovel, or pickax now dug ditches and built furniture. The veterans of the Great War policed the ghetto, artisans were engaged to design furniture, and there was a tailor's shop that made uniforms for German soldiers. It was the tailor shop to which Anna was assigned.

The Germans who guarded the camp were not overtaxed because, on the whole, the inmates were elderly and infirm. It was common knowledge that here time alone would achieve that which elsewhere required more active measures. There was one section into which those who lived in the ghetto were not allowed, nothing less, Anna discovered, than a stop on the way to Auschwitz. Trains arrived daily, often left on the tracks overnight, and the cries of misery from within the boxcars floated eerily in the night air, reminding every inmate of the ghetto that whether by time or by circumstance, the fate of European Jewry was sealed. Listening to those in the boxcars was a special kind of torture, but there was nothing that could be done. SS with vicious guard dogs patrolled the tracks, and to help would have meant instant death, not only for the one who tried to help but for the inmates of the cars as well. And if anyone should escape there were immediate reprisals. As many as twenty might be shot on the spot.

"YOUR FINGERS ARE SORE," the kindly gentleman observed as he leaned over Anna Wertheim. She looked up into the amber eyes of the man introduced as Aaron Rosen. He was her age, she surmised, perhaps a few years older, but slender and fit, with a fair complexion and a white beard. Giving the immediate impression of being educated and well bred, he was the tailor in charge of the shop.

"I'm afraid I wasn't trained to do anything practical," she admitted. His eyes remained glued on hers, and he ran his hand absent-mindedly through his beard. "Anna. That's your first name, is it not?"

She nodded.

"Anna, Anna, you don't remember. No, why should you?"

He was smiling, and she liked his smile. She studied his face but nothing in it gave her a clue as to why he seemed to know her. "Have we met before?"

"Twice," he replied. "But long ago, my dear, long ago when the world was young."

She tilted her head and searched her memory, but his face summoned no memories. "I'm sorry," she confessed, "but I do not remember."

"The first time we met I was a young student with a scholarship from the Obermann Foundation. We met at a dance at their home. You, I believe, were a bride, so I hardly expect you to remember the dance you danced with me. Ah, but I remember, I remember those eyes. I fell in love with you then, Anna Wertheim, and I feel gratified to discover you today as lovely as you were then."

Anna blushed and lowered her eyes. How strange to be reminded of her girlhood, to feel the flush of embarrassment at her age and in this place. "And the second time?" she inquired.

"The second time we met was after the publication of my third book on the history of Jewish mysticism. I came then to the Obermanns to give a private lecture. You sat in the third row and looked terribly bored. I never knew why I was invited; no one in the audience cared for the topic and few thought of themselves as Jews."

Anna's face brightened. "I remember the lecture," she said, "though I'm afraid I don't really remember the lecturer."

"At least you're honest," he laughed. "I know your son, Robert."

The mention of Robert's name caused a shiver of anticipation. She suddenly felt close to this man, linked to him because he knew her son. Anna reached up and touched his sleeve impulsively. "When did you last see him?"

Aaron Rosen frowned at the sudden anxiety in her voice. "Not recently," he hurried to say. "I last saw him two years ago."

The expression of hope faded from her face. "I'm worried about him. He's adventurous." She smiled a little. "I've always had the feeling that Robert kept secrets from me. Not because he wanted to deceive me, but because he thought I wouldn't understand, or care."

"I think it is more likely that he didn't want you to worry."

"You know something," Anna pressed. "Tell me. Whatever it is, I want to know, too."

"Robert knows he is a Jew. He has given much to our cause."

Anna knew her mouth had opened slightly and she moved to disguise her surprise, but it was too late. Aaron Rosen was quick to understand.

"Robert was my student at Oxford and he visited me often in Germany. He became interested in Zionism some years ago and worked with Aliyah Beth, the organization for the illegal immigration of Jews into Palestine—well, illegal as far as the British are concerned."

"Palestine?"

"It will one day be our homeland, our nation. Israel reborn."

"I always suspected something. He used to disappear for months sometimes. Then too, he was always very interested in politics." She shook her head sadly, looking away. "I know so little. I never called myself a Jew; it was only after *Kristallnacht* that I came to think about these matters."

He smiled gently and touched her shoulder. "Would you like to learn more?"

"Yes."

He nodded. "We will talk after the evening meal. First, Anna, let me show you how to sew without hurting your beautiful hands."

"They are useless hands."

"No hands are useless, only untrained. I am fortunate that my father was a tailor. How else would a scholar learn to sew?"

He sat down beside her and began to instruct her. Anna watched, fascinated with this man who seemed to know more about her own son than she did.

Once back among the women in the barracks they called home, she found herself teased mercilessly. "How fortunate to be tutored by the greatest living Jewish scholar," the wife of an elderly rabbi joked. And young Marianna, who was only half-Jewish, added, "I think there is a romance brewing." Lotti, whose bed was just above Anna's, laughed. "And there is another advantage. Aaron Rosen is so prominent he has his own apartment. He drinks his tea from real cups and receives extra rations from outside." The rabbi's wife nodded. "But he shares them. He is a generous man."

Anna only smiled shyly. The truth was she looked forward to talking to Aaron Rosen again, and not just because he offered to teach her. He aroused something in her, something she had never felt before and was unable to describe. How foolish of me! she thought. We have only just met. But his eyes had bored through her

257

and he seemed to read her mind. It was as if she had known Aaron Rosen all her life, but not until this moment noticed him.

Chapter Fourteen

1

THE VENERABLE CRYSTAL CHANDELIER that hung in the dining room of the Bristol Hotel reflected the gaiety below. Rarely during the summer of 1942 did men and women living in London celebrate, dig out their prewar finery, and kick up their heels.

Champagne was the drink of the evening, and the dinner, served on the finest Royal Dalton china, had consisted of breast of chicken smothered in a delicate sauce of herbs and spices. For dessert, fresh sliced oranges, courtesy of the United States Air Force, a rare treat in wartime Britain.

Adria had worn an emerald green taffeta evening dress with a snug-fitting top that had a daringly low back and plunging neckline. Her hair was still styled in a page-boy cut like the one so popularized by Joan Crawford. Around her neck she wore a single strand of pearls, a gift from her father years ago when he had returned from Hawaii.

Following the sliced oranges and brandy, Lieutenant General Dwight Eisenhower, recently appointed commander of U.S. troops in Europe, rose to make the presentation speech.

"You have given Americans a feeling for the horror of war by depicting its human casualties in a way few have managed. From London in the darkest days of the Blitz, during the siege of Tobruk, and in North Africa with the British Eighth Army, your lens has recorded life in the trenches, and moments of defeat, frustration, and victory. On behalf of the Wesley Photographic Foundation I am pleased to present you with this award for outstanding work in the field of photographic journalism for your photographic essay, "A Desert Victory."

Adria had blushed, spoken a few words of thanks, and been grateful when the general asked her to dance.

"You are a splendid photographer," he had praised, "And when the time comes and we liberate France—even though now it may be far in the future—I want you there. Are you willing?"

Adria had enthusiastically accepted.

"I'm surprised your father's not here, the general commented. "I would have thought he'd move heaven and earth to see his daughter so honored."

Adria looked away, grateful she didn't have to lie. "He's in Cardiff, sir. He's recently remarried . . ." her voice trailed off.

The general sensed her discomfort and changed the subject back to photography and the perils of being an army photographer. He then launched into history, telling her about the young artists who had been employed to sketch the civil war.

The general, Adria thought, was a sensitive and charming man. Everyone seemed to agree with her on that point, attributing his rapid advancement to his personality and diplomatic ability. The latter, of course, was rare in the military, and now if ever, a diplomat was needed. Not a few of the allies' best generals—Patton, Montgomery, and even her old find De Gaulle—were prima donnas. Ike, as his friends called him, was a master at handling relations between the Americans, the British, and the French. Some criticized him and called him a paper shuffler, but the truth was, he was a master strategist, who could, if necessary, charm the volatile General Patton into accepting his will. But then, she mused, Ike had been chosen over three hundred sixty-six other candidates for commander of the U.S. forces in Europe.

"You seem a little preoccupied," the general commented as he guided her toward the center of the floor.

Adria smiled. "I guess I can't get used to the sound of music instead of gunfire."

"It takes time. I think you made a wise decision to come back to London to accept the award. You needed to get away. How long had you been in North Africa?"

"Eleven months," Adria answered. "I flew back a few nights ago."

"Well, that qualifies you for rest and recuperation."

"I plan to stay at least two weeks."

"And then you want to go back to the Eighth Army?"

Adria smiled. He had given her an opening to ask for what she had wanted to ask earlier. But then he had asked about her father and she had missed the opportunity. Not again, she decided, taking a deep breath. "General, I'd like to have U.S. army credentials. I'd like to be in on Operation Torch."

The general grinned. Operation Torch was his baby, the planned allied invasion of French North Africa. "We're not going right away," he said.

"I'd heard that, but I don't mind waiting. My editor thinks—and I agree—that it would be better if I were with the American army now that we're in the war."

The general smiled slyly. "You know the rules. American press are all pooled. The Army decides where they go and when. And all material is subject to army censorship. Of course there is intelligence clearance, too, but the Brits must have cleared you already."

Adria laughed. "Not a difficult job, I imagine. I've been on file in the Pentagon since the day I was born."

"You and all the children of career military men."

"Actually, I think the American press regulations are nearly the same as the British rules."

"We have more press, so we have to be stricter. Can't have a press corps larger than the army. Once you're accredited, you work for the army first and your editor second. It's the price you pay for the sumptuous free room, board, and communications." The general smirked.

"Otherwise known as a hard cot, k-rations, and a field telephone," Adria responded dryly.

"Exactly right. As for the censorship, well, the Brits do the same. Major casualties are not announced until three months after they happen."

"That's harder on reporters working for dailies than it is on me."

"I'm sure. I get a lot of complaints."

"I'd still like to be with the U.S. army."

The general winked. "Keep me apprised of your location. I'll make the arrangements when the time comes."

"Thank you," Adria said.

"And I thank you for the dance."

It was after midnight when Adria returned to her hotel room. She ran her fingers over the silver plaque, then placed it on the table next to her bed. She had finally dozed off into a deeper sleep when she heard the pounding on the door.

Adria sat up abruptly, disoriented by the heavy blackout curtains which blotted out the sun. The clock said it was slightly after nine. She shook her head and climbed out of bed, hastily pulling on her robe. "Just a minute," she called out. Not bothering with her slippers, she hurried across the ice-cold tile floor of the foyer and opened the door a crack to peer out. Then, with a cry of surprise, she flung the door open. "Robert!"

He stepped into the darkened room and closed the door, took her in his arms, and kissed her deeply. First her lips, then her neck, finally her ears. Her arms were around him tightly. She could not quite believe he was real, that he was actually here and holding her.

"I got Charles's message that you were all right. I prayed and prayed you would be." Tears were running down her face and she knew she was beginning to sound incoherent. "I thought you were still in France," she gasped.

"Oh, officially I still am." He winked and smiled engagingly. "I shouldn't be here, but I couldn't resist."

Her lips formed a question and his finger touched

them sensually, tracing the outline of her mouth. "Don't ask me any questions, Adria. I can't answer them. Take this meeting on faith. I can't stay in London, but you can come to Scotland with me. We will have a week. Say you will."

Adria looked into his face, and although the room was dark, she could make out the thin, white lines on his cheek. They were scars. She touched one lightly, "What have they done to you?" she sobbed, shuddering in his arms.

He shrugged. "In time they'll heal completely." He drew her once again into his arms and Adria rested against his broad chest. "Of course I'll come," she breathed. A week with Robert! A week without bombs dropping, without war, a week in a place untouched by destruction. "I love you," she said, again touching his cheek.

2

THE WERTHEIM ESTATE IN Scotland consisted of a rambling stone house with eleven bedrooms, four baths, a library, reception room, parlor, and dining room. It sat atop a grassy knoll half-obscured by trees dressed in their summer foliage. Acres of woods and rolling moors provided fodder for the hundreds of sheep that grazed everywhere, and beyond fields of purple heather attracted hundreds of birds who came to feed on the sweet stalks.

The July days were reasonably warm, but the nights were unusually cool. When the sun dropped behind the hills, mists gathered in the bogs and Adria conjured up the ghosts of the Highland Scots defeated at Culloden and could easily imagine the eerie wail of their pipes across the deserted moors.

Apart from the shepherds who lived in huts dotted around the estate, the only staff were old Mr. and Mrs. Campbell, who looked after the house and cared for the occasional visitor.

"Tired?" Robert asked as they reached the top of the grassy knoll.

"Not at all! I think I'd have to walk five miles just to walk off that breakfast."

"Mrs. Campbell outdid herself. She doesn't realize she's feeding two people who are used to a lot less."

"I'd get fat if I stayed around here very long," Adria said, smiling at the memory of breakfast. Mrs. Campbell had served up a course of kippers followed by eggs and fresh-baked rolls, jam and real butter, and coffee with real cream. "Real butter and cream! God, I'd forgotten what they tasted like."

"Well, we better get plenty of exercise, because rumor has it Mrs. Campbell has killed the fatted calf for dinner."

"We're having beef?"

He laughed. "Only a metaphor. We're having lamb as only Mrs. Campbell can prepare it."

Adria sat down on a nearby rock and looked out over the peaceful valley below. "I'll be too spoiled to go back."

Robert stepped to her side and ran his hand through her hair. "Don't talk about it now."

"I have to say I wish you wouldn't go back."

"There's no choice. Not one I could live with anyway."

"They tortured you. I can't forget that, can't kill my fear."

"Do you know what I did in prison?"

Adria shook her head.

"I named all of our children."

Adria laughed in spite of herself. "Will there be so many?" she asked, turning to look into his eyes.

Robert grinned and ran his finger slowly down her back. She was wearing a low-necked white peasant blouse and a full skirt. It made her look voluptuous, just the kind of woman a man fantasized about meeting in the heather. "Think of the pleasure of conceiving."

"And *you* think about giving birth," she returned.

"Well, we can stop at three if you insist. What we'll do is give all of them very long names so I can use up all the ones I thought of."

"Let's hear an example."

"Well, I think our first son should be called Nathan."

"I like that," Adria agreed.

"Of course there's Charles to consider. We'll have to call him Nathan Charles. Then there's my father and grandfather—that would make it Nathan Charles Abraham Benjamin Wertheim."

"Very impressive."

Robert laughed and pulled her to her feet. "One might even say off-putting."

"Sometimes you sound so British," she said in a mock accent.

He made a face. "You don't say off-putting in America?"

She crinkled her nose back at him, "No, we say stuffy."

"I know a glen near here. The grass is as soft as cashmere and there's a babbling brook that leads into a small spring-fed lake surrounded by wild flowers. Tell me, have you ever been made love to outdoors?"

She shook her head and took his outstretched hand.

"I have this fantasy of meeting a beautiful woman in the heather. And I take her to the glen and I undress her slowly and caress her naked body and make love to her on the grass. Then we both swim naked in the cold water and I admire her taut nipples and rounded hips."

Adria blushed, "You are an erotic lover, aren't you?"

"You don't approve?"

She touched his lips with her fingers. "Did I say that?"

3

THREE MONTHS BEFORE, IN early May, Charles Wertheim had attended a high-level meeting of MI6. Like all such meetings, it took place in the bowels of Whitehall and was attended by pale men whose work necessitated long hours inside.

The seven men who made major decisions were somber and considerate; they weighed all possibilities. Like himself, they were generally unsmiling men, men who had to weigh seriously schemes that might have made others laugh. Ah, how many wild plans had he heard expounded by wild-eyed men? There had been plans to poison Hitler, plans to assassinate the entire German general staff, and even a plan to subvert Hitler's astrologers and cause them to misread the heavens so Hitler might be led into an Allied trap.

In most cases M16 rejected the ideas of the various European dissident groups as too dangerous or ineffective. But the Czech's plan had been different, offering minimal risk and virtually no British involvement.

"If they are successful, their action will shake the entire German command." Charles Wertheim himself had uttered those words not three months ago, but on this beautiful July morning, he felt little more than numb. Silently, and for wholly personal reasons, he cursed the two young Czechs, Jan Kubis and Josef Gabeik, for brilliantly succeeding in their bold act of assassination. He himself had supported the plan, but today he wished they had failed.

The two Czechs were members of the Free Czechoslovak Army in England, and they had approached British intelligence with an audacious scheme. They proposed to parachute into Czechoslovakia and assassinate Reinhard Heydrich, the chief of the security police, the SD, and deputy chief of the Gestapo. An ambitious man, Heydrich had persuaded Hitler to name him "Acting Protector of Bohemia and Moravia." He had installed himself in the ancient Hradschin Castle in Prague and took great pleasure in riding about in an open Mercedes sports car.

"Once in Czechoslovakia we will have a great deal of assistance," the two would-be assassins had pleaded. There were discussions and finally a decision: the two were parachuted into Czechoslovakia by the RAF and provided with a British-made bomb. On the morning of May 29th, as Heydrich drove from his country villa to the castle in Prague, the bomb was tossed from beside the road. It blew Heydrich's car to pieces and shattered his spine. "Hangman" Heydrich died on June 4th.

"The vengeful sword," Charles murmured. In the manner of ancient Teutonic rites, the Germans loosed a terrible retaliation, more brutal than anyone in England could have imagined. According to the information that had just reached him, over one thousand Czechs were immediately shot; the little village of Lidice, near Prague, had its entire male population burned alive and its women deported to concentration camps; but even more horrible—no, more personal—was the fact that three thousand people from the privileged ghetto of Theresienstadt had been shipped east for extermination and some six hundred killed immediately.

Charles Wertheim sat back in his blue chair and tears rolled down his cheeks. On the coffee table were his intelligence reports of the German revenge and in his hand, a notification from the Red Cross that his beloved mother had been traced to Theresienstadt, where she was being treated well. But his intelligence reports were only hours old, while the report from the Red Cross dated back two months.

Charles clenched his fist and shook his head. Why hadn't she come to England? And almost worse than knowing where she was—if she was still alive—was the fact that he would have to tell Robert on his return from Scotland. Charles stood up and walked to the fireplace, then paced to the window. Robert's frame of

266

mind was vital to his work. Perhaps he, Charles, should bear this terrible apprehension alone. Off with the woman he said he loved, Robert would return in perfect condition to carry out his duties. Nothing, Charles decided, should distract him. If Robert thought their mother had been killed by the Germans he would want to kill every German in sight, and a vengeful man was a dangerous man. Hatred could make one careless.

4

WARM INSIDE AND OUT, Adria reclined beneath a sheep-skin in front of the fire. Between them was a wooden table, and on it, two filled brandy snifters. The room was a large bed-sitting room and the only bedroom open besides the one at the opposite end of the house occupied by the Campbells.

"Are you stiff?" Robert asked. They had spent the afternoon horseback riding across the moors.

"No. Besides, it wasn't as rough as crossing the desert in a jeep." Adria glanced at the finely carved cuckoo clock. It was six in the evening of their last day. In the morning they would return to London and Robert would again disappear from her life.

"I'm already beginning to miss you," she confessed. "I want this war to end. I want to be with you."

Robert turned to her, his eyes downcast. "Adria, there are things I haven't told you."

Her heart seemed to stand still. Was he going to talk about another woman? No, he wasn't like that. "Tell me now," she said softly.

He came to her side and sat down on the floor. "Before the war I worked for a Jewish organization. We smuggled Jews into Palestine. The man you delivered the magazines to in Barcelona was part of that network."

Adria's expression clouded. "It must have been dangerous. I know the British tried to stop immigration."

"So did the mufti. The Zionist organizations—do you know what Zionism is?"

"Vaguely—a movement for a Jewish homeland. Wasn't it started in Germany in the last century?"

He nodded. "That's right. In any case, the Zionist organizations paid to settle Jews in Palestine. In some cases they paid for protection as well as for land. There were always Jews in Palestine of course, but now there are over a hundred and fifty thousand, and when the war is over more will want to go there."

"What about the Palestinians?"

Robert arched one brow and nodded knowingly. "That's a rather complicated question. You see, there's more than one Zionist organization. We're a nation without a country. We already have political parties and we don't agree. I belong to a party that believes that with time and negotiations we can establish a bilateral Palestinian Jewish State with equal power sharing and government responsibility. Our historic claims are real, and so are the claims of the Palestinians." He shook his head. "Of course there are Jews who want a religious state and there are religious Jews who believe there should be no state till the Messiah comes. There are Jews who don't care about the Palestinians and Jews who believe in partition to separate the Palestinians from the Jews." He smiled. "We have a saying: 'put three Jews in a room and you soon have four political parties.'"

Adria laughed at the irony. "So you wanted to confess your Zionist beliefs to me?"

"I'm afraid it goes deeper than that. I want to marry you, but I want you to understand that I have a commitment to the establishment of the State of Israel. I work with the British now in spite of their rules against Jewish immigration, and I believe that we can pressure them to open Palestine for immigration after the war."

"And if you don't succeed?"

"Then I will be on the other side. What I'm saying is that I intend to go to Palestine and work for the establishment of the State of Israel. I want you by my side, but I want you to understand what I'm asking."

Adria propped her head up with her arm and the sheepskin slipped downward, revealing her bare shoulder and the curve of her breast. "I'll be with you wherever you go," she said softly. Then smiling, "Surely the birth of a nation requires a photographer."

He looked across at her. "I hunger for you," he said in his low, deep voice. "I've never known a woman like you."

Adria ran her finger across his cheek, the scar a reminder of his treatment at the hands of his Nazi tormentors. "Some nights I have dreamt of being with you and it was so real I thought you were holding me in your arms. And now being with you is like a dream." She moved slightly to be closer to him. The sheepskin below and above her felt sensuous on her nude body.

He leaned over and kissed her lips, his hand slipped beneath the sheepskin and touched her soft flesh, cupping her breast. "I keep making love to you, and when I am done I want to begin again." He pushed away the covering and kissed her breast, watching as her nipple hardened. Her eyes were like misty jewels.

Adria shivered beneath his touch as well as at his words.

He touched her lips in the way he did when he didn't want to talk anymore, leaned over again, and drew away the rest of the covering. Lying down next to her, he pulled the sheepskin over both of them.

She closed her eyes as he ran his hand across her flat stomach and down to caress her thighs.

Touching her flesh was exotic. His fingers more sensitive since his months in prison, he could feel the blood pulsating through her veins and he knew when she was at the height of passion.

Adria moved to accommodate his gentle explorations. He warmed and chilled her simultaneously, he made her want to cry and laugh, he filled her with desire until she wrapped herself around him and urged him to release her pent-up passions once again. He in turn devoured her with kisses and toyed with her till she writhed with desire. Then at the moment when she could stand no more, a moment he sensed as if he were in her body, they came together lost in one another, complete in each other's arms.

5

THE APACHES (PRONOUNCED A-PASH) were the young ruffians of Paris. They gave birth not only to the violent symbolic dance of the same name, but to a style of dress now adopted by most of the cabaret singers of France. Faithful to the fashion, Celeste Deschamps wore a skin-tight leather skirt, an equally tight red and white horizontally striped top, a black Basque beret, black silk stockings, and spike heels. It was for tourists, but the German officers liked it.

She moved around the room playing up to the German officers and in a throaty voice sang the popular song, "Lola—The Naughty Lola" in German. Its words were suggestive and the German officers laughed and reached out for her, some making obscene suggestions, others patting their knees in invitation.

When Celeste finished her song she returned to the table she was sharing with four SS officers. Two were old and lecherous, two were young, inexperienced, and, she reluctantly admitted, almost decent. All of them were drunk on red wine and satiated with the pleasures of occupied Paris. And all talked freely, which was why Celeste spent time with them.

She slid into her chair and smiled engagingly even as Von Hendle's hand immediately began caressing her knee. My body means nothing, she told herself. It is for a free France—it is for Michel. She repeated her reasons over and over to herself. This was how she entered the trance that made it possible to allow the German to fondle her. She could not think too much about Michel, the young Jewish doctor to whom she was engaged and who had been deported two months after Madame Wertheim. "They're resettling Jews in Russia," the rumor went. The Germans even made a film on Theresienstadt and showed it in French theaters. "Jews get own town," the subtitles read as the camera swept across the landscape and honed in on the industrious ghetto. Celeste would have liked to have believed it; she would have liked to have believed that the trains heading east were not as ominous as she knew them to be. Most of all she wanted to believe that Michel and Madame Wertheim were safe.

"Your German is good," Von Hendle told her.

"Only when I sing a song I know. Actually I don't speak German well at all," she lied in French. Abraham Wertheim had provided for her education and he insisted that she study English, French, and German just as his sons did. This way the Germans spoke to her in French but German among themselves.

"You should learn," he grunted.

Celeste smiled. "Oh, but it's so hard. The verbs take so long to get to."

He laughed and pinched her cheek with his free hand. "So, you have just arrived from Berlin," he said, addressing Bruen, the younger lieutenant.

"Yes; I worked in Göring's office."

Von Hendle nodded as if acknowledging the importance of the young man's position. Celeste forced herself to smile at him, also thinking he must be important. The SS were everywhere now and the Germans even spied on their own. She had been warned by the SOE agent in Paris that the most dangerous intelligence organization was the Abwehr. He also told her that the Abwehr and the SS were locked in competition, and that day by day the SS gained in importance.

"Anything interesting out of Berlin?" Von Hendle asked. "You must at least have the latest gossip."

The young man smiled and laughed, his pale moon-shaped face flushed from so much wine. His blue eyes were dull, and before he had finished his first few words, his companion, Lt. Goetz, had warned him to keep his voice down. "I have heard," the young man said, "that Heydrich's plan is to be put into effect. *Endlosung*—the final solution."

"Really?" Von Hendle raised a bushy eyebrow in interest and again squeezed Celeste's knee.

"*Ja,*" Bruen continued. "Heydrich may be dead, but his plan lives on."

Lt. Barth, who was also older, frowned and repeated the German word. "*Endlosung.*"

Celeste tried to look disinterested, though she felt herself beginning to shake even as she fought for control.

"It hardly seems wise to me," Lt. Barth muttered. "Killing creates martyrs. Why not be happy to deport them? Inferior race or not, they are no danger."

Goetz shook his head. "Better to be rid of them altogether."

Von Hendle agreed, "*Ja,* it's good."

Celeste found her dark eyes focused on Von Hendle's revolver. He had removed his holster and the gun was right next to her, slung over the back of her chair. She edged her hand over and felt the cold steel of the handle. An image of her lover flashed across her mind. They would kill him. They would kill every Jew in Europe. *Endlosung*—the final solution. The word rang in her ears and an image of the trains moving east flooded over her. Her fingers caressed the gun. She could kill all four of them, maybe some other German officers in the club, too. How many could she kill before someone killed her? Did it matter? When they had marched into Paris with their tanks and guns there had been miles of them, miles of disciplined, jack-booted Germans. Michel was gone and she knew in her heart he would not be coming back. She felt suddenly defeated and tired. Had she deceived herself all these months with the Resistance? Had she let German soldiers paw her and sleep with her for nothing? Was any of the information she gathered valuable?

"You do not like our plan to rid the world of the Jews?" Lt. Von Hendle asked, joggling her knee and leaning into her face.

Celeste forced a weak smile and thought, I'd like to kill you, pig. I'd like to see your monstrous body lying on the floor. But why didn't they all look like monsters? Indeed, they were ordinary in every way save one. They could scratch their names across a paper, condemn men, women, and children to death, and not seem to feel a thing.

She remembered Herr Hoffman, a German noncommissioned officer who had been killed at the gare de l'Est only a few weeks ago. His murder had brought on massive executions in reprisal. They had the upper hand. The murder of four German officers could not avenge Michel or Madame Wertheim, and it would only result in more senseless killing. Celeste felt some strength coming back. What she and the others were doing was buying time. Maybe there was some hope, maybe the people in the camps would not all be killed. Celeste edged away from Von Hendle. "Time for another song, mon cher," she said looking down to hide her hatred.

6

KNOWING THAT SHE WOULD join the Americans when they invaded North Africa, Adria left London on August 8, 1942, to rejoin the British Eighth Army, which now had orders to hold El Alamein against the assault led by General Rommel.

Adria moved her left foot, then her right to keep them from going to sleep. She was strapped into a jump seat at the rear of the cargo plane, opposite a middle-aged man with a dark complexion and eyes and thick, graying hair. He was wearing fatigues that bore the insignia of military intelligence. The plane hit yet another air pocket and the man looked slightly nauseated.

273

"There are some salt crackers over there," Adria said, pointing. "The salt will settle your stomach."

He nodded and looked at her curiously. "Do this sort of thing often?"

Adria smiled. "I try to stay on the ground."

"I gather you're a photographer," he said, noting her cameras. "Been at the front before?"

"I was in Tobruk for eleven months."

"My God, a veteran. This is my first time out, I'm afraid. Hated like hell leaving the hallowed halls of Cambridge."

"I wouldn't have liked that either."

"Duty calls. I was drafted, and after one week of basic training the army discovered I had no talent for the usual things. Then someone looked at my file and they discovered I speak five languages, including Arabic, and here I am. God I hate heights. I begged to come by ship."

"Well, it's night so at least you can't see out the window. Why don't you just pretend you're on a very uncomfortable bus?"

"I'll try that." He swallowed a few times. "I'd have thought they'd let a woman travel a bit more comfortably."

Adria laughed. "They don't make exceptions for me. Actually, I'd expected to be traveling more comfortably. General Gott, the new commander of the Eighth Army, was due to fly out tonight and I'd hoped to be on his plane."

"Did they bump you?"

Adria shook her head. "No, I was on my way to the base airport from London and my cab broke down. It took me ages to get another and I missed the plane."

"Bad luck," her companion agreed. "Look here, I've terribly bad manners. My name is Omar Middleton."

The incongruous name made Adria smile, and clearly Mr. Middleton understood.

"My mother was Palestinian and my father British," he said by way of explanation.

"Adria Halstead," she offered.

A look of recognition came over his face. "Of course! How stupid of me. I've seen your work."

Adria smiled. Palestinian—she thought of Robert and all he told her their last night together. "I wanted to talk to you about it before," he'd said, "but I kept putting it off."

"Have you ever lived in Palestine?" Adria ventured.

"For a time. Of course I used to visit my mother's people before the war."

"I suppose you know the Jews want to establish a homeland in Palestine."

"I know it and I dread the prospect."

"You don't think the Jews and the Palestinians can get along?"

"They've been getting on for thousands of years, but if there's an influx of European Jews and they want a state, the Palestinians will fight for their land. Why not?"

Adria nodded. She had no desire to start an argument. In any case Robert had talked about the possibility of war.

"Have you an interest in Palestine?" Mr. Middleton inquired.

"It's an interesting issue. I'd like to learn more about it, that's all."

He laughed. "Well, I'm not as intransigent as some. Personally, I would hope level heads can prevail. There are already many Jews in Palestine, and I imagine some sort of bilateral state could be agreed on when the British pull out."

Adria smiled. Robert, too, had talked of a bilateral state. She glanced at her watch. "We'll be in the air for hours. You should try to sleep."

"I'm afraid I'm very British. I've adopted the prime minister's ways. If I'm going to sleep, I'm going to tipple. May I offer you a little brandy?"

Mr. Omar Middleton withdrew a silver flask from his flak jacket and held it out to her. Adria took it and poured a shot into the paper cup which had previously held water. "Thank you."

He too poured a shot. "To our new General Gott," he toasted.

After two more drinks Adria leaned back and closed her eyes, drifting into a light sleep. She was awakened by the noise of the door that separated the pilots' compartment from the rest of the plane. The copilot, a cigarette dangling from his mouth, stood framed in the doorway. "All buckled up back there?" he shouted.

"Yes!" Adria called out, as Mr. Middleton opened his eyes.

"We're landing," she told him.

"Not a moment too soon," he responded sleepily.

The plane circled and tilted, circled again, and then Adria felt her ears pop as they lost altitude. In a few seconds she heard the grind of the landing gear as it dropped, and a few minutes after that the wheels hit the uneven runway and the plane bumped along to a stop.

Unstrapping her harness, Adria gathered up her cameras and backpack. She bent down as she walked through the center of the plane to the door the pilot had opened. A ladder had been moved into place below and on the runway she could see a parked jeep, its lights extinguished.

Adria stepped out into the clear, cool, North African night and inhaled. She walked toward the jeep and heard "Adria! Adria! Thank God!"

Jeff Borden was standing up in the jeep. He vaulted over the side and ran to meet her, his face actually pale. "God, am I glad to see you!" He hugged her impulsively.

"What's the matter?" He looked truly upset, as upset as she had ever seen him.

"I thought you were flying in with General Gott."

Adria frowned. "My cab broke down; I missed the plane."

"Shit! I was worried out of my mind. I thought you were dead."

"Dead?"

"General Gott's plane was shot down by Jerries."

Adria opened her mouth in surprise. "I had no way of knowing," was all she could manage. "What's going to happen now?"

Jeff took her arm and guided her toward the jeep, Adria hardly aware that Omar Middleton followed. It was a strange feeling she had, and she wondered if, like a cat, she had nine lives. If so, three were gone, one in Spain, one in Italy, and one now. But for a flat tire she would have been on that plane.

"Rumor has it Montgomery will take over the Eighth now," Jeff told her. "I hear he's a real prick."

Adria didn't comment. "Jeff, I'd like you to meet Mr. Middleton, who was on the flight with me."

Jeff extended his hand, "Welcome to our desert hellhole."

Middleton nodded and Jeff tossed his bag in the back of the jeep telling him to sit by the driver. He helped Adria into the back seat, then climbed in with her. "Home, James!" Jeff shouted to the young private who was the driver.

Adria leaned back as the jeep bumped along the tarmac toward the main road into town and looked at Jeff's profile. He had really been worried about her and it made her feel guilty. Still, as soon as he'd seen her he had recovered. "If you thought I was on General Gott's plane, why did you meet this one?" she asked.

"I heard from the guy in the control tower there was another plane coming in, figured it was worth waiting. Besides, you always mess things up. I thought you might have missed the first plane."

She smiled to herself. "Has it been rough out here?"

He turned and looked in her eyes. "Lonely. You look great, Adria. You ought to spend less time at the front."

"I had a good rest."

"And you saw him, didn't you? I can tell that look of contentment, you know. You haven't looked that way for a long time."

Adria bit her lip. "Yes, I did. He's all right. He escaped."

"Lucky man. Hey, listen, one of the reasons I wanted to see you was to say good-bye."

His voice is full of bravado, she thought. He was trying too hard. "Are you going somewhere?"

"Yeah. Yeah, I am. I'm going to be flying with the RAF out of England for awhile. I've wanted to try some aerial photography for some time now. I'll be leaving tomorrow night. Hell, I was afraid you wouldn't get back in time for me to say good-bye."

I should ask him if that's what he really wants to do, she thought. But Jeff wasn't the type to admit he'd been hurt and in a way she admired him. "We'll have to have a farewell drink," she suggested.

"Sure, good idea," he answered somewhat glumly.

Chapter Fifteen

1

CHRISTINA BARTON HAD LONG deceived herself. But on December 7, 1941, her beliefs were shattered. If the sudden attack on Pearl Harbor shocked her, the events of December 10 and 11 alarmed her, when two of her close friends in the United States were arrested along with two hundred German-American Nazi sympathizers. The FBI swoop was sudden, unexpected, and reasonably complete, and barely a German agent survived. Next, her father, a former Senator and prominent Washington lobbyist, fell silent, later becoming vocally anti-German. For months following the arrests Christina had waited for a visit from either American or British intelligence, assuming her position to be precarious at best.

She was not arrested or even questioned. Nevertheless, in March, 1942, after a particularly nerve-wracking day when she imagined she had been followed, she made a vow. "You have always come first," she told her mirror image, "and from now on, I shall see to it that Erich is given only harmless information." It was bad enough to have to play loving wife, to live in fear was too much.

She began by vetting the contents of her husband's briefcase, selecting only non-sensitive data. But Erich grew suspicious, and on and off Christina provided him with everything in spite of her vow. Then in October she hit upon ways to change the information in Nelson's notes. Correct information could be easily traced to her, she reasoned, but incorrect information could come from any number of sources. Still, it was a dangerous game. The Americans might arrest her—she had, after all, initially passed on vital information—or the Germans might suspect she was holding back and force her to cooperate more fully by threatening to expose her. But as the months passed without incident, Christina grew more comfortable.

January, 1943, brought never-ending cold rain to London, but also a respite from the bombing. Dense fog protected the city, and though it was thoroughly damp and miserable, everyone seemed grateful for the silent nights. Christina congratulated herself. Nelson did not have the slightest inkling that she read his notes and forged new ones. It was these she photographed for Erich, and he too, seemed satisfied.

Then on January 5, Erich summoned her for a rare face-to-face meeting. She had no choice but to attend, and sitting across from him in the rented hotel room, she felt nervous and tired. Erich, by contrast, looked relaxed as he contemplated his folded hands. Steepling his fingers he looked up at her with his cold blue eyes. "You have been passing me false information," he said without emotion.

His assertion ran through Christina like a knife, and she struggled internally for control, running her hand through her hair. Finally she forced a smile and

279

shrugged casually. "I've been photographing all his notes as usual. Perhaps he suspects something, perhaps MI6 suspects something." She almost believed it herself now, and she grew bolder and more strident. She continued, "Friends of mine were arrested at home; perhaps the FBI notified MI6? Oh, dear God, Erich, do you think I'm under suspicion?"

Erich's eyes seemed to drill through her, but then he smiled. "Perhaps. How does Nelson treat you?"

A wave of relief swept through her. Now she had to follow it up. She bit her lip and threw herself into a fear not altogether feigned. "He's been a little distant lately," she lied. "What shall I do?" she asked, struggling for just the right amount of tremor in her voice.

The smile faded from his narrow lips and his eyes became hard and angry. "You might realize that this is not a Hollywood film about spies and agents. I'm afraid, Christina, that you are not quite the actress you think you are, and certainly no master forger. Oh, it fooled me for a time because I never saw the developed film. But we have experts in Berlin, my dear, and they do bother to evaluate and check intelligence information. Some months ago I was informed that what you were passing me was nothing more than bad forgeries revealing false information. I am your control, my dear. Can you imagine how much this news distressed me? But I waited to see what you would do."

Christina's normally pale skin grew even whiter. The rouge on her cheeks looked like crayon marks and her ruby red lips trembled. She opened her mouth and the words tumbled out, "I had to protect myself! They would have known it was me. I'm certain I'm being watched! Nelson even told me he'd been assigned a new assistant; he thought *he* was being watched! I would have been caught!"

Erich's expression remained cold and hard. "He's quite right. His assistant is with U.S. Naval Intelligence."

"See! I *would* have been found out."

"But in the meantime we could have sunk half the

arms being poured into England. I'm sorry, Christina. You have deliberately lied to me and to my superiors. It is a lie you will pay for."

Christina's lips parted, in a silent plea.

"I suppose you thought our personal relationship held some special meaning for me?" His eyes were deadly cold now, and his voice low.

Christina stared at him. Was she really surprised? No, Erich was a pragmatist.

"If you did, you were quite wrong. I would rather sleep with any one of half a dozen good German girls I know than you. One I am especially fond of is very beautiful, much more so than you ever were. No, you are simply a matter of convenience when I am in London." He was deliberately striking out at her, trying to hurt her as much as possible. Still, she felt not pain but sheer panic. He was quite capable of killing her, and until now she hadn't considered him quite that calculating.

Erich Schmidt stood up and paced a few steps. "You are a conundrum. You cannot stay where you are because you will soon be arrested. Even though your recent information has been false, the earlier material will be traced. You cannot be trusted not to crack. Then, too, from your point of view, the consequences of being caught are not pleasant. Killing you would allow the scandal to unfold and certainly there would be excellent propaganda value. On the other hand, I hesitate to kill someone who might still be of use."

Christina shivered, drawing her hands around her own bare arms.

"Are you cold, my dear?" He moved toward her and draped a heavy sweater from the arm of a nearby chair around her shoulders. "You shouldn't dress so lightly. You know there's no central heating, practically no heating at all now."

"Stop it! You're toying with me!" Tears began to fill her eyes.

"Yes, I am playing cat and mouse. But I must consider all of the alternatives. And actually, I think I have quite an ideal solution to our problem, from your point of view."

"What do you mean?" She pressed her lips together.

"I think I shall allow you—'under escort,' of course —to 'escape' to Germany. I can manage to have a sub to pick you up off the Irish coast. It's quite an interesting way to travel, really, if you don't get torpedoed. Once in Germany, your sexy, soothing voice can be used to broadcast 'information' to British and American troops. And I think the scandal of your 'defection' will be quite effective."

"My father will be arrested—"

"Now, now. You know you're more concerned with yourself. And alas, your father is of very little use to us now."

"I don't want to go to Germany," Christina whimpered.

Erich Schmidt smiled. "First I think you will write a little confession." He took some paper and pen from the desk drawer. "I shall dictate it, if I may. Your mind does seem muddled."

"I don't want to go to Germany."

Erich made a sudden movement with his wrist and a long stiletto appeared in his hand. Before she had a second to move or to scream, it was next to her throat. "Did I give you a choice, darling?" he asked threateningly.

Christina shuddered, afraid even to breathe. Her terror-stricken eyes met his and he smiled, slowly moving the blade away. "Shall we proceed?"

Christina nodded dumbly.

2

BETWEEN THE DULL GRAY barracks of Theresienstadt rivulets of water had run downhill to the river below. Now the cold had frozen the mud into rutted pathways, and a light snowfall had covered the ground.

Anna walked along the crumbling wall of the old

stone fortress, stopping abruptly when she saw a formation of icicles where some water had run down the wall. The weak winter sun made them sparkle like a nest of jewels between the stones.

"What are you looking at?" Aaron Rosen asked, catching up to her.

"These icicles. It's been so long since I saw anything beautiful."

He smiled at her warmly. Her wavy white hair was tucked under a kerchief and her magnificent eyes were wide, like a child with a new discovery. Like the others in the camp, she wore a brown dress of crude material, and her shoes, like his, had been stuffed with scrap paper where the soles were worn through. Over her dress was a wool blanket, wrapped like a stole. But in spite of her dress, and the hardships she had endured during nearly two years at Theresienstadt, she was still a beautiful woman.

"They're melting," he said. "If this thaw continues the ground will soon be running mud again."

She inhaled deeply. "It's good to be outside for awhile. It's so stuffy inside."

"It's unusual to find a moment alone in this place." He sat down on a flat stone, "Come, sit down here beside me, Anna."

She came to his side and sat down on the rock. "We have to go back to the barracks soon," she commented as her eyes surveyed the sun and she guessed at the time.

"Soon, but not this second," he answered. It was a rare moment and he intended to use it. "Anna, I want to marry you," he said, taking her hand in his.

"Marry? Oh, Aaron I'm too old and set in my ways. But your asking makes me very happy. It's a great compliment."

"It was not meant to be a compliment, my dear Anna. The fact is, I am an old but lustful man, and frankly, you are a beautiful woman. Besides, I have loved you since the first time I danced with you. You,

Anna, have enchanted me, and I won't take no for an answer."

Anna looked into Aaron's amber eyes with surprise. But she did not resist when he kissed her hand, then her cheek and finally her lips. He pulled her into his arms, and his hands ran through her hair, brushing her kerchief aside.

"We are not *so* old," he told her. Then, his voice lowering, he added, "Anna, things will get worse before they get better. There's less food now, less heat, and fewer guards. More people are being moved to the east, to extermination centers. More people are dying. I want to be with you for however long we have."

She pulled away and looked into his face. "I'm not going to die so easily to please the Germans," she said with determination. "Nor are you."

"Well, I certainly intend to do my best to stay alive," he replied.

"If I do marry you, you realize we may be together for some time," she smiled mischievously. "I warn you, I am a possessive woman."

He grinned at her. "I doubt you will catch me straying."

Anna lifted her hand and touched his cheek, and a slight smile crept around the corner of her mouth. "Does that mean I won't catch you, or you won't stray?"

He laughed. "I won't stray."

"Then I shall marry you," she promised, then sighed. "I wish there was some way to tell Robert."

"What about your other son, Charles?"

"Oh, Charles would be shocked," she laughed. "In fact, I'd like to see the look on his face when he finds out."

Aaron grinned broadly and stood up, encircling her waist. He lifted her off the stone and kissed her. "Let us go and find the rabbi! Let us not waste another precious moment."

3

ADRIA HAD REJOINED THE British Eighth Army in August, 1942, near El Alamein, remaining with them till November 4th, when General Montgomery succeeded in winning the seesaw battle for Egypt. His victory in early November was complete and the German Afrika Korps in full retreat.

On November 9, as promised, she flew to join the American forces that had landed on the Algerian and Moroccan coasts. Algiers had been taken by nightfall on November 8, so Adria joined the battle near Oran, where resistance from the French Vichy government proved stronger than the Americans had anticipated. By late November the major battles were occurring in Tunisia, where the Americans and Germans became locked in another of North Africa's seesaw battles.

In January Adria received orders from General Eisenhower to return to Allied-held Casablanca. There she found two surprises.

"You are absolutely the last person I expected to see," Adria exclaimed, looking into Charles Wertheim's eyes. Resplendent in a crisp white tropical suit and British pith helmet, he had met her military flight from Tunisia, packed her bag in the back of his car, and ordered the driver to take them to the palace.

Adria leaned back against the richly upholstered seat of the prewar Rolls Royce. Still dressed in battle fatigues and disheveled from her night flight, she felt entirely out of place. "What are you doing here?" she pressed. "What am *I* doing here?"

Charles turned his head slightly and smiled. "All things in good time, my dear. But to keep you from losing all patience here." He handed her a brown envelope and Adria quickly ripped it open.

My darling,

Tonight this letter will leave for England with a person I shall call Max, a downed pilot on his way home. Of course it is coded for his protection. He will give it to Charles who will have it decoded, retyped, and delivered to you wherever you are. By the time you receive it, it will have been read by at least ten people. Do you know how hard it is to write a love letter that will be seen by so many?

Months have gone by and you are no less real to me. I think of you daily and wait anxiously for a time when we can be together again. I am well and progress is being made. If I could write you every day I would. Believe that I love you and miss you. Know how anxiously I am waiting to hold you in my arms.

Love,
Robert

Adria felt tears welling in her eyes. She glanced at Charles, whose face revealed little. I wonder if he's read it? she asked herself. "Thank you for bringing it," she said softly, even as she began to reread it.

"I would have had it relayed by radio if I hadn't known I'd see you here." He looked out the window. The car turned up a palm lined road.

She smiled. "It's good to have, even if it is in someone else's handwriting."

"Under the circumstances I'm afraid there is no such thing as privacy."

The driver turned the Rolls into a narrow private drive, its entrance guarded by two Marines and a barred iron gate. Along the road on either side of the guards barbed wire was woven into the existing fence. Charles flashed his identification and explained who Adria was. The Marine checked his clipboard, apparently found her name, and checked it off.

"Sorry, sir. We'll have to check Miss Halstead's luggage."

Adria frowned. "I thought the palace was a hotel Charles. Why all this security?"

"I'll explain everything soon," he promised. Turning to the Marine, he said "Her bag is in the boot. Oh, you American's say trunk, don't you? The driver will open it for you."

Silently the driver got out of the car and opened the trunk. The Marine went through her pack, then asked to see her camera bag and cameras. Checking each of them quickly and efficiently, he handed everything back and saluted. The car engine was again started and they continued up the date-palm-lined driveway.

Within half a mile the car came to a stop in front of an elegant white hotel built in the Moroccan style. They climbed out of the car and again gave their names to a waiting guard.

"Miss Halstead to villa number three," he turned and pointed down a flower-lined path. "That way, they're all numbered. Lord Wertheim, villa number five. It's just beyond three in the same direction." He snapped his fingers and two servants took their luggage, trudging on ahead of them.

"This is becoming very mysterious," Adria said. "And whatever it is, I have a feeling I'm not dressed for it."

Charles smiled. "The second of my two suitcases I had packed for you by a woman whose taste is impeccable. I think you'll find everything you need."

"Charles, what is this? I insist on knowing."

"Ah, here we are." Stopping in front of a small white villa, he directed the servant to leave her bag and one of his, then sent him on to number five with his other bag. "I'll come in for a moment, if you don't mind. We'll have a drink and I'll explain everything."

The inside of the villa was quite luxurious. It had a bedroom, a private bath, and a sitting room with a small, fully stocked bar and bucket of ice.

"What would you like?" Charles inquired.

"Something cold and some answers." She had to hand it to Charles Wertheim. When he wanted to be

287

mysterious, he certainly knew how. And, she thought, he can be charming, too.

"A gin and tonic then. Very good in warm climates."

"You didn't have to bring clothes for me, I could have shopped here. But thank you."

"No, I'm afraid you couldn't have. Once on these grounds, you have to stay here till the conference is over."

"Conference?"

"Conference. Today your American president will be arriving. Our prime minister and the combined chiefs of staff are already here."

"Roosevelt?" Adria was incredulous. "Here, in Casablanca?"

"And Winston Churchill."

"General Eisenhower asked for you personally. There are four other pool reporters. Of course you can't attend the conference, but you will take pictures when requested, and within a month your photographs will be released to all news media. This is a major strategy conference, very, very hush hush till its over. I'm certain you understand."

Adria smiled. "Of course." Charles Wertheim handed her a tall, ice-filled glass with gin and tonic water. "Thank you." She curled up on the sofa and sipped at her drink. "They're planning for an invasion, aren't they?"

"You know I can't answer that question."

"I know."

Charles Wertheim sat down in a chair across from the sofa. "You'll have a few days good rest here, you know. There's even a pool in the garden behind the house."

"I'm looking forward to a bath and to a bed instead of an army cot."

"I imagine." Charles cleared his throat and looked about uncomfortably. "Miss Halstead, there's something else I have to talk to you about, something terribly unpleasant."

Adria looked at him steadily. His expression had

grown serious. "Robert? But you brought me his letter—"

"Not Robert. Your father."

Adria's mouth opened slightly. Her father? What on earth had Charles Wertheim to do with her father? And why did he always call her Miss Halstead?

"Please call me by my first name," she said. "I didn't know you knew my father."

"More specifically, this concerns your stepmother," he amended.

Adria now felt totally perplexed. "Christina?" She hastily added, "Let me assure you, I never considered *her* my stepmother, though I suppose she is, legally. I haven't seen my father since he and Christina were married."

"Nonetheless, this is a matter about which you must be informed." Charles Wertheim leaned back, lit his pipe, and seemed to be searching for words. "I'm afraid I can't think of a way to put it delicately. Your father was sitting in on admiralty meetings before America entered the war. Naturally, once America became our ally, his attendance took on a much greater importance, and in keeping with the joint command, he was privy to a great deal of confidential, and I may say extremely sensitive, information."

Adria tilted her head. She could not imagine where this conversation was leading. "I suppose he must have been," she murmured, for lack of a better comment.

"Well, it seems that your father is married to a German agent. Worse, he appears to have been careless with classified material."

Adria's mouth opened in surprise. "Christina, a German agent?"

"Quite. A few weeks ago, her father was arrested by your FBI, but he suffered a fatal heart attack before he could be questioned. It seems he was a stalwart of the German American Bund, perhaps even an agent himself."

"He was once a senator," Adria said in surprise.

"Fortunately, ex-. But it was his daughter who did the real damage. She's defected to Germany, got out through Ireland we think. She left a note implicating your father, confessing—or perhaps I should say boasting—that he was the source of leaks we have been aware of for some time."

"My father is a loyal American!" Adria protested. "The one thing he wouldn't do is what you're accusing him of. What Christina says he did."

Lord Wertheim sighed deeply, his heavy shoulders visibly rising and falling. "Women can be very subtle, in bed and out. I give him the full benefit of the doubt. I think he was used and used badly. She seems to have photographed his notes. It is even possible he was drugged. There is, however, one mystery. Sometime after Pearl Harbor—about four months after—the information leaked to Berlin became inaccurate. We think Miss Barton may have been trying to protect herself."

Adria leaned back, stunned.

"Perhaps," Charles added, "your father should have read that American poster that's all over the place, you know the one, 'a slip of the lip will sink a ship.'"

Unconsciously, Adria doubled her fists, conjuring up the image of Christina Barton's tight, smug little face. Christina had once stepped between Jeff and her, she had indirectly caused her parents divorce, and now she had ruined her father's career, if not his whole life.

As if reading her mind, Charles Wertheim said, "I doubt she will have a pleasant life in Germany. I think she was forced to leave by her controller. He must have realized she wasn't passing accurate information. Doubtless they thought they'd get maximum propaganda value if she left a note confessing and explaining that she was going to Germany to help build the New Order. We foiled that, of course; we had her under surveillance and we intercepted the note before it reached the press."

For the second time within the hour Adria felt tears welling in her eyes, this time cold tears of anger. She was certainly tired from her long journey aboard the military transport plane, but she was also devastated by what her father must be going through. "What will happen to him?" she finally managed to ask.

"I only know that all the information has been passed on to the American Office of Naval Intelligence. They, by the way, already had their suspicions and had a man on him. Of course, he has been temporarily relieved of his command. I would suppose he would either be asked to resign his commission, or perhaps be transferred to some remote or non-strategic area. Patagonia, perhaps."

Adria pressed her lips together and fumbled in her purse for a handkerchief. "You must forgive me," she said. "I'm very tired and this is almost unbelievable."

"I understand. What are you going to do?"

"When this conference is over I'll try to get back to England. I have to see my father."

Charles Wertheim nodded. "May I share some good news with you?"

Adria tried to smile. Charles was managing to look truly sympathetic. "Please do."

"I've received word from the Red Cross that my mother is still alive in Theresienstadt."

"I'm terribly glad," she told him. "Does Robert know?"

"I've sent him a message."

Adria finished her drink and stood up. "I'd like to rest now, if there's time. Charles, I want to thank you for telling me all this personally."

"I didn't think you should hear it from a stranger." He looked down at his watch. "You have about four hours before the arrival of President Roosevelt. You'll want photos of the prime minister and the president shaking hands on the runway. Then during before-dinner drinks, perhaps at dinner, and, of course, a few shots while they're having their brandy. Tomorrow you'll be given a list of the times you may take pictures."

Adria nodded. "I'll clean up and take a short nap then."

"If you need anything you know where to find me."

Adria watched as he picked up his briefcase and sauntered up the path toward his own bungalow. She assumed that British intelligence had planned and was responsible for the secrecy of this meeting. Well, Charles was to be congratulated. The rumor mill was strong and healthy and there hadn't been even a whisper about Roosevelt coming to Casablanca.

4

THE USUAL FOG BLEW off the Thames while dark rolling clouds threatened more wet snow. Londoners, thousands of whom had now had their homes destroyed, spent their daylight hours living as if nothing were amiss. The only perceptible change was that most now dressed in extra layers of clothing and many carried a small satchel or valise with a change of clothes and a few precious belongings in case they had to go to the air raid shelters. Otherwise, the well-dressed men of Fleet Street still walked briskly, umbrellas in hand, and tipped their hats. The populace still gathered in pubs at noon and in the early evening for darts and a warm beer. Rationing, shortages, and persistent bombings had done nothing to change the British.

It was the first of February, and news of the daring Casablanca conference filled the papers for the first time. Franklin Roosevelt was hailed as fearless. Wheelchair-bound for many years, the American president was the first American president since Lincoln to visit a battle front, the first to have left the United States in time of war, the first to travel to Africa while in office, and the first to travel by airplane. The conference had lasted ten days, and on the last day a large number of correspondents had been summoned to a Casablanca press conference in the desert beneath a protective covering of fighter planes. Joined by de Gaulle, the leaders announced they had agreed on the

1943 war plans and that the goal was "unconditional German surrender." Passing newsstands, Adria felt especially proud. Hers were the only pictures of the leaders during casual moments of the conference.

Adria walked up three flights of stairs to her father's apartment and paused outside for a moment. Better now than when I first found out, she thought. Not only had she had time to think, but the Navy committee investigating the affair had met and issued its decision. Her father had been found the 'victim' of a foreign agent, and while he had been severely reprimanded for lack of caution, his personal loyalty had not been questioned.

Adria knocked and heard her father's call to come in. Damp and cold, the small Hampstead apartment also smelled of stale smoke, unemptied ash trays, and unwashed dishes. It was cluttered and thoroughly messy, very unlike her father, who was normally 'regulation' to the letter.

Admiral Nelson Halstead stood straight and tall with his back to the door, looking out the window as wet snow fell from the dark skies. But his posture was a matter of training, and when he turned, his face told a very different story. He had deep lines under his eyes and he held his head less confidently. His cheeks seemed to sag slightly and his eyes were bloodshot from lack of sleep. He looked ten years older than when Adria had last seen him. And his voice, on the verge of cracking, told more of the story than his face, the brusqueness gone out of it. Adria didn't need to be told that her father was a defeated man, a man suffering not just from the charges leveled by others but from his own bitter self-accusations.

"Frankly, I had hoped you meant what you said about not wanting to see me again."

"Daddy." She heard the pleading quality in her own voice. She hadn't sounded like that since she was a child.

"I can't blame you for hating me," he said softly. "Your mother—I treated her badly. I don't know how

293

to explain that to you. She was too sacrificing, too smothering. She didn't give me room to breathe. Of course, I seem to have made a mess without her."

"I understand about Mother," Adria said softly. "She doesn't mean to be choking, but she is. I fought it, too. I don't blame you for that anymore."

"Well, the old saying is right. 'There's no fool like an old fool.' Christina had me hoodwinked. But you know, that's what hurts. I loved her."

Adria's fingers were curled around the side of the table, holding back an, "I told you so."

Her father looked down. "I'm a bastard," he said, "a prideful bastard. Look at the irony. I've spent this war tied to a Goddamned desk while you've been out distinguishing yourself on the front lines. Your photographs are sensational, Adria. I'm so proud of you. Guess I never told you that before."

Adria stood and stared at her father. Tears were streaming down his cheeks, and he covered his eyes with his arm to hide the fact that he was crying.

"I've ruined my career and disgraced you. It would be best if you left, best if you broke off your relationship with me."

Adria crossed the room and threw herself into her father's arms, hugging him fiercely, thinking how much she really loved this blustering, austere, stubborn man. "I couldn't do that," she whispered and broke into tears. "I'm your daughter, and we need each other."

Nelson Halstead held her for a long while, then fished for his handkerchief. "I'm requesting active duty in the Pacific," he said. "Even though I know I'll be demoted."

Adria nodded. Softly she suggested, "Write mother."

"She'd be a fool to take me back."

"You could try."

He hugged Adria hard. "I'm a lucky man to have a daughter like you."

A daughter—Adria squeezed him back. "Write me, Daddy. Please."

He nodded silently and released her, both trying to smile through their tears.

Chapter Sixteen

1

My Darling,

In some ways it seems like yesterday that we were together, in other ways it seems a hundred times the seventeen months which have elapsed. In my mind I write you every day and imagine your answers. But as you know I can only send you a message when fate delivers a messenger into my hands, and it is impossible for you to reply. How I would like to tell you everything, but my letters must, of necessity be short. I am well. I have heard you are the same from Charles. And I love you, want you, and wait anxiously for the day we will be together.

Love,
Robert

ADRIA FOLDED ROBERT'S letter and added it to the other five. She kept them tied together at the bottom of her camera bag, always with her. They were decoded, censored, and passed on to her only after they'd passed through the hands of intelligence agents, radio operators, and typists, but it did not matter. When she received a letter she knew he was still alive.

"You're mooning, love," said Rick Shattner, the Australian reporter, as he leaned over the table and sat down without invitation.

The sidewalk café in Palermo was crowded with military personnel, and the waiters bustled back and forth, hurriedly taking orders and delivering trays of pasta. Adria smiled at her fellow correspondent. The press corps were all close and got along well. They weren't all together all the time, but when one left a specific area there was usually a replacement sent and so eventually you got to know everyone. "I didn't know you were in Palermo."

"A little rest and recuperation," he replied. "Nice of the generals to liberate the places with the best climate first." He laughed and ordered a Campari on ice.

Adria nodded her agreement. 1943 seemed to be a turning point in the war. Sicily had fallen to the Allies in August, and Italy had surrendered in September. Not that the Italian surrender meant an end to fighting in Italy, when the Germans were deeply entrenched. Nonetheless, the Allied fronts in southern Italy were firmly established, though stalled by tough German resistance. Adria had been with the American troops when they captured San Pietro on December 17; then, bone tired and battle weary, she had left for Sicily, vowing to spend Christmas and New Year's resting on the liberated beaches. "I came for the same reason myself," she confessed.

"I thought you had a rather dark tan. How long have you been here?"

"Since December nineteenth."

"Malingerer. Heard from Jeff Borden?"

Sometimes I wonder where he is myself, she thought. I seem to run into everyone but him. "No," she answered, thinking, I'm sure I'd be the last person to hear from him. Jeff, she had long ago concluded, was avoiding her.

"I heard on the rumor mill that he's headed for Italy, thought he might have contacted you. As I remember, you were friends in North Africa."

Adria half smiled. Rick had been one of the reporters that night in Tobruk when she had followed Jeff out of the shelter during the air raid. Probably everyone who'd been with the press corps in Tobruk thought she and Jeff were lovers. "We are friends," she said quietly. "But we don't keep in touch that often."

"Headed back to San Pietro?"

Adria shook her head. "I was, but I have a new assignment."

"Ah, the mysteries of the military! Could it be that the Allies are going to make the long-rumored landing on the west coast of Italy to break the impasse?"

"I don't know, and if I did I couldn't tell you. All I have is a set of orders to report on January twenty-first."

"To whom?" he asked, lifting one eyebrow.

"It's a secret," Adria said, winking.

Rick Shattner crossed his legs, leaned back in the wire chair, and looked at her appraisingly. "How about a night on the town?"

He was wearing shoes without socks, the mark, Adria thought, of an Australian reporter. None of them wore socks. "Are you asking me for a date when there are all these lovely Sicilian women to chose from?"

He drank some of his Campari and nodded. "Have you noticed all the Sicilian men with long knives? No, thank you. The professionals all have V.D. and the nonprofessionals are off limits."

"I'm off limits, too," she said, smiling. "I'm engaged." It wasn't exactly true, but it served to discourage men who approached her. And Robert *had* asked her to marry him.

"Well, how about just dinner and some dancing? Very platonic, I promise."

Adria nodded. "Around seven?"

"Perfect." He then leaned closer. "You're American. Tell me, is it true that the Americans offered that Mafia boss, Lucky Luciano, a deal for his cooperation in taking Sicily?"

"I've heard it is, but I think he would have cooperated, anyway. They say the Germans and the Mafia didn't get along."

He laughed and hit the table with his fist. "Probably the understatement of the century."

Adria stood up and brushed off her skirt. "Till

seven," she said, smiling. She waved again as she turned the corner and walked toward her hotel. The sun was warm, there were flowers everywhere, and the narrow streets of Palermo were nearly untouched by the war. In her purse was a telegram which read simply, "Report to U.S. VI Corps, England by 1400 hours, January 21." Three days from now she would fly to England and report. Rick was probably right. In all likelihood the Allies were going for the long-discussed amphibious landing on the west coast of Italy. But Adria could not help hoping that instead they would be landing on the coast of France.

2

THE NIGHT WAS COLD and Adria unzipped her flak jacket and slipped it over the back of the chair in the wardroom where the ship's officers gathered for chit-chat and coffee. Press were always offered wardroom privileges while aboard, and the round-faced Filipino mess boy brought her a cup and saucer without her asking. He poured the coffee from a large silver urn, offered cream and sugar, and smiled broadly. "Anything else, missy?"

Adria shook her head and looked at her cup. Even the addition of cream left it dark; it was good, strong Navy coffee, the kind her father joked about when he said, "It's not coffee unless the spoon stands up by itself."

A wave of nostalgia passed over her. I grew up here, she thought. Since she was a child she'd been eating in ship's wardrooms, and she was used to the ever-present Filipino mess boys in their white coats, the aroma of coffee, the battleship gray walls, and long tables covered with white cloths. She glanced around the spacious room. The walls were covered with photographs and paintings of ships. It looked like every wardroom she had ever been in, all interchangeable in her memory.

"Adria, you're not seasick are you?"

Carrying his coffee cup, Captain Hughes sat down and signaled for the mess boy to refill his cup.

"No, sir."

"Good. You're not supposed to get seasick when your father's an old salt. How is he?"

"He's fine. Somewhere in the Pacific." Mentally she thanked heaven that her father's indiscretion had never become public. "I get letters all the time, but they're heavily censored, so I have no idea where he is." She didn't elaborate, but almost a third of the last letter she'd received had been crossed out with India ink. Of course that wasn't unusual; the military censors were very careful about ship locations.

Captain Hughes laughed. "I got a letter from my son—he's on the *Princeton*—and it began. 'Dear Dad.' Then it was blacked out till he mentioned his Christmas present, and blacked out again until the 'Love, Jack.'"

Adria smiled and sipped her coffee. "Has our destination been released yet?"

"I've got the aerial maps down in the situation room if you'd care to look at them. They're no secret now, and you'll be taking pictures of the same thing when you get on the ground."

"I'd like that."

Captain Hughes stood up. "Follow me. I'll give you a private briefing."

"I don't want to bother you," she said.

"No bother. If the Executive Officer can't run the ship by now we're in real trouble." He glanced at her, "Oh, you can bring your coffee. We drink as much there in the situation room as in the wardroom."

Adria followed the captain, down a narrow gangplank and through the heavy door into the situation room, a small space with about ten desks and charts all over the walls. The captain pulled down a large picture taken from the air.

"Anzio, a resort town," he said, pointing to a village. "We'll be landing here and here." He indicated two areas of shore. "These buildings are on the outskirts of

Anzio, and as you see, on the shore. One is a gambling casino."

Adria nodded. "How far is Anzio from Rome?"

"Thirty-two miles. Here, let me get down an area map." He pulled down a large relief map.

"It's really hilly," Adria commented.

"Yeah. Well, this is the problem. From Anzio to this road is about sixteen miles inland. The road goes to Rome, of course, and that's sixteen miles north. But there's this village, Cassino, and the mountain behind it. The mountain guards the road, and we think its got a large number of German gun implacements. In fact, starting right about here," he indicated the first strip of hills between the coast and the road, "it could be hill by hill fighting."

"You don't sound very optimistic."

Captain Hughes shrugged. "The hills are out of range of our guns. We can secure the beachhead, but further inland is General Lucas's, and the army's problem. He wants to put everything ashore at once. I think he's crazy. If we catch the Germans napping, we ought to take as much territory as fast as we can. The Germans have a lot of troops in Italy and they can mass very quickly because the rail lines are still operating."

"Are we going to catch them napping?" Adria asked.

"Our last flyover showed nothing but peace and quiet."

"Then I bet you're right."

The captain smiled. "Look, we wouldn't be having this conversation if I hadn't known you since you were seven. Admiral Lowery says our job is to deliver the troops. I don't have to tell you that the army and the navy do things differently. I'm just giving you a private, very personal opinion."

"I appreciate that. It won't be repeated."

"Good girl. Listen, we have some apple pie to go with that coffee, and I have an idea you might not be seeing any apple pie for quite a while." He took her arm and led her back toward the wardroom.

* * *

300

Just after midnight on the twenty-second of January the landing craft slipped into the still, dark waters. Admiral Lowery was one hundred per cent on schedule. In perfect unison, the first wave was heading for shore by 0200. Then, as scheduled, there was a five-minute rocket barrage on the shore, answered only by silence. No machine guns responded from shore, no planes strafed the beachhead or bombed the ships. General Lucas smiled gleefully, turned to his second in command, and ordered him to send the message: "Paris-Bordeaux-Turin-Tangiers-Bari-Albany," which meant, "Weather clear, sea calm, little wind, our presence undiscovered."

Adria went ashore with the second wave of troops. It was lighter now, and she set to work immediately as the Rangers seized a large yellow building in the center of the beach. It was the gambling casino adjacent to the resort town of Anzio that she had seen on the aerial photographs. Adria took the first ground views as the Rangers stormed the door of the totally deserted pleasure palace.

It was in the pastel light of dawn that Adria saw Jeff Borden lumbering toward her. He waved his kerchief, and when he got to her, he picked her up and hugged her. "Adria! We must have been on different ships! Hey, look at this! Look around! Not a damn Jerry in sight! We've got it made!" He moved his hands expressively, "Can you see the headline! *Allied Units Land Behind Nazis in Italy!* Adria, we're only thirty-two miles from Rome!"

Adria tried to smile back. It was true that there was virtually no resistance in the sleeping town. Equipment was being unloaded by the shipful. She thought back to the aerial maps she had seen, the hilly terrain between Anzio and the main road to Rome. The Germans might have been caught off guard by the invasion, but unless the road were reached quickly, the invasion force could not cut off the large number of German troops to the south.

* * *

Robert's dark trousers were old and worn, frayed at the edges and stained with blotches of coffee, his dark jacket ill fitting, its sleeves slightly too short and, frayed. Under his beret his hair had been dyed gray, and make-up had been cleverly applied to make him appear an old man. He rode his ancient bicycle hunched over, and chewed on the end of an unlit, but half-smoked cigar. He looked like a thousand other old Frenchmen, who carried their meager belongings in bags atop a beaten up, rusty bicycle.

But the eyes that surveyed the streets were not old. They took in everything. Robert turned the bicycle off the main boulevard and headed toward the safe house in the Parisian suburbs.

As he turned onto the quiet, residential street, a group of children greeted him with cries of, "Grandfather! Grandfather!" Not that he knew them or was related to them, French children all called old men "grandfather." He waved back weakly, reflecting that the disguise must be very good indeed to fool them.

He brought the bike to a clattering halt in front of the house, climbed the steps, and knocked, being careful to stoop and to hold the railing tightly.

Beckoning him in, only when the door was closed did Gaston venture a smile and a comment. "To dress that way is one matter, but must you also chew garlic?"

Robert smiled. "The look without the odor would be unconvincing," he replied in French.

"I assume you got my message. There's been a wireless transmission for you."

Robert nodded and followed Gaston to the ladder in the kitchen. They climbed and emerged into a rough and unfinished storage room littered with boxes. Beyond the boxes was a low door and behind it the radio room.

Gaston shuffled through some papers and withdrew a single sheet. "It is still in code," he remarked. "I never leave decoded messages about."

Robert nodded and pulled out a chair near the table. "When did it come?"

"Last night."

"It's short," Robert commented, tucking it inside his pocket. "Before I go, shall we have a coffee?"

"If you can take it without milk. The store was out."

"I can stand it." Robert followed his friend back down the ladder and into the kitchen, where Gaston boiled some coffee.

"The BBC reports heavy Allied bombing raids on Dresden," Gaston said, "and on Berlin, too."

"Slowly, but surely," Robert muttered. He looked into this dark coffee and wondered if it would all be too slow and too sure to save the Jews who were interned by the millions.

"When the time comes, my friend, we will have our work cut out for us. Especially here in Paris." Gaston smiled broadly. "General de Gaulle is an insistent man. He broadcasts now all the time. He says the French will liberate the French. He says he will liberate Paris."

"French politics prevails," Robert replied with a wry smile. "And I rather suspect the general, too, will prevail.

"I do believe people will follow him," Gaston ventured.

Robert drained his coffee cup. "I do believe you're right. I have to go, my friend, and do not worry. I think I may be gone for at least a week."

Gaston nodded and watched as Robert once again assumed the posture of the old derelict.

As rapidly as he dared, Robert pedaled toward his own small room on the left bank. The code books were not kept with the radio. He reached his room within the hour, and once behind the bolted door, began immediately to decode the message. It began with one line: "The Hounds are Running." That was his code and meant the message was for him, the Fox. Finished, it read quite simply, "cloth of gold."

Robert smiled broadly. It was an historic reference to The Field of Cloth of Gold: the great embassy and tournament held between Francis I and Henry VIII at

Calais in June, 1520. The apron of Calais was then held by the English.

Robert wondered if this message meant more than he thought. By pre-arrangement it signified a rendezvous in Calais with a British submarine, which would be ready to take him aboard for three consecutive nights. That much of the message was for certain; what he wondered now was if that was to be the Allied landing spot as well. He shrugged. He would know soon enough. That was why he was being brought to England.

3

ADRIA WAS A HALF mile back of the main assault force. It was still dark, but periodic mortar fire and flares lit the sky like an electrical storm in spring. The air was heavy with the smell of smoke, the stench of death, the odor of cordite from the bombs. She glanced at her watch. It was five-thirty A.M., and she had been on her feet since ten-thirty the previous night. Seeing a crumbled wall, she sat down behind it, closing her eyes for a moment's rest.

During the early euphoria after their unopposed landing five long months earlier, Jeff had started up the road to Rome with a unit from the Indiana National Guard. "I'm a Hoosier," he called back to her. "Hey, look, Indiana takes Italy!"

But five months of fighting had proved it wasn't that easy, and Jeff now called the Anzio beachhead a piss pot, his way of expressing frustration. The generals, the officers, and the men, of course, were equally depressed. Still, the press corps could not desert the battle, even as it shaped up to be one of the worst of the war. Indeed the situation demanded their presence, even if the worst news was censored or held for release.

By 0500 on the day of the Allied landing Field Marshal Kesselring, the German commander, had ordered the 4th Parachute Division near Rome and several units of the Göring Division to block the roads from Anzio to the Collo Laziali. He reported the invasion to the German high command and immediately 715th Division from France and 114th Division from the Balkans were ordered to Italy. Kesselring also activated a new division from several lesser units in northern Italy. General von Mackensen was ordered to send reinforcements and by nightfall the 65th Division from Genoa, the 362nd from Rimini, and the 16th Panzar Grenadier Division from Leghorn were all on their way to the Anzio area. All this had been done before 0730, pitting a total of nearly one hundred thousand German soldiers against the thirty-seven thousand allied troops that had landed at Anzio. Within twenty-four hours, the phrase "unopposed landing" had fallen into disfavor in Anzio.

And there had been mistakes. General Lucas had chosen to solidify his beachhead rather than move quickly to take territory, giving the Germans time enough to move into position. General Lucas was replaced by General Truscott and the beachhead was held only because of over 250 Allied bombing raids. The Germans had gone so far as to sink two hospital ships in the harbor, sending their already wounded and crushed cargo into a sea of burning oil and wreckage.

It had taken till March to drive on to the village of Cassino. The village lay at the base of a mountain and on top of the mountain was an ancient abbey, all pockmarked with German gun implacements. The Americans and British hesitated to bomb the historic abbey, but in February President Roosevelt himself ordered it destroyed.

In spite of the bombings, the Germans began an offensive in March, nearly succeeding in driving the Allied army back into the sea. During those weeks, Adria had lived in caves with the 2nd Battalion near Pozzolana, in tents behind the lines, and in old houses, foxholes, and trenches. The fighting between March and May had been continuous; supplies were short, and all attacks on Cassino had been repulsed. In total, one thousand, two hundred tons of allied bombs had been dropped. Cassino, its population having fled, was completely destroyed, and the deserted abbey was left with only one wall standing.

Adria's eyes snapped open and she pulled herself up, ready to go on. She cautiously walked toward the rutted path they called a road and stopped to wave down a truck that was rumbling along. Adria was pulled up and into it by the soldiers at the rear.

"It's nasty up there," one of them said in a broad midwestern accent, pointing toward the front.

"I've been here from the beginning, and I'm not going to miss the end," Adria said, adjusting her helmet.

"Jesus, a dame," someone muttered in the dark.

Adria ignored the comment, used to it by now. The truck slowed. "This is as far as we go!" the driver called out. "Jump and run. About three hundred yards ought to put you in the thick of it!"

Out the men went, their heavy equipment clattering as their boots hit the pebble strewn road.

Adria jumped too. She ran toward a formation of jagged rocks. The Allies were "sweeping the mountain"—clearing out snipers and machine gun nests as they went, advancing in waves, one after another. There was shouting and cursing, screaming and even the occasional laugh.

Adria leaned against a jagged rock and shivered. She was only a few hundred yards from the main advancing force, and she stopped momentarily to get her bearings. Seldom did she smoke, but now she lit a cigarette, crouching so the light could not be seen. She inhaled deeply and tried, if only for a moment, to close out the sounds of battle.

Shells lit the darkness, and in the east, the thin line of dawn ran across the horizon like a white ribbon on dark velvet. Machine gun and rifle fire crackled. Above the din rose the all too frequent call, "stretcher bearer!" or "medic!"

Adria stubbed out her cigarette, wondering why she had even bothered to light it. Cautiously she moved forward, all too aware that in the sweep toward the top of the mountain, German sharpshooters might have been overlooked.

Nearby, crouched to photograph the twisted face of a dead soldier, she saw Jeff's unmistakable hulk. Looking up, he acknowledged her with a wave.

Then the noise and light suddenly increased. The big guns were firing now, and mortar fire and flares kept the sky light. In the distance Adria could see the jagged wall of the abbey silhouetted, and she stood up and began taking pictures. She and Jeff were of the new school of photography—quantity would yield quality. She shot almost her entire roll, advancing the film and shooting as fast as she could.

"Shoot, drop, and roll! Get down!"

Adria turned toward Jeff's voice, but he was too fast. He landed squarely on her, flattening her. The sound of machine gun fire blotted out her scream; then a grenade exploded nearby. Adria struggled desperately to turn her head, gasping for air. Only a second after she had filled her lungs did she realize Jeff hadn't moved. Dampness touched her back and she struggled out from beneath him, already screaming, "Stretcher! Medic!"

Adria saw the gaping hole in his stomach and she screamed again. The bullet, exploding on impact, had entered his back and blown a hole right through him. As she struggled free, she had rolled him over. "Stretcher!" she called out again.

Looking up at her, Jeff moved his lips, struggling to speak. "Save it for someone who needs it. Hey, did you get your damn picture? Shit, I knew you'd never learn to roll."

He was half smiling and she cradled his head. "You need the stretcher—Don't you die, don't you dare die!" Tears were streaming down her face and she shivered uncontrollably as the blood drained from her face. I'm going into shock, she thought as she struggled for control.

He moved his hand and touched her cheek, wiping a tear away. "Does that mean you care?" he asked, coughing. Blood was gurgling out of his mouth now, and she could hear him struggling to fill his lungs, fighting death even as it crept over him.

"Of course I care!" She leaned over and kissed him, his blood on her lips.

He grinned weakly, ghastly pale. "I had a mind to get back together with you when this was over," he gasped. "Wanted to take you to this swell restaurant in Rome . . ." He coughed again and more blood oozed from his mouth.

Adria screamed again. It was as if they were alone. Where the hell was the medic?

"Love you, Adria, baby," Jeff said. His eyes were fighting to focus.

Tears ran down her face, "I love you too," she replied. And at that moment it was somehow true. His head fell sideways and his breath ceased with one final gurgle. "Stretcher!" She screamed into the night. Then she screamed, "You can't die! You can't!" Jeff had taught her everything. He'd taught her to be a professional, and in a way he had taught her to love.

In the distance she heard shouts of victory, the tanks advancing as they rolled toward the abbey. Five long months, she thought. Over a hundred thousand casualties, not counting tonight's drive. Twenty thousand men dead—two-thirds of Jeff's beloved Indiana National Guard. The combined force of men from fifteen Allied nations were shouting now; the road to Rome was finally opened. Ought to get up and take pictures, she thought, but she couldn't move. Jeff's blood was soaking through her clothes and she didn't care, she didn't even care that Monte Cassino had finally fallen. For once her cameras hung limply around her neck.

A medic pulled her up and they rolled Jeff onto a stretcher, covering him as if he were in a cocoon. Adria stared dazed and the medic took her hand and led her back toward the field hospital. They passed two dead German soldiers, their bodies spread out atop their hidden machine gun nest.

"Jeff!" Adria held out her hand as the two medics

carrying the stretcher passed her. She couldn't stop crying.

"This way, miss." The young medic looked like a fair-haired child as he prodded her along. He pushed rather than pulled her into a stuffy tent. "Shock," he said matter-of-factly, then left.

An orderly took her arm, rolled up her sleeve, and jabbed a needle into her. "Jeff?" Adria asked, as the face before her blurred and became his. "You saved my life . . . you got killed saving my life!" She fell forward toward the orderly, who caught her and lifted her onto a cot.

4

ADRIA TOSSED IN HER delirium, her thoughts confused and her drug-induced dreams seeming almost real.

Frame by frame, the battle for Monte Cassino replayed in Adria's mind. She relived the weeks she had existed in the shepherd's caverns that were dug into the ridge line. The large caves withstood shelling, and many were connected by tunnels. Extending for miles, the caves reminded Adria of a giant sand castle that had somehow dried out and hardened with time. The dream ended with a battle as the Germans fought fiercely to push the Allied troops back into the sea.

As in reality, she was one with her cameras. Her lens had captured the scrawny cats of Anzio as they poked through the debris in the flattened town square, the hollow eyes of children, orphaned and hungry, the soldiers giving chocolate bars to urchins. Last—always —the casualties of war: dismembered bodies, hands clawing at the earth for shelter from flying shrapnel, and the gaping mouths of soldiers as time after time they cried out for the stretcher bearers.

She dreamt of two young soldiers who had been trading comic books at lunch, deaf and blind by dinner time from an exploding grenade. But in her dreams she was protected because she was framed behind her camera. It was all a picture, light and shadow, distance and focus, unreal until she watched Jeff die in her arms. In her final nightmare thousands of faces appeared as they were consumed in fire, each one of them Jeff.

Then she would scream in her sleep, try to force open her eyes, and feel another needle in her arm. Then there was precious blackness, a long and thankfully dreamless sleep. Adria tossed sideways, then again on her back. This time she forced open her eyes and pushed herself up in bed, prepared to fight off a needle that did not come.

She shook her head. Where was she?

She was alone in a huge room with a cathedral ceiling. Bright sunlight flooded through immense floor-to-ceiling windows draped in gold, and next to the large double bed in which she lay was a tray bearing juice and toast.

She was about to shout when the door opened a crack and an elderly woman dressed in a blue uniform peeked in. "Oh, you're awake are you!" Her short, fat arms went to her hips, and she smiled impishly.

"Where am I?" Adria blurted out.

"Glad to see you're so lucid. I heard they kept you sleeping till they got you here. You're in London, in the home of Lord Charles Wertheim. Now, I say, doesn't that make you a lucky girl?"

Adria blinked. Was it possible? "How long have I been asleep?"

The woman shrugged, "About fifty-two hours. They flew you on a plane and brought you directly here. His Lordship sent for me to see to your nursing needs. Little shell shock the doctor said, and Lord Wertheim said the hospitals were needed for wounded, so here you are."

The woman advanced on her and Adria pulled back. "I don't want another shot," she protested.

"Wasn't going to give you one, dearie. I would suppose you're about sleeped out, and you seem all right to me. Besides, all those drugs just make your dreams worse. Now I just want to plump up those pillows. His Lordship said he wanted to talk to you when you came round."

Adria nodded. "Is there a mirror? My things—where are my cameras?"

"All safe and sound in the closet. I'll get a mirror and your kit. You don't have to worry, love, the army bundled you up with all your belongings and sent you first class."

Adria leaned back against the pillow and smiled. "I'm sorry, I didn't ask your name."

"Blossom."

"Blossom," Adria repeated. It was as incongruous a name as one could imagine. Blossom was short and round and spoke in a cockney accent. "Blossom, do you think I could have a bath?"

"I think that's a first-rate idea. Mind you, I sponged you off when you arrived, but that's not likely to replace a good soak is it? Bath's right through that door. I'll go and draw the water."

Adria waited till Blossom had disappeared and she heard the water running, then folded back the covers and stepped out of bed. She stood still for a moment getting her balance, shaking her head again as if to clear it. Too many sedatives, she thought, but she walked across the room toward the bath, feeling more normal with every step.

Blossom tested the water with her hand. "'Bout right," she announced.

Adria sank into the tub and allowed the water to keep running. It was heaven, deep and hot. Blossom meanwhile rummaged through the cupboard and finally withdrew a bottle. "Scent," she said with satisfaction, as she poured it under the tap.

Adria leaned back in the deep tub, submerged up to her chin. She inhaled and the distinctive aroma conjured up a picture of Madame Wertheim. It was her bath oil, Adria thought, no doubt left on some long-ago visit.

After half an hour, Adria emerged from the tub.

Blossom helped her dry her hair and dress. "You look like a different person," she declared with satisfaction.

"I feel like one, believe me. Is Lord Wertheim at home?"

"In the den," Blossom replied. "Just go down to the ground floor. It's the second door on the left."

Adria made her way down the winding staircase and along the hall, stopping outside the den to knock. The voice that answered sent a shock wave through her. "Robert!" she cried, as she flung open the door.

Robert embraced her, then bent to kiss her.

Adria moved her mouth against his and ran her hands over his chest. Was she having another dream? She pulled away slightly and looked into his worried face. "I can't believe you're here," she whispered. "I want you and need you so. Your being here is . . . is overwhelming," she said breathlessly.

"Chance is kind to us. Oh, God I've missed you."

He kissed her again and Adria clung to him. "You can't go back. You can't go back this time. Robert, please. I'm so afraid of losing you. I'm more afraid now than I was before."

"Why now?" he asked, still holding her tightly.

"I love you more and more and I just lost someone close to me. It's strange being surrounded by death and dying. It doesn't become real until it's someone close."

"Was the someone close named Jeff? You called out his name several times."

Adria nodded. "I don't know how to explain him."

"You don't have to."

"I do. I want to tell you about him."

"We'll have time to talk after dinner."

"Oh, God I'm so glad you're here. I'm so taken aback and glad!" She hugged him tightly. "I love you so much."

He smiled and hugged her back, "Unless I'm mistaken you haven't eaten for awhile."

"You're not mistaken and I am hungry."

Robert took her into the dining room where Charles waited. He rose when she entered, inquired after her

312

health, and poured her some dark red wine. "I splurged," Charles confessed. "Told cook to use all our ration coupons and buy a good piece of beef. What you need is a little red meat, my dear."

Adria eyed the rib roast and smiled. "I've been eating army rations for five months, and this does look wonderful."

Charles began carving with gusto.

"He craves it as much as you," Robert said, leaning over. "Charles's only objection to rationing is that it enforces equality. He can't buy any more beef than the maid can."

Charles looked up and sniffed. "I can't say much for equality, but we must all make sacrifices."

Adria suppressed a smile, but Robert didn't bother.

Dinner was mercifully short and Charles Wertheim, seeming almost embarrassed, excused himself directly thereafter, claiming he had not been to his club for over a week.

Dressed casually in gray slacks and a V-neck cashmere sweater, Robert gazed lovingly at Adria as she curled up in the corner of the sofa.

"I seem to have been delirious for several days," Adria said thoughtfully. She smiled faintly. "It's a strange feeling to lose time—not to be able to remember."

Robert poured two brandies from the decanter. "You kept calling the name 'Jeff'. You don't have to tell me—that is, I don't want to pry."

Adria felt tears in her eyes. She shook her head, then whispered, "I have no secrets from you."

"I know. But perhaps you don't want to talk about it just now."

"It's all right. Jeff Borden was a photographer. I apprenticed with him during my last year of training."

"I've seen his work. He was with *Life*, right?"

"Among others. Most of his work was sold to newspapers and syndicated."

"And he was your teacher," Robert said.

"Yes. He was relentless and a perfectionist. He used to tell me I was so bad I should be taking pictures of children on ponies. He used to make me so mad." The tears started to run down her cheeks. "And because he made me so mad, I improved. Once in New York I screamed, 'I'll show you!' and all he said was, 'I hope so.' He was very brash and self-centered. He would do anything to get the pictures he wanted."

"And you once loved him," Robert said moving closer to her.

"Once I did. Then he became the brother I never had."

Robert sat down beside her and put his arm around her.

"He used to make me practice so I wouldn't get killed when we were on the front lines. 'Shoot, drop, and roll!' he was always shouting at me, and he made me learn how," Adria sobbed. "I forgot and he knocked me out of the way—he was killed saving my life."

There should be words to comfort her, Robert thought. But they were too often trite, too seldom conveyed what was intended.

"I've seen so much death . . . But Jeff's death was so personal, even more personal than Carlos's execution. And I watched Jeff, trying so hard to hang on to life . . ." She began crying again and Robert drew her into his arms and held her tightly. "That's why I can't bear to let you go."

"Adria," He touched her hair and ran his hand gently over her cheek, brushing aside her tears. "I could stay here and bury myself in your arms, but if I did I couldn't respect myself, and in the end you wouldn't respect me either. There are people in France who are depending on me to bring back the information they need to plan the liberation. Days wasted are lives wasted, Adria. The SS has taken over Lyon, and their newly assigned commandant, Klaus Barbie, has executed hundreds of men, women, and children. Were I captured in Lyon today, I wouldn't stand a chance, and

314

there are even more terrible things happening. The Germans are no longer simply deporting Jews. We know—we've heard from the underground in Poland—that the Jews are now being exterminated in large numbers. And Celeste herself obtained information about the 'final solution.'"

Adria leaned against him and put her arms around him. "I can't help being selfish," she whispered.

"I don't have long in London," he replied. "Up till now the underground has been a hindrance to the Germans. But we must have a coordinated plan for D-Day, be ready to strike behind the lines when the Allies land. I'm part of those plans."

Adria nodded, her head buried deep in his chest.

"I have to return in forty-eight hours."

"It's too soon." She clung to him, her hands moving across his back.

His lips found her mouth and then her throat. He kissed her deeply and she returned his passion savagely, terrified at the thought of parting again.

"When Paris is liberated," he whispered. "I'll meet you at the house Celeste brought you to—you remember where it is?"

"Yes," Adria whispered.

"On the third day after the liberation—"

"And then—no more good-byes?"

He cupped her breast and bowed his head to kiss her again. "No more good-byes," he promised.

5

A BRISK MAY BREEZE whipped around the corners and blew Celeste's skirt as she walked quickly to the safe house. She was to meet the liaison from British intelligence, code-named the Fox, but of course the Fox was no mystery to her; he was her half-brother, Robert Wertheim, just returned from England.

Celeste pulled her cloth coat tighter against the wind. The streets of Paris seemed dull to her eyes, now that the city was truly under the German boot. Sometime before her arrest, Madame Wertheim had given Celeste all her jewelry. "Sell it for whatever purpose you need," Madame had instructed her. Celeste had, selling them to buy food for the underground, to obtain money for bribes, which were often necessary, and to buy arms. Everything had gone save one ring, a precious heirloom, a diamond surrounded by red rubies surrounded by more diamonds and set in platinum. She glanced at the ring on her left ring finger, intending it for Robert. It would, she thought, make the ideal engagement ring.

Celeste approached the old town house and looked about. No one followed her, and the house looked as it always had. She climbed the steps, turned her key in the latch, and let herself in. Chantal and Gaston, who lived here, must be out. Walking down the hall, she froze in the parlor doorway, her hands falling limply to her side, lips open in a silent scream.

Chantal was on the floor, face down in a pool of blood. Gaston slumped across a chair, a bullet hole in his forehead. In front of the fireplace, a tall, immaculate, stone-faced SS officer stood covering her with a pistol. He was a man she had drunk with often, a man who had given her valuable information, a man she had slept with. Celeste shivered involuntarily, and whispered, "Karl . . ."

"Bitch!" he hissed the word between his teeth, and in two strides was standing directly in front of her, his giant hand pulling her hair. With the pistol he slapped her face hard, and Celeste dropped to the floor, whimpering as blood gushed from above her left eye.

"Dirty little French bitch!" He kicked her hard in the ribs. "Yes, I suspected you, and I followed you here last week. Today I came early and found your friends. Also a short wave radio. Otherwise the house is empty, but we will wait, my sweet. I think you are expecting someone, yes?"

Celeste shook her head, "No, no one is coming."

He dropped to one knee and loomed over her, his

eyes filled with fire and his thin lips twitching. "Then we have time. Come, have a little drink with me."

Pulling her by the hair, he propelled her to large kitchen where a half-liter bottle of red wine sat on the table. Clearly he had already had some. He poured a glass and gulped half of it; the rest he threw in her face. Celeste closed her eyes and forced back tears. She tried desperately to blot him out, but his hands were all over her. Roughly he tore away her clothes and forced her to the hard floor. He bit her breasts till she screamed, then with savage force, parted her legs and brutally rammed himself into her, tearing at her flesh and hitting her face till she nearly lost consciousness. Suddenly he pulled himself away from her and jolted up, slapping his hand across her mouth. Celeste struggled in vain against Karl Eberhardt's hand, hearing Robert's footsteps.

The door of the kitchen was flung open and Robert stood there, his own pistol drawn. Had he seen the bodies in the living room? Nearly blinded by blood from the slash across her forehead, she could barely see him. Eberhardt pulled her in front of him as a shield. "Shoot!" Celeste screamed, "shoot through me! Kill him!"

"Drop your pistol on the floor and kick it over here," Eberhardt demanded. His own pistol pressed into Celeste's back.

"Shoot him," she begged.

Robert's face twisted, a mask of conflicting emotion. Then, slowly he dropped his pistol and kicked it over to Eberhardt, who quickly took out the ammunition clip and threw the weapon to his right. Celeste sagged in Eberhardt's grasp, moaning, "no . . . no . . ." even as he pushed her away like a half-dead animal. She lay in a heap a couple of feet from his legs looking up at him.

He didn't kill her—that thought flashed across Robert's mind. He wants us alive. He must realize we're more important than the others.

A second, a minute, Celeste wasn't sure. She summoned her strength and lunged at Eberhardt's ankles, sinking her teeth into his leg as hard as she could and tasting his blood through his trousers. He stomped and let out a curse in German. Again Celeste sank her teeth into Eberhardt's leg and again he attempted to free himself, but Celeste held on with all her ebbing strength.

Robert saw Eberhardt's head turn toward Celeste and take aim at her. It was a split second and Robert jumped to Eberhardt's right side, but he was not quite quick enough. "No," he shouted, even as Eberhardt fired and Celeste rolled away, clutching her stomach. Eberhardt kicked free of her just as Robert grabbed Eberhardt's wrist, forcing the gun to point downward toward the floor; with the other hand Robert punched Eberhardt in the face. Eberhardt's head snapped back and his nose started to bleed, but though stunned, he kept his balance, successfully blocking a kick towards his groin. Robert twisted the wrist that held the pistol so that it was pointed at Eberhardt's head and the German's eyes grew wide with terror. Letting go of the pistol he swung at Robert's head, knocking him to the floor. Robert felt the side of his head throb as he fought to stay conscious.

Robert saw the pistol just ahead of him and reached out to get it. Instantly Eberhardt was on him, digging his knees into Robert's back as he too tried to reach the Luger. Robert gasped and managed to twist himself around to face his enemy. Warm blood dropped on Robert's face from a now snarling, wild-eyed Eberhardt. Robert reached up and seized the German's throat, even as the German seized his. Robert gasped for breath as he squirmed to move Eberhardt off him and through a half-open eye he saw the pistol just to his left. With all his strength he squeezed the fingers of his right hand into Eberhardt's bulging neck. He reached for the pistol with his other hand . . . he was less than an inch from being able to grasp it . . . his fingers stretched, feeling the tile floor. Eberhardt likewise reached out to stop Robert. This caused Eberhardt's weight to shift a bit, giving him more reach. Robert now tried to squirm to his left and pull Eberhardt to the right. Using his left knee he pounded Eberhardt's ribs as his left hand, fingers stretching . . . clawed for the gun he knew was there. Another half inch . . . a half inch to live or die.

Chapter Seventeen

1

"YEA, THOUGH I WALK through the valley of the shadow of death, I will fear no evil; for thou art with me; thy rod and thy staff they comfort me.

"Thou preparest a table before me in the presence of mine enemies: thou anointest my head with oil; my cup runneth over.

"Surely goodness and mercy shall follow me all the days of my life: and I will dwell in the house of the Lord for ever."

The priest closed his Bible and crossed himself, as the men assembled before him mumbled, "Amen," in unison. Like the men he ministered to, the priest was dressed in battle gear, wore a helmet covered with leaves, and had his face blackened with grease. He was unarmed, of course. Adria snapped a series of pictures, zooming in on the men's faces, trying to capture different expressions. Two of her four cameras were loaded with high-speed infrared film, so she didn't require a flash.

"Hope prayers work," someone muttered. Another lit a cigarette and a third strained to see some snapshots of his family in the predawn darkness. There are two hundred men on this landing craft, Adria scribbled in her notebook. She often took notes for use later when she was writing captions. Nothing too detailed: atmosphere, nuances, anything she thought important. She looked at the faces around her and wondered what these men were thinking. Some seemed visably frightened, others were full of bravado, the majority silent and contemplative. And herself? She was apprehensive and her hands were cold. Strange emotion, fear, she thought. Not rational. All her life she had feared thunder instead of lightening, but it was lightening that could kill. In battle she cringed at the sound of the guns, but it was said that you never heard the bullet that killed you. She shook her head. In a few minutes she was going to wade ashore and be part of a major battle, yet it frightened her less than the thought of staying overnight in a room filled with skittering mice.

She looked upward momentarily, reassured that there were no enemy aircraft in sight.

The many landing craft were so close together it seemed a miracle they did not collide. As far as Adria could see there were ships silhouetted against the sky. Huge barrage balloons hovered to keep low-flying German aircraft from strafing the men who were now preparing to wade ashore.

"Awesome," was the adjective for this invasion force. The greatest amphibious operation in military history, it included 5,409 fighter planes, 3,497 heavy bombers, 1,645 light and medium bombers, 2,316 transport planes, 6 battleships, 23 cruisers, 122 destroyers, 360 PT boats, and hundreds of frigates, sloops, and other combat craft, as well as 6,480 transports, landing craft, and special-purpose vessels. Within minutes, the first of nearly 200,000 men would be put ashore between Cherbourg and Le Havre.

Adria squinted into the distance, making out the shoreline of what was code-named Utah beach. She was with the U.S. First Army under the command of General Omar Bradley who stood only a few feet from her. Like his men he was in full battle gear, having stated his intention of going ashore with them rather than following when the beachhead was secure.

Adria adjusted her helmet slightly. The combination of the heat, grease, and the metal on her forehead made her perspire in spite of the fact that it was quite cool.

"Better get your cameras in their watertight bag," General Bradley said as he stepped to her side.

Adria nodded and began packing her cameras into the rubber backpack. The tide was out, but they'd been warned earlier in the briefing that although the water shouldn't be more than three to four feet deep, it might be deeper in some places and swimming could be required.

Watching her, General Bradley smiled. "You realize you're more battle seasoned than these troops, don't you?"

"Yes, sir."

"I wasn't overjoyed when you arrived in Tunisia, you know, but then I found out you were an admiral's daughter, and I told myself you must already know the military ropes. Well, you've done well, Adria."

"Thank you, sir."

He grinned at her. "You may be under my command, but you're not one of my men. Call me General Bradley. And while I know this is your second beachhead I will tell you this now. When you get past the surf, hit the sand. And don't move till we've secured the first quarter mile."

"Not even a little bit?"

The general smiled, "Well, only if there's no shooting near you."

"I don't know how we've managed it, but I don't think the Germans have spotted us."

"That's the first miracle," General Bradley said. Then, scowling, "No optimism. You were at Anzio."

"Yes, I remember." I wish I didn't, she thought.

"Now let's see, I usually tell my men to keep their powder dry. Guess I'll have to tell you to keep your film dry. And your fingers crossed. I'm going to start the countdown now."

The general made his way to the highest level on the landing craft and gave the hand signal to prepare for landing. Some of the men had been crouched, others sitting, but now they all stood and adjusted their weapons, tense silence replacing nervous chatter.

Adria took one last look off the landing craft. There were so many ships. Tears suddenly filled her eyes; they were tears of pride. She felt full of emotion, and for the first time in her entire life felt the importance of the moment. "A witness to history," she whispered.

"Down!"

The great wooden front of the craft opened and the men swarmed into the shallow water, guns above their heads, and waded toward shore shouting.

Adria felt the wooden plank beneath her boots, then the cold water as it hit her knees and soaked through her battle fatigues. She ran through the water with the others, her head down, heart pounding, as machine gun fire crackled from the shore. A young man beside her dropped face down in the water; another screamed, "Medic!" And they all kept on running.

Adria felt the damp hard sand beneath her feet—solid ground once again. She ran a few more feet up the steep beach and then fell down behind the first line of men. Almost instinctively she began digging in the sand with her hands, trying to bury herself. The gunfire was close and she writhed frantically trying to make a deeper cavity for her body.

Men ahead of her fired continuously, then crouched and inched forward. A wave of bombers passed overhead, their bombs falling so close she thought they would hit the beachhead. The big fourteen-inch guns on the *Nevada* were firing now, too. Their anti-personnel shells burrowed some twelve inches into the ground, then exploded, destroying close to half an acre of land and anything or anyone on it. Adria put her hands over her ears, but she could not completely close out the sound and she couldn't close out the smell at all. The ground beneath her vibrated and shook as the gunners pounded their shore targets and the stench of blood mixed with the salt air and the smoke. The noise was horrible, incessant, shattering.

Minutes passed like hours, but inevitably the line in front of her advanced. More and more GI's had come ashore, surrounding her.

A foot away a communications officer set up his radio equipment and began taking and relaying instructions. "Tell them to make a drop half a mile east," an officer told him.

"Roger," the radio man replied. Then, into his radio: "Able Baker—come in—come in . . . come in White Eagle . . ."

"Stretcher!" Two medics ran by her and Adria edged into a crouched position and brushed the damp sand off her pack. Beneath a line of rocks in front of her an aid station was being set up.

"Move it up!" a sergeant snarled. "Get up, move it! We ain't got no time to build sand castles!"

There were two, three, then six lines in front of her. There was shooting, and overhead, a Thunderbolt fighter aided by a Spitfire had taken on two Messerschmitts in a dogfight.

Adria sat up, undid her pack, took out her cameras, and slung them around her neck. She knelt in the sand and snapped half a roll of film of the men coming ashore. Then she turned and took the aid station, and a closeup of the communications officer. She took photos of the dead and the wounded too, and a picture of one young soldier eating a Hershey bar while he reloaded his rifle. "D-Day, June 6, 1944," she captioned the spread.

2

IT WAS NOW WIDELY acknowledged that British and American Intelligence had done their jobs remarkably well, deceiving the Germans into believing the invasion would take place at Pas-de-Calais. There *was* fighting the first few days, but by June 8—D-Day plus two, the U.S. First Army had linked up with the British Eighth Army near Port-en-Bessin, Bayeux, five miles from the landing beaches, and cut the rail link to Cherbourg. By

June 12 all the beachhead landing groups were linked along a fifty-mile-wide front. The Germans surrendered to the British at Perugia and the Americans advanced on Cherbourg.

Inside the port city the underground instituted an uprising, and street-fighting broke out as the Americans approached. On June 27 all German resistance ended and Cherbourg was taken over by the U.S. 4th Division, so that by July 1 the whole of the Cherbourg peninsula had been secured. But the push toward Paris bogged down in mid-July in the area of Saint Lô, overlooking the once peaceful valley of Vire. At another time the view from the ramparts might have been a pastoral scene from a painting by Constable. Not now, Adria thought bitterly. The Americans launched carpet-bombing and used napalm daily, leaving the earth scorched.

First Army headquarters was an abandoned rural school. How quickly it had been converted, Adria thought. One day it had been a slightly damaged building consisting of two classrooms and an office. Children's pictures had hung on the walls, and math problems remained scribbled on the blackboard. Then overnight the damage was repaired and its roof and outside walls received a coat of camouflage paint. Army trucks backed up to the door and unloaded portable room dividers and desks, in trays and out trays, as well as ashtrays. The bureaucracy of battle followed close on the heels of the warriors, it seemed, and where students had only recently studied, there were now public relations officers, requisitions officers, clerks, communications men, and transport experts, as well as the corps of engineers. Down came the children's pictures, to be replaced by bulletins and charts, maps, posters, and duty rosters.

Adria stood in front of Major General Henderson's battered oak desk, wondering if it had been here or if it had come on one of the trucks. His giant ashtray was filled to overflowing with smoldering cigarette butts, the smell of which mingled with that of burned coffee.

Major General Henderson was the press officer, and she had heard that before the war he had been a rookie reporter on a midwestern newspaper.

"The army is killing French civilians by the thousands," she complained.

Major General Henderson's lips were pressed together, his uniform less than fresh, his eyes bloodshot. "And?" He raised an eyebrow.

"Only a few days ago we used napalm on our own men. Lieutenant General McNair was among the casualties. That's a big news story."

"What do you want, Miss Halstead? Do you want us to tell the American public that we've shot ourselves in the foot? Your so-called big story has been censored. You know that. You also know that if you object to your story being censored you are free to fill out form C-101 and submit it in triplicate. It *is* possible that in a year or two the ban on the story might be lifted."

Adria felt angry, but as strongly as she felt, she knew there was nothing she could really do except register a complaint. "We did more than shoot ourselves in the foot. There were a hundred casualties. We've inflicted more casualties on ourselves than the Germans have inflicted on us. Furthermore, the carpet-bombing is killing French civilians—very possibly members of the underground."

"Miss Halstead, I admire your work. You're a talented photographer. But you are not a general and you are not directing this operation. Do you think we're thrilled when our own men die because of ineptitude, or that we enjoy killing civilians?"

"No, I—"

"You think we should be more careful," he said sarcastically. He shook his head and withdrew a cigarette from the crumpled pack he kept in his shirt pocket. He tapped it on the desk to pack the tobacco and then lit it, drawing in the smoke and exhaling. "I will tell you what they tell me to tell the press. The Germans are trained and seasoned troops. Ninety percent of our men had six weeks' basic training and whomp! they were landed in the middle of a war, and six weeks is not enough. Hell, half of our officers—myself included—are ninety-day wonders! We're right out of college. I have a real interesting pamphlet here from the War Department—" Adria watched as he opened one of the familiar green pamphlets with the symbol of the eagle on the cover. He flipped through the pages rapidly. "Ah, here we are. A little medical study that's been carried out. Sixty-five percent of our men—got that? Sixty-five percent, suffer from violent beating of the heart, shaking and trembling, are sick to their stomachs, break out in cold sweats, vomit, and lose control of their bowels just before or during battle. Now, try to understand that mistakes are going to be made when we use green troops."

Adria lowered her eyes. Major General Henderson was annoying, but he was right. She wanted to say more about the carpet-bombing, but she knew he would only tell her that the underground had helped plan the invasion and knew full well what to expect. "I suppose," she finally agreed.

"Come hell or high water, we have to take Saint Lô, Miss Halstead. It's a vital communications center and it's on the Vire River. Our strategists believe it's the key to the rest of France. Look, you want a story, I've got one for you. Our intelligence sources tell us the Germans are behaving like savages. A few weeks ago the SS killed every man, woman, and child in the village of Oradour-sur-Glane, near Limoges. All six hundred villagers were herded into a church and burned alive because the SS couldn't find one of its commanders who had been kidnapped by the underground. The sooner we take Saint Lô and move on, the more lives will ultimately be saved."

Adria nodded silently. This was the first she had heard of the village killings, and she felt properly chastised. "Time," Robert had stressed, "is the important factor. Each day more French civilians are being killed, each day more Jews are dying in the camps."

"Now listen," Major-General Henderson said,

"there's a Frenchman holed up down the road with C company. He's with the underground and you did ask to speak to any of them if any reached us."

"Thank you," Adria said. Turning, in the doorway, she added, "I'm sorry."

Henderson waved her away. "Take the jeep out front."

Adria left and headed for C company. How many members of the underground had she spoken to? None of them knew where Robert was, and she prepared herself for another disappointment.

Now well behind the lines, C Company had erected a tent city, a field hospital, even a temporary canteen. It was in the latter that Adria interviewed Jacques Dunant. Clean-shaven and seemingly unmarked by his experiences, Dunant was also young, a recent recruit, Adria assumed.

"I'm looking for a man known as 'the Fox,'" Adria told him. "Have you seen him? Do you know of his whereabouts?"

The young man grinned, "Mademoiselle, everyone has heard of the Fox."

Adria's heart leapt, although she had met dozens of members of the underground who claimed never to have heard of the Fox. "Do you know where he is?" she pressed.

The young man drank from his coffee mug and nodded. "In Paris. He went there some weeks ago and was to remain until the liberation. He will help organize an uprising among the population when the allies are close."

Adria smiled, relieved to know Robert was not in the area of the carpet bombing. Still, she felt disappointed that he was not closer. Robert had told her they would meet on the third day after the liberation of Paris, but she had always hoped it would be sooner. Stuck as they were in Saint Lô, Paris seemed a long way off.

"He is your friend?" Jacques asked, raising a knowing brow.

Adria blushed. "He is my friend." Jacques meant

327

"lover." To change the subject she asked, "May I photograph you and hear some of your story?"

Jacques stroked his clean-shaven face and agreed. "My family is safe in Cherbourg now, so I can now talk."

Adria took out her note pad and checked the film in her camera. Andy Martin wanted some stories on the underground to accompany her photos of the march across France.

3

IN SPITE OF THE horrendous overcrowding at Theresienstadt, the Germans had assigned Aaron Rosen to a small apartment consisting of two rooms with their own toilet, comfortable chairs and a bed, as well as real crockery and cooking utensils.

He had protested that the sick and infirm needed such luxury more, but the Germans refused to move him. Following their marriage, Anna moved in with her husband. Aaron and Anna lived as they did because the world was to know that Jews like these two were treated well.

In the months before their marriage Anna had come often to Aaron's apartment to study, learning then just what kind of man he was. Aaron Rosen refused German requests to sit on the camp governing committee, a committee really run by the Germans. Instead he voluntarily worked night and day on the camp welfare committee, a group he himself had organized from the tailor shop. Moreover, Aaron Rosen received more parcels than any other inmate of Theresienstadt, parcels from France, England, America, and South America. They came via the Red Cross and often contained food, medical supplies, clothing, hygiene products, and even books. Sometimes there were even cookies and candies, but mostly tins and tins of sardines. The contents were sorted and divided, going to the other inmates, to where they were needed.

And if Anna marveled at Aaron's organization and

generosity, Aaron was as much in awe of his new wife. Where had a woman of her breeding learned to cook potatoes so many ways? Anna was the most inventive of women, and her temperament was even just as her outlook was eternally optimistic. "God's commandment to the Jews is to live," Anna told the discouraged. Then she added, "Aaron taught me that."

Anna finished washing the last of the cups. She replaced them in the small cupboard and then carefully poured the dishwater through a sieve and into a large jar. Water was always a problem in the camp and she never threw it out till it was utterly impossible to use anymore, instead straining and reboiling it. Dishwater was used and reused, as was water for personal washing, stored in other jars. Anna had developed her own system for making each precious drop last as long as possible.

Wiping her hands on her apron, she sat down at the table. Aaron's amber eyes watched her lovingly. "You know I've observed many people under difficult conditions. It amazes me that those who lived well before all this do best now."

Anna smiled. "Poverty is a new adventure for us. For the others it is simply the way they have always lived."

"I suppose there's something in that," he said thoughtfully. "Well, I'm afraid you will have to continue to play at poverty after this is over. Palestine is a hard land."

"I shan't mind. But I will want to see my family first."

"Ah, that is a must for both of us."

Aaron often spoke of his sister in England, of his nieces, nephews, and cousins. In turn, Anna had told him about her sons, her relatives, and her cousins in America.

"Dealing with freedom may be difficult at first," Aaron said thoughtfully.

"You speak as if you know something," Anna said, touching his hand. "Aaron, do you?"

"The beginning of the end . . ." he said. "Anna, you

must not tell anyone yet; false hopes could be dangerous. But I have heard from a member of the Czech underground that the Allies have landed successfully in France."

Anna gasped and siezed his hand. France soon liberated! Her thoughts were suddenly filled with images of Robert. "When?" she pressed. "Where in France?"

"Normandy. The BBC reports they are headed for Paris."

Anna sighed. "Oh, I wish I could hear the BBC again."

"My Czech friend says the news is always reported well after the event. But German troops are being moved to the western front, and the Russians are making gains, too. But I fear the Germans might try to kill us all before they retreat."

Anna shook her head. "No," she said firmly. "We are commanded to live." She squeezed his hand and walked to the small window, looking out at the drab camp buildings etched against the starlit sky.

Aaron walked to her side and put his arm around her waist. "You have faith."

"There is a simple poem I read once. I didn't understand it until I came here. It went, 'Two prisoners looked out from behind their bars—one saw the mud, the other the stars.' It is important not to notice the mud, Aaron."

He leaned over and tenderly kissed her hair. In a few moments she would cross the wretched compound to spend two hours nursing the sick as she did every night. "Hold on," she would tell them. "Hold on because soon we'll be free." And if the dying cursed the Germans, Anna would quote the camp rabbi, "Vengeance belongs to God, not to man," she would say. Aaron Rosen hugged his wife. "I love you," he said, kissing her cheek.

4

ROBERT WERTHEIM'S FOREHEAD WAS covered with fine beads of perspiration, his hair was disheveled, and his clothing wrinkled. On August 23, the fifth day of the insurrection of Paris, it was unbearably hot even inside the normally cool Swedish consulate.

Standing behind the thick curtain, he peered out into the street. It looked calm enough, but in the distance he could hear sporadic gunfire. He checked his watch anxiously. Raoul Nordling, the Swedish consul, should have been back by now.

The door of the consul's office opened a crack and Robert turned. Instead of the consul, he saw his weary secretary, a balding man in his mid-fifties. "Would you like some refreshment while you wait?" the secretary asked.

Robert shook his head. "No, thank you."

"Moments of rest are few these days." The secretary gestured toward the leather couch. "I can vouch for it," he winked. "I've been sleeping on it for a week."

Robert smiled and sat down to satisfy the man.

"If you change your mind about refreshment, there is a bar behind the desk in that cabinet. Please help yourself. And if you need anything further I'll be at my desk."

"Just let me know if you hear anything from the consul."

"Of course."

The door closed and Robert leaned back and closed his eyes. Certainly it had been many days since he had slept more than a few hours at a time, exhilaration, apprehension, and anger combining to keep him awake. He had a kind of raw nervous energy brought on by the events of the last five days. The damnable confusion that held Paris by the throat was exactly what he had worked to prevent, but events had overtaken him, and he was now compelled to go with the tide. The question of *who* would liberate Paris loomed large with most of the partisans. Robert shook his head. The insurrection of Paris—the uprising orchestrated by the various underground movements—was as divided as French politics in peacetime, perhaps more so. But there were other considerations, and for Robert the main one now was the Germans plan. In response to Hitler's orders to destroy the city, the bridges were wired with explosives and protected by German tanks. Many historic buildings were also wired, and Robert, as well as most partisans, knew that if Paris burned, the populace of two million would be so infuriated that they would attack the Germans with their bare hands. In such a blood bath, more French than Germans would die.

Still, victory *was* at hand, and the pure joy of that thought kept him going. "You should be here now, Celeste," he said to himself. He pressed his lips together and mist filled his eyes as for a minute he relived the terrible scene. Eberhardt's strong hands were strangling him until a shot rang out and the big German's grip loosened even as he fell backward. Crouched against the wall, his half sister Celeste held the Luger in her hands, shooting Eberhardt through the head with her last ounce of strength. Celeste had gestured toward the ring and whispered. "It's yours." Robert kissed her forehead and ran his fingers through her blood-matted hair, holding her tight when she gasped and went limp in his arms. He had taken the ring and covered her with a sheet from the bedroom, then left the house, never to return.

Robert forced himself up off the sofa and his sad recollections from his mind. It was after nine. Where the hell was Nordling? Perhaps he'd been killed accidently by the Resistance or stopped by the Germans . . . Perhaps, perhaps . . . At this moment Nordling was the only man who might save Paris from burning.

On August 18, Paris was the prize that threatened to create a civil war between the French Communist Resistance and the Gaullists. The uprising had begun that morning when information reached the underground that the Allies were sixty miles away and that General de Gaulle's Free French Army, led by General Leclerc, was even closer.

"Ah, General, you have caused me much difficulty," Robert mused. But no matter how much de Gaulle angered him, Robert also admired the man. De Gaulle understood the French and he understood how to manipulate the many political factions to his advantage. The Free French Army consisted of some sixteen thousand troops fighting with the Allies, but de Gaulle refused to take orders from Eisenhower. "France," he declared, would be liberated in the name of the Republic and not in the name of the Allied high command. And he, de Gaulle, commander of the Free French, would liberate Paris with General Leclerc. Then and only then would the Allied commanders be allowed to parade through the streets for a "symbolic" liberation celebration.

Meanwhile, in Paris itself, the insurrection began. The Communists took over twenty district offices in Paris, the Conseil National de la Résistance—the CNR —the Comité Parisien de Liberation, and the Alliance, and other resistance movements took over police stations, hotels, hospitals, and other government buildings. The French flag was raised on all "liberated" buildings, German units were attacked, and the citizens of Paris, as throughout their history, responded to the "call to the barricades."

Fortified in certain areas of the city, the Germans counterattacked and were greeted by Molotov cocktails, hand guns, and even bows and arrows. Disputing internally, the resistance was at least united against the Germans.

On the first day more than fifty Germans were killed and a hundred wounded, the bodies strewn about the boulevards and squares along with French corpses. It was at this point that Raoul Nordling had entered the scene, going to General von Choltitz, the commander of German forces in Paris, and proposing a cease-fire. "You haven't enough troops to defend your position against two million Parisians," he argued. "History will not forgive you for burning Paris." Within twenty-four hours, General von Choltitz had agreed to the cease-fire.

"He's been in Paris too long," Nordling told Robert when he reported on the meeting, "and he loves the city. I don't think he will follow Hitler's orders."

"Will he surrender Paris?"

"Troops are being pulled out now. But he won't surrender till he absolutely has to."

Five days passed. The Communists did not respect the cease-fire because they had not been consulted by the other resistance groups before Nordling began negotiations. There were arguments and counter arguments. This very afternoon, the cease-fire agreement had run out, resulting in sporadic fighting everywhere. Nordling had returned to the general to try to negotiate a surrender so Paris would not be destroyed by either the Germans or the invading Allies.

The door of the consul's office opened again and his secretary entered. Robert stood up. The secretary's face was not simply pale, it was ashen.

"What is it?" Robert asked anxiously.

"It's the consul. He's suffered a heart attack."

"Is he—?"

The secretary shook his head. "Not dead. He's in hospital."

It's over, Robert thought. The Germans would set off the explosives, Paris would be taken building by building in hand-to-hand combat. The Allies wouldn't hesitate to bomb and the city would be completely destroyed. "Oh God," he mumbled.

"Sir," the secretary said, touching his shoulder, "there's still a chance."

"What chance? Nordling was the only hope."

"General von Choltitz issued the consul a pass to go through German lines to General Leclerc. He's offered to surrender to Leclerc or any Allied general, but he will not surrender to the Resistance. He told the consul that he would order the city destroyed first.

"But the consul cannot use the pass, if he's in the hospital."

"The pass is made out simply to R. Nordling. The consul's brother is here and his name is Rolf. He has offered to go in the consul's place."

General Eisenhower had already reluctantly given Leclerc permission to enter Paris first, and he had also expressed the hope that the city would be spared. "Send Rolf Nordling then," Robert said. And in twenty-four hours, whether or not Leclerc has been reached, notify General Choltitz that Leclerc is on his way."

"General von Choltitz has warned that there are pockets of SS who will not obey the surrender order."

Robert half smiled. "The Resistance will clean them up when Leclerc is at the gates of Paris."

"And not before?"

"We're waiting for more guns," Robert said. "And to see who will accept the surrender and who will not." He pressed his lips together and shook the secretary's hand. "I have work to do," he said, excusing himself.

Chapter Eighteen

1

SPIES FOR THE RESISTANCE in every village between Paris and the Allied armies called daily with troop movements. They reported every detail of the fighting in Paris and of the melting German resistance.

Adria gulped down some hot black coffee from her thermos as the open jeep sped through the darkness. She and two print correspondents had left the main American force two hours ago to join General Leclerc in the forest of Rambouillet twenty miles from Paris. The Resistance had let it be known that Leclerc was ready to move.

"God, it's warm," Rick Shattner muttered, his Australian accent clipped.

"But quiet," Gorden Ames, a British correspondent, said gratefully.

"What a lovely war!," Shattner said with an ironic laugh. "Not a German in sight, Allied armies poised to enter the city, and all this brouhaha about who's going in first!"

"De Gaulle has won," Adria put in. "We might as well be good sports about it."

"You be a good sport. Your man Eisenhower shouldn't have allowed this. This victory belongs to Montgomery and Patton, not to the Free French Army. Monty's having a royal snit and Patton's chewing nails," Ames said angrily. Then added for good measure, "You just can't trust the French."

Adria laughed. Ames was *so* British! And the fact was, he was having a royal snit too. At the moment she didn't care who did what or what the implications were, she cared only about getting to Paris. She and Robert would soon be together. And German resistance had melted! That left her free to be selfish.

"We should have left for Paris weeks ago," Rick said. "Hemingway did. He got right through the German lines and he's been in Paris fighting with the Resistance. What stories he'll have!"

"And will we be able to sort his fact from fiction?" Ames asked.

"Look!" Adria pointed up ahead. They were in the forest of Rambouillet now and ahead was the end of the long tank column commanded by General Leclerc. The driver halted the jeep and climbed out with the three correspondents. They all showed their identification and the driver, a member of the Resistance, spoke in French rapidly. Then he turned and spoke to them in English.

"They'll be pulling out at dawn. They will divide themselves into three columns. One will enter Paris via Versailles, one through Porte de Sèvres, the northwestern gate, and one to the southeast through the valley of the Chevreuse. Assuming all goes as planned, General de Gaulle will parade down Montparnasse sometime after four P.M."

Adria thought about the city. The other two correspondents didn't know it as she did, then, too, they weren't photographers. I want the best pictures, she thought. "I'd like to go with the column headed through the northwestern gate," she said. It would pass through a large residential area and, she reasoned, the populace would flood the streets. The others nodded and each chose a different column.

"You wish to ride in a tank?" the young Algerian officer asked.

"No, I'll go in one of the trucks," she told him in French. He smiled and led her to a troop carrier. "Try to sleep in the back," he advised. "It will be a while before we enter the city."

Adria's eyes snapped open at the first wild shouts of "De Gaulle! de Gaulle!" "My God, I did sleep," she mumbled as she pulled herself up and went to the back of the truck. The soldiers were outside; some marched while others rode on the tanks.

She blinked in the bright sunlight. They had just crossed the city line and were inching down Avenue de la Grande toward the Arc de Triomphe. Adria leaned around as far as she could, straining to see ahead. All she could see was a veritable ocean of people swarming over vehicles, swamping the soldiers with hugs and kisses and embracing one another and dancing.

"Vive de Gaulle! Vive la France! Vive la République!" they shouted and pointed at the Cross of Lorraine that was on all the tanks. Then a soldier atop a tank unfolded the tricolor of the Republic and the people went wild as the flag caught in the early morning breeze. Women threw themselves across the tanks and were pulled up by soldiers. Flower petals filled the air as bouquets were tossed from balconies. Children linked arms and sang, "Allons enfants de la patrie, marchant, marchant," the stirring words to *La Marseillaise*.

Men, women, children, even the soldiers cried openly.

Adria wiped her cheek with her hand. With each inch the convoy moved forward, the mass of humanity seemed to increase. I'll be here all day, she thought. How far were they from the Arc de Triomphe? A quarter mile at the most, she reckoned. De Gaulle would enter the city through Porte d'Orleans and go to the square opposite the station on Boulevard Montparnasse. It was across the Seine, but not more than two miles. Surely, if she avoided the main streets she could make better time on foot. Then too, as different Free French Units were entering the city from different directions, she could get a greater variety of photographs if she took to the streets, rather than remaining with this particular group. Indeed, if by some side street she could get in front of the Arc de Triomphe, she could photograph this group coming through it. Adria jumped off the truck and pushed her way through the tens of thousands that now flooded the Avenue.

The streets around the Arc de Triomphe were like a pinwheel and she headed for Avenue Foch and then around the pinwheel to Rue Kléber, which ran north of the Trocadero Gardens. She heard people shouting about German resistance, and a woman told her the people of Paris had erected barricades to prevent a German counterattack.

Hoping the side streets were less crowded, Adria turned a corner and headed east. "Closed for the liberation", signs in the windows of closed shops proclaimed, and she stopped to photograph one.

She pushed on, but was suddenly stopped by a screaming mob running toward her. Adria pressed against the side of a building. There was gunfire at the end of the street and she saw a German truck careening round the corner. From windows over the street rifle fire cracked and then a flaming torch was thrown. The fabric that covered the truck burst into flame. Adria shot and shot again, holding her camera over her head when the crowd blotted out her view. Then a tall Frenchman lifted her and she continued taking pictures. German soldiers ran from the burning truck and citizens swarmed over them, beating them with their fists. A girl grabbed a German helmet and paraded around in it. Then Adria screamed. A child, not more than six, held a machine gun he had taken from an unconscious German. He aimed it wildly and in a burst of gunfire, three German soldiers and four French civilians fell. The child, his mouth open dropped the gun and began to wail, "Papa! Papa! Papa!"

Adria snapped her final picture on that roll and signaled her human step-stool to let her down. She thanked him and turned around, running back toward the boulevard, pausing only once to catch her breath. The child's face came back to her and she shivered. There still was fighting and the city was in utter chaos.

In the end, Adria reached Montparnasse simply by taking the Metro. It too was crowded with celebrants, but at least it avoided the streets. At four-thirty the general appeared to wildly chanting crowds. Adria had positioned herself in the window of a building opposite with her long distance lens at the ready.

"De Gaulle! De Gaulle! De Gaulle!" The general made his lanky body into the symbol of the victory sign. The crowds loved it, and they cheered on and then broke into *La Marseillaise* again.

It seemed to Adria as if everyone in Paris was in the square, as if they all had flowers to throw, and as if they had hidden their flags away, waiting for this moment. Then General de Gaulle raised his hands and turned to walk into the station. The crowd parted as if it were the Red Sea and he was Moses. Another figure walked toward the general and Adria peered through her long distance lens—it was as good as binoculars—she thought. The figure was as tall as the general, and the two of them embraced emotionally. Then in a flash

Adria realized that the other man was the general's son, a naval officer.

Next General Leclerc appeared and he handed General de Gaulle a sheaf of papers—the surrender papers? Adria took several pictures in rapid succession. De Gaulle again rose and greeted the crowd. Again he made the victory sign and he waved the documents. Then he walked down the steps and bent to slip into the front seat of an open Hotchkiss, the Rolls-Royce of French automobiles. The car eased off and the crowds followed it chanting the general's name in unison.

At seven, when it was too dark to take any more pictures, Adria headed for the Hotel Ritz. The elegant hotel had a room even though the lobby was crowded with other correspondents and a motly collection of Resistance fighters, all clearly drunk.

Adria looked around the lobby and blinked increduously when she saw Ernest Hemingway dressed in a colonel's uniform. He was with OSS Chief David Bruce and appeared to be the leader of the drunken band. The elegantly dressed director of the Ritz smiled indulgently at the festivities. "When did they get here?" Adria asked.

"Oh, Mr. Hemingway, my friend, came an hour ago with the Resistance contingent. He came to declare us liberated. I welcomed him and asked if I could get him anything and he replied, 'Seventy-three dry martinis.' I should think they're all well past that number now."

Adria smiled. "How like him," she replied, taking her room key.

"I'm sorry we're short of bell boys," the director said.

"It's all right. I only have my pack. I can find my own room."

"Well don't tell anyone I let you," he replied. "We have our standards."

"You've only just been liberated," Adria replied, laughing. The Ritz, like Maxim's, was an institution.

Adria made her way to her room on the fourth floor. She collapsed on the bed. A little rest and I'll go to the

Club Morocco, she decided. If she could find Celeste, perhaps she could find Robert.

2

CLUB MOROCCO WAS LOCATED in the Latin Quarter and Adria took the Metro to the station on Rue Monge and walked south a block to the nightclub. She forced her way into the packed club. A tiny chanteuse with short, tightly curled hair sang *La Vie en Rose* while French soldiers wept openly.

"Mademoiselle, buy you a drink?" A French soldier shoved his companion and made way for Adria at the crowded bar. The patrons suddenly linked arms and broke into the rousing national anthem. The French had been unable to sing it for four years. Now they could not stop. She had heard it all day on every street in Paris.

Smoke curled in the air. The flickering light bulbs offered little illumination. Adria took advantage of the space offered her, but shook her head. "No, thanks," she replied in English, momentarily forgetting to speak French.

"You're American! Ah, tomorrow all the Americans will come to Paris, eh? We will have the liberation all over again! Do let me buy you a drink. Tomorrow when your countrymen come, the price of wine will triple." He smiled broadly.

Adria laughed. "No, let me buy you one."

She leaned over and asked the bartender for two glasses of red wine. He responded quickly since the request had come in French. The soldier grinned.

"I would usually insist on paying," he said leaning toward her, "but tonight I am letting women do anything they want for me."

Adria blushed, but ignored his comment.

The bartender returned and set down the two glasses of wine. Adria leaned over. "One moment," she asked. "I'm looking for a Mademoiselle Celeste Deschamps. Can you tell me where she is?"

The bartender had a square, unsmiling face. He wiped his brow, but his facial expression did not change. "About six feet under in the churchyard," he answered unemotionally.

"When?" Adria blurted out. "When did she die?" She tried to hide her shock and suppress her fear.

"She was murdered by the SS in May."

Adria paled. She was not to meet Robert for another two days—if he were still alive. Oh God, where was he? Robert had returned in May—Robert would have met Celeste. She felt faint and then she felt a hand on her shoulder. Adria turned and looked into the face of a Frenchman. His eyes were bright and his expression serious.

"May I speak with you?" he asked in French.

Adria nodded and slipped off the barstool, following him across the room and into a secluded booth hidden by a moth-eaten red velvet curtain. There, in this alcove, sat five men around a table. They were all drinking wine and talking in low voices. When she was ushered into the alcove, they ceased talking immediately.

"What do you want?" Adria asked.

"I overheard you ask about Celeste," the man who had brought her said. "What business did you have with her?"

"She was my friend. I'm looking for her brother— her half-brother."

The men at the table smiled and muttered to one another. "The Fox," one of them said aloud.

Adria felt a surge of hope, "Where is he? Is he all right?"

"He wasn't killed with his sister," one of them told her.

"We're with the Resistance," the one who had brought her explained. "I saw the Fox this morning, but he was headed for the Palais de la République. There have been many casualties there, I am afraid."

Adria felt her heart sink once again. She searched their faces. "Has no one seen him since?"

They shook their heads and muttered their apologies.

"I must go there," Adria said with determination.

"You can't—it is cordoned off; there is still fighting there. Come, Madamoiselle, let one of us take you back to your hotel. The streets are dangerous tonight."

One of them laughed. "We have more than freedom. We have anarchy."

Adria looked from one of the men to another. Their clothes were soiled and their faces dirty. One had blood on his shirt, and they all had guns. Not the most reliable sources of information, she told herself. But then she knew they were right about the streets. "Thank you," she said. "I'd appreciate a ride back to my hotel."

Outside, she climbed into the canvas seat of an old Renault just like the one Robert had driven the last time they'd been in Paris together.

Adria leaned back. The night sky was ablaze—she couldn't tell if the spectacular display was from fireworks or mortar fire. And, she thought ruefully, that question nearly summed up Paris. Sheer anarchy had a terrifying edge—she had seen it in the face of a child with a machine gun.

The Renault clattered along Rue Monge till it crossed the bridge into Île de la Cite. The ship-shaped island was ten streets long and five streets wide. Adria could see the grim turret of the Conciergerie of the Palais de la Justice rising against the night sky. She and Robert had driven along this very street . . . passed these same landmarks. Tears filled her eyes. Thank heaven Paris had been spared. She thought of Monte Cassino—how terrible it would have been if Paris had been bombed into ashes. How terrible it would be if Robert were killed on the very day of liberation. . . . She shuddered and bit her lip as the car turned onto the Champs Elysées and then eased to a stop in front of the hotel.

Her silent, nameless Resistance fighter opened the door of the car. "Can I see you to your room?"

Adria shook her head. "I'll be fine, thank you so much."

For a moment she stood in front of the hotel and looked down the magnificent avenue. It was pitch black; the blackout that had lasted four years continued. Then Adria gasped. Something remarkable happened. Suddenly the lights went on across the street, then on her side of the street, then in the distance. A joyous cry came from inside the hotel and from other places along the avenue.

Adria turned and went into the lobby. On a phonograph from the bar, Vera Lynn's crystal clear voice was singing, "When the lights go on again, all over the world . . ."

Please be alive, Adria prayed. Please be safe.

3

ON AUGUST 26 THE Allies entered Paris for what was now sarcastically called, "the symbolic liberation." Again Parisians flooded the streets in the tens of thousands, and while the welcome they had given de Gaulle had been a greater outpouring of emotion, that they offered the Americans and British was impressive.

Adria forced herself to work all day, photographing the procession of American tanks, GIs being swamped by French women, and near the flower market on the Left Bank, she found some female collaborators whose heads had been shaven and who had had swastikas drawn in ink on their scalps. She searched Paris for the unique, pictures which would reveal the extraordinary mood of the city and the emotions of its people. She worked till her feet ached from walking and her arm hurt from holding her camera, then she returned to toss and turn in her room.

The next morning Adria made herself go to the *coiffeur* at nine A.M., passing an hour and a half while the doting hair stylist trimmed, washed, and set her hair. Next Adria went shopping, even though she could not concentrate, finally purchasing a light green summer dress. Unable to bear waiting a single second longer, Adria hurried to the house on the edge of Paris, the house at which she and Robert had agreed to meet. "Three in the afternoon on the third day after the Liberation of Paris" was what he had said.

Adria climbed up the steps from the metro and headed toward her destination, well aware that it was only 2:30. If Robert didn't come, where would she look? Paris was teeming with refugees. The French military forces were disorganized and members of the underground scattered. People were being let out of camps where they had been incarcerated for months. The numbers of people trying to find one another would be staggering.

Of course Robert had predicted the confusion, which was why they had made such a careful plan. He had wanted to allow time for snipers to be cleared out, but as it turned out there had been few of those after the first day.

Adria rounded the corner and headed down the street. But long before she reached it, she saw the house in the distance. It stood gaunt against the summer blue sky, gutted by fire, its once wide veranda broken and sunken, its steps splintered planks. In its ruins children gathered charcoal and searched for treasures. Adria quickened her step, and as she did so, she called out to the children in French. "What happened here?"

A small boy came up. "The Germans burned it down," he answered. Then added, "and shot the neighbors."

Adria shook her head, dreading the answer. "Was anyone in the house?"

"They took away two men and two women, all dead," the child replied.

Adria shivered and looked around. Celeste—and who were the others? She felt desperate and frightened as she looked around. No one was coming, the street was deserted. She sank to the grass lawn in front of the house and sat down. I must wait, she told herself. Her mouth was dry inside, her heart beat wildly, and her fingers felt numb.

The children eyed her as if she were a mad woman, then returned to the grim work of trying to find some little treasure left by the dead. Adria watched them, her hope fading by the moment even as her fears rose. No one, no one was coming.

Then an older child, dressed in knickers and riding a bicycle, rounded the corner, stopping in front of the house. He doffed his hat. "Mademoiselle Halstead?"

Adria struggled to her feet on rubbery legs. "Yes, yes," she replied eagerly.

"I've come to get you."

"Did Robert send you?"

The boy shrugged and waved half an American dollar. "I get the other half when I bring you."

Adria followed him willingly. Cheerfully he pointed out sights along the way as if he were a guide and she was a tourist.

They walked for over a mile and stopped in front of one of the many clinics set up around the city to treat civilian casualties. He led her down an aisle of cots and stopped in front of one.

Adria dropped to her knees, tears of relief running down her face. "Robert, oh my God, I thought you were dead!"

He grinned and gave the boy the other half of the bill, then he touched her hair. His leg was bandaged and so was the top of his head. "I'm quite alive," he said reassuringly, "and I'm told there's no permanent damage." Then more softly, "You're a vision, Adria. Are you real? Are you really here?"

Adria kissed him passionately and he hugged her. "I was so worried. I tried to find Celeste. . . ." Her tears continued unabated.

Robert bit his lip and in a halting voice recounted how Celeste had died. "She saved my life as Jeff saved yours."

"How were you hurt?" Adria finally asked.

"Resistance fighting after the ceasefire, cleaning up some pockets of Germans. The SS regarded General von Choltitz as a traitor for not burning Paris, and some of the SS held out and refused to surrender. I was wounded at the foreign office when a suicide squad of Germans attacked us. I took a bullet in the leg and I'm afraid I banged my head rather hard when I fell."

Adria leaned her head on his chest. "I love you."

Robert kissed her again. Then he took her hand and slipped the ring Celeste had given him on her finger. "This is from Celeste—her last gift. It was my grandmother's engagement ring. No more good-byes," he told her. "Not ever again."

Adria looked at the beautiful ring and then pressed her lips to his. "Never," she repeated.

9/5/93

MORE FICTION AVAILABLE FROM
HODDER AND STOUGHTON PAPERBACKS

NATASHA PETERS

☐ 43106 1   Wild Nights   £3.50

PAMELA TOWNLEY

☐ 42135 X   The Stone Maiden   £3.50
☐ 48927 2   Nearest of Kin   £3.50

ANNE TOLSTOI WALLACH

☐ 41603 8   Private Scores   £2.95
☐ 05460 8   Women's Work   £2.95

MURIEL DOBBIN

☐ 43069 3   Going Live   £3.99

BENJAMIN STEIN

☐ 48488 2   Her Only Sin   £3.99

All these books are available at your local bookshop or newsagent, or can be ordered direct from the publisher. Just tick the titles you want and fill in the form below.

Prices and availability subject to change without notice.

Hodder & Stoughton Paperbacks, P.O. Box 11, Falmouth, Cornwall.

Please send cheque or postal order, and allow the following for postage and packing:

U.K. – 55p for one book, plus 22p for the second book, and 14p for each additional book ordered up to a £1.75 maximum.

B.F.P.O. and EIRE – 55p for the first book, plus 22p for the second book, and 14p per copy for the next 7 books, 8p per book thereafter.

OTHER OVERSEAS CUSTOMERS – £1.00 for the first book, plus 25p per copy for each additional book.

Name ....

Address ....

....